PRAISE FOR POINT ROBERTS

"A severed hand, wild rituals, a town full of secrets—*Point Roberts* is a cascade of mysteries you will have to know the answers to. This twisting, turning, wild ride is at times whimsical and light, at times dark and disturbing, and always heartfelt. The Great Northwest shimmers to life in this spirited tale."
—Carmiel Banasky, author of *The Suicide of Claire Bishop*

"*Point Roberts* is a wistful descent into a legacy of murder and madness that will keep readers guessing. It's spooky and just offbeat enough to capture wild imaginations. Even amidst the distinctly odd scenario, readers can easily root for these earnest souls who band together to solve the murders. This elaborate tale will entertain readers who enjoy intricately networked characters and a tinge of the weird."
—*Independent Book Review*

"Alexander Rigby's *Point Roberts* is a white-knuckle murder mystery that delivers all of the thrills, chills, and stunning reveals that fans of the genre crave. It is also a tender family-of-choice novel, in which a cast of deeply sympathetic misfit characters search for love, acceptance, and a place to call home. Readers won't want to put down this sensitive, deeply engrossing page-turner."
—Jake Wolff, author of *The History of Living Forever*

"An engrossing read from beginning to end, *Point Roberts* has an intriguing premise and a well-paced plot. The narrative alternates between the points of view of Liza, Theodore, Colette, Grant, and Maude, who have complex backgrounds that fit the somber mood of Rigby's narrative. The truth the protagonists seek, however, is much more twisted than they anticipate."
—*Readers' Favorite*

"A twisty, atmospheric mystery, *Point Roberts* features a motley crew coming together in a truly unique setting. Reading it will make you want to visit the very real place at the heart of this well-imagined story."
—Alexandra Oliva, author of *The Last One*

"Readers will enjoy this cold case murder mystery that unfolds in a unique and distinctive setting. Rigby's use of multiple civilian sleuths to solve the decades-old crimes makes *Point Roberts* feel original and organic, with characters that are diverse and memorable."
—*BookLife*

POINT ROBERTS

ALSO BY ALEXANDER RIGBY

Bender
What Happened to Marilyn
The Second Chances of Priam Wood

POINT ROBERTS

A NOVEL

ALEXANDER RIGBY

Alden
The Allegory Ridge Press

This is a work of fiction. Names, characters, organizations, places, events, and incidents are either products of the author's imagination or are used fictitiously.

Copyright © 2021 Alexander Rigby

All rights reserved.

No part of this book may be reproduced, or stored in a retrieval system, or transmitted in any form or by any means, electronic, mechanical, photocopying, recording, or otherwise, without express written permission of the publisher.

Published by Alden, The Allegory Ridge Press
Seattle, Washington
allegoryridge.com

Alden

Cover design by Edward Bettison
Interior design by Rachel Marek

ISBN (hardcover): 978-1-7358017-0-4
ISBN (paperback): 978-1-7358017-1-1
ISBN (ebook): 978-1-7358017-2-8

Library of Congress Control Number: 2020918101

For Grammy Darling

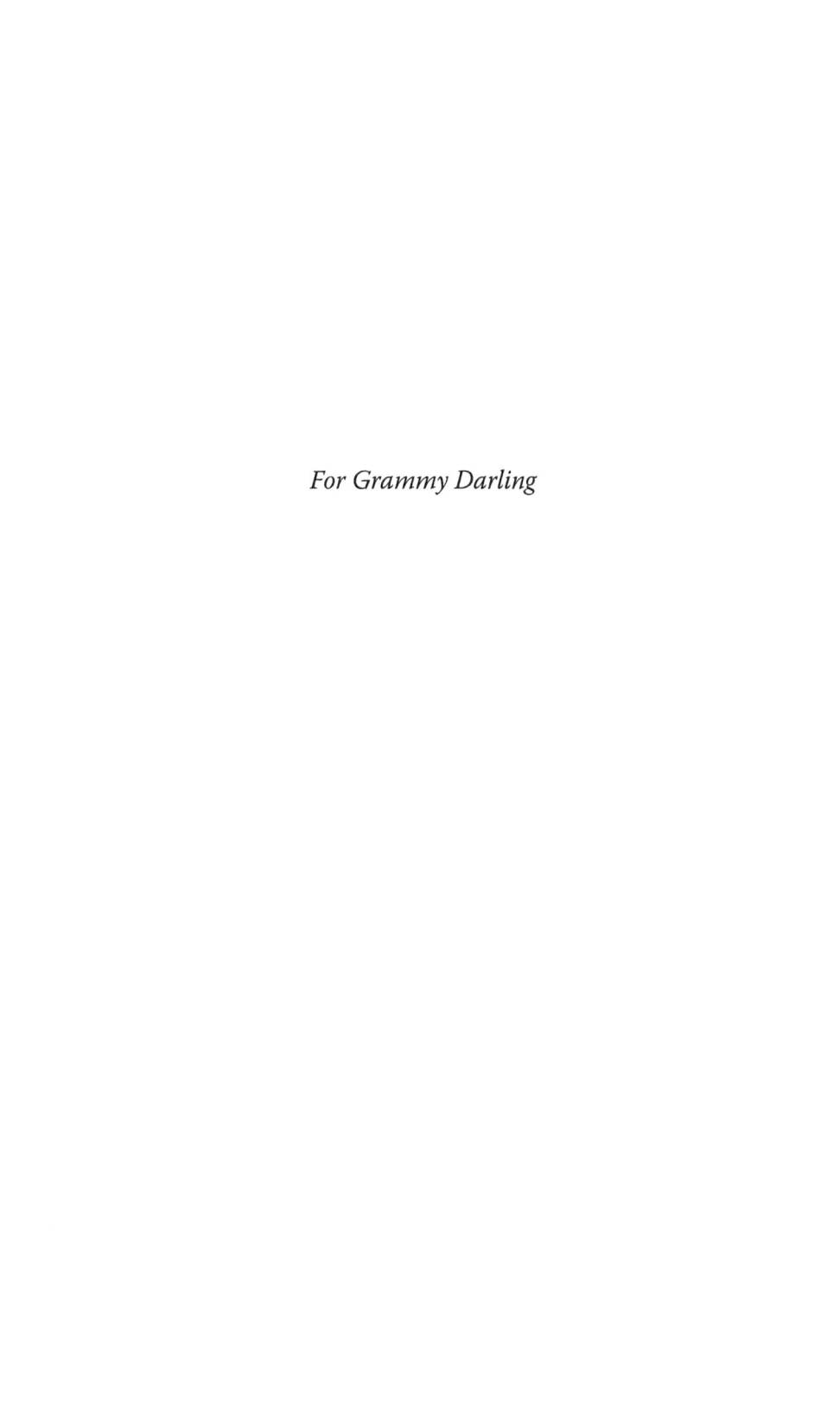

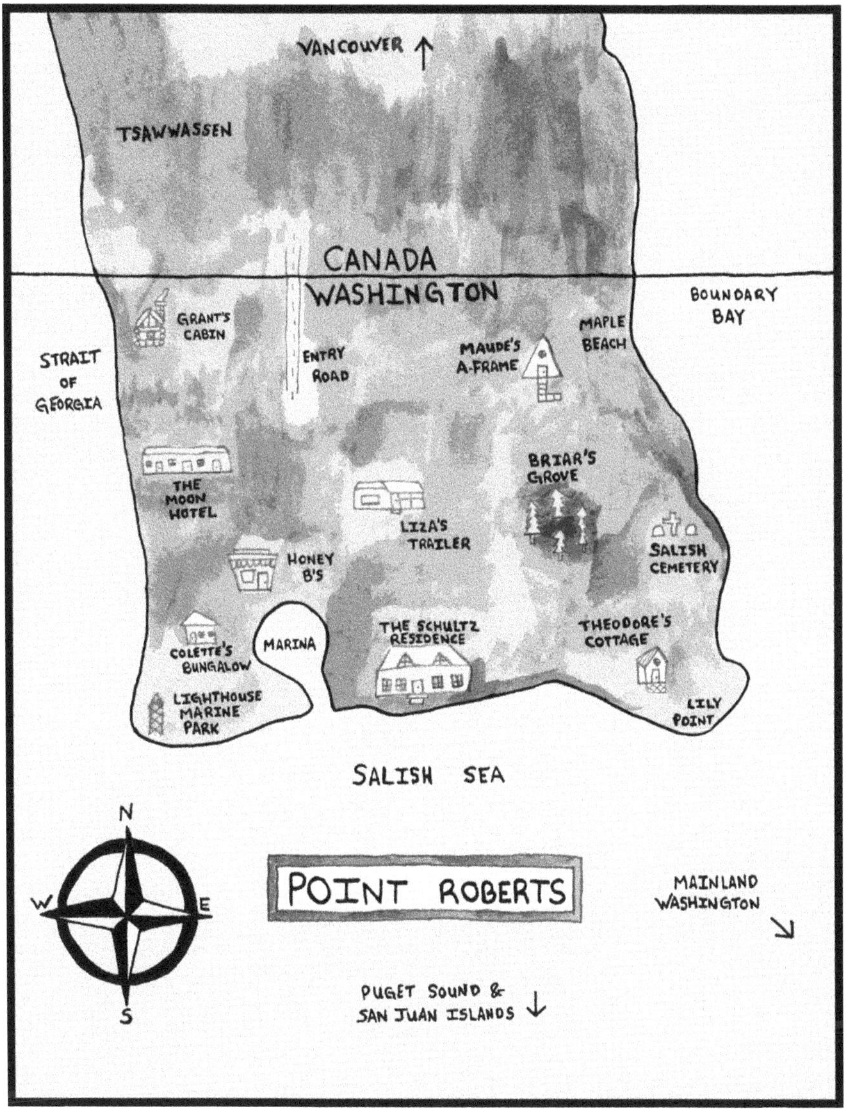
VANCOUVER
TSAWWASSEN
CANADA
WASHINGTON
BOUNDARY BAY
GRANT'S CABIN
STRAIT OF GEORGIA
ENTRY ROAD
MAUDE'S A-FRAME
MAPLE BEACH
THE MOON HOTEL
BRIAR'S GROVE
LIZA'S TRAILER
HONEY B'S
SALISH CEMETERY
THE SCHULTZ RESIDENCE
THEODORE'S COTTAGE
COLETTE'S BUNGALOW
MARINA
LIGHTHOUSE MARINE PARK
LILY POINT
SALISH SEA
N
W
E
S
POINT ROBERTS
MAINLAND WASHINGTON
PUGET SOUND & SAN JUAN ISLANDS

PART I

THE TOWN THAT SKIPPED FEBRUARY

CHAPTER ONE

LIZA

On the first day of February, the sea became her enemy. Marooned on Point Roberts with nowhere to go, Liza Jennings was trapped among gruff, weird-looking strangers who glared at her with icy scowls. The only way she knew how to make sense of what had transpired was by heading into the woods, aiming to find solace in the giant moss-covered trees. As her muddy boots squelched against the saturated forest floor, she listened carefully to the whispers that came to her through the cracks of half-open clams, oddly embedded in the branches above.

    A few strands of Liza's curly red hair fell in front of her face, causing her to take a deep breath as she pushed them away. Forcing herself toward the shore, she moved further from the past she wished to forget. She made her way down the winding path, which curved around a steep ravine where the corpses of old, enormous pines withered and decayed. Eventually, the trees that were still firmly rooted in the ground began to thin as she ambled on, and the water in the distance decided to share a preview of its navy hue. Once she emerged from the thicket, the soggy brown trail slowly evolved into a multitude of beige-colored granules, which made Liza lift her feet higher as she walked, trying to keep the sand from slipping into her boots. The sound of gentle waves lapping the coast came to her as she arrived at sea level, and in that moment, she pretended this sweet melody was a gift from Mother Nature, played just for her.

If only the earth could be her guardian. Instead, Liza was stuck with new foster parents who refused to answer her questions about why the mayor had closed the border and outlawed the use of boats anywhere in the exclave's vicinity. After the perplexing announcement had blared on the news that morning and her queries had gone unanswered, she'd stormed out of their dilapidated trailer on Benson Road in frustration. She hoped her journey down to Lily Point—where deciduous and coniferous trees comingled before leading to a stone-covered beach—could reveal a secret or two, because if no one else wanted to tell her what was going on, perhaps the ocean would.

When she finally made it to the shore and gazed out into the distance where the towering white peak of Mount Baker punctured the luminous blue sky, Liza reluctantly accepted that it would be twenty-eight days before anyone was allowed to enter or leave the peninsula again. Nothing about Point Roberts made any sense, but whether she liked it or not, this strange town was now her home. She knew she couldn't run away this time. There was no way out.

The multicolored pebbles shifted beneath her boots as she took a step back to avoid a strong oncoming wave. Her gaze still lingered on the horizon, where an uncharacteristically clear sky slammed into the invisible edge of the salt-filled waters, which pulsed in discord. Liza had always loved the sea, but now that it was functioning as an impassable gateway, keeping her prisoner, her feelings toward it were conflicted. Some of her earliest memories were of walking with her pa along the bay in Bellingham, searching for stones to add to his extensive collection. She had lived in Washington State her entire life, the rain that came down so frequently just as much a part of her essence as the bright red hair that made her stick out in a crowd.

And while Point Roberts was still a part of the Evergreen State, it felt a world away from where Liza had spent her childhood. The small town was located on the edge of the Tsawwassen Peninsula, just barely protruding beneath the forty-ninth parallel, where the border between Canada and the United States had been placed in the mid-nineteenth century. Point Roberts was surrounded on three sides by water that stretched on for a few miles; the fourth side—the only thing keeping it from being an island—was the international border between the two countries. Even though Liza still had no idea why Mayor Schultz had closed the town off, she understood how it would be easy enough to keep people in and intruders out.

With no high school in the town itself, she and the other local teenagers had to ride a bus up through Canada and back down into the mainland of the United States just to get to class every weekday. Liza wondered if they would have the entire month of February off since no vehicles were going to be permitted to drive across the border. She hoped to God that her foster mother, Mary, wouldn't have to homeschool her. It'd probably make her dumber.

Pa had died in 2013 when Liza was thirteen, resulting in her being put in the foster care system. Over the past four years, Liza had lived with six different families, located everywhere from Seattle to Spokane. After her third time running away from what her counselor deemed "a perfectly suitable living arrangement," he'd decided to send her where it'd be nearly impossible to escape. She hadn't realized how accurate his claim would be.

Seagulls flew overhead, squawking in dismay as they swooped above Liza, her gaze finally drawing back from the mountain-adorned skyline. There was no one else on the beach, no unruly strangers to scold her, no one for her to question what the hell was going on. Her foster parents hadn't been surprised when the announcement came on the news that morning. It was as if this was the most normal thing, a ritual every Point Roberts resident had come to accept.

To Liza, it was an unbearable tragedy, a rusted lock clamped tightly on whatever little freedom she had left.

She began to walk alongside the collapsing crests that continuously hit the shore, the water just a few inches away from where her boots crunched on the rocks that were littered everywhere. Liza had come down to Lily Point a few times previously, in the couple of months since she'd first been placed in Point Roberts shortly after Thanksgiving, but the weather had never been so clear before. The pebbles covering the beach shined more vibrantly in this light. The deep-red rocks that were present sat in stark contrast against the many black-and-white congregations, which were the kinds most commonly found.

Liza bent down to pick up a particularly beautiful crimson stone that was the size of a baby's fist, rolling its smooth edges over repeatedly in the palm of her hand. Her mind unwillingly dragged her back to the last memory she had of Pa, who would have claimed this to be a perfect pebble.

"You know Liza, every day passes quicker than the last, so by the time we're old and gray, we wake up before we're even in bed," he told her as they trudged through a forest of her past, trying to make an important point.

"You mean it feels like you wake up before you're even asleep?" Liza inquired of his riddle, given to her just a few weeks after her thirteenth birthday as they hiked together on the Oyster Dome Trail outside Bellingham. "How can that be?"

"Well, my dear, there are other ways to rest the mind and soul. Some of us go through life like we're half-conscious, asleep as we walk, barely recognizing those around us. Before I adopted you, I lived a solitary life wandering around the country, working odd jobs, stopping to explore any national park I came across. I was surrounded by exceptional beauty—white mountains, expansive valleys, towering pines—but having no one to share it with always made it seem to matter a little bit less."

"Is that why you wanted me?" Liza asked as they emerged from the woods, ascending to their destination atop the rocky promontory, where a magnificent view of the San Juan Islands spread out across a royal-blue sea.

"Of course." Pa sighed, trying to catch his breath now that they had reached the pinnacle of their challenging hike. "You know I've never been the romantic type, so finding a partner didn't seem like the best idea. A daughter, on the other hand, was the kind of challenge I couldn't pass up. So when you happened to appear in my life, I—"

Suddenly, a loud swooping noise truncated Pa's explanation as his attention was pulled to the sky above them, where two hawks circled in rapid succession.

"Well, would you look at that," he exclaimed, his voice full of wonder. "And to think we have this show all to ourselves."

They were the only two standing on the outcropping, the unobstructed views of the islands surrendering to them beneath the hawks' circular route. Liza felt dizzy after watching the birds for a few moments.

"Let's go out closer to the edge to get a better look," Pa suggested.

It was the last thing he ever said to her.

At sixty years old, Pa was no longer in the best shape of his life. After the strenuous hike, he was out of breath. The hawks overhead caused his steps to be unsteady as he remained distracted, watching their path in the sky instead of focusing on his footing. He moved toward the drop-off in flickering movements, while Liza followed behind. They arrived at the precipice of his life and rested there for the count of a single roaring heartbeat before one of the hawks descended from the sky. It slammed against Pa's chest as it wrenched at the piece of beef jerky that had been resting in his shirt pocket.

He lost his balance immediately, his eyes connecting with Liza's in shock before he fell backward, plummeting over the unforgiving cliff, unsure of why he was falling, before hitting the rocky forest floor hundreds of feet below. His body crumpled into a mass unlike itself, desecrated into something wholly unknown.

Liza screamed. Alone on the outlook, the fear in her voice echoed through the trees behind and below. That was the day everything changed, the day she started to hate the pines, hemlocks, and Douglas firs. Yet she had always believed the sea was still on her side, as it had never betrayed her. Not until this February.

⁓

She blinked hard, bringing herself back to the present as she squeezed the red rock in her hand. Whenever she was frustrated, confused, or scared, Liza found this final memory of Pa flooding back to her like a nightmare that wouldn't fade. She'd continued her search for stones since the day he'd unwillingly left her, because she knew he would have wanted her to.

Liza could usually block out that terrifying, unwanted goodbye on Oyster Dome when she picked up a pebble Pa would have been proud of, but if she paired her search with any strong negative emotion, the scene replayed itself like a film skipping on repeat. The dark parts of her past that she wished to forget would never truly leave her. It wasn't that she wanted to forget Pa, because their memories together were what she held most dear. Instead, she wished she could let go of what had happened to him, the abrupt end of his life, which haunted her like a ghost in a derelict castle.

Placing the stone into the pocket of her yellow raincoat, Liza continued along the coast, the sun warming her face as she breathed out heavily, the air filling her nostrils with the smell of salt as she tried to convince herself everything was going to be okay.

But would it be?

Since Pa had left her forever, the undoing of everything that had ever been done had eaten her up and spat her out on the side of the road like unwanted trash. Liza had considered herself garbage ever since, as many of her foster parents had shouted such profanities in her direction. She wished for this unending choir to cease, hoping for something easier than what was, but soon realized she wouldn't be anything but a stranger among strangers, never meant to stay anywhere for long. It was for this reason she had to run. No one else wanted her. She was simply a lost girl, passing along the edges of the sea.

And now the sea had trapped her in Point Roberts for the month of February. The waves crashing on the shore served as her prison guard, keeping her from breaking free.

A strong wave pushed forward, accelerating swiftly so that Liza was unable to move out of the way before the water hit her. Her toes became submerged, but luckily, the thick rubber boots she was wearing protected them from getting soaked.

As she veered closer to the beach, Liza tripped over something the tide had brought forth, a loud clunking noise emanating at her feet.

She toppled forward onto the shore, using her hands to brace her fall as she swore loudly, hitting the ground with a soft thud. Stretched out, parallel with the wet ground, Liza kicked her feet violently to free herself from the large pile of seaweed that had wrapped its tentacles around her boots, pulling her down. She had sat up to remove the final few pieces that were still stubbornly clinging to her, when a bright orange color caught her attention. There was something mixed in with the mound of seaweed. Something manmade.

"What the—?" Liza exclaimed, unsure what she was looking at.

She sat up farther, pulling back the slippery seaweed that entangled the rectangular shape, the slimy sea foliage feeling both coarse and scaly against her hands. Once she had removed enough, Liza grabbed the mysterious object and lifted it off the ground.

It was a book.

An orange book in a clear plastic box.

Liza opened the box and pulled the book out. It was a large, heavy, extremely thick book whose pages were sticking out at mismatched angles, the edges roughly cut, as if someone had put it together by hand. The cover was made from a sturdy piece of leather that was fastened shut with a locked metal latch, so it couldn't be opened without a key.

On the cover, the words **The Fifteen** were written in a messy, cursive scrawl. No other words were present.

Liza pried at the lock, trying to see if she could rip the book open. When the lock didn't budge, she pulled the rock from the pocket of her raincoat and slammed it down against the metal, a sharp clacking noise coming from where the two collided. After trying this a few more times with no success, Liza gave up, realizing the lock wasn't going to magically spring open just because she wanted it to.

She turned the book over in her hands, seeing if there was any other way to access its contents. At first, the back cover looked completely bare, but then Liza noticed a tiny piece of seaweed in the bottom right corner still suctioned on. She plucked it off. Once removed, the word **TOP** was revealed; the handwriting was similar to the words on the front, albeit at a much smaller scale.

Taking a closer look, Liza wondered if maybe it wasn't a word at all, as tiny periods separated each letter.

T.O.P.

Were these the author's initials? What else could it mean? She had no idea where this book had come from. It could have floated for hundreds of miles before arriving in Point Roberts. She had to find a way to get into the book, as the contents would likely offer up an explanation of whatever *The Fifteen* meant. Since it wasn't going to be possible to get the lock open down on the beach, Liza knew it was time to start heading back to the trailer on Benson Road, now with more questions than she had left with.

"What'd you find there, little missy?" a raspy voice creaked from above.

Without thinking, Liza shrieked and bolted to her feet, swinging the book madly, accidentally bashing it into the face of the woman who'd questioned her. Liza had not anticipated her sudden appearance. The book had captivated Liza so fully that she hadn't even heard the woman approach.

Blood gushed from the stranger's nostrils as she cried out in pain, her wide-brimmed hat tilted askew over the sprouts of her long auburn hair. "What the hell didya do that for?" she asked, her voice gurgling as Liza began to run.

She had to run.

Her legs became unsteady as her boots slipped over slick rocks; her heart was beating fast as she clutched the orange book to her chest. The adrenaline released from the encounter pumped through her veins, urging her to get away from Lily Point as fast as possible. She didn't know why, but for some reason, she had the strongest feeling this book was important.

Dangerous, even.

Liza sped hurriedly away from the coast, immersing herself back into the long grassy reeds that sat farther away from the shore. The rocks and sand began to disappear, evolving into an ombré trail before changing entirely into the dark earthy colors of the woods. The woman continued to shout down by the water, but with each step Liza took, her voice grew quieter. Liza kept running uphill, past the decaying pines that had fallen dead into the steep ravine, the still-growing trees thickening their embrace around her as the green moss multiplied in her view.

A cacophony of whispers echoed in Liza's eardrums as the snowy-white clams sang in the branches overhead. She did not stay to decode their anomalies, knowing full well that it was in her best interest to get back to Benson Road. There she could hide in the pink bedroom her foster parents had provided, the moth-eaten curtains adorning the windows capable of blocking out the light, blocking out the bad, blocking out the absurdities of Point Roberts and the ridiculous rules that had arrived this February.

At the top of the hill, the path diverged in two directions, gravel covering the previously barren earth. Liza bolted to the left toward the small houses on the edge of the park. After a few more ardent strides, she left the trail, cutting into the woods, passing a tiny purple cottage placed delicately on the outskirts of the forest.

So shook up from her stressful morning and the encounter down at the beach, Liza didn't notice the handsome middle-aged man, standing on the front porch of the purple cottage, who watched her race by.

But he noticed her.

And more importantly, he noticed the large orange book she was carrying.

He'd seen it before.

And he had hoped to never see it again.

Sighing heavily, the man headed back inside as Liza continued to run—away from the past she wished to forget, toward a future she could never have imagined.

CHAPTER TWO

THEODORE

"What do you mean you don't know where his ashes are? He was only cremated a week ago, for goodness' sake!"

Theodore Price was losing his patience. As he yelled into the phone at the confused young woman who worked at the local funeral home, he could picture her on the other end, twirling her long blonde hair around her fingers in frustration. He recognized her voice from when they'd met at his husband's viewing.

"I'm sorry Mr. Price, they seem to have been temporarily misplaced. I'm sure we'll find your husband's ashes in no time. It is February 2, after all. You know how people get at the beginning of this month. Someone probably wasn't looking in the right place down at the crematorium."

"I don't give a damn how this month affects people," Theodore snarled, trying to maintain a firm voice even though he could feel a distraught sob aching to come up. His partner of thirty years had succumbed to a hard-fought battle with

AIDS, and the last thing he was going to let happen was some girl at the funeral home telling him Bill's ashes were missing and that the ridiculous rules of Point Roberts in February were to blame. "I'm going to call you back tomorrow, and I hope to high heavens you've located Bill's remains."

With that, he hung up the phone, not wanting to hear any more excuses from the opposite end of the line. He was so tired of everyone else shying away from the consequences of their actions. Theodore had made mistakes in his life, but he wasn't the kind of person to shirk his responsibilities. On the contrary, he often found pleasure in taking on what seemed trying or difficult, which was only one of the reasons he had spent so much time researching the cases of the Fifteen.

Now that his health was deteriorating, Theodore found himself at a crossroads. His own HIV-positive status had yet to progress to AIDS, as his late husband's condition had before his death, but he was kidding himself if he thought he had the same amount of energy as he used to.

Bill had always been there, supporting him and listening to his theories about what strung the murders together. He'd been his confidant, acting as his research partner as they tried to figure out how the victims were connected, and why the killer had never been caught. It had been fourteen days since Bill had passed, and every instance of life without him felt lessened since he'd permanently left their little purple cottage at the edge of the woods.

Theodore had been alone before, sure, but not since he was a young man in his twenties. He didn't know how to go on without Bill by his side.

He took a sip from the cup of mint tea that had been resting on the kitchen counter, moving with it as he headed toward the main living space, where high-arched ceilings were held up by massive wooden beams. As he glanced out the large picture window that looked out over the nearby woods, he saw flashes of the red-haired girl running past the day before, clutching that orange book like it was the holiest bible she had ever come across.

Theodore had no idea how she'd found the book.

His book.

In front of the window where he stood was a tall, thin table, its surface covered in multicolored stone tiles that created a beautiful mosaic of his purple cottage and the surrounding pines. The sharp blues of the sea were laid out in intricate patterns, lapping at the corners. Bill had made Theodore this table for their twentieth anniversary. It was covered with several house plants—Bill's babies—most of which appeared to be dying now because Theodore had refused to water them since his husband's death.

If Bill was gone, what was the point of keeping his plants alive? Theodore certainly didn't have a green thumb. In the past, when Bill had asked him to water his plants, Theodore had either oversaturated them or let them get too much sunlight. The indoor foliage drooped and decayed whenever he was in charge of their well-being. He had never been very good at taking care of living things.

No wonder he hadn't been able to save Mallory that day.

Pushing a particularly leafy plant aside so he could set his tea on the table, Theodore placed the cup directly over the purple stones that represented his home and then sat down in his favorite armchair. The stylish maroon piece had been purchased from an antique dealer on a visit he and Bill had taken to Seattle ten years prior. Ever since they'd brought it back to Point Roberts, it was the place where he sat to contemplate the most challenging aspects of his life.

Bill's deteriorating health.

His failed attempts to publish another successful novel.

The rejection his parents had delivered the day he told them he was gay.

Mallory's death.

The Fifteen.

And now there was something else to ponder over: the teenage girl who had sprinted past his house yesterday in such a hurry, holding the book he had thrown into the ocean the night Bill died.

Wilbur—the name Bill had given to the taxidermied zebra head they'd accidentally acquired on a trip to Kenya—stared down at him from its perch high up on the cottage's main wall, where souvenirs from their travels hung in close succession. The zebra always seemed to glare at him whenever his thoughts turned to the Fifteen. Theodore tried to avoid its gaze, as his eyes passed over the warm-colored tapestry of oranges and reds from Peru, the framed geisha's kimono from Japan, the photograph Bill had taken of the Sydney Opera House, the dramatic oil painting of Charles Bridge in Prague, and of course, due to Bill's insisting, the first edition of Theodore's debut novel, illuminated in a light box.

The Undesired Immortals. It had sold over a million copies.

He would gladly return any portion of his early success if only he could have Bill back. Together, they had seen the world, and now he had been forced into an undesired solitude, tucked away in his bright purple cottage on the edge of the forest.

Yesterday was the first time since the funeral he'd gone out on the front porch. He wished he hadn't. Theodore was tired—part of him almost hoping his health would decline as rapidly as Bill's had—and he didn't want to have to think about the murders anymore. He had already sacrificed so much of his time trying to find the elusive missing link that would reveal the identity of the Point Roberts Slayer, who had killed his sister and fourteen others.

When the redheaded girl ran past his cottage, Theodore had been tempted to call out. To beg her to stop, to give him the book, to return it to the sea. Yet he hadn't. He'd been unable to speak, unable to face the madness all over again. Bill's death had ignited something in him, and he had tried to use that spark to burn away everything he knew about the Fifteen. He wanted to let them go, even though they had never wanted to let go of him.

Theodore understood now—for whatever reason—that it wasn't time to stop. The book had survived his attempted drowning and was now in the hands of a teenage girl he'd never seen before.

He had to find her.

The orange book in her possession contained information on all fifteen victims: who they had been, how they had lived, and how they had died. All the evidence the police had found, the connections that tied the victims together, and all the possible suspects filled the pages of the book that Theodore had so carefully constructed. The first victim—his sister, Mallory— had the most extensive coverage, as every other heinous crime stemmed out from there like a giant salt-stained spider web. Every murder was still unsolved and had been since the last one occurred in 1989.

The first year Point Roberts was on lockdown for the entire month of February was 1990. Because every single one of the fifteen murders had occurred during February, at the rate of five per year between 1987 and 1989, the town had been closed off from the world during the second month of the year ever since.

The mayor claimed that this—his brilliant plan—was why the murders had ceased.

Theodore wasn't so sure.

Hoping to silence his thoughts, Theodore moved his attention to the old-fashioned radio that sat on an end table next to his chair. He quickly turned the large knob to power it on, seeking a tune by Elton John, Barbra Streisand, or another one of his favorites.

Instead, what he got was a blaring news announcement. It was the last thing he wanted to hear, but at the same time, he felt unable to turn it off.

> The border crossing at Tyee Drive will be closed to any through traffic until midnight on Wednesday, March 1, 2017. The border is also closed to any foot traffic. No Point Roberts resident is permitted to exit the peninsula through this border crossing. The border wall along Roosevelt Way will be manned with additional guards and surveillance. The beaches along Monument Park and Bay View Drive will also be sectioned off and guarded, twenty-four hours a day. Mayor Emory Schultz urges all citizens of Point Roberts to please refrain from trying to leave the peninsula at the Canadian border, or by any other means.

"Fucking Emory Schultz," Theodore muttered aloud, unable to hide his disgust. How he despised that portly old man.

The announcement on the radio continued.

> Anyone caught trying to get into Canada will be arrested and taken to the Point Roberts Prison to face criminal charges. The mayor would like to remind everyone that last year, there were no arrests, and we would like to keep it that way again this year. By this point, all boats should be checked into the Point Roberts Marina. Any boat found docked elsewhere

> on the peninsula will be impounded immediately, and the owner responsible for failing to check the vessel in will be arrested and taken to the Point Roberts Prison to face criminal charges.

"For goodness' sake! Now they're arresting people over boats too?" Theodore exclaimed wildly, unable to keep his thoughts to himself even though there was no one else in the room.

> Any boat or vessel seen in Point Roberts waters, whether incoming or outgoing, will be immediately apprehended. Both the United States and the Canadian Coast Guards are aware of our February protocol. The Point Roberts Airpark is closed to all flights, both departing and arriving. Normal operations will resume on Wednesday, March 1, 2017. The vigil for the Fifteen will be held tomorrow evening, February 3, at 5:00 p.m. at Lighthouse Marine Park. All Point Roberts citizens are encouraged to attend.

Theodore groaned. "There's no way in hell I'm going to that vigil. You know it'll be hosted by Emory." After he said it, he turned to his right, where the blue chair Bill usually rested in sat empty. For a moment, it was almost as if he'd forgotten his husband was no longer in the cottage, there to listen to every word he murmured. He needed to stop talking to himself.

> This announcement will continue to play through tomorrow, February 3, on

both public radio and every local television station at one-hour intervals throughout the day. Beginning at midnight on February 4, it will be illegal to discuss anything relating to the Fifteen in public. Anyone caught discussing the topic by the on-duty district parlancers will be taken into custody. No questions asked. Thank you, and have a lovely afternoon.

The announcer's voice clicked off, replaced by the swishing repetition of static before the crooning voice of Frank Sinatra came on, slowly taking over the room. Theodore closed his eyes, trying to erase the outrageous radio announcement from his mind.

Since the February closure of Point Roberts first began in 1990, the town's small population had gotten even smaller, with lots of folks moving away. But many people in Point Roberts had stayed, becoming complacent with the laws that went into effect every February, happily accepting the stipend the city paid them to remain. They were satisfied that no murders had occurred since the town started locking itself down each time the second month of the year reared its ugly head.

But not Theodore. He was a skeptic, unable to accept the town's self-inflicted isolation as the reason for why the murders had ceased. He knew too much to buy the crock of bullshit that Emory Schultz had whipped up and imposed upon the unassuming townspeople. And now that Bill was gone, he had no one to air his frustrations to, but that alone couldn't dissuade him from his belief that something else was going on.

Something sinister.

On February 27, 1989, the evening of the last murder, Bill—the town's sheriff at the time—was called to the scene of the crime on Edwards Drive. A woman had been viciously stabbed in her home. A shattered window and broken back door provided evidence of forced entry, an obscene amount of her blood was splattered across the kitchen in Rorschach-like patterns, and a large knife had been left behind, covered in crimson. The first responding officers had been unable to locate the victim's body in the house, but from the amount of her blood discovered, the coroner who'd been called to the mansion on the coast was certain she couldn't have survived.

All they ever found was her severed left hand.

When Bill arrived back to the cottage a little before midnight, Theodore was waiting for him by the door, his hands clammy from how tightly he'd been gripping the documents he'd gathered on the first fourteen murders. They didn't know it then, but the nightmarish reality they'd been enduring for the past three years was about to come to some sort of end. A so-called solution would be announced the very next day, and a fable of mythic proportions would begin in Point Roberts as it started a new era.

Once Bill opened the front door and walked inside, Theodore pulled him into his arms, shrouding him in love. Theodore held him tightly, making sure he could feel the pulse of his own heart thumping in rapid succession against Bill's crisp uniform.

After their embrace lingered for a few more moments in silence, Bill kissed Theodore fully on the lips and then retreated, removing his sheriff's hat and taking a seat at their dining room table. Without saying anything, he lifted his arm, motioning for Theodore to sit down in the chair beside him.

"What happened?" Theodore asked as he joined Bill at the table.

The cuckoo clock above the kitchen sink suddenly screeched out in alarm, as if it had been present when the woman had been stabbed again and again and the reality of what had occurred was too ghastly to summarize adequately.

It was midnight.

"I swear to God, if we don't get rid of that clock soon I'm going to rip it off the wall and smash it to pieces," Bill said gravely, the tone of his voice steady, unwavering.

"It was my mother's. You know it's one of the only things she's given me."

"Well, at the very least, can we please take the batteries out?"

"I suppose that would be a fair compromise," Theodore admitted as he reached out and placed his hand on his partner's bicep, using the firm muscles of Bill's arm to pull himself closer. He swallowed the brief tranquility that had fallen over them when the echo of the cuckoo's cry lifted, urging the conversation on. "Was it as awful as you feared?"

"It was worse." Bill sighed, reaching out to grasp Theodore's hand. He looked at him intensely, his gaze resolute but tinged with an expression of utter exhaustion. "There was blood everywhere, but her body wasn't in the house. They're still over there, searching the beach and the surrounding grounds, but I had to come home. I had to see you."

"Oh, Bill. I'm so sorry. This is so fucking terrible. I don't know what to say. This has gone on for so long, the repetition of it is worse than any nightmare I could have ever imagined. Even when it was just Mallory, before anyone else was killed, I didn't know if I could go on. Now that it's become such a long string of—"

"That's just it," Bill interrupted, truncating Theodore's soliloquy. "Mallory. There's something I have to tell you, the reason I came back while I still have men at the scene."

"What is it?" Theodore asked, his brow furrowing as he leaned away from where Bill sat, untangling his limbs from the physical connection they had shared. He didn't like it when anyone else said his sister's name aloud. Not even Bill. It hurt too much for him to hear anyone else mention her, no matter the context.

She'd been gone for two years, and Theodore was still haunted by the memory of his sister's murder. He hadn't been able to stop the killer as Mallory died in front of him.

Bill looked at him in a surreal way, his expression unlike anything Theodore had ever seen painted across his face before. "Whoever took that woman, they wrote a message in her blood."

"What did it say?" Theodore asked, his curiosity dominating his disgust.

"It was Mallory."

Theodore choked on his saliva, coughing violently without warning. When he was able to regain his breath, no words came to him.

"That's all that was written, nothing more, nothing less," Bill explained. "This is the first time any of the murders have been connected so deliberately."

The cuckoo clock squawked—its tone remaining hostile nearly thirty years later—ripping the past away from the present while forcing the two to collide. Theodore had put the batteries back in for the first time the day after Bill died.

Now he was starting to regret that decision.

He quickly got up from his chair and grabbed his teacup, guzzling the few tepid sips he had left, the tea bag's grainy texture brushing up against his lips where it clung to the edge. He headed toward the door, where his pair of yellow rain boots begged to be reunited with the thick wool socks he usually wore.

Theodore had to get out of the house. There were too many memories here, both wonderful and horrible. His little purple cottage—the lavender color he'd decided on was so striking in the darkened woods that neighbors and passersby always questioned the choice to paint it such a shade.

"Because it was the most flamboyant thing I could find," Theodore would tell them, his answer always the same.

Without looking back, he exited the space, stomping along the dirt path outside to where his old Subaru sat waiting, a trusted mechanical steed that had never failed him. He turned the ignition on, the engine sputtered to life, and he slowly backed down the driveway, making sure to avoid the tall firs that lined the passage in tightly grouped pairs.

Heading west, Theodore left his corner of Point Roberts behind, making his way to the new bakery that had recently opened on the other side of town. He refused to look south as he drove, where large houses loomed in the distance, sitting on the shore like beautiful abandoned wives. Most of the owners were wealthy people who lived up in Vancouver. They were smart enough to stay out of Point Roberts during the month of February.

After Mallory's murder, he'd wanted to leave himself, to run away to another part of the Pacific Northwest and never come back, but his new relationship with Bill kept him tethered to the town. And now, thirty years later, he couldn't imagine living anywhere else. No matter how fucked up Point Roberts was, it was his home.

Besides, February was always the month he found the most inspiration to work on *The Fifteen*. His next book.

Or at least it was going to be before he threw it into the sea. His publisher had been asking for the manuscript for years, and now they would probably never get it.

Maybe someone at the bakery would know who that red-headed teenager was. So far, asking anyone he came across was the only idea he had to trace her whereabouts.

When Theodore pulled into the bakery's parking lot, he had trouble finding a spot, an abundance of cars crammed into the tiny area. Once he'd parked in a space tucked in the corner alongside the building, he stepped out of his car and headed inside, the brass bell chiming against the glass as he opened the door.

The aroma of freshly baked bread and pastries smothered the air, and patrons sipped coffee in bright yellow booths lined up against wide windows. He didn't recognize anyone present, and the majority of customers chose not to make eye contact with him. They were looking out the windows toward the marina, which was overflowing with confiscated boats.

"Bonjour monsieur, what can I get for you today?" a blonde-haired woman said from behind the front counter, beckoning Theodore's attention forward to where trays of fruit-filled Danishes and doughnuts covered in sugar silently gloated over how delicious they appeared.

Theodore had heard that a woman from Montréal was the one who'd opened Honey B's, but he didn't think she'd actually speak French to her customers. Apparently, she was the real deal.

Before answering her, Theodore inspected the options on display, trying to decide if either the flaky croissants or the tiny coffee cakes looked best. Once his choice was made, he looked up, prepared to order and ask the question he'd brought with him.

The woman stood there like an elegant mannequin, her grace and beauty just now making itself obvious as he took in the sight of her. It was hard to tell exactly how old she was, as her high cheekbones and unwrinkled skin likely helped shave off a few years. Theodore guessed she was in her late thirties or early forties; her long golden hair was pulled back in an immaculate bun that sat on top of her head. He noticed her tall stature right away, as her intense blue gaze penetrated his at a similar level. She delicately cleared her throat, trying to urge Theodore to say something so they could stop staring at one another.

"I'm sorry, it's been a difficult morning," he admitted freely before pointing to a large croissant at the top of the glass cabinet and ordering a small coffee. The woman assured him it was no problem as he watched her supple fingers grasp the metal tongs to retrieve the croissant from its chamber. She poured him a coffee and then brought the two items to the counter, where Theodore hurriedly paid as the woman thanked him graciously.

He was halfway to the yellow booth that had just opened up before he realized what he'd forgotten; Theodore spun back around to find the woman still standing at the counter, a tray of stacked pastries now in her hands. She'd been watching him walk away, her interest piqued.

He returned to her.

"Yes? What is it?" She could see the question written on his face, even though it was in a language that was not her own.

"Have you seen a teenage girl around here? She looks to be about seventeen, with frizzy bright red hair, skinny legs, and an affinity for books."

The woman tilted her head, her lips pursing in concentration, racking her brain for the description Theodore had just delivered.

"Well, I—" she began, before pausing dramatically. "Can I first ask why you're looking for her?"

"She has something of mine. A very important manuscript," Theodore went on, just wanting the woman to answer his question. He didn't have time for this. Newcomers in Point Roberts always seemed so clueless. "I'm not sure if you know who I am, but my name is Theodore Price. I'm the writer—you know—the one in all the interviews. I'm the only person who ever saw the murderer, and it's imperative I get this manuscript back. It's about the Fifteen."

The woman appeared unimpressed at first, her expression unchanging.

And then suddenly she fainted, bringing the metal tray of scrumptious-looking beignets with her down to the ground, causing an unpleasant clanging sound to reverberate across the black-and-white tiled floor.

"Oh, for heaven's sake," Theodore mumbled before rushing behind the counter, becoming the baker's unwilling assistant.

CHAPTER THREE

COLETTE

The smell of burning bread filled the bakery as coagulations of smoke filtered out from the oven door that Colette was desperately prying open. A screeching alarm pulsed across the smoldering air in quick patterns, causing Colette's already pounding headache to reach new levels of distress. Since she'd fainted at the counter yesterday afternoon, she'd been unsteady on her feet, and the bump on the back of her head throbbed in random intervals. She struggled to balance herself as the addition of the chirping alarm and thick smoke increased her dizziness.

When she pulled the baguettes from the oven, they were completely charred, their usual golden color scorched to a shade almost black. She'd never burned anything so badly in all her years as a baker.

Colette tossed the tray of baguettes onto the wooden island that was centered in the prep space, where piles of uncooked dough, fresh fruit, and thick layers of flour were scattered in jumbled piles, forming an archipelago of the unprepared. She ripped the oven mitts off her hands, setting them beside the tray before wiping her dusty fingers on the front of her apron. Honey B's would open soon, and she still had so much to do.

What had she gotten herself into?

Had opening up a bakery in a town she'd never been to before been a terrible mistake?

Colette missed Montréal and hearing the sound of her native tongue bouncing off the city streets. She longed for it in the same way she had longed for Paris as a child when her parents first dragged her across the Atlantic.

Now she lived in yet another country, a foreigner in a land that seemed just as confused as she was about where it belonged. Point Roberts was part of America, but Colette knew it could just as easily have been a part of Canada if only certain boundaries had been drawn differently.

Colette wasn't satisfied with the rules that had strangled the town, but at the very least, she was glad her bakery would be busy during February. After all, there was barely anywhere else for people to go.

She needed to make more bread.

After dumping the ruined baguettes into the trash, Colette began to knead the uncooked dough on the counter, hoping her next batch would come out as they should. She lost herself in preparations, shaping new baguettes and hollowing out pockets in the circular Danishes so she could add in generous dollops of the fruit mixture she had concocted earlier.

She scuttled about the bakery's kitchen like a pinball tossed around the inside of an arcade machine. While she worked, the soft glow from the rising sun reached in through the wide windows at the front of the building, highlighting the warm wooden accents against the bright white walls and yellow booths. Meanwhile, the turquoise stools along the counter sat in carefree solidarity.

Colette's encounter with Theodore Price the day before lingered in her mind as she drizzled cinnamon rolls with icing, the clock clicking closer to opening time. It was as if the memory of his face were floating alongside the tiny remnants of smoke that refused to dissipate.

Her fainting spell had overtaken her swiftly, the mention of the Fifteen sending Colette over the edge in a way that had surprised her. It wasn't just that, though. As she regained consciousness on the floor a few moments after Theodore came behind the counter to assist her, his handsome face came into focus. She knew him.

Of course, she didn't actually know him, but she had watched many of his interviews on various news programs in the past. Any time a show like *Dateline* or *20/20* covered the Point Roberts murders, Theodore Price was always featured. He was considered to be the town's expert on the matter, and he was always willing to talk—at least until recently.

Colette had overheard a customer just the other day gossiping about how Netflix wanted to film a multipart docuseries about the Fifteen but it was on indefinite hold because Theodore refused to participate and the producers felt they couldn't make it without him. He was such an integral voice on what had transpired all those years ago and how Point Roberts had functioned ever since.

It was the reason she'd stared at him when he'd entered Honey B's. She knew she recognized him, even though she couldn't place him at first. He was still a very attractive man for being in his midfifties, the wrinkles on his face written in delicate lines that were incapable of erasing his distinct, angular features or the intensity of his gray-blue eyes. Nevertheless, even with his thick brown hair, he appeared much older than he had in the last image she'd seen of him.

Theodore had seemed perturbed with Colette from the start, but for whatever reason, when she fainted, his demeanor changed. Her weakness softened him. He helped her up from the floor of the bakery, steadying her in slow movements as he allowed her to grab onto him, walking her over to the yellow booths in short, steady steps. Two teenagers had snagged the last empty booth, but he ordered them out of it in rapid-fire words, causing them to disperse without question as they approached. Theodore guided her into the seat as he told her to take deep breaths. He scurried back behind the counter and returned with a large glass of water and a plate full of pastries and slices of bread.

"Have you eaten anything today?" he asked.

"I think I forgot," Colette sheepishly admitted.

As she ate, he didn't bother her with any other questions about the redheaded girl he'd come looking for. Besides, she hadn't seen any teenager matching the girl's description.

She wanted to ask Theodore a million questions, about the book on the Fifteen he was writing, how this unknown girl had acquired it, why he had refused to participate in any new interviews about the murders, and if he knew anything about Elsie that the police had yet to disclose.

Instead, the two of them sat in silence as Colette swallowed large gulps of water, washing down the bites of sugar-covered beignets in rapid succession. She knew not having eaten anything all day was probably to blame for her collapse, but she also realized that the introduction of Theodore Price into her life had shoved her over the precipice. Part of the reason she had come to Point Roberts in the first place was to try to find answers about her childhood friend's murder, and the town's most valuable source had presented himself directly to her.

And instead of getting any new leads, she'd made a complete fool of herself.

Once she finished the last piece of bread on her plate, Theodore spoke again, the chatter from the other customers around them who had barely reacted to Colette's ordeal regressing further back to an even lower hum.

"Are you feeling better?"

"I think so." She sighed and reached toward the window to grab a paper napkin so she could clean her sticky fingers. "Thank you so much for—"

"You're welcome," Theodore interrupted as he stood up without warning. "If you see that girl, will you please call me?" He handed her a piece of paper as she nodded silently, his eyes registering her gaze, imprinting this new connection onto a formerly blank card and filing it away. "I have to go now." And without any hesitation, he left her.

Colette tried to stop him, but by the time her cry of "Wait!" squeaked out from her throat, the chime of the bell was already ringing against the closing bakery door.

~

Now—the day after that messy interaction had occurred—the bell rang again as Colette placed the final tray she'd had time to prepare into the oven. As if on cue, her first customer was trudging through the doorway just as the clock struck eight o'clock. Opening time.

"Well, doesn't it just smell delightful in here this morning?" the man who entered asked rhetorically as he made his way toward Colette, who was moving away from the ovens to greet him at the counter. The man's energy sucked all the air out of the room, as even the few molecules of smoke that had refused to scatter were suddenly rocketing up his oversized nostrils.

Emory Schultz had not visited Honey B's in the few months since it had opened, but Colette always knew that one day he would make his grand entrance.

The mayor of Point Roberts never let any place escape his commandeering presence, or so the citizens of the town always said.

Colette feigned a smile as Emory arrived directly before her, only making eye contact with him briefly before he began studying the pastries and breads on display in the glass case they stood on opposite sides of.

He was a large man, his stomach extending out far past where the average person's should, yet his belly did not hang loosely above his waistline. Instead, his hips and pelvis ballooned outward to meet it in the middle, creating a rotund figure. Colette watched him in silent awe as he breathed heavily on the glass, his face only inches away from where her pastries sat, the see-through barrier fogging up more and more with his every exhalation.

Emory's bulbous nose appeared to be enjoying every scent it was experiencing. Colette watched it twitch in pleasure as he continued to peer at the goods she had available. It was like he barely noticed she was there.

"Is anything in particular striking your fancy?" Colette finally asked, breaking the awkward tension.

"Oh, everything looks spectacular," Emory wheezed, his squeaky voice coming out as if his throat had the narrowest opening possible. "But what do you recommend?"

That was the thing about Emory Schultz. He was easily the most despised man in Point Roberts, but he had a way of making people feel as if their voices mattered more than his own.

It was the reason people voted for him again and again. They had initially hated how their town was closed off every February, but because the murders had stopped ever since he implemented the rules, they'd placed their trust in him. They didn't have to like him personally—in fact, his very appearance and demeanor were a major turnoff for many people—but he was a good listener, and he made it seem like he really cared how people felt. He never turned down a request for a private audience with a citizen.

Still, he wouldn't change his policies. He was a man set in his ways, a fat king sitting atop a delicious crop he'd never let his sheep take control of again.

"Well, since this is your first time in, I'd recommend going with the beignet or the croissant. They're what we're known for," Colette said flatly.

"If that's the case, I'll take two of each, and some jam, please."

"Of course," she answered, sliding back the glass panel to access the fresh pastries he'd ordered. "Anything else?"

"Oh, that will be all," Emory sighed, looking at Colette intensely as she placed his items on a tray on the counter between them. "How do you know it's my first time here?"

Colette rolled her eyes slightly. "I'm the owner of the bakery, Mr. Schultz. I'm here whenever we are open. Besides, I'd remember if a force as formidable as you had come into my shop previously."

Emory chortled, pulling out his wallet to pay for his order. "So you know who I am? I can never be sure with newcomers."

"I've lived here for almost a year, Mr. Schultz. I'm not sure if that classifies me as a newcomer."

He paused dramatically for a moment before his fingers started stroking the folded green bills held in his grasp. "But this is your first February, isn't it, Ms. Bernard?"

"Yes, but what does that—"

"Then I would say you are a newcomer. You don't really know Point Roberts until you've seen it in February. My favorite month of the year," Emory admitted without guilt.

Colette found this such an unappetizing thing to say, especially coming from the mayor. She didn't give a damn whether he thought he had stopped the murders or not. His rules weren't going to bring her friend back.

"You have a very nice shop here. I've been meaning to visit ever since you opened in October. But you know how responsibilities can add up quickly, making you lose track of time."

"Well, you're here now, Mr. Schultz," Colette said, unable to pretend she was enjoying this.

"Please, call me Emory," he said as he extended a crisp twenty-dollar bill.

"If you wish," Colette whispered, unmoving.

"Shall I call you Colette?"

"I'd prefer Ms. Bernard," she admitted with little emotion. How did he know her name?

"Alright, then," Emory said rather awkwardly, lifting the hand that clasped the bill up and down as if to get Colette's attention since she had still not taken it.

"It's on the house."

"Oh, no, that wouldn't be fair," Emory pleaded, his voice reaching its highest octave yet.

"I insist," Colette said, her voice shaking as she worked up the courage to say the words she knew she had to speak next. "Are you ever going to give the public access to the Fifteen's case files? I believe people have a right to know all the details."

"My, my," Emory murmured. "I didn't know you had an interest."

"Elsie Dawkins. Victim number seven; 1988. She was only thirteen. She was my best friend. You could say I have an interest."

His demeanor changed then, his immense girth shifting from side to side as he rebalanced his weight. The pleasant and carefree look he'd been presenting up until this point melted away as a stern grimace of apprehension overtook the mountainous terrain of his face.

"You're not family. I'm sure you know only family members are allowed to see the case files."

"But by this point you have to admit that—"

"That is the rule, Ms. Bernard. It's not changing." Emory interrupted tersely, taking a step away from her, making it clear he was ready to leave. "Now, can I have a to-go bag? I need to get back to my office to make some final preparations before the vigil tonight."

Colette reached for a paper bag and slid one in his direction. It flew across the counter and hit him in the center of his enormous belly before plummeting to the ground.

"How kind of you," Emory rasped as he bent down to pick the bag up off the floor. Colette remained glued to the spot where she was standing, waiting to see if the mayor would lose his temper. Instead, he quietly placed his pastries into the bag and repainted his face so he appeared as if he were very fond of her. "I do hope you'll come to the vigil tonight. If you are as interested in the Fifteen as you say, there's no better event to attend."

"I wouldn't miss it," Colette muttered, even though she knew it meant she would have to see this infuriating man again.

"How grand! Well, this was such a pleasure, Colette. I'd heard a charming French beauty had opened up this place; who knew that you'd be even more attractive in person than I'd imagined," Emory said as he turned to go; he walked toward the door before giving her a chance to reply.

Nonetheless, she made sure to have the final word, even if he wasn't looking at her.

"It's Ms. Bernard to you, dear Emory. Now please, get out of my store."

The mayor couldn't help but guffaw at this, plodding onward to exit without retort, the bell chiming as he left, while Colette slid down to the floor, entirely exhausted from the exchange.

No matter what happened—she convinced herself then and there—she wouldn't let this man win.

Colette left the bakery earlier than usual and began the mile walk from Honey B's southwest to Lighthouse Marine Park in the dimming afternoon light. With a thick golden shawl draped around her shoulders, she moved in rushed, determined steps, passing around the edge of the marina where sailboats and other vessels bobbed in tight quarters against one another. Her route eventually curved away from the marina and took her along Edwards Drive, where she walked in shadows drawn by the giant houses along the coast. Every so often, views of the beach would peek out from between the mansions Colette left in her wake, the diffused orange glow of the setting sun warming her face in strangely consistent patterns.

The day at the bakery had proved to be a busy one, allowing Colette to put her confrontation with Emory at the back of her mind as she went about serving her customers. She knew this wouldn't last though, as the mayor would soon be making his way to center stage again at the vigil to which she was heading.

The vigil for the Fifteen was the only public event Point Roberts hosted during February that actually acknowledged the fifteen murders that had taken place in town—the very reason for the rules that were implemented in the second month each year.

When Colette reached the edge of Lighthouse Marine Park, she could see the swell of people huddled along the beach, where giant tiki torches surrounded the throng on all sides. An elevated stage rested before them, separating their bodies from the ever-shifting tides. The slick grass beneath her heels quickly changed into coarse sand as Colette made her way into the crowd, trying her best to remain steady on her feet as she planted herself in the middle of those gathered. No one was speaking audibly—the only whispers present were overtaken by the sound of cresting waves behind the stage, where a single microphone stood perched beside a large frame that displayed photos of the fifteen victims.

The sun sank closer toward the horizon with each passing moment as Colette glanced at those who stood around her, their dark-colored tunics and jackets presenting a kind of monotony against the brightness of the gilded shawl she had wrapped around her torso. Most of their eyes faced the sand at their feet, their heads bowed as if in deep reflection, contemplating the circumstances that brought them to the beach. She looked for Theodore Price or a redheaded teenager, but saw neither.

And then suddenly, with an intense shock that sent her head spinning, Colette caught the gaze of another parishioner. The concentrated look on his face made it seem like he'd been watching her evaluate her surroundings since the moment she'd arrived. The whites of his eyes glowed in deep contrast to the darkness of his skin; the puffy red coat he wore was the only other colored garment present besides her own that made any difference.

Colette was intrigued by this unknown man, even though he simultaneously frightened her a bit. The weight of her body shifted as she unconsciously began to move slowly toward him, only sliding past one other person before a familiar voice spoke into the microphone, interrupting her progress as she turned back to face the stage.

"Mallory Price. Susan Kaiser. Brent Locke. Jennifer Barnes. William Fisher. Christopher Smith. Elsie Dawkins. Willow Mendez. James Turner. Toshi Oshiro. Diane Wertburger. Judy Dennison. Eddie Wayne. Alan Henry. And my beloved wife, Amelia Schultz."

Emory Schultz stood before them on the stage, his wheezy voice taking in a gulp of air after calling out the last name. His gargantuan shape completely blocked out the light of the disappearing sun.

"These, our loved ones, our friends, our neighbors, are the Fifteen. These wonderful people had their lives cut short due to an unimaginable evil, and we miss them every day," Emory went on before clearing his throat dramatically. "Candles, please."

Colette turned to the outskirts of the crowd, where police officers along the edges of the gathering began passing out small candles, their tubular wax bodies adorned with circular pieces of cardboard to catch the drippings that would soon melt down their sides. Once Colette was holding her candle, its wick ignited by a flame that was passed on to her by the person to her left, she turned back to where the man she'd locked eyes with earlier had been standing.

He was still there, but his gaze was no longer trained on her. Instead, it was focused on the mayor, who stood elevated before them, continuing his speech as the final candle in the crowd began to burn.

"As we light the flame in our hearts to remember those we've lost, we hold these candles in our hands to put that inner love on display. The sun sets on another day," Emory proclaimed, taking the microphone from the stand and moving to the side of the stage so that the final moments of waning sunlight could dance over the faces of those gathered before day evolved into night. "A moment of silence, please."

The crowd grew even quieter then, the lower volume not from their lack of speech, but from the stillness of their statures. Colette stared at her feet as everyone around her stood frozen, transfixed. She barely knew anyone in Point Roberts, and she certainly didn't have any friends here—her only friend who'd ever lived in the town had been killed decades ago. Yet during these moments of silence, as the numbness of her fellow citizens abandoned their gloomy hearts and leeched onto the boldness of her spirit, she felt like she knew their pain.

Until one man interrupted it all.

"Why are we still doing this, Emory? We all know the Point Roberts Slayer is long gone. People want to know the truth about why we still close Point Roberts down every February. What are you hiding?"

It was the Black man in the bright red coat, the one Colette had noticed earlier. His voice was strong and resolute; each syllable he spoke was succinct and crisp as if he had been planning what he was going to say for the past few days.

"How dare you interrupt this vigil with such questions," Emory cried from the stage, his tone flustered and embarrassed. "Where is your respect for the victims?"

"I *am* thinking about the victims," the unusually tall man said as he moved forward through the crowd, people stepping out of his way without a second thought. Colette watched as he dropped his candle onto the sand, stomping out the flame to extinguish it. The bodies in front of her began to swallow up the sight of him, his booming voice the only thing that allowed her to track his movements. "I'm thinking about my grandfather, William Fisher, victim number five. A man I never met because some insane person took him from me. I'm thinking of him and each of the other fourteen victims. But I have to ask, Emory, who are you thinking of? I doubt it's your wife. Hell, the police gave up pretty quickly on ever finding the rest of her body, don't you think?"

"Shut your mouth!" Emory shouted, pacing back and forth before pausing at the spot where the other man arrived directly in front of the stage. He wanted the mayor to focus on no one else but him.

Colette tried to push her way forward, hoping to get closer to the conflict, but no one else in front of her budged. Everyone in the crowd was overtaken by what was transpiring on the edge of the sea.

"What is going on with the investigation? Are there any new leads? I'm a family member of one of the victims, and even with access to my grandfather's case file, I feel left in the dark. I can't imagine how the rest of these people feel."

"This is so out of line," Emory interrupted, unable to pretend he had any interest in listening to what the protestor had to say. "This is supposed to be a reflective time to honor the victims."

"I think the victims would appreciate some answers. Some justice. Are you even concerned about solving the murders anymore? Or do you just enjoy the fact that you can control us every February by shutting our town off from the rest of the world? You know that's what a lot of—"

"This vigil is over!" Emory screeched into the microphone, his high-pitched voice shrieking in frantic tones, ringing through the ears of everyone who stood before him.

No one moved.

Ten seconds passed. The other man did not speak up.

"I said this vigil has concluded! Anyone who does not disperse at this time will be arrested, no questions asked!"

That got people moving.

It was as if a dam had burst, and the people around Colette had become water molecules rushing frantically to slip back into the passage of a river they had once flowed in. The citizens of Point Roberts were too scared to stand up to Emory Schultz, regardless of how corrupt he was. Colette couldn't help but think of these people as cowards as she remained glued to her spot in the sand, the crowd dispersing into the newly darkened night in quick succession around her until she and one other soul were the only two drops that remained.

The man in the red coat turned away from the stage as Emory ambled down it, joining the police officers who were waiting for him. He shifted his attention away from the mayor and placed his gaze back on the curious French woman he'd never met.

He quickly walked toward Colette, the look on his face growing harder to read the closer he got. Even though she was scared, she didn't move.

"What are you still doing here?" he asked as he reached her side.

"I could ask you the same thing," Colette said softly.

"Do you want to get arrested?"

"Of course not. I just wanted to talk to you."

"Well, we can't do it here," the man told her sternly as he walked away.

"Where are you going?" Colette asked as she began to jog at his side to keep up with his long strides.

"To get ready for the event."

"I thought this was the event?"

"Emory's vigil? Hardly. The séance starts at midnight, between the third and fourth days. Consider this your invitation. Not many get one."

"I have no idea what you're talking about," Colette gasped through hurried breaths. They were both running north now, traipsing over sand littered with driftwood, which soon turned into grass before transitioning to solid pavement. "Can you please slow down?"

He stopped abruptly, and Colette slammed into his solid frame before she could stop herself, then toppled to the ground. He reached his hand out to her and pulled her up.

"If you're looking for answers, come with me."

CHAPTER FOUR

GRANT

Grant Fisher's cabin was an absolute mess. There were mounds of dirty laundry piled in nearly every corner, a towering stack of encrusted dishes on the brink of toppling over in the sink, and speckles of cat litter strewn across the wooden floors. The only reason the cabin was inviting at all was due to the warmth emanating from the fireplace, not far from where Colette sat at a table directly across from Grant. In the space between them, he had lit a stick of lavender incense; the aroma was releasing itself into the air in visible, hypnotizing slow motion as burned sawdust was abandoned on the table.

They'd arrived back from the vigil out of breath, their lungs heaving due to how far and fast they'd run, racing across the two miles from Lighthouse Marine Park at the bottom of the peninsula to Grant's log cabin on a ridge above the shore near Monument Park.

They were only two or three hundred feet away from the Canadian border, the line they were forbidden to cross.

It was dark outside now, the remaining traces of twilight entirely erased. They hadn't discussed anything as they jogged north; the facts of who Grant Fisher was were only revealed once they arrived at the cabin and he offered Colette his name and she offered hers in exchange—a mere prelude to his engrossing story.

At twenty-seven years old, Grant Fisher had a sense of wisdom beyond his years. That wasn't to say his thoughts always came about in a coherent or easy-to-follow manner; they often formed at random, spilling out of his mouth in haphazard patterns that made them difficult to follow. But still, the ideas he was responsible for were the kind that elicited change, that got others thinking their actions actually mattered. He had formed a society—not a cult, he was very insistent in explaining the group wasn't a cult—that was working behind the scenes to try to string together leads to solve the murders of the Fifteen.

As he sat at the table and told Colette about how his life had led him to this very instant, he stroked an orange tabby cat that lay in his lap and continually purred with glee. From the current state of his apartment, Colette was able to surmise he lived alone, but the sequence of events that had brought about this life of solitude was still distressing to learn about.

"My grandfather, William Fisher, victim number five, was killed two years before I was born. I've been told by countless people that my parents were never the same after his death. I didn't get to know the happy, upbeat couple so many described to me over the years. Instead, I had two deeply depressed parents that enjoyed drinking more than they enjoyed hanging out with me. They left Point Roberts as soon as I turned eighteen, and I haven't seen them since. I could go into the horror stories of my upbringing under their watch, but I think I'll save that for another time. That reminds me, I never offered you any water," Grant exclaimed as he hopped up from the table, the cat meowing loudly as he pounced to the floor. Grant moved to the kitchen and filled up two glasses for them, returning to Colette's side and extending a glass to her, which she gladly accepted and began to chug. Grant sat back down in his seat.

"Where was I?"

"Your parents left when you were eighteen," Colette said quietly, her lips moist from the remnants of water that had sloshed down her throat. She pulled her golden shawl, which had slipped down while she was drinking, back up onto her shoulders.

"Ah, right," Grant said before he took a sip of his water and set it on the table. His orange cat hopped back into his lap for more affection. "I've been alone ever since. I have no siblings, no other family to report to. After high school, I had to get away from Point Roberts, even if it was just for a little while. Being the only Black boy in town had started to get old. I joined the navy, and before long, I was sailing around the Pacific. My fellow sailors always joked with me about my last name, saying I took to the water more naturally than anyone else they'd ever met. For most of my years in the navy, my last name was shortened by two letters. Everyone called me Fish.

"I left the navy at the end of 2013, and I've been back in Point Roberts ever since. I captain a fishing vessel called the *Louisa* out of the marina. I'm on the water every month of the year, every month but February."

"Do you ever get lonely?" Colette interjected.

"Of course, but I have Binx here, and my fellow fishermen on the *Louisa* when we're at sea."

"What about a companion?"

"I haven't gone on a date in years," Grant confessed. "No woman wants to deal with my schedule of being away for weeks at a time out on the water."

"I see..."

"What brought you to Point Roberts from France?"

"Oh, I haven't lived in France since I was a young girl," Colette answered sheepishly. "I moved here from Montréal early last spring. To be honest, I had just gotten out of a messy relationship and needed a fresh start. It had been my dream to open a bakery, but I couldn't afford the rent in Montréal. Point Roberts has always been on my radar, since my childhood best friend, Elsie, moved here with her parents in the mid-eighties. As I'm sure you know, she was killed the year after your grandfather. The fact that her murder has remained unsolved never sat right with me. When I found the space for Honey B's and saw that it was available for so cheap, I decided to take the leap. I wanted to start over here, create a successful business, and hopefully find answers about Elsie's death in the process."

"Well then, you must come to the séance tonight," Grant exclaimed with enthusiasm. "You can meet the other members of the society. Collectively, I believe we have more insider knowledge about the Fifteen than anyone else on the peninsula."

"Is Theodore Price part of this society?" Colette asked.

Grant's expression changed then, the whites of his eyes brightening as his dark skin blushed. He cleared his throat and took another sip of water before responding. "Theodore Price is not part of the society."

"But I thought Theodore knew more about the Fifteen than anyone else?" Colette continued.

"We do not need Theodore Price," Grant answered, his tone sterner than it had been previously. "When I started the society in February 2014, it only consisted of myself and three other individuals. Last year, the society had ten members. Tonight is our first meeting since last February, and each member is allowed to bring one other person. We only hold meetings during this month. The rest of the year, we interview other people in Point Roberts who we think might have leads, or might be hiding something. We do so discreetly. Our goal is to find answers and to end the regime of Mayor Schultz. As you were no doubt able to conclude from my interaction with him, I'm not a fan of the man."

"I just met him this morning, and I would have to say the same," Colette admitted.

"I am convinced the reasons for his yearly closures of the town are far more complex than he leads us to believe. He's hiding something."

"What do you think he's hiding?" Colette asked, uncrossing her legs and placing her feet flat on the floor. The crunching sound her shoes made smashing small pieces of cat litter was noticeable to each of them.

"For those answers, for the truths we're determined to uncover, you'll have to attend the séance at midnight. I've already invited you as my guest."

"And for that I'm grateful, really I am, but you keep calling this meeting a séance, and I don't see what that has to do with anything. Are you trying to communicate with the spirits of those we've lost? It just doesn't seem practical."

Grant stood up, Binx once again plummeting to the floor as if he had been thrown through the windshield of a crashing car. He landed in a furry heap. His appendages crossed in mish-mashed directions before he was able to recover and scamper away.

The lavender incense on the table had burned to the bottom of the stick, the dust it had left behind forming a tiny ridge of residue.

Colette looked confused, but Grant was able to see past that.

He could sense her fear.

As Grant moved to the back of the cabin and walked through the doorway to his bedroom, he tried to assuage Colette's worries. "Ms. Bernard, these are questions that can be answered—at least in part—if you attend the gathering tonight." His voice was muffled as he rummaged around in the room she could not see, but his words still reached her ears loud and clear.

She didn't know if she wanted to attend a meeting in the woods, in the middle of the night, with a man she had just met.

"Please, call me Colette," she shouted back at him, trying to raise her voice over the commotion that was coming from his bedroom. "And maybe you're right. But I do know one thing, we both want answers about the Fifteen. We want the Point Roberts Slayer brought to justice. Maybe we just disagree on how to proceed."

Grant reemerged then, walking back to where Colette remained seated at the table, a billowing golden robe with an enormous hood draped over his arm.

It was the same color as the shawl she had wrapped around her shoulders.

She popped up from her seat so the two of them were both standing, facing one another.

"This is the reason I was staring at you in the crowd," Grant explained as he looked from the mysterious robe in his grasp to the shawl that Colette was pulling tightly across her chest.

"I have to go," Colette said abruptly, walking away from Grant and heading to the door.

"But what about the séance?" Grant asked, unable to hide the disappointment in his voice.

"I'll come back," Colette told him, unsure of whether or not she meant it. "You're not the only one with an animal to feed. It's nearly eight o'clock. My dog, Buster, is probably starving."

"Okay," Grant said, trying to understand, even though he didn't want her to leave. "But please be back before eleven, we'll have to leave shortly after then to get to the gathering on time."

"Understood," Colette replied, heading to the door and throwing it open, walking out into the cold dark night to return to her empty house, where a dog named Buster had never existed.

∼

In the dense thicket of woods behind the elementary school, a congregation of sixteen people stood gathered in a tight circle, and a steady rain falling from the darkened skies hit ten golden robes with heavy drops. It was a minute or two past midnight, officially the fourth day of February and somehow the first time Point Roberts had seen any precipitation during what was usually one of the wettest months of the year.

The towering pines and firs blocked some of the rain, allowing those gathered to avoid getting completely soaked in the deluge, but the shower was still ever present, like an uninvited seventeenth guest. The ten members of Grant's society were the ones cloaked in golden robes, while the six new recruits that had come to see what this was all about stood in regular rain jackets, their faces painted with shades of confusion and apprehension.

They stood around a ring of fifteen small torches that were unlit, embedded firmly in the moist ground, near piles of small stones. The torches enclosed a larger hearth in the center of it all, where an impressive bonfire blazed, the rain incapable of stifling its significance.

A few more minutes passed and those assembled said nothing, the sounds of the crackling fire engaging in a noisy boxing match against the repetitious pings of the storm. The other nine members of Grant's society who had been here before looked to him for direction, wondering why he hadn't started the séance promptly at the stroke of midnight as was his usual fashion.

They didn't know he was waiting for someone.

Grant's eyes scanned the area one final time, looking into the shadowy distance beyond the group where giant trees stood one behind the other, overlapping and shielding them from any unwanted intruders. Even though Colette hadn't returned to his cabin at eleven, he still thought she'd show. He'd left a note for her on his front door with directions on how to find him. She had seemed so passionate and intrigued during their conversation, but now that it was nearly ten minutes past midnight, he knew he had to give up on her appearing and start the proceedings.

This was the deepest part of any woodland in all of Point Roberts.

What if she had gotten lost?

Grant straightened his posture, pushing his broad shoulders back so his scapulae clapped together. His muscular chest puffed out, the soft fabric of his gold robe pulling tighter against his upper torso, so any wrinkle present disappeared. He stood firm and strong, proud of this showing for the first meeting of 2017. His six-foot-six stature offered a domineering presence to those who anxiously waited for him to speak.

He pulled his hood down, emerging from its shadows so everyone could see his face unobscured. As he cleared his throat, he ran his fingers through his thick black hair, which sat dramatically piled atop his head, making him appear at least two inches taller than he already was.

Grant Fisher was a force to be reckoned with, but that didn't mean he never got nervous. Especially at times like these.

"This society is gathered here tonight to honor the lives of the Fifteen, and to use our wit and might to find the answers that will bring them justice," Grant began, his voice loud and clear against the pattering rain; the attention of the other fifteen assembled didn't waver from where he stood at the helm.

"Nine of you have been here before, but to the six of you who stand uncloaked, this is your first time at Briar's Grove.

We are a secret organization seeking justice for this town, since we know the police officers have been Emory's docile servants ever since Sheriff Bill Bruno retired. Our gatherings are held here, deep in the woods at night, because it's illegal to discuss the Fifteen in public. It's been thirty years without answers, but our numbers have continued to grow since our first gathering in 2014, as we've aimed to reach at least fifteen. It appears we have finally made it."

At this proclamation, Grant paused, and the nine other members in golden robes pulled down their hoods, showing their faces clearly to one another for the first time since the fire had started burning. They were men and women, both young and old, covering nearly every living generation of Point Roberts' citizens, with different facial features and characteristics that made it easy to tell them apart.

"This isn't a group for those who are easily scared; unabashed gusto and brazenness are the two most important qualities for new members to possess," Grant went on, happy to see the nine faces he recognized well, savoring the fact that he was addressing them during a formal meeting for the first time since the previous February.

"The ten of us who stand here in golden cloaks were all assigned a member of the Fifteen when we joined, and we have each taken the responsibility to research every element of their murders. The victims have been assigned in chronological order. I have Mallory Price, Arthur has Susan Kaiser," Grant explained, motioning to a balding older white man who raised his hand with fervor, before continuing, "and so on and so forth. During February, during these gatherings, we share what we've learned throughout the other eleven months of the year, performing rituals to strengthen our cases further, solidifying them into the earth. New members will be assigned Diane Wertburger, Judy Dennison, Eddie Wayne, Alan Henry, and Amelia Schultz, as long as you successfully complete the initiation ritual, the main goal of tonight's meeting."

"And what does this initiation ritual entail exactly?" a woman with dark wavy hair and a multicolored rain jacket asked, interrupting Grant before he was able to explain.

"Asking questions to get to the root of the matter, check one for brazenness for Ms. . . . ?"

"Bianca," the middle-aged woman said in earnest, introducing herself to the group of strangers clustered around her. Her pale skin looked nearly alabaster in the glow of the fire. "And while we're at it, I have another question. Why isn't Theodore Price here? I thought for sure he'd be a member of this group, it's the main—"

"We do not need Theodore Price," Grant said gravely, cutting her off before she could finish, offering no other explanation before addressing her first question. "To explain the ritual would take away from its significance. Instead, I think it's best if we begin. Do the rest of you agree?"

The other nine in golden robes nodded while the six newcomers looked at one another in mild alarm.

"Very well, then, let's begin. To those of you who wish to join the Briar's Grove Society, please follow my instructions; those already inducted are not permitted to speak until the initiation ritual is over."

Grant began to hum loudly, the vibrato at the center of his gut ricocheting up his throat, where it banged around inside his neck like a bowling ball in a glass house. The hums were long and powerful, overtaking the sound of the rain as he paused for a count or two between each one, eventually fifteen separate sounds coming forth from his mouth.

As the last hum faded entirely from the confines of the forest, Grant and the other nine in golden robes moved in choreographed patterns, whipping their arms about in dramatic movements. They began voguing with their upper limbs as if creating invisible shapes around their faces, causing a kind of organized chaos with their extremities as they squatted toward the ground and then spun around. They continued to twirl in dizzy arrays in place before all ten of them began to skip around the large bonfire, extending their legs and cavorting in the night as they each cried out the names of their respective victims.

The woman who'd introduced herself as Bianca stood frozen to the ground as she watched this procession, her mouth noticeably agape.

Once the movements had ceased, those in golden robes were back at the spots in the circle from which they had started.

"This is too weird!" one of the initiates shouted, a thirty-something Asian man who looked horrified. "I didn't sign up to dance around in the dark," he added, leaving his spot in the circle, heading into the woods without another word.

"Well then, to the five of you who remain, you must now disrobe," Grant said, just loud enough that his words were audible against the rain and wind. "There must be nothing between our skin and these golden robes. We must all be naked underneath."

The other four who had yet to share their names didn't move, but Bianca did as she was told and began to peel back the multiple layers she wore. She didn't know what the point of this was, but she was determined to find out what these people knew. And the only way to find out anything new was to pass this initiation, to become a member of the Briar's Grove Society.

When the others saw her disrobing, they hesitated for a few moments more, but then began to undress. Grant passed out five golden robes to the new members, who awkwardly tried to hide their nakedness while putting the robes on their freshly nude bodies. Once everyone was dressed, fifteen people in gold cloth encircled a bonfire that refused to be extinguished.

"We stand here vulnerable and dressed identically so that the Fifteen who are no longer with us can reach across from the other side and understand how dedicated we are to this cause as a team," Grant explained. "In these woods, we let go of our reservations in our search for truth and justice. Our desperation and anger at the fact that the Point Roberts Slayer is still at large allows us to release our frustrations in unusual, profound ways."

Following Grant's lead, the other nine initiated members lifted their arms from their sides as he did and placed their hands on the shoulders of the people on either side of them. They created an interlocking circle of known individuals and strangers, a golden ring outlining the fire that remained in its hearth.

After standing connected for a minute in silence, Grant removed himself from the group, heading directly toward the embedded torch in the ground before him, the name Mallory Price etched on its copper hull. He pulled it from the earth and removed its cap, revealing the wick, and tipped it into the fire so it could begin to burn. Once it was lit, he returned his torch to the spot from which it had originated, rejoining the circle and his fellow brethren; Arthur went next, igniting the flame that bared Susan Kaiser's name. The other members followed in this pattern until ten torches were burning around the outskirts of the fire.

Grant then instructed the five new initiates to step forward and grasp the torch closest to them. He ordered them to dip the wicks into the bonfire simultaneously, so that the last five victims would finally have their flames, and in turn, their equal representation in the Briar's Grove Society.

They did as they were told, and as they rejoined the others back in the connected circle, Grant relished in the glory of this achievement. For the first time, all fifteen torches were burning in the night.

Glimmering light danced across their faces in warm orange hues as the flames reflected off the succession of steady raindrops that had collected on each person's skin. At this point, their robes were soaking wet, yet still, there they stood, fifteen bodies on fire.

Grant pulled his hands away from the members on either side of him, everyone else following his action in quick succession so they were each singular entities once again.

"And now, to display our dedication, and to take away some of the pain the Fifteen endured at the hands of an unknown assailant, we offer ourselves as a sacrifice, hoping to create pain upon our flesh so they suffer no more. To forge ourselves together, we must perform this trust exercise. This is the final test of initiation before the five of you become members and can share in the vast knowledge we possess."

That was all Grant said before he picked up one of the stones at the base of the fire and threw it at Arthur's chest.

Arthur knew it was coming and allowed the stone to hit him without trying to dodge it. He momentarily lost his balance, making a sound that suggested the wind had been knocked out of him.

When he was able to regain his composure, Arthur picked up a stone and hurled it at the squat mousy-haired woman who represented Brent Locke, victim number three. The rock hit her directly in the left breast, and she choked on the impact, not allowing herself to shout in pain.

Before Bianca knew what was happening, she watched in a state of uncomfortable discontent as the ten initiated members threw stones at one another, inflicting pain on purpose.

Had they taken their dedication too far?

Right before it was her turn, in the direct aftermath of the largest stone yet hitting one of the new members in the stomach, a scream echoed from somewhere farther back in the woods.

Grant recognized who it was immediately, as the face of Colette appeared to him from behind a giant fir, illuminated by the flames he had set.

She had arrived late to their séance, finding it at the most inconvenient time, when she had no context to understand what the hell was going on. All she saw were fifteen robed bodies hurling stones at one another around a massive fire as tiki torches burned.

Covering her mouth with her hands in fear that her scream would doom her to death, Colette retreated, running back into the woods that had led her to this traumatizing scene, her long blonde hair slicked to her terrified face, drenched with rain.

"Colette! Wait!" Grant shouted as he broke away from his congregation, wanting to give her some context for what she'd witnessed.

Before he got past the group, a firm hand reached out and latched onto his bicep, the fingernails digging through his robe and into his skin.

"Grant. Don't go after her. We have to finish," Bianca said to him sternly. "I may be new, but I believe in what we're doing here."

Grant stopped in his tracks, staring intently into Bianca's eyes. For the first time in his life, he cared about something—no, someone—more than his society, but running after Colette would likely accomplish nothing.

He would have to explain himself another time.

He remained with his flock and watched as Bianca stood erect, preparing for her turn. She took the stone that impacted the front of her right shoulder as if she'd been expecting it since the day she was born. She barely flinched.

This was a woman who had experienced real pain before.

The initiation then ended as it came full circle, Bianca picking up a medium-sized stone from beside her torch and chucking it at Grant, hitting him in his left thigh.

At this point in the séance, under normal circumstances, Grant would allow everyone to introduce themselves, and solidify the connection between each of the new members with their assigned victim.

Instead, proving this was no ordinary evening, not even for the Briar's Grove Society, Bianca broke with the protocol she did not know, realizing that if she didn't tell them now, she might not have the courage to tell them at all.

"Before we go any further, I just want to say I think it very fitting that I'm representing Amelia Schultz," she said to the group, their eyes drinking her in as her voice trembled. This was it. She gulped and then continued. "After all, she is my own flesh and blood."

"What are you talking about?" Grant asked, his tone angry, suddenly questioning the power he'd felt emanating from Bianca earlier.

"My name is Bianca Schultz. I am the daughter of Emory and Amelia. You have never heard of me because I was hidden in the basement of my parents' house for the first seventeen years of my life. In 1989, the night of my mother's murder, I was able to escape. This is the first time I've been back to Point Roberts since."

Grant was at a loss for words.

"I think I may have some of the answers your society has been looking for," Bianca said. "It starts with the wife of victim number ten, a woman who still lives in Point Roberts. Her name is Maude Oshiro."

CHAPTER FIVE

MAUDE

Children in town called her the Point Roberts Witch. Not because she was actually evil or really cast magical spells on them—turning young boys and girls into snow-white ferrets and pimply toads, as the rumors went—but because she was a weird, reclusive old woman who lived in a spooky-looking house from which she never emerged. The only view anyone ever got of her was when she peered out of the two gigantic windows at the front of her dark-brown A-frame house, where it sat elevated on a hill overlooking the quiet hamlet of Maple Beach.

She was always watching. It was her favorite thing to do. The only thing to do.

Maude Oshiro had been observing her neighborhood with close scrutiny every day since February 1988. Every day since her husband, Toshi, was murdered.

Once he was gone, she decided she would no longer go outside, her comfortable home devolving into a self-imposed prison. And she had stubbornly stuck to it, even as twenty-nine years passed her by.

On the morning of February 5, a light drizzle dropped from the darkened clouds above. Maude sat in her chair in front of her windows, watching people walk by in brightly colored raincoats on the sidewalks that led to and from Maple Beach. She didn't know where they were going, and frankly, she didn't care—as long as they didn't come onto her property.

She didn't want to be bothered.

Maude had spent so much time alone over the last three decades that she barely remembered what it felt like to interact with another person. It wasn't that she hadn't been in close proximity to others, as her trusted mailman still delivered her many magazines regularly, and there was the woman she had hired to deliver her weekly groceries and take out her trash whenever necessary. But she had never actually spoken with them, at least not audibly. She would faintly smile at them and nod to acknowledge their presence whenever they arrived, but that was it.

Anything that came or left her house was pushed through the oversized mail slot Maude had had installed. She never even had to open the door.

Before Toshi was killed, Maude was a well-respected citizen. Her husband was the town's pediatrician, and she worked as his nurse and assistant. Together they ran a beloved family practice that helped keep the children of Point Roberts healthy. Back in those days—when she wasn't wearing scrubs with patterns of zoo animals or balloons covering her from head to toe—Maude dressed in gorgeous dresses, fine jewelry adorned her neck, ears, and wrists, and her hair was always immaculately coiffed into a chic dark bob.

Now, at seventy years old, Maude had a long scraggly mane; the jet-black hair she'd once been known for had transformed into a gray mess of tangles. With pronounced wrinkles under her eyes, liver-spotted skin, and the neutral-colored muumuus she wore every day, she was a shell of her former self. Nothing about her appearance could be deemed inviting.

It was no wonder the children who saw her ogling through her windows were afraid of her. She made quite the impression.

Little did they know, she was afraid of them too.

She had once loved children, working with them daily and trying her best to make them feel better. Yet in the years of her seclusion, the children she'd helped had forgotten about her, and new ones had taken their place. They tormented her with ridicules and blasphemous names as they dared each other to come right up to where she sat at her windows and throw things at her face.

If she could ask for anything, Maude would request never to hear another one of them scream, their cries bolting from their throats because of her ghastly appearance.

Still, none of the trespassing children had ever gone past her front steps. Her home had kept her safe.

As a first-generation American, Maude had ensured her home was designed in the same traditional Japanese style that her parents had raised her in. She may have let herself go, but her house remained immaculate. The space was made up of several wide adjoining rooms that could be opened up to one another with sliding doors made of bamboo. Some of them were covered with intricate hand-painted scenes of idyllic forests, where tiny Japanese people stood in awe of Mount Fuji rising above the tree line. Her ceilings were covered in smooth planks of wood, while the floors were cold slate tile throughout, often covered with woven grass mats and plump pillows to sit on. For all the horizontal and vertical lines that were present throughout the space, the A-frame roof that rose diagonally appeared as a direct contradiction.

It hadn't been her choice. When building their house, she and Toshi had compromised by allowing him to design the exterior, while she had been responsible for the interior.

It was just another reason why she felt she couldn't leave. The outside of their home had always been Toshi's domain. She couldn't bear to care for it, fearing doing so would make her heart break even more than it already had.

His formerly curated gardens now stood in complete disrepair, as she had refused to hire anyone else to tend to them, not wanting anything to bloom unless it was under the guidance of Toshi's hands.

As the morning rain continued, Maude wheezed as she noticed three young boys leave the street and head up the stairs toward where she sat watching them.

They were coming onto her property.

She guessed they were around ten or eleven years old, two of them short and scrawny, while the boy in front wearing a bright blue jacket was stockier and taller. He was the leader. She watched as he ordered them to follow him. His mouth moved quickly, and the two smaller ones, carrying apprehensive looks on their faces, followed him up the stairs embedded in the hill toward where Maude's house sat.

When the boys continued to get closer than any other children had in quite some time, Maude began to worry. She rose from her chair so she could get a better look at what they were up to.

The tall boy led the way, his rain boots trampling over the decay of Toshi's garden as he pointed at where Maude now stood, showing the others that the witch he'd told them about really did exist—or so she feared.

She felt objectified and slightly terrified, but she knew there was nothing she could do to stop them. They were outside, and she had no way of going out there to confront them. She couldn't leave her house.

Maude watched as the boys stopped at the bottom of her porch, standing before the front steps where all the other children had always ended their journeys, too afraid to step into her domain.

"We see you witchy-poo!" the tall boy shouted with glee, as the other two boys shrank behind him. "We know you're in there! Why don't you come out here and show your face? Why don't you stop watching over us and casting spells? We know you used your magic to kill the Fifteen!"

Maude gasped. These kinds of confrontations with curious children over the years had always been unpleasant, but none had ever come with accusations like this. Tears welled up in her eyes as she tried to steady her trembling legs.

"They don't know you," Maude whispered aloud to herself, trying to regain some sense of control over the situation. "They're just confused young boys—"

And that's when they started to throw things at her.

Maude watched in horror as the tall boy picked up a few rotten apples from the ground beneath one of Toshi's old apple trees and launched them at the large window she was standing behind. It was as if he wanted to do her harm.

The apples weren't solid enough to shatter glass, but each one seemed to hit with a louder thud, the succession of missiles quickening in rapid fire as the other two boys joined in.

Maude didn't move, her very sense of self riddled with projectiles hurled by children who thought she'd killed her husband and fourteen others.

She was frozen in fear.

Growing weary since none of the apples were breaking the glass, the tall boy jogged up the front steps, standing on her porch, only a few feet away from where Maude stood inside, the glass the only thing separating them.

He was in a place no other child had been before.

Maude knew then that this time would be different.

He stared at her, with a flicker of discontent shining in his eyes. She looked back at him somberly, praying he would go away.

And then he threw another apple, this one perfectly ripe, solid, and firm—the proximity of his position allowing his goal to be achieved.

The old windowpane did not shatter, but boy, did it crack.

He shouted in celebration, and before she knew what she was doing, Maude lunged toward her front door, flinging it open for the first time in years, a screeching creak assaulting her ears, interrupting the boy's cries of success.

The cool February air hit her nostrils, the freshest air she'd breathed in decades filtering into her lungs. As the state of transfixion almost pulled her outside, she hit an invisible wall, unable to move any farther.

Maude remained too afraid to leave her house.

But still, she could speak.

"What on earth is the matter with you?" she asked the tall boy on the porch who was staring at her, taking in the unruly sight of her up close, no barrier between them.

She never got an answer.

Instead, another question came from an African American man who had rushed up the stairs on the hill to where the three boys had begun their reign of disarray.

"What are you kids doing bothering Mrs. Oshiro like this? I saw you hurling things at the window from the street! You have no right to be on her property, let alone act this way!"

Another question unanswered, as the tall boy shouted for the others to run and they began to flee, sprinting past the man who'd intervened. Maude watched in awe as he let them pass, restraining himself from reaching out and wringing them by the hoods of their rain jackets.

After a few moments passed, it was just the two of them, the thinning dribble of raindrops growing quieter as the darkest clouds began to blow out across the Salish Sea.

"Are you alright, Mrs. Oshiro?" the man asked as he got closer, stopping a few feet away from the bottom of her porch, the place where so many had stopped before.

"I'll be okay, just a little shaken up. Thank you for stopping them. I don't know what would have happened if you hadn't," Maude said, the sincerity of her gratitude ringing across the emphasized syllables she spoke.

"Of course. Damn kids these days. I swear those video games they play make them violent."

"Perhaps. I suppose I need to go in and call someone to come fix this window," Maude said as she gestured to the cracked pane of glass to the left of the doorway she still stood behind. "Thank you again, Mr. . . . ?"

"Fisher. Grant Fisher's the name. It's nice to meet you, Mrs. Oshiro."

"Likewise, young man. I hope the rest of your day is better than this," Maude said as she forced a smile, moving backward so she could close the door and be alone again.

Grant hustled up the steps and put his hand on the large oak door to stop it from closing, startling Maude so much she nearly screamed.

Two new people on her porch in one day. That was a record.

"I'm sorry to bother you Mrs. Oshiro, but I was actually headed over here to see you before I even noticed those boys bothering you. If I hadn't been walking up your stairs, I'm not sure I would have seen the havoc they were causing."

"Is that so?" Maude asked demurely, allowing Grant's steady hand to keep the door open.

"Can I come in to talk?"

"I'd prefer not. I'm sorry. The house is a mess," Maude lied, even though she was sure Grant could probably see the clean space behind her.

"Would you like to come and sit out on the porch with me then?"

"No, thank you," she said quickly. Maude was grateful for Grant's actions, and she figured she owed him whatever it was he sought, but that didn't stop the exchange from exhausting her unused social chops.

"Alright. Well, I suppose I can just get right to it then." Grant sighed, his tall, broad stature towering over Maude's tiny figure. The young man and the old woman stood on opposite sides of the open doorway, at the precipice of unraveling everything that had plagued Point Roberts for thirty years. "I met a woman named Bianca, and she claimed to be the daughter of Emory and Amelia Schultz. She told me her story over a drink at the bar last night, and some of the most intriguing parts involved you, your husband, Toshi, and your son, Jon Templeton. I was hoping you'd be willing to talk to me."

The sound of the door slamming reverberated in Maude's ears before she even realized how aggressively she'd swung it shut in Grant's face.

The core of her chest burned in intense pain as if acid had drenched every one of her organs.

She did not move again. She could not move.

Grant walked away from the door to the cracked window. His face came to her through the glass, splintered with the broken lines that cut his appearance into triangular portions as if she were peering at him through the empty spaces of a spider web.

"Please leave me alone!" Maude yelled, covering her face with her hands as sobs overtook her ability to speak.

"I'm sorry! I didn't mean to disturb you, Mrs. Oshiro. I'm part of a society trying to learn the identity of the Point

Roberts Slayer, to solve the murders of the Fifteen. I wouldn't bother you if I didn't think your testimony was imperative to finding the truth!"

"I said go away! I don't want to talk about any of it. It's too upsetting," Maude admitted, revealing the simple truth of why she was unwilling to divulge the information she knew could help.

"Perhaps another time, when you can set the time and place? I shouldn't have ambushed you like this," Grant conceded as he began to retreat down the porch steps slowly.

"Maybe. I don't know. Just not now. Not now," Maude repeated, loud enough that Grant could hear her from outside. She watched him leave reluctantly, seeing the disappointment weighing down on his shrunken shoulders, which had been pushed back with pride when he'd first arrived.

She returned to her chair, the broken window in front of her serving as an unpleasant reminder of what had just transpired. She didn't have the energy to call and get it repaired.

Instead, she began to sway back and forth in her seat, thinking back to the last time she saw her son, Jon Templeton—a name she hadn't heard spoken aloud in decades, even though she thought about him every single day.

***

"I'm going to help Bianca escape," Jon told Maude as they sat on the floor of her home, sipping matcha tea from cups that had whimsical floral patterns.

It was the end of February 1989, a year after Toshi's death, and Maude's only remaining solace in life came from the company of her adopted son, Jon Templeton. He had come to visit her often since she began her self-imposed exile, traveling the short distance across town from the studio apartment he lived in by himself.

At only nineteen years old, Jon was an intelligent and charismatic young man who worked at the local grocery store. When Toshi was still alive, he'd often helped out at the doctor's office too. Maude had urged him to leave Point Roberts after high school, to move on to bigger and better things than the cursed peninsula could provide, but he'd decided he couldn't leave her side, afraid of how she would waste away after his adoptive father was brutally killed.

And then he met a girl, and everything changed.

"Escape? Escape what?" Maude asked incredulously, knowing very little about the girl in Jon's life. She had never met Bianca.

"There's a reason why Bianca hasn't come over here to meet you. Her parents won't let her leave the house."

"What do you mean? Is she grounded?"

Jon grabbed his cup of tea and brought it to his lips, tipping his head back as the thick green liquid poured down his throat. He placed the cup back on the saucer and stared intently into Maude's soft hazel eyes.

"She's not allowed to leave her house. At all. She's a prisoner. And I have to set her free."

"If she's never left the house, how did you even meet her?" Maude asked, the holes in Jon's proclamation spreading exponentially across the forefront of her mind.

"Dad told me about her. He was the only one the Schultzes let visit Bianca from the outside. He was her doctor. Once he was gone, they asked me to replace him."

"Jon, you're scaring me," Maude said, her voice wavering. "So many terrible things have already happened, I don't know if I can bear any more. If what you're saying is true, it sounds like getting Bianca out of that house could be dangerous."

"I imagine it will be," Jon admitted, unable to sugarcoat the reality of the situation.

"Why on earth would her parents do such a thing in the first place? And if the girl needs treatment, she needs to see a real doctor now that your father is gone. As smart as you are, Jon, you're no doctor."

"I know, but it's not about that," Jon said, lowering his voice as if he were afraid someone might overhear them. "I think they knew Dad had told me about Bianca, and wanting to keep their secret, they passed his mantle on to me."

"Why would your father go along with this? Why didn't he go to the authorities? The poor girl! Never going outside? What a terrible life to live," Maude cried, her tone growing more dramatic with every word she spoke.

"Says the woman who hasn't been outside in a year," Jon whispered, his voice flat.

Maude dropped her cup of tea, the green liquid spreading across the slate floor as she moved quickly and slapped Jon across the face. Her hand stung as she brought it back to her side, instantly regretting what she'd done as a bright red hue colored the point of impact on his cheek.

"I think that's my cue to leave." Jon stood up from the floor, heading to the front door where he took his rain jacket off the coat rack and slung it over his shoulders.

"Oh, Jon! I'm so sorry! I didn't mean that. I just got worked up and—"

"It's fine. I have a plan in place. I'll be okay. I'm going to get Bianca out of there, and then we're going to get the hell out of Point Roberts. You may not hear from me for a while, but I'll contact you when I think it's safe. Take care of yourself, Mom."

With that vague explanation, Jon Templeton left the home he grew up in—where, from the ages of four to eighteen, he'd been showered with endless love by Maude and Toshi Oshiro.

It was the last time Maude ever saw Jon.

That night, Amelia Schultz was killed in her home on the beach, her severed hand the only piece of her ever found.

Jon never contacted Maude again.

She still didn't know if he was alive or dead—a murderer, an accomplice, or the unrecognized sixteenth victim of the Slayer.

At the edge of a full-blown panic attack, Maude was hyperventilating at an alarming rate. The young boys' assault, the uncomfortable conversation with Grant Fisher, and the mention of Jon's name, which brought back the painful thoughts of what might have happened to him, all added up to be too much for her to handle.

To calm herself down, she'd need to make a drastic change she never thought she'd have the courage for.

She had to go outside.

But first, Maude had to make herself presentable.

She moved to the bathroom at the back of the house, taking off her drab muumuu and throwing it to the ground so she stood naked, facing the mirror above the sink. She pulled out hair-cutting shears from the adjacent cabinet and began chopping at the long gray locks that hadn't been trimmed in ages. Before long, Maude returned her hair to the shape of the chic bob she'd once been known for. She found an old package of black hair dye she hadn't used, ripped it open, and applied it. Thirty minutes later, she jumped into the shower, trying to wash away all the years she'd lost.

When Maude emerged and dried off, she caught a glimpse of herself in the mirror, barely recognizing the woman who stared back at her. She looked nearly ten years younger.

She headed to her closet, pushing past the neutral-colored muumuus she always wore to find a bright yellow dress shoved in the back. She pulled it out and slipped it on, the fabric still fitting her like a glove. Maude dug through her old jewelry box and found a few of her favorite pieces, hanging large diamond earrings from her lobes and placing a matching silver necklace and bracelet around her throat and wrist. The final step was to return to the bathroom to apply the lipstick and eye makeup she hadn't worn in forever.

Feeling adequate enough to be seen in public for the first time since 1988, Maude moved gracefully to her front door, a newfound sense of confidence coming not from the ensemble she had put on, but from the steadfast bravery she'd been able to muster to make the change in the first place.

She didn't think about leaving the house, knowing if she pondered over it too much, she would grow discouraged. Instead, Maude walked out the front door and headed down the porch steps as if it were something she did every day.

The clouds in the sky had broken up, the rain had dissipated, and the sun filtered through to highlight the exposed parts of her skin. Maude took it as a sign that this was meant to be.

The stairs down the hill to street level were much steeper than she remembered, taking longer to descend than her bones recalled from her past life. She had to remind herself that it'd been twenty-nine years since she'd last done this.

When Maude reached the bottom, placing both of her turquoise flats firmly on the black asphalt, she breathed a heavy sigh of relief. She'd done it; she'd broken free of her self-inflicted captivity.

With only a moment to enjoy the accomplishment, Maude's triumphant return to society was truncated by the force of a redheaded girl who ran into her at full speed, knocking Maude to the ground and tarnishing her spotless yellow dress.

The girl also tumbled down in the crash, her facial expression becoming as twisted as the curls in her hair. She looked to Maude to apologize, the words coming out forcefully.

"I'm sorry, I—" the teenager began.

Maude wanted to scold her for being so careless and for ruining her special moment that had been twenty-nine years in the making, but she noticed the pain written on the girl's face—not from their collision, but from a difficult life afflicted with sadness.

Maude knew that look. She had seen it in the mirror every day for as long as she could remember.

"It's okay. It'll be okay," Maude assured her as the teenager got up quickly, brushing off her yellow raincoat and picking up the sizable orange book she had dropped in the crash, offering her hand to Maude to help her regain her footing.

Maude let the girl pull her back to her feet so they stood facing one another, their eyes in parallel planes of existence.

Before Maude had the chance to say anything else or ask the girl where she was going in such a hurry, she sped off just as swiftly as she'd come.

Maude watched her go, remaining silent, allowing the scene to play out before her as if she were watching it from above, still protected behind the windows of her home.

When the reality of the situation washed over her again and she remembered where she was, she couldn't help but take a few steps forward.

This would be her new beginning.

Whether she liked it or not, there was work to be done. Maude knew she held the key to the answers so many had been searching for.

It was time to speak out, not to just anyone, but to a select few.

Maude started walking down the street, unknowingly making her way to four people who would change her life and set the town of Point Roberts barreling toward a reckoning thirty years in the making.

PART II

STRANGER STRANGERS

CHAPTER SIX

LIZA & THEODORE

When Theodore opened his front door the morning of February 6 and found the girl standing there—her curly red hair a disheveled rat's nest piled on top of her head, her hands clinging to the orange book like it was the last existing copy of her favorite novel—he blinked hard twice to make sure he wasn't imagining her appearance. It had been five days since he'd last seen her, and despite scouring every inch of the peninsula, driving around in his Subaru and exploring the more remote corners on foot, he'd basically given up on finding her.

"Is your name Theodore Otis Price?" she asked, realizing he was at a loss for words.

"Yes, yes, it is," Theodore stammered as he remained in the doorway, staring at the teenager and his book, which she hugged tightly to her chest. "And may I ask who you are?"

"My name is Liza Jennings. I think this belongs to you," Liza said as she extended the book toward him. "T-O-P," Liza whispered as she pointed to the letters on the back cover.

Theodore's eyes glazed over his initials and then moved to the front as Liza flipped it over, two words scrawled in his cursive handwriting now facing him. "I've come here to talk to you about the Fifteen."

"Where did you find it?" Theodore asked, his startled tone shifting to a sour note as the milk he'd drunk earlier that morning curdled in his stomach. He didn't know how to talk to teenagers.

"Someone put it in a plastic box and threw it in the ocean," Liza admitted sheepishly, pulling the book close to her again since Theodore hadn't reached out to take it. "It rushed in with the tide and knocked me over when I was walking along Lily Point a few days ago."

"I was the one who threw it in there. At the time, it seemed like a good idea. I thought I never wanted to see it again. Did you read it?"

A puzzled expression came over Liza's face as she wondered why Theodore would throw away something he had put so much time into. Even though she had so many questions, she decided to answer his rather than offer up her own. "I wasn't able to get it open," she told him, clicking the still-intact lock back and forth against the latch with her fingers. "I've only lived in Point Roberts for a few months, and this February business has confused the hell out of me. When I found this book, the title gave me the only clue I needed. I went to the library and typed in 'the Fifteen' and 'Point Roberts' and have been reading about the unsolved cases ever since. I figured the book must belong to you. You've done so many interviews about the murders, and of course your sister, Mallory—"

"Please don't say her name," Theodore interrupted, pausing Liza's unspooling recollections of how she ended up on his doorstep.

"Oh, I . . . I'm sorry. I didn't mean to—"

"It's fine." Theodore urged her on with his hands, swirling them in a continuous motion. "I just don't like it when people say her name," he said, surprised at himself for admitting this embarrassing truth.

"I understand," Liza said, trying to empathize with his pain, even though she couldn't truly understand his heartbreak. "I kind of lost myself in the library, reading so much about the Fifteen and why Point Roberts closes down each February. It was hard to pull myself away. I felt stupid for not going there when I woke up on the first and found out the town was shut down, but I guess going to Lily Point and finding your book led me there anyways."

Theodore rolled his eyes, not at what Liza had said, but at his oversight. In all his time searching for the girl, he had never once checked the library. He had unconsciously skipped over it, having spent too many frustrating days there over the years.

"I'm sorry, did I say something wrong again?" Liza asked, noticing the perturbed look on Theodore's face. The last thing she wanted to do was make this man her enemy. She needed him.

"No, it's just that . . . Well, I was looking for you too. I saw you run by here that day, and I noticed you had the book. I've been trying to find you so I could get it back."

"Well, here you go, Mr. Price. That's why I came over here, to give it back to you," Liza said as she held it out for him once again; this time Theodore accepted it back into his care. "Like I said, I haven't been able to get it open anyways." The quizzical look on her face made it clear she wanted Theodore to open it for her now, but neither of them did anything to push past this threshold.

"What made you decide to come here this morning?" Theodore asked as he shifted the large book to his side, holding it up against his hip.

"Oh, well, the librarian finally allowed me to see your birth record after I'd been pestering her about it all week, and the name Theodore Otis Price was spelled out for me. T-O-P. It was the first and only place I'd seen any mention of your middle name—a sure sign of what I'd already guessed."

"It's such a horrid middle name, can you blame me for hiding it?" Theodore asked with a smile, finding himself warming up to this strange young girl as if he had known her all his life.

"I had a dog named Otis once, at one of my foster homes. He was great."

"My point exactly." Theodore laughed. "Otis always makes everyone think of a beloved mutt." He paused then before starting to draw himself back into his purple cottage, giving the signal to Liza that he was ready to retire indoors. "Thank you for bringing this back to me. It means a lot."

"Yes, of course, Mr. Price," Liza said, her face blushing as she swung the rucksack off her back and unzipped its main compartment, pulling out a well-worn copy of *The Undesired Immortals*. Theodore's first novel. "Would you mind signing this for me? I've been reading it in between stretches of researching the Fifteen. It's one of the best things I've ever read."

Theodore stared at the book, the memories attached to writing it flooding back to him as he began to sink underneath their weight, slowly becoming immersed in a murky lagoon.

He'd written it while Mallory was still alive. She'd been the first person to read it.

"Please, call me Theodore," he said, allowing a sense of familiarity to come between them. He wasn't sure why, but he had taken an immediate liking to the girl when she'd arrived on his doorstep, even though the past few days she had been an unknown nuisance that felt like the bane of his existence. Liza had a certain charm about her, and he could tell that she was a loner, like him. "And that's very kind of you to say. I'm sure you've read many other books far better than this one."

Liza started to say something else, but he put up his free hand to silence her, shifting his feet so he could readjust the heavy book at his side. "But I'd be happy to sign it for you. It's the least I can do. I have some pens inside. Would you like to come in?"

"I thought you'd never ask," Liza said, covering her mouth right after the words were released from it, surprised at her own curtness.

Theodore chuckled at her blunt admission. "I guess we have been standing here chatting long enough. Please," he said as he pushed the front door open wide and beckoned Liza to follow him in.

∽

Once indoors, Liza followed Theodore past the kitchen to the main living space, where he stopped and hovered by a table littered with decaying plants that sat before a window showcasing the towering pines outside. Theodore said nothing as he paused here, instead allowing Liza to take in the sight of his place. She set her rucksack on the hardwood floor and moved toward the taxidermied zebra that was hung on the main wall, its eerie gaze penetrating her every worry. Her eyes darted from the deceased mammal to the other artifacts Theodore had gathered here, amazed at the exotic belongings framed in front of her. They were clearly from faraway lands she had never been lucky enough to witness.

"Have you been to all the countries these things came from?" Liza asked without turning around.

"Many years ago . . . ," Theodore replied.

As Liza began to turn to face him, the copy of *The Undesired Immortals* in the highlighted box caught her attention. Underneath the book, an engraving in thick golden letters read, "To Theodore, for over one million copies sold. All my love, Bill."

"Do you live alone?" Liza asked, facing Theodore again as she fully came to grips with how handsome he was. It was as if his home had brightened the features the outdoor light had glossed over. He appeared both strong and gaunt at the same time. She was weirdly fascinated by his presence. It was like he had the unforgettable looks of a long-dead president she had admired all her life. Theodore Price was the kind of man whose face was a timeless war piece; something battles had been waged over in alternate timelines where men had been willing to accept the beauty of the masculine form. Forget Helen of Troy, Theodore's jawline alone could have sunk every ship in the sea.

"I do."

"Who's Bill?"

"He was my husband."

"Was?"

Theodore let out a heavy sigh, not wanting to discuss Bill but knowing there was no way to avoid it.

"I'm sorry. I keep being so forward about everything. I don't know what's the matter with me."

"It's okay, Liza. It's normal to have questions," Theodore told her, his tone far warmer than it would have been to anyone else who had inquired similarly.

The girl had gusto, and her inquisitive mind held nothing back. She had come here for answers, seeking solutions like she was an amateur detective fumbling in the night. She reminded him of a younger version of himself.

"Bill died of complications from AIDS a few weeks ago. He was in poor health for a while. I think, at the end, he was ready to go."

"I'm so sorry. I had no—"

"It's alright. Even though it was hard, we both knew it was coming." Theodore thought about telling Liza of his own positive status, but decided that information was too heavy for the teenager to find out about in their first conversation.

"That's terrible. I'm so sorry, Theo. Can I call you Theo?" Liza asked, her words spilling out of her mouth.

"Sure you can," Theodore told her, even though he never let anyone else abbreviate his name.

For whatever reason, with this girl, it was different. He didn't know why exactly, but he felt that her arrival was the key he needed to solve the mystery of the Fifteen. To put it to rest, before it was too late. Before he was dead.

"Can I ask how you found my house?"

"Well, to be honest, the person who told me how to get here was pretty rude. I don't even know who he was, but he—"

"What did he say?"

"He told me to head down to Lily Point and look for the gayest purple I'd ever seen," Liza divulged, her words becoming quieter as they reached their end.

Theodore chuckled, unable to hide his amusement. Liza feigned a smile, unsure how this made him feel. "What a fine way to describe it. That's what I was going for." He moved toward his favorite maroon armchair and plopped down in it, placing the orange book in his lap and running his fingers over its edges. He motioned for Liza to take a seat in the overstuffed blue chair near his, the place where Bill used to recline. No one else but he and his husband had been in this house for years. Yet when Liza obliged and took her place in the seat he'd directed her to, Theodore convinced himself this was right.

An awkward silence came over the room as their minds searched for the next appropriate thing to say. Theodore wanted to know more about Liza, to find out where she'd come from, and what—if anything—she had to offer up on the Fifteen.

Her enthusiasm for answers beat him to the punch.

"Do you still have the key?" she asked, her eyes glued to where Theodore was stroking the book as if his touch alone could massage it open.

"I threw that in the ocean too."

Liza's face went white then, her look of disappointment unmistakable.

"Luckily, I have a spare," Theodore said with a smirk.

"Can we open it?" Liza went on, getting right to her point. These four words were the manifesto of what she'd hoped to achieve with her visit to the edge of the woods. Now that she had delivered them, the strings inside her heart began to quiver.

"I don't see why not. I just have to find the damned thing," Theodore answered, standing up as he placed the book down on the armchair. His right hand lifted to his forehead and pushed through his thick brown hair, scratching the back of his skull in contemplation as he moved to the tiny kitchen to search through the whitewashed wooden cabinets and drawers that spread from wall to wall. A minute or two passed until he exclaimed in delight, "Aha! I've found it!"

Theodore moved to the dining room table and motioned for Liza to join him, instructing her to bring the book over so they could lay it on a flat surface and inspect its many pages. Once at his side, Liza dropped the book on the table, its sheer volume hitting the wood with a resounding thump that echoed in her ears.

She was finally going to get answers. The kind of answers the library didn't have.

Theodore placed his hands on the book's leather cover, pushing past some of the thick mismatched pages whose deckled edges stuck out beyond the cover's trim. Once he had the lock firmly in his grip, he slid the key into it and popped it off. Removing the metal guardian and setting it aside, Theodore flipped the cover open to reveal the first page to Liza.

Like a gatekeeper who'd been hiding precious pieces of evidence, Theodore lowered the drawbridge to his crystal castle, irrevocably bringing Liza into the fold.

There would be no going back.

Theodore took a step back without saying anything, letting Liza flip through his manifesto—an accumulation of research, physical evidence, details from interviews, theories, and utter conjecture.

As she placed her hands on the interior of the book for the very first time, Liza's eyes opened wide. She registered the softness at the pages' edges, where the seawater had dampened them, their contents having dried since she'd torn it away from the clutches of the tide. Luckily, the paper was almost like cardstock, and from what she could tell, the plastic box Theodore had placed the book in before throwing it into the ocean had protected it from getting ruined.

There was so much within the book it was hard to digest it all. The opening pages weren't organized in any manner Liza could understand. Newspaper clippings, black-and-white photographs, scribbled notes, diagrams, and drawings of sticklike figures depicting victims being stabbed, strangled, shot, and killed in every way you could imagine were stretched across the introduction. There were pieces of string glued on individual pages, connecting threads between pictured suspects and victims of the Fifteen. Theodore had made mosaics of the crimes, collaging fragments together in a haphazard manner that combined his ideas, theories, and evidence in some intangible mix.

It wasn't until twenty-five pages in that Theodore finally started to get organized. Here, scrawled in the loopy cursive handwriting that Liza recognized all too well from the front of the book, were the words *Victim #1: Mallory Price.*

"I didn't have a plan when I started this book," Theodore explained, looking over Liza's shoulder to see where his sister's high school senior photo was glued to the page. Mallory's friendly gaze peered back up, so pure and kind. "It began as a place to collect my thoughts and theories as well as the evidence I found while the murders were happening in real time. I could barely keep up that first year. I mean, imagine, five murders happening within one month in a town as small as this. It was insanity."

"She's so pretty," Liza said when he paused, unable to censor her thoughts.

Theodore brushed off Liza's comment, not acknowledging it as he continued his explanation. She needed to know how this book had come to fruition, especially if he was going to let her rifle through its contents. "When the murders stopped in March of '87, I had a chance to organize everything. When I started to focus on the five murders separately—as you see here with my sister, Mallory—things came more into focus. The pattern continues throughout the book, as two more Februarys created new pages where I dumped all I could, only able to organize and digest it in ten separate accounts later. The end of the book tries to fit the pieces across all fifteen into something that makes sense. I've been adding and subtracting to it for nearly thirty years."

"It's incredible," Liza said with enthusiasm, her fingers moving to turn the page away from Mallory's photo to review the rest of the book Theodore had just described.

Before she could make her move, Theodore's hand slammed down onto the table. His closed fist pounded the corner of the page, only a few inches away from where Liza's fingers had been before she wrenched them away in fear.

"I'm sorry, did I—"

"If we're going to do this, we have to start at the beginning and take it one step at a time. There's so much to go through . . ." Theodore sighed, gently nudging Liza to the side and pulling out the two chairs tucked underneath the table.

He took a seat and nodded at Liza to do the same. They sat side by side, the book open before them. Their holy grail. "And to really understand the cases of the Fifteen, we have to start with Mallory," Theodore explained, his fingers tracing the outline of his sister's photograph.

Liza said nothing. Instead, she watched Theodore in silence, whose despair was so evident to her.

"All I want is to solve these murders. To find the Point Roberts Slayer. It's been so long—decades. And still there's been no justice," Theodore growled through his teeth, his angry tone directed not at Liza, but at the lack of punishment for whoever was responsible for killing his sister and fourteen others. "Bill always used to help me. In fact, a lot of the declassified evidence came from him. He was the sheriff of Point Roberts for a long time. But now he's gone, and I have no one . . ."

"You have me," Liza whispered warmly, bumping her shoulder against his in a playful way, trying to break the tension that had overtaken the room. "I'll be your partner. I may only be seventeen, but I like to think I'm smart. I've had to be resourceful over the years, as I've been tossed from one foster home to the next. Even though Point Roberts is a weird place, I feel like I have a purpose here for the first time in my life. I want to use my investigative skills to solve something—to make something better."

Theodore smiled, encouraged by Liza's enthusiasm even though he couldn't help but doubt his decision to get her wrapped up in this. He liked the girl. Her unbridled energy made him feel something he hadn't felt since before Bill's death: hope.

"You really want to help me?" Theodore asked. "These murders are dark, they're confusing and convoluted, and some of the pictures in this book are a hell of a lot harder to look at than this one of Mallory." He wanted to make sure Liza knew what she was getting herself into.

"I do. I really do, Theo," Liza told him, using the shortened version of his name again, which sounded so right to his ears even though she was the only person who'd called him by it in years. Bill had always preferred his full name. "I want something to work on."

"Well then, it seems we've formed an unlikely duo. And I must admit—I'm glad you're here. I've been lonely since Bill's been gone."

"I'm lonely too," Liza confessed, the inside of her eyes flashing back to memories of Pa, her time with him the only chapter in which she'd felt she belonged. She chose not to bring this to Theodore's attention, knowing that talking about her adoptive father would only cause the memories in her eyes to evolve into streaming tears.

"I'm glad we're keeping each other company," Theodore said. "Now I suppose we should get to Mallory's murder."

～

On the third evening of February in 1987, twenty-four-year-old Theodore Price was walking home with his sister Mallory after they had gotten food at the local diner, the space that was now occupied by Honey B's. A high school senior, Mallory was a bubbly, well-liked girl who was known for being as intelligent as she was pretty. During their conversation at the diner, Mallory had acted strange, her usually animated personality coming across in monochromatic shades of gray. It was as if someone had put her in an invisible straitjacket, holding back the new truths she desperately wanted to reveal.

After all, the very reason Mallory had asked Theodore to meet with her was because she had something to tell him. And by the sound of her voice on the telephone when she'd called him that afternoon to request his attention, Theodore knew it was something serious.

So at the diner when Mallory admitted that her concerns were only related to a few difficult school projects, Theodore could tell she was lying. He knew his sister too well not to notice the look of farce stretched across her perfectly symmetrical features.

What he didn't know was why she'd changed her mind about telling him what she'd discovered.

It would be a secret that would go with her to the grave, as Mallory Price was murdered that evening, right before her brother's eyes.

If only Theodore had convinced Mallory to reveal what she'd found out before it was too late, perhaps no one would have been killed in the days and years to come. Instead, Mallory Price became the first victim of the Slayer, who stole souls exclusively during the year's second month.

The night she was killed was a chilly one, and as the two siblings turned off Tyee Drive and left the streetlamps behind, a blanket of darkness swallowed them in gulps. Their eyes gradually adjusted to the lack of light, tricking them into thinking their path was more illuminated than it was.

As they walked back to their childhood home where Mallory still lived with their parents, Theodore agreed to stay the night, even though he had moved out years ago. Mallory had been begging him to sleep over since they'd first convened at the diner, her frightened tone becoming incessant there in the gutted heart of the evening, so that she'd finally gotten him to say yes.

She needed him.

With a half mile or so to go, on an unpaved road covered in slick dirt, Mallory and Theodore walked side by side. Their long woolen coats were draped across their shoulders, creating heavy silhouettes, their shadows unknown. With his arm wrapped around his sister, pulling her close as their walk neared its terminus, Theodore tried his best to keep her warm, the shivers down her spine shaking more violently with each step they took.

It wasn't even raining.

Without warning, a figure interrupted their solitude, unexpectedly emerging from behind one of the thickets of trees that ran along both sides of the road, where no other houses, lights, or onlookers would be present to witness what happened next.

The unknown assailant wore a terrifying white mask with a long-pointed beak over their face, their eyes hidden behind concave black ovals. A long red cloak covered their body so they had no real distinguishable shape. When their hand pulled the fabric covering their torso aside to reveal a glistening silver knife that shined even in the darkness, it took less than a second for Mallory to release an ear-shattering scream.

"What do you want?" Theodore asked, his voice quaking as the shriek his sister had let out still rang through him.

The figure said nothing, brandishing the knife they held with sleek leather gloves as they ran the fingers of one hand along the edge of the blade.

Mallory spoke then, not to the unknown nightmare who stood before her, but to the brother she adored so fiercely at her side. "I should have told you the truth, Theo. My worries have nothing to do with school. It has to do with—"

Before she could say anything further, the figure pounced, striking Mallory so she fell on the road, the knife slamming into her abdomen as she cried out in pain. Acting on impulse, Theodore propelled his fist into the attacker's masked face, hoping to get them off his sister before they could inflict any more damage.

The figure acted as if they didn't feel the blow—even though their mask was now slightly askew—retreating from where Mallory lay in the middle of the road, blood spilling from her stomach. They turned their attention to where Theodore stood, shifting his weight on his legs back and forth, his arms raised. He only had his fists to defend himself.

He swung again, this time colliding with air as the assailant ducked his punch and dug their knife into Theodore's shoulder. He shrieked as a searing pain seeped through his veins, the intensity of the wound hitting him so strongly he collapsed. He crashed onto the street, unable to stop himself from falling.

The cloaked figure returned to Mallory. They moved swiftly, inflicting multiple stab wounds to the girl's body, causing blood to gurgle out of her mouth right there in the middle of the road that meandered through the depths of Point Roberts' woods.

"Mallory!" Theodore screeched as he tried to pull himself back up. The sight of his sister's crumpled, blood-soaked body was terrifying. Only a few minutes earlier they had been linked, walking home with their arms wrapped around one another.

Seeing his sister in this condition was a view more shocking than anything Theodore had ever experienced. It was a trauma that would imprint itself upon his memory to taunt and terrorize him in the decades to come, no matter how many times he tried to erase it.

As Theodore knelt beside where his sister lay—begging her to cling to life, unaware she was already gone—the masked figure fled, returning to the blue car they'd hidden behind the trees. The rumble of the engine brought Theodore back to reality.

"Mallory, hold on, please hold on! I have to get help. I have to try and stop them!" He didn't know what else to do, even though a part of him wanted to give up and bleed out on the road at his sister's side.

Instead, he ran after the blue car speeding down the road, blood flowing from the gaping wound in his shoulder. A steady flow dripped from his arm, leaving a trail of his identity in heavy drops along the dirt road he sprinted across.

Everything before him was blurred, but even in the chaos of this disastrous night, Theodore was able to recognize the one thing that mattered.

The blue car wasn't unknown to him. It belonged to a man he knew—Mallory's boyfriend of over a year: Robert Turner.

Suspect number one.

～

When Theodore finished recounting the horrific event, he closed the book with a thud, the pages collapsing upon the bright smile emanating from Mallory's senior photo, so she was hidden in darkness once again.

Liza didn't know what to say.

She had listened in awe to his recollections of the night he lost his sister, drinking in every detail so she'd be sure to remember it forever. No matter how horrid the story Theodore had described, she knew she had to pay attention if she was going to help him. Maybe as she continued to learn more about the Fifteen, she would be able to piece together something he had missed.

Theodore looked at her, his sinewy limbs shifting as he moved away from the table and back to the living room, pacing past the shriveling plants in front of the wide window.

Liza followed after him.

"But Robert Turner didn't stay a suspect for long, did he? Even though you saw his car?" she asked from behind Theodore, the colorful artifacts on the walls seeming to swirl around them. They were both feeling a little dizzy.

He turned around to face her as he stopped pacing, their bodies half-heartedly aligned.

"That's correct. He had an alibi, and while I doubted his innocence at first, it soon became clear he'd had nothing to do with it. Bill concluded that whoever killed Mallory had stolen Robert's car to try to frame him."

"That's terrible. Why would someone . . . Wait, Bill? As in your Bill?" Liza asked, remembering the name of Theodore's late husband, which pushed itself in front of the other queries swimming around the sea of her mind.

"Yes, Bill Bruno—Deputy Bruno at the time—my Bill. That was the only good thing that came out of Mallory's murder. It's what brought Bill and me together. He interviewed me countless times during that first February, and a relationship started to form between us . . . although we had no idea what we were doing, but enough about that—"

"It'd be nice to hear more about you and Bill."

"Maybe another time. I think we've had enough for today. I'm feeling drained."

"Who do you think did it?" Liza blurted out, changing gears as she realized their conversation was about to fade, using one of her last opportunities to get more answers.

Theodore was tempted to let the name Emory Schultz roll off his tongue and stumble out, even though he had no real evidence connecting their buffoon of a mayor to the murders, just the strongest inkling he was hiding something. Instead, he told her a more tangible truth.

"I've had my theories, but they've been proven wrong again and again. So I don't think it's wise to tell you anything unless I have the facts to back it up," Theodore said sullenly as he opened the door of his cottage, the brisk winter wind pushing itself into the space and enveloping them both with the pungent aroma of sodden evergreens. "As it stands now, I still don't know. No one does. Robert Turner was the first suspect, and after him came Sean Jensen, then Jason Dawkins, and Marcus O'Reilly, but none of them stayed at the top of the list for very long. After those four men, the evidence and theories just became a ridiculous jumble that's not even worth—"

"I want to hear everything you have to tell me, no matter how ridiculous," Liza confessed, following after Theodore, who had jammed on his yellow boots and rain jacket before walking out the door at the end of her response.

He approached his Subaru parked in the driveway and swiveled around to face her. A thin mist of precipitation began to wet the skin of his lips.

"It's been heavy enough for today I think, Liza. Why don't we continue tomorrow?"

"Okay, sure. I have nothing else to do."

"Fabulous. Now, where do you live? I'm going to drive you home."

"I'm over on Benson Road, but you don't have to do that. I'm fine walking back."

"Benson Road?" Theodore asked, the mist that had fallen on his face freezing his handsome features and breaking them into pieces with icy daggers.

"Yeah, my foster parents live in a trailer there near the intersection of Mill Road."

"That's the street my parent's house was on. That's the street where—"

"Oh my God," Liza interrupted, realizing that Mallory's murder had occurred somewhere on the street she lived on.

"We're driving," Theodore said hastily, pulling the car keys out of his jacket pocket and unlocking the Subaru's doors. "Get in."

Liza did as she was told, opening the passenger door and plopping her rear in the seat beside her new friend, a man more than twice her age, a man who usually spoke to no one.

In that confined space, as Theodore put the car in reverse and they backed out of the long driveway, Liza acknowledged that she'd never been so mesmerized by another human being.

And even though he didn't want to admit it, from this first day alone, Theodore already knew he adored her.

The next day, Liza sat waiting on a dead girl's bed in the trailer on Benson Road. The bedroom she was forced to call her own had once belonged to the Rettons' daughter, Justine. She wasn't one of the Fifteen though—that much Liza knew, even if she didn't know how Justine had died, because the Rettons refused to tell her. Nevertheless, Liza was able to accept the fact that some people died in Point Roberts without getting murdered.

Liza had convinced Theodore to meet her at the trailer to discuss their next steps since both her foster parents would be gone during the day. As the morning dragged closer to the time they'd agreed on, Liza got anxious, her impatience forcing her eyes to shift around the bedroom, taking in the sight of everything that was the antithesis of who she was.

The walls were painted bright pink, with windows draped with lacy curtains full of giant holes, so the light that came in created unusual shadows and patterns. There was an old poster of Hannah Montana hanging above a fuchsia-colored desk covered in Lisa Frank stickers, and a pile of dusty stuffed animals stacked in a heap in the corner, none of them having been held in years.

The only piece in the room she'd added herself was the photo of her and Pa posing among mountains in the North Cascades. She'd taken the photo with her to every foster home she'd lived in.

If it had been up to Liza, her room would have been painted a calming shade of blue or green, with the black-and-white photos Pa had taken of Puget Sound the only features adorning the walls. She would have put a bookcase in the corner where the stuffed animals lay, filling it up with everything she'd ever read.

It wasn't up to her though, as nothing in her life had ever been. She was just a passenger, floating down the stream of her own never-ending dilemma. Unable to jump ship, unable to change course, she would go where the water took her.

Theodore Price's surprising kindness had made her feel like her life held value for the first time since Pa died. He'd made her feel like her voice mattered, like her ideas and questions about the Fifteen had the possibility of taking them in a new direction.

She stared out the lace-covered window beside her bed and watched dark stormy clouds pulse and stretch in the sky overhead. Thick raindrops were falling and sliding down the long blades of grass that stood uncut in the yard past the portal she looked through.

Liza knew she probably shouldn't get too attached to Theodore, no matter how much she liked him. If she did, she'd probably jinx it and he'd die too, just like Pa.

The cases of the Fifteen had transfixed her, and she was excited to work with Theodore. She craved answers to this mystery, and finding them through him was her best bet at solving the murders that penetrated her every waking moment.

It was only the seventh day of February, but already the reason for Point Roberts' annual closure had taken over her imagination, capturing her bones and throwing them in a cage somewhere in the depths of the sea she couldn't swim to.

A loud knocking arrived, startling Liza out of her state of oblivion and forcing her into action. She untucked her legs from beneath her, left the bed, and walked down the wood-paneled hallway to the front door.

Theodore stood on the other side, his tall stature unmistakable even through the opaque golden-colored glass. For such a shithole trailer, the Rettons had opted for the fanciest looking door.

Liza flung it open, welcoming Theodore inside as she stood on the living room's disgustingly thick shag carpet in her bare feet, the tiny fibers tickling the spaces between her toes, almost causing her to laugh.

The look on Theodore's face stopped her urge to giggle as he appeared hesitant and worried. He remained standing outside the trailer, the orange book held tightly in his right hand, resting up against his hip.

"Are you sure this is okay?" he asked.

"Of course it is," Liza told him, repeating that her foster parents weren't home and wouldn't be back for hours. "Please don't worry. They won't even know you were here."

"Alrighty. I hope I don't get you into trouble," Theodore said as he walked inside.

He was more concerned for her than he was for himself. Liza's heart grew three sizes larger. He liked her, he really liked her.

Liza guided Theodore to the dining room—the least embarrassing part of the mobile home—where a large oak table sat uncovered, waiting for them to take a seat at it and jump right back into their investigation.

Theodore wasted no time, opening the book to the pages detailing the second victim's murder: Susan Kaiser.

With Liza sitting right beside him, her elbows firmly planted on the table so she could elevate her gaze above the book—ensuring she wouldn't miss a single detail—Theodore began to tell her what he knew, the tone of his voice more neutral than it had been when he recounted what'd happened to Mallory.

A week after Mallory Price was killed, a middle-aged woman named Susan Kaiser was shot in the face in her kitchen while making an apple pie. There was no evidence of forced entry, so it appeared that Susan must have welcomed the perpetrator inside. The murderer left nothing behind, and it became almost impossible to link anyone to the crime. No one else was home, and none of Mrs. Kaiser's neighbors saw anyone come or go from the property. Due to the nature of this seemingly random act of violence, the Point Roberts police didn't think it was connected to Mallory's death, mainly because they were still questioning Robert Turner, who was in their custody at the time of the murder.

Although the wound inflicted upon Mrs. Kaiser's face was one of the most grotesque the Point Roberts Slayer ever delivered, it was their cleanest killing. The murderer even found the bullet that burst through the back of Mrs. Kaiser's skull and removed it from the scene.

Eventually, Bill Bruno put two and two together and delivered his theories to the elderly town sheriff. They were dealing with someone who had reasons, someone who was killing people in Point Roberts with purpose. It just wasn't clear what those reasons were, or what had driven them to madness.

"How did they connect Susan Kaiser's murder to the rest if there was no evidence left behind?" Liza asked once Theodore stopped his explanations.

"That fall, when Sheriff Ambrose retired and Bill was promoted to take his place, we only stood at five murders, and none had occurred for months. We didn't know who was responsible, but we were relieved to think they'd come to an end."

"Did something happen when Bill took over?"

"Bill located a witness Sheriff Ambrose hadn't questioned, a Canadian visitor who'd only been in town that day. A man who distinctly remembered hearing a loud boom as he drove past Mrs. Kaiser's residence had noted a blue car in her driveway; the license plate that read 'TOOCOOL' was etched permanently into his mind: Robert Turner's car."

"But I thought you said Robert Turner was being questioned when Mrs. Kaiser was killed?"

"He was," Theodore said quietly as he swiveled away from the table, closing the book and turning his attention to her fully. "And he still claimed his car was missing."

"Oh my God," Liza said, trying to hold back her glee as this connecting thread made her feel like they were getting somewhere. "Why was none of this about the car in the paper? I don't remember—"

"Emory Schultz—our mayor—made the police keep certain pieces of evidence from the public. This was one of the things they kept secret. I only know about it because Bill shared it with me."

"I had no idea," Liza confessed, getting up from the table to pour herself some orange soda, suddenly parched. She took the two-liter bottle off the kitchen counter and turned the cap, making it hiss open before she filled a large cup to the brim. She asked Theodore if he wanted any, but he declined. "The articles I read said Susan was lumped into the Fifteen because no other murders occurred in Point Roberts during those three years, so it was agreed she was a part of it."

"And indeed she was," Theodore whispered to the ground as Liza returned to her seat, brought the large cup of orange liquid to her lips, and began to chug in the most graceful way she could muster.

When she was done swallowing—the cup now empty—a silence lingered, the dust settling on them even as they stirred.

"I think we need to come up with a plan," Liza said, changing course.

"A plan?"

"On how we're going to try and solve this shitstorm. To bring justice to Point Roberts once and for all," Liza said, her voice getting louder as she stood up again.

"Sit back down, please," Theodore requested. "You're starting to sound like a character from some thriller show on ABC. I don't like it."

"I'm sorry," Liza said, plopping her bottom back on the dining room chair, feeling defeated by the man she now considered her mentor.

"I'm beginning to wonder if this is too dark for a seventeen-year-old girl. This is probably a mistake," Theodore said, moving to pick up his book.

"No!" Liza yelled, reaching her hand toward his, wanting to slam it down onto the book so he couldn't take it, but instead delicately placing her hand over his. The warmth of his flesh transferred onto hers. "Please don't go. Please don't leave me. I can handle this, really I can. I've handled much worse in my life."

The look of longing in Liza's eyes as their hands touched was too much for Theodore to ignore. He couldn't pull away from her now, not when they had already progressed this far.

"Alright, we can keep going, but we need help. We're not going to get far if it's just the two of us. Believe me, Bill and I tried for decades and barely got anywhere. We need more people, people who can provide different viewpoints—ways of thinking that we might not come up with ourselves."

"And how are we going to find these people?"

"Well," Theodore thought for a moment, his idea not fleshed out. "What if we both find one other person we can trust? Someone in Point Roberts who will aid our cause? You find yours. I'll find mine. Then we can meet back up, the four of us."

"I like that idea," Liza admitted. "But I don't really know anyone else in Point Roberts besides you and my foster parents, and I'm sure as hell not involving them."

"Probably smart of you."

"Yeah, but—"

"I guess you're going to have to make some friends. Go out there and talk to people. They might appear gruff, but I swear, even with all the madness in this town, there are some good ones."

"Okay . . ."

Liza didn't know how she'd find a friend in this town, let alone someone she could trust with something as monumental as this. But Theodore already knew who he was going to ask. Colette—the blonde baker who had been so interested and inquisitive—would, of course, be the perfect choice. He may have been somewhat dismissive of her during their first interaction, but that was only because she had reminded him too much of Mallory.

The telephone rang then, startling Liza out of her stupor as she jumped from her chair.

The phone rang and rang, but she didn't move to answer it.

"Are you going to get that?" Theodore finally asked.

"There's no way it's for me."

"Still . . . you should probably answer it."

"Okay, okay," Liza said reluctantly as she moved to the kitchen and took the receiver from its cradle.

"Retton residence," she answered, saying the words her foster mother, Mary, had instructed her to deliver whenever she picked up the phone.

"How lovely the two of you are together. Liza Jennings and Theodore Price. It has a nice ring to it, grouping you two in one breath," a deep voice spoke into her earpiece, the words warbled by some kind of speech modification device so Liza couldn't place it even if she tried.

"What? How do you know he's here?" Liza asked, a powerful gust of wind shaking the frame of the trailer as if on some diabolical cue. A storm was coming.

"I've been watching you," the voice said.

"Who is it?" Theodore mouthed at Liza, now standing at her side, having gotten up from the table when he heard what she'd asked the unknown caller.

Liza didn't answer him; her attention was focused on the phone.

"What do you want?" Liza asked.

"Oh, just to say hello," the voice said, laughing wildly. "After all, we'll be getting together soon. I think you two will make the perfect sixteen and seventeen. Until then, do take care of yourselves. You haven't got much time left."

The click of the caller's receiver rang in Liza's ear. The arriving dial tone punctured her guts, her entrails spilling out on the floor, making her feel like she would trip over them if she moved.

She gulped and slammed the phone back into its place on the wall, pulling Theodore toward her and hugging him tightly as she rested her head on his chest. He was startled by the embrace, but let it happen.

"Theodore, I think we have a problem. An even bigger problem than what we started with."

There had been a twenty-eight-year hiatus, but just like that, someone was claiming the murders were going to resume. Even closing off the town of Point Roberts from the outside world couldn't stop the maniac responsible for the deaths of the Fifteen.

They were already inside.

CHAPTER SEVEN

THEODORE & COLETTE

"He reminds me of a giant meatball."

"A meatball?" Theodore asked Colette as they sat together on a bench at the edge of the marina, amused by her proclamation but also confused. "That's one I haven't heard before. It's hard to believe he's really the president."

"I still can't believe he beat her," Colette admitted, staring out toward the marina where quarantined ships and sailboats bobbed in the water, a gentle breeze causing them to sway back and forth. It wasn't raining, but the afternoon was mostly overcast. The sun tried to poke through where the clouds were thinnest, but failed for the most part, being continuously swatted back by the cumulus and stratus who didn't wish to share the sky. Colette tried to read some of the names on the boat hulls closest to where they sat but had trouble making out what they said. Her eyes weren't as good as they used to be, but she still felt too young for reading glasses. She clung to her fleeting youth.

Colette sighed and pulled her golden shawl tighter around her shoulders as the breeze picked up, the clouds above whipping past more swiftly and the sail lines clacking against the ships' tall poles. "With all the terrible things he's done in just a few short weeks in office, I can't help but think of the similarities, you know?"

"Similarities?" Theodore asked, the quizzical look on his face sincere.

"Maybe they don't stand out to you that much, but they do to me. This is my first February here. There's the wall the president wants to build on the southern border, versus Point Roberts' massive wall against the north that already exists. Then there are the similarities he shares with our disgruntled leader, Emory. They're both behemoths, tyrants who have latched onto power and seem drunk on it. Still—in both places—the people voted them in."

"Well, Colette, you have a point, but I don't think getting fired up about that bright-orange man in DC is going to help our situation here. The US is at a tipping point, and I think we might be too. That's why I wanted to talk to you, to discuss the Fifteen and where the search for justice lies today. For the first time in a long time, we might be getting closer to the truth. Things have changed since I last saw you, and even though I wasn't ready to talk with you then, I'm ready now."

"I'm glad to hear that, Theodore. I've had a few things happen since we last spoke too. Things I think you should know about."

Just ten minutes earlier, Theodore had come face to face with Colette in Honey B's, the sweet aromas of her French pastries swaddling him in a warm embrace.

He wanted to get to know her. But more importantly, he wanted her to join him.

When Colette saw Theodore walk into her shop, the bell chimes ringing as he entered, she couldn't hide her excitement. Her giddiness was brought about by the delight of his presence, but also from the relief that it wasn't Grant Fisher calling again. The young man had stopped by multiple times since the night she'd found him in the woods, but each time he appeared, she'd gone to the back of the bakery, refusing to speak to him.

Colette had been wondering if Theodore would return ever since he'd abruptly left her. And then all of a sudden, there he was. This was the man she wanted to talk to more than anyone else. When he arrived, she had flour residue all over her face, and bread dust in her hair, but she didn't care.

Theodore convinced Colette to take a break and venture outside to speak with him in private. Since she'd hired additional help because of how busy the bakery had been since the beginning of the month, she could leave her ovens for a while without the fear of the place filling up with smoke again like it had the week before. After accepting his invitation, she ran to the bathroom to clean up her appearance and then walked with him outside, following him to the bench where their conversation had plunged into the depths of everything.

Theodore had guided Colette to the shore of the Point Roberts Marina on purpose. He knew they would have some privacy here since all the boats were locked up for another twenty days. People tended to steer clear of the ships in February, not wanting to be tempted to sail them away. It was unlikely anyone would be in their vicinity. Parlancers rarely patrolled the area, because everyone else avoided the marina.

They were alone.

"Why don't you go first?" Colette asked, her eyes moving away from the boats to the large orange book resting on Theodore's lap. Neither of them had addressed its presence, but she knew how important it was, clearly noticing *The Fifteen* written in cursive on its front cover. It was the manuscript he'd told her about, the one he'd been missing. The one he claimed the redheaded girl had taken. Somehow, it had made its way back to him.

"Well, as you can see, I got my book back," Theodore started, moving his hand over the front cover, tracing the letters of *The Fifteen* with his fingertips. "I've spent the past two days hanging out with a seventeen-year-old girl named Liza. I searched all over the peninsula for her, but I never found her. She found me."

"And she brought your book back?"

"She did. And although it didn't seem like the best idea at first, we've decided to become partners. We've gone through the book and discussed everything I know about the first two murders. We plan to go through them all, one by one, and see if we can find something that's been missed. Liza's very energetic about it. The kid's got a lot of spunk, that's for sure." At this, Theodore smiled a bit, the corners of his lips curling upward as he thought of the congenial bond he'd begun forming with Liza. "We're going to approach the cases of the Fifteen by assembling a trusted team of a few people who might be able to bring something new to the investigation. I was hoping you'd join us."

"Oh my," Colette whispered.

"I'm sorry, did I totally gauge your interest wrong?" Theodore asked, looking concerned, his body shifting on the bench so he leaned away from Colette.

"No, of course not. It's just a bit much to take in. You Americans are so direct," Colette said, fidgeting uncomfortably. Even though she felt like she could trust Theodore, she was somewhat hesitant. She was intrigued by the knowledge he held on the Fifteen, and while his offer was tempting, joining him would be akin to jumping off the end of a dock with a heavy anchor chained to her ankles. She needed to know more. And it wasn't just that. She didn't even know this girl, Liza. What if they didn't get along? She hadn't had any relationships with teenagers in her adult life. From the way Theodore talked about her, it sounded like they were already close. Colette was nervous that Liza would hate her, simply from looking at her. It wouldn't be the first time a girl had been intimidated by her.

Even as her conscience begged her to consider her options, her heart threw itself aboard a moving boat. She released her ankles from the anchor's chains and jumped onto the boat's bow, gliding through the waters of her life as she lifted her arms at her sides.

"Alright, I'll join you two. You just have to promise me one thing."

"What's that?"

"You're not part of the cult, are you?"

"The cult?" Theodore asked, puzzled by the words that left Colette's lips, the sound of her French accent reverberating away from where they sat, bouncing from one ship to the next, heading out to sea.

"It's what I wanted to talk to you about—what's happened since I last saw you. I met a man named Grant Fisher."

Colette revealed how she met Grant at the vigil. She told Theodore about the conversation they'd had at his cabin, and what she'd witnessed in the woods when she went to find him and see what his society was all about.

"When I saw them throwing stones around that bonfire, I ran away as fast as I could. He's come by the bakery a few times since, trying to talk to me, but I've been too nervous to leave with him, and he didn't want to talk in front of others."

"I hate to admit it, but I know all about Grant's society," Theodore told her. "He's asked me to join in the past, but I've always declined. I consider myself an authority on the Fifteen, so I didn't feel the need to join in on their antics. But I've been feeling stuck for a while now—until recently that is. Perhaps my husband's dying was the kick in the gut I needed to push me out of my comfort zone."

"Oh, I'm so sorry to hear that, Theodore. I didn't—"

"It's okay. His loss pains me every day, but he was sick for quite a while. Bill was ready to go."

A temporary silence glided across the marina then, allowing them to take a moment to contemplate what to say next. Colette was hoping to avoid any more details about Grant and whatever the hell it was he'd been doing in the forest. Even for a woman who felt secure in herself and her sensibilities, what she'd witnessed in the woods made her stomach churn, melting the butter of her insides. And Theodore preferred to move away from any more talk of Bill's death. There were other deaths to discuss.

Potentially his own.

"There's something else I should mention before we go any further: a call Liza got yesterday when I was with her at her trailer on Benson Road."

"What kind of call?"

"Someone threatened her. Their voice warbled with an audio-cloaking device. They knew the two of us were together, even though we'd just met the day before. They told her that we'd be victims number sixteen and seventeen." Theodore gulped; just saying it out loud made it all the more ridiculous, all the more real.

"Oh my God," Colette said, unsure whether or not to take the threat seriously or categorize it as some sick prank.

"Who knows who this person is, or what their intentions are, but it might be dangerous to associate yourself with us."

"I'm up for the challenge," Colette told him, not letting herself overthink the danger of what might come her way, instead allowing her heart to pulse more powerfully than her brain once again. She had come to this town for a reason. She wanted answers, not only about what had happened to her dear friend Elsie, but to the rest of the Fifteen as well. While the thought of joining Grant and his society made her feel uneasy, joining Theodore felt like the right thing to do.

"I was hoping you'd say that," Theodore confessed, his shoulders slackening as he relaxed. It seemed he'd added another citizen to his cause. Colette Bernard was in.

⁓

The naked body of Brent Locke was found on the shores of South Beach in the early morning hours of February 15, 1987, by a woman who was walking her poodle. At first, she thought he was some drunk lunatic who'd fallen asleep by the sea, but when her dog eagerly pulled her closer to where the man was sprawled out, one look into his blank open eyes made it obvious he was dead.

When investigators arrived to secure the crime scene, and the coroner first examined the corpse where it was found, it became apparent that Brent had been strangled to death. His Adam's apple was surrounded by darkened ligature marks, his throat a turtleneck of bruises.

A third victim had been discovered, and as news of the murder spread across town, the citizens of Point Roberts started to lose it, breaking out into a kind of mass hysteria.

Two murders in one month was terrible enough, but three was a resounding screech, a cacophony of crows eternally cawing somewhere in the treetops, unable to be found.

Later on in the medical examiner's office, the coroner found dried semen on the victim's body, which did not appear to be his own. The coroner also found multiple tears in Brent's rectal cavity, causing him to conclude that Brent had been raped shortly before he'd been strangled to death.

The dinner Brent had shared with his boyfriend the night before on Valentine's Day was still digesting in his stomach. It would never make it past his small intestine.

Deputy Bill Bruno was the first officer to question Sean Jensen, Brent's boyfriend of over three years. Bill didn't tell Sheriff Ambrose he knew who Sean was, afraid that if he did, the sexual relationship he'd once had with Sean would come to light. Since Sean was a suspect, any prior connection between them would unravel Bill's involvement with the case. Bill was still deeply in the closet, and he planned to keep it that way. Nevertheless, he wanted to protect Sean from the other officers who'd conclude he'd murdered Brent as the result of some "queer lover's spat."

Bill wanted to find out what had happened to Brent, but he didn't want Sean to go down for it if he was innocent. He couldn't imagine Sean being a killer.

Sean never denied that he had sex with Brent the night before, telling Bill the semen on Brent's body had to be his. They were in a relationship after all. He claimed it was consensual, if a bit rough. He urged Bill to believe him, trying to convince the deputy that the coroner had made a mistake in classifying what he'd found as evidence of rape.

Sean loved Brent, and now that he was gone—murdered and discarded on the beach—Sean's life began to collapse around him. The summit of Mount Baker started smoking in his periphery as a volcanic eruption exploded in his heart.

Bill tried to keep an open mind. The evidence found was circumstantial, and multiple people in town confirmed that Brent and Sean had been in a loving, committed relationship. There could be a simple reason why Sean's semen hadn't been washed off Brent's body.

The last time Sean saw Brent was in the middle of the night, half-asleep, worn out from the passionate sex they'd had after enjoying wine and the delicious seafood pasta Brent had made. He remembered looking at the face of the man he loved, his partner's eyes closed as they lay in bed together, their bare legs intertwined. When he woke up in the morning, Brent was gone. To where, he did not know.

And then an anonymous tip came in from someone who claimed they'd witnessed Sean dragging Brent's naked body through the sand on South Beach. This was before the police had publicly announced Sean as a suspect.

From this point on, Bill couldn't help Sean any further. All bets were off.

～

"My, my, my. What do we have here?" A high-pitched voice asked in somber tones, as it swiveled around from behind the bench where Theodore and Colette sat. The large body of Emory Schultz blocked their view of the sky, blotting out any lingering sunshine.

Theodore slammed his book shut, the pages on Brent Locke's murder he'd been showing Colette compounding upon themselves. They'd been talking openly about the case of the twenty-five-year-old who'd been dumped on South Beach. The third victim in a string of fifteen.

He hoped they hadn't been heard.

"Not many people come by the marina this time of year. You know, with all things considered," Emory wheezed, his hands awkwardly resting on top of his stomach. No matter how hard he tried, his stubby limbs couldn't get comfortable. His body was constantly at war with itself.

"Which is a shame, don't you think?" Colette asked him, her tone pleasant on the surface, but laced with an air of aggressiveness. "It's such a lovely place to sit."

Inside, Theodore was screaming, but he couldn't speak. His aversion to the mayor calcified his bones. He and Colette needed to leave, as quickly as possible. He couldn't risk this interaction turning into a full-blown conversation.

"That was exactly my thought today. I decided to break with tradition and head over here, to clear my mind and take a seat on this bench to think over a few things. It appears you two beat me to it."

"Well, we were just leaving," Theodore said, his bones unfreezing. He stood up from the bench and looked at Colette, trying to convey a sense of urgency. It was imperative they escape the situation without letting Emory engage with them any further.

Before he knew what was happening, Theodore felt the book being wrenched out of his grasp, tugged on from behind and captured by grubby little fingers.

He moved into action, twisting away from Colette and turning to face Emory, looking down on the bald, portly man with an expression of fury he couldn't hide. He wouldn't lose the book again.

"Give me back my book, Emory!" Theodore screamed. There was no point in playing coy.

"Oh my," Emory said, contemplating the book in his hands as he admired the words on the cover. "I thought I'd heard you two discussing the Fifteen as I was approaching, but my hearing isn't as good as it used to be, so I couldn't be sure. I guess this book proves my suspicion. How unfortunate." Emory shifted the book to his side then, moving his enormous frame a few steps away from where Theodore stood next to Colette. He dug his hand into his pocket, shifting his belly aside as he pulled out a cell phone. "Since no parlancers are on duty here,

I'll need to call the Point Roberts police. The two of you will have to be arrested. I know you're new, Ms. Bernard, but my dear Theodore, you certainly know the rules."

"No!" Colette shouted, pouncing forward like a lynx and pushing Emory in the stomach, causing him to double forward, the book popping out of his hands and falling to the ground.

Without hesitating, Theodore scooped it up, turned to Colette, and shouted, "Run!"

The book was back in his possession as they sprinted away from Emory. Theodore began thinking about where he could hide it, since it wouldn't be long before Emory would send the police to arrest them. Bill was no longer around to protect him. But at least if he had time to hide the book, everything he knew about the Fifteen wouldn't be shared with the man he loathed.

"Wait! I have a deal to offer!" Emory shrieked from where he remained along the edge of the marina, not even trying to catch up with them.

Colette stopped running, too intrigued by what Emory might say to continue her escape.

"Don't listen to him! He's a liar! He won't offer us anything."

"I just want to see—"

"Give me the book, and I'll make an exception. Give me the book, and I'll pretend none of this happened."

Theodore doubled back and jogged to the space where Colette had stopped, fifty or so yards down the street that led away from the marina toward Honey B's. Emory was far enough away that he wouldn't catch them if they decided to leave again, but still, his presence was too close.

"We have to take it," Colette whispered to Theodore, making sure her voice was quiet enough that Emory wouldn't be able to hear them over the wind that had picked up. "I know you don't want to, but getting arrested is going to be far worse than losing this book. Who knows how long they'd keep us in custody."

Theodore's brow furrowed as he recognized Colette's valid argument, even though it stung. He had just gotten his book back, and now she was trying to convince him to part with it again.

"I know, but maybe we can barter with Emory. Give him something else instead."

"You know that won't work. He wants the book. We have to rip the Band-Aid off," Colette said, moving swiftly and pulling the book from Theodore's grasp, who had to force himself to let it go.

Colette walked the book back to Emory, dropping it on the bench without looking at him or saying a word, instead staring out to where the boats still gently bobbed, finding some consolation tucked away within their sails. Having made her deposit, she turned back and joined Theodore as calmly as she could, the two of them leaving the marina's domain for good. Theodore walked with Colette as he tried to stifle a projectile of bile that wanted to sing a tale of melancholy past his lips.

Emory cackled behind them. The book was his.

This was a battle he'd won.

Theodore threw up in his mouth then, but made himself swallow it down.

"I know you must be feeling sick about this," Colette said as she took his hand in hers, his fingers ice, hers laced with warm marmalade. "But I promise you, we'll get the book back. In less than twenty-four hours. Consider it a challenge. We'll figure out a plan together."

"We have to."

"We *will*."

And even though it seemed impossible at that moment, he believed her.

By 11:00 a.m. the next day—after discussing their plan all morning—a course of action was underway.

Colette walked into the Point Roberts township building and stood before the front desk, where a frumpy secretary with oversized spectacles scrutinized her from behind a large stack of paperwork.

"Can I help you?" the woman asked, clearly annoyed she had to speak to Colette, or perhaps simply perturbed by the way Colette's appearance contrasted against her own.

Colette's blonde hair framed her face in gentle waves, as if she'd just come back from a sunshine-filled day on the coast, and her skin gave off a golden glow. The dress she wore was light blue with a white floral design stretched across the fabric, like antique wallpaper displayed in a museum for its vintage beauty. She held a box of fresh pastries, their heat emanating through the cardboard and onto her hands, which were already sweating—not from the heat, but from sheer nervousness. Colette's rouged lips opened to announce her business. Her white teeth looked as if they belonged in a Crest toothpaste commercial—once again differing from the secretary, whose unfortunate snaggle tooth was biting down on her lower lip in anticipation.

"Oh, I've just popped by to drop off some pastries for the mayor," Colette said as casually as she could.

"How nice of you," the secretary sneered. "You can leave them on my desk. I'll be sure he gets them." In reality, she planned to eat them all herself.

"If possible, I'd like to personally deliver them to him," Colette requested sheepishly, as if their entire plan did not depend on this very encounter coming to fruition.

It was before lunchtime. She hoped Emory would still have a healthy appetite.

The secretary rolled her eyes but decided to oblige. If Emory learned she'd turned away a pretty woman who wanted to deliver food directly to him, she'd never hear the end of it. She picked up the phone on her desk, paged Emory, and waited for him to answer.

"There's a woman here with some pastries for you. She insisted on delivering them to you herself. Her name? Oh, I guess I haven't asked," the secretary said before covering the phone with her hand and turning her attention to Colette. "What's your name?"

"Ms. Bernard. Colette Bernard."

"Her name is Colette Bernard," the secretary said. "Okay. Yes. I'll tell her." And then she hung up.

"He'll be right out. He said to wait here."

"Thank you," Colette replied, secretly breathing a sigh of relief that Emory had decided to leave his office. This would make her job much easier.

The plan went something like this: Colette would distract Emory with her false peace offering of pastries, apologizing to him for her behavior. She'd ensure he was enticed not only by the smell of her baked goods but by the way she presented herself and playfully charmed him. Meanwhile, Theodore would sneak into the township building through the rear entrance, using a key he had left over from Bill's time as sheriff, slink quietly into Emory's office, grab the book, and get the hell out as quickly as he could.

Colette had asked Theodore to steal the case file on Elsie Dawkins, but he wasn't sure how easily he could find it, so he made no promises. Reclaiming his book was dangerous, but he had to get it back. Knowing Emory was rifling through its pages made Theodore feel dizzy, much like he'd felt after throwing it into the sea, but exacerbated to an even deeper level of uneasiness since this time, losing it hadn't been his choice.

Once inside Emory's office, he planned to look for something that could give them leverage. He just wasn't sure what that would be. Theodore had long suspected the mayor was hiding something crucial, and he hoped to high heaven there was evidence in his office to back up this idea. They had to find something he'd kept hidden from the public, or he and Colette would have nothing to hold over him—nothing to threaten him with or expose. They had to convince Emory to let them keep their freedom and the book.

As soon as Colette heard a door click open down the hallway and saw Emory's large figure emerge from his office and begin walking toward her, she subtly shifted her stance and reached into her dress pocket to send the already written text message to Theodore. It was time for him to move into action.

Emory trudged down the hallway, the creepy smile on his face getting wider as he got closer to where Colette waited for him in the lobby. She was purposely standing far away from the secretary's desk so the woman couldn't eavesdrop. As the mayor arrived in front of her, Colette caught a glimpse of Theodore slipping into Emory's office down the hall, the door remaining slightly ajar as he disappeared behind it.

Wasting not even a moment, Theodore was inside.

Half the battle was won.

Yet her conversation with Emory was just beginning.

"I must say, I'm surprised to see you here this morning, Colette," Emory admitted, the sound of his wheezy voice rattling in her ears. She looked down on him, her tall, thin figure accentuated by the high heels she'd worn. She wanted to be as high above him as possible. "And to think, you brought treats! Have we turned over a new leaf?"

The excitement in his voice made her nauseated. She wanted to reach into the yellow box of pastries and smash the huge cinnamon roll covered in thick, gooey icing right into his face—but she resisted. The desecration of baked goods wouldn't help her now. She had to act as if she were sorry, even though she was far from it. She had to become an actress with the starring role in a well-thought-out play.

"Ah . . . yes. Well, I've thought a lot about what happened yesterday by the marina and even our first interaction at Honey B's, and I've come to realize I haven't been very nice," Colette explained as she shifted from heel to heel, the pastry box in her hands held right before Emory's pie hole. The corners of his lips glistened. He was salivating. "I want to apologize for my behavior. As we say in French, *je suis désolé*," she said through half-gritted teeth, not letting him notice how hard it was for her to say these words. She laced them with an air of overcompensating sweetness that was not a part of her usual nature. "I've brought over some of my best pastries, ones that I don't think you've had a chance to try yet. I thought that—"

At this moment, Colette dropped the box of pastries, pretending to have lost her balance as she adjusted her stance. She'd dropped them gently, making sure the box didn't tip upside down. As long as the box was on the ground and she had to retrieve it, her purpose would be achieved.

It was sad she had to use such tactics, but she had an inkling that Emory was attracted to her. Bending over in her short, fitted dress—her long legs on full display—would distract him further.

As she bent over to pick up the pastries, making sure her ass was pointed directly at Emory's face, she giggled nervously, as if she were embarrassed by what she'd done.

Instead, she was strangely empowered. They'd barely spoken, and already she'd given Theodore plenty of time.

"I usually don't wear high heels like this," Colette told the mayor as she stood erect once more, the box of pastries back in her grasp. "So silly of me."

"Please, it's quite alright," Emory told her, smacking his lips on the last word in audible delight. "Now why don't you open that box and show me what you've brought?"

He was as aroused by the sight of her as he was by the tempting treats still hidden from view. He wanted more.

Emory's office was surprisingly clean. For a man who never presented himself in a polished fashion, the room Theodore found himself in was organized with the utmost care.

Theodore's attention was drawn to the two large bookshelves in the corner of the room, which were wedged beside large windows looking out on the empty back parking lot. Each of them was overflowing with binders labeled with the names of the Fifteen. Serving as bookends were carefully arranged stacks of Twinkies and Ho Hos still in their plastic wrappings, their fluffy, cake-like exteriors acting as foundations to hold back the terrifying details of how fifteen lives were taken.

Theodore walked over to the bookshelves and grabbed two binders. One labeled "Mallory Price," the other, "Elsie Dawkins." He knew he didn't have time to look at them here, so he decided to take them, shoving them both into the canvas tote bag he'd brought.

As Theodore turned his attention to the mayor's desk, he analyzed the multiple piles of papers covering it. Each stack was placed parallel to another, the different documents working together to create a grid. Emory's pens were arranged by color, ranging from black to blue to red, and his stapler, Post-it notes, and tape dispenser sat together in a neat little row like a family.

In the middle of it all, Theodore's book sat open on the desk in plain sight, as if everything else the mayor possessed was serving as a chorus to his distinguished opera soloist. Emory Schultz had always possessed a lot of information about the Fifteen, but he'd never had Theodore's book or the insight that came along with it.

And that's how Theodore wanted it to remain.

He snatched the book, grasping it with both hands as he noticed it was open to the pages about the fourth murder that had occurred in 1987, when Jennifer Barnes had been smothered to death with a pillow in a room at the Moon Hotel.

No one had heard her screams.

Closing the book and trying to forget the pandemonium that had overtaken Point Roberts after Jennifer was killed, Theodore plopped his orange manifesto into his bag atop the binders and began to scan the desk for anything else worth taking. It had already been a few minutes since he'd entered the office, and he knew he shouldn't overstay in case Colette's chat with Emory didn't last for as long as they'd planned.

His eyes glazed over paperwork that detailed Point Roberts' laws and regulations for the month of February, city water bills, written correspondence with the police department, proposals for new buildings in the center of town, housing deeds, a grant for expanding the protected areas of Lily Point, and what appeared to be a bunch of receipts with a bright yellow Post-it note placed on top of the stack.

Theodore took a closer look, squinting to make out the ungainly cursive script Emory had written across the note.

Where is Jon Templeton?

Not familiar with the name, Theodore became intrigued, rifling through the pile, where more than thirty receipts from Smith's Grocery Store were paper-clipped together. Each of the receipts dated back to either 1987, 1988, or 1989.

These receipts had to mean something.

The last names of the customers were marked in purple highlighter. They'd all purchased the goods listed by using store credit, their names recorded on the receipts so that the clerk could add the totals to their balances to be paid at a later date.

As Theodore shuffled through the receipts and started to take in what he was looking at, he could barely breathe. The bag holding his book and the two binders resting on his shoulders grew heavier, its strap digging into his skin.

Fifteen different last names were highlighted.

Each one corresponding to a victim of the Fifteen.

The dates of their purchases made within a week of when they died.

They all matched up.

Every. Single. One.

Theodore didn't have to look up any of this information to double-check the conclusions he was coming to. He knew the exact dates of when each of the Fifteen had been killed by heart.

So when he began to notice that the name Jon Templeton was printed at the top of every highlighted receipt, it all started to click.

This had to be more than a coincidence.

Had the mayor figured out the identity of the Slayer?

Theodore grabbed the stack of receipts, shoved them into his bag, and headed for the door, knowing the few minutes Colette had promised to give him were about to expire.

He left Emory's chambers as hastily as he'd entered them, his book back in his possession, with a new lead and even more questions. As he snuck back into the hallway, he could hear Colette and Emory chatting at the front of the building, Colette's gentle voice making its way back to him. Once he reached the building's rear exit, he waited to hear the mayor's voice again, wanting to use it as cover to open the door and leave.

But when Emory's voice shouted, "Goodbye, my dear Colette! Thanks again for that sweet surprise," he knew he had to rush out the door.

For the second time in two days, he found himself running away from Emory Schultz.

The cold drizzle overtook him as he sprinted from the township building and went down the hill to where he'd hidden his Subaru behind an enormous bush. His boots plodded against the moist grass, and he almost slipped when he lost his balance.

Once at the car, the doors already unlocked, he ducked into the driver's seat, tossing the tote bag into the back and bringing the engine to life, driving toward the building he'd just left even though it wasn't part of the plan.

He and Colette had arrived separately, and that was how they were meant to leave, hoping to give Emory's inquisitive nose no reason to suspect they were working together.

Theodore needed to change their itinerary.

Finding a clue as monumental as the receipts had altered the game.

If this Jon Templeton lead really was something and Emory walked back into his office with the book and receipts gone, he feared Colette would be taken into custody, regardless of whether or not she had the secret evidence in her possession.

He'd urged Colette to drive to the township building so she could get away quickly, but she convinced him to let her walk. With Honey B's only a short distance away, she argued that Emory would suspect something was up if she didn't travel to see him on foot.

She was walking calmly down the sidewalk, having made it just a little bit past the township building, when Theodore spun up beside her, rolling down his window and yelling at her to get in.

"What are you doing?" she shouted in surprise. "This wasn't part of the plan!"

"Screw the plan! Get in!" Theodore bellowed, the look on his face convincing Colette not to question him again. She shimmied around the front of the Subaru, whipped the car door open, and plopped into the passenger seat as Theodore began to drive away.

Just then, the air was interrupted by Emory Schultz, who emerged from the front of the township building and started shrieking down the street. Theodore gripped the wheel tightly. The window was still open and light rain splattered the car's interior. His eyes on the road, he tried to focus on what was in front of him, aiming to ignore the obese man who was now attempting to follow after them on foot, his arms waving in terrifying motions as he tumbled down the sidewalk like a mountainous bowling ball unable to gain speed.

"He looks like he wants to kill us," Colette said, turning her head farther back as they gained more distance from the mayor, entering a realm of temporary safety. "And I just got him to like me again. I guess that won't last long."

"I think we're going to be okay for a while, now that we're getting away from him," Theodore said, his nerves rattled but his confidence restored. It wasn't long before they reached the outskirts of town, turning onto the road that led to his purple cottage in the woods.

"Did you get the book?" Colette asked rhetorically as she reached into the backseat and pulled Theodore's tote bag forward, removing its contents and placing them in her lap. The orange book was the first item to present itself. She took it in her arms and held it close to her chest like it was a long-lost pet. "I told you we'd get it back, didn't I?"

"You did. And there's more. Look what else I got," Theodore directed as they continued driving along a back road lined with tall stretching evergreens that made the gloomy day even darker.

"You got the case files! Theodore! This is huge!" Colette exclaimed, her excitement palpable, so distracted by what her new friend had accomplished that she didn't even have the focus to open the binders up.

"Yeah, and something else too. Something unexpected. I think it's evidence, something that might lead to a new theory of who the killer was, and why these murders happened. If I had to guess, Emory's kept this knowledge secret for a reason.

He won't want the public to know about it, so we can threaten to release it if he pursues us. It gives us leverage. We have the book back, and we're not getting arrested. At least, I don't think we are."

"I don't understand, what . . . ," Colette started before trailing off. She moved the book and the binders to the floor in front of her and shuffled through the receipts Theodore had taken, the Post-it note and highlighted names calling out to her.

"Who's Jon Templeton?"

"That's what we have to figure out. And I have an idea of who might be able to help us, although you probably won't be happy to hear it."

Theodore turned into his driveway then, hitting a large pothole he usually remembered to miss.

"Merde!" Colette cried in alarm. She wasn't wearing her seat belt, and her head had nearly hit the top of the car.

"Sorry!" Theodore apologized, his purple cottage looming before them, filtered through the tiny raindrops that had sacrificed themselves from the sky and fallen onto his windshield.

"So what's your idea?" Colette asked. "Are we going to get Liza and whoever else she decides to bring into the fray involved with researching this?"

"No, it's not that." Reaching the end of the driveway, Theodore put the car in park and exited the vehicle, knowing he needed to tell her, no matter how unfavorable Colette might find it.

When she opened her door and got out on the opposite side, he faced her across the car's hood and looked at her bright blue eyes, her red lipstick, and golden-blonde hair. She was presented to him in a palette of primary colors.

She was so very lovely. He knew this. And even though he was not attracted to her in the ways of the flesh, her beauty sizzled just the same.

She was no longer a stranger to him.

"You have to talk to Grant Fisher again. And even though I don't like admitting it, I think we could learn more about the Fifteen if you join the Briar's Grove Society."

"You want me to join a man who makes people wear strange golden robes in the woods and throw rocks at one another? There is no way I can possibly—"

"Colette. They're the only other people in Point Roberts who might be able to help us. Do you want to find answers about what happened to Elsie and the others or not?" Theodore interrupted, knowing that saying her childhood friend's name would egg her on, causing her to find strength in the crevices she thought she'd dusted out long ago.

"You know I do. I want that more than anything."

"Then the Briar's Grove Society is the next step. Grant Fisher may not use methods I approve of, but he's determined to solve these cases. And that's the kind of guy we need on our side right now. I've spurned him too many times to show up at this point. It makes sense for you to go."

Colette gulped, her eyes pulling away from Theodore's as she reached into the car to collect the book, binders, and receipts, placing them back into the tote bag.

She knew he was right.

Without acknowledging this out loud, Colette started walking toward the house. The rain slicked her hair so that her blonde waves became stretched out like skinny pancakes, losing their volume as they stuck to her temples. Her high heels sank into the damp earth, causing her gait to become unsteady, but she did not fall.

"Alright, let's get inside. It looks like we have to come up with another plan."

She used the key he'd given her earlier in the day and walked into his cottage as if she'd lived there for years, as if she'd been the one who'd picked its dramatic purple shade.

Theodore stood by the car for a moment more, hardly able to believe the firm resolve she'd just presented when her face had been aghast only moments before.

He left the rain and followed her in.

CHAPTER EIGHT

COLETTE & GRANT

For a place called Lighthouse Marine Park, the lack of any lighthouse present along the shore had always been startlingly apparent to Colette whenever she walked here. Instead of a grand column of white stone encasing a thrumming lantern, there was a hideous steel conglomeration covered in bright yellow hazard signs with a flashlight-looking device strapped to its top. Apparently, this structure was what allowed the park to keep its name, as it scared away any ships, birds, or passersby who dared to get close enough to it.

Still, Colette found that coming to the edge of the sea brought her clarity when she needed it most. The sandy coast at this corner of Point Roberts was only a fifteen-or-so-minute walk from the small bungalow she was renting.

As the rain pelted her, Colette pulled the hood of her jacket closer to her brow, trying to shield herself from getting entirely soaked. Her thin nylon jacket did a decent job keeping her dry, but it wasn't warm enough on its own. She'd bunched her golden shawl underneath it, which served as an added layer of protection to keep her from shivering.

She needed to invest in better gear.

Colette had come to the beach to clear her head and calm her rattled nerves. She didn't want to be afraid anymore. She had been afraid for too long, ever since that fateful summer in Montréal when her relationship with Victor went sour.

Too many screaming matches, too many bruised wrists, too many slaps across the face.

When she'd ended up in the hospital early last year, Colette knew she had to leave Victor for good. She could no longer cling to any of the excuses she'd once used to justify his monstrous behavior. Leaving the apartment she'd shared with her boyfriend of three years wasn't enough, though. Colette knew Victor would seek her out if she stayed in Montréal. The chaotic passion they'd shared would tempt her to fall back into his arms, even though those very appendages had caused so much damage.

So she had left Montréal entirely, taking a leap and using that disaster of a relationship as the catalyst she needed to move to Point Roberts and open up Honey B's.

Colette had left, but she refused to say she'd run away.

She was stronger than that.

As these recollections reminded her of the danger ahead in Point Roberts, Colette traipsed across the saturated granules of sand, the waves collapsing in repetition. The rain picked up with a gust of wind, causing the drops of precipitation to swell in size as they swung themselves harder through the air. Colette's hood flew backward, permitting a dense layer of rain to overtake her unprotected face, copious amounts of black mascara running down her cheeks within a few seconds.

Waterproof makeup, another thing she needed to invest in.

It was time to start heading home. This had been enough rain for one day, if not a lifetime.

Her thoughts turned to what had transpired with Theodore and Emory over the past two days as she began walking up the beach away from the water. She crawled over piles of bleached driftwood wedged up against where the sand met the grass.

As she walked past a group of melancholic picnic tables and benches carved with the initials of teenage lovers long since gone, she was tempted to take shelter among them where they sat abandoned beneath covered alcoves, but she thought better of it. She had to keep moving. Besides, it wouldn't be long before her expected guest would arrive at her doorstep.

Colette took a deep breath as she reached Edwards Drive, following the winding street back toward the center of town, where warmth and the dry indoors were calling her name. She passed gorgeous houses along the coast, each manor appearing statelier than the next. She tried to pay them no mind, but when she found herself in front of number 209, her soaked boots stopped in their tracks. She gazed into the windows of the extravagant homestead, the place where Emory Schultz resided.

He still lived in the house where his wife had been murdered.

Victor had made it hard for her to trust men, but Emory was a whole different story. Emory made her want to swear off anyone with a Y chromosome entirely.

Except for Theodore. He was different.

But what about Grant? Where did he lie along the spectrum?

She had yet to make a final decision about him.

There were some things she did know, though. She would join the Briar's Grove Society like she and Theodore had discussed. And Grant Fisher would be allowed into her life. It was for this reason she'd left her house this morning, hoping the harsh weather could coax her into submission by knocking out her apprehension.

Even though a part of her wanted to go pound on Emory's front door, Colette knew she had to continue, her gait quickening as she left his house and all its mysteries behind. The rain was starting to seep through her jacket, the heaviness of her golden shawl multiplying as it, too, became damp.

She began to jog, her lungs barely noticing her increased pace, as if they'd gotten used to all the random bouts of running she'd already performed this month. It had only been a week since she'd sprinted away from this same area of town, following Grant from the beach to his cabin near the border.

There was something about Grant that both terrified and enticed her. That night a week ago, she had been attracted to him—there was no denying that. His energy pulsated through her core as if he somehow knew a part of her she hadn't bared. Their conversation made her feel connected to him in a way she had planned to abandon, but then just as she was considering opening herself up, she stumbled across him throwing stones at people in the forest.

She ran away from him that night, just as she was running now while the memory of Grant calling after her returned. His towering, elongated stature stretched both above her and beyond, and his fiery gaze thawed the ice gnawing at her spine.

~

Colette's bungalow was a modest one bedroom painted a pale shade of coral, with brown wooden panels flanking the moldings of its many windows. As she prepared herself a cup of coffee inside—the heat cranked high to help dry the soaked apparel she'd been wearing outside in the rain—she paced back and forth from the kitchen to the crackling fireplace, while the pot she'd put on slowly filled up with dark liquid. Her bones were frozen. Turning the thermostat up hadn't felt like enough, so she'd decided to burn some logs in the hearth as well, hoping it'd lessen the time needed for her golden shawl and rain jacket to release the moisture they'd coupled with.

Besides, Colette knew the guest she was awaiting had a positive affinity for fire.

She was nervous. Grant Fisher was due to arrive any minute, and Colette was going to have to muster up some courage to cover all the topics she'd promised Theodore she'd bring up. Grant was coming into her space, the place where she felt safest.

Yes, she had decided to invite him in, but that didn't lessen her anticipation.

Colette had decorated her home in a manner that could be described as frilly yet strong. White lacy doilies covered stark gray end tables, and prints of French landscapes painted in soft pastels were framed by thick pieces of wood notched with heavy grooves. An oversized mauve-colored sofa was paired with pillows showcasing geometric designs, and her kitchen displayed artwork by both Georgia O'Keeffe and Jackson Pollock. And while her main living space had been written as a recipe of contradictions, her bedroom was adorned almost entirely in white, barren of any personality whatsoever.

The place where she slept had to be kept simple. It was the only way to keep the nightmares at bay. Both those that crept out of her past and those she felt lurking behind every corner of the days to come.

Her coffee pot beeped as it reached its filling point, stopping Colette in midstride as she turned back to the kitchen to empty its contents into her favorite mug. The knock on the door came shortly thereafter, so she moved with the full mug in hand and opened up her home without a second thought.

She didn't want her anxiousness to get the best of her, but perhaps doing things quickly without overanalyzing everything could be a beneficial trait to add to her makeup. Perhaps to solve a cold case involving fifteen murders, one had to act before thinking, so any doubts were stopped before handicapping one's consciousness.

Colette swung the door open and found Grant Fisher standing before her in the rain, the drops pummeling him just as they had her only an hour ago. Yet the young man didn't appear wet, his coat deflecting the moisture away from his core, repelling it back to the earth from which it'd spun. She looked up at him, his angular face gazing down at her without comment. His dark complexion was lightened by the morning aura as the rosy-colored paint on the outside of her bungalow was reflected onto his skin.

"Are you going to invite me in?" Grant asked after a few moments passed in silence, the sound of the rain the only pattern present.

"My goodness, yes. I'm sorry, please . . . do come in," Colette uttered awkwardly, embarrassed that she'd stood there like a deer in the headlights.

They were about to dive into the thick of it.

There would be no going back.

⁓

"To be honest, it was one of the most disturbing things I've ever seen," Colette told him, unable to sugarcoat how she felt about the ridiculous antics the Briar's Grove Society was participating in when she stumbled upon their séance.

"I understand your concerns, but the initiation has a purpose. It creates a bond between the members that allows us to trust one another, to stay strong, to persevere through the trenches of information as we search for justice."

"It wasn't the fire or the flamboyant cloaks—I kind of like those. Actually, I like them a lot," Colette said, unable to hide a slight grimace from Grant, their conversation barreling ahead as they sat facing one another in her cozy living room. "It's the violence. And the chaos it could bring about if it goes any further."

"It never goes any further. What you saw is as intense as BGS ever gets. You happened to stumble upon the meeting at its most dramatic moment," Grant explained, his eyes firmly locked on Colette's, the intense expression he held begging her not to shy away from him. "I experienced a great deal of violence at the hands of my parents when I was young, and although during those times I felt weak and terrified, I grew bigger and stronger and was eventually able to stop an attack before it began."

Colette knew all too well what pain could do to a person, especially when it was inflicted by the hand of a loved one. It seared like hot metal against the skin.

Unwilling to admit that a part of her understood what Grant was saying—because she was not yet ready to divulge that piece of herself—Colette stood up from the purple sofa she'd been sitting on. She tore her eyes away from Grant's watchful stare and moved to the wide window that looked out on a meadow across the street. Tall emerald strands of grass shifted in the wind. The rain was beginning to slow, the clouds having wrung themselves out, but still the sky maintained a murky hue.

"I didn't tell you about our methods, because I was afraid if I explained the initiation process, you would never have joined us in the forest," Grant said quietly, his tone the most subdued it had been since he'd arrived at Colette's bungalow.

"Instead, you allowed me to wander upon it as if I were just casually stumbling upon a scene from some terrifying M. Night Shyamalan film," Colette countered, her tone direct and cold. "I don't agree with your methods, but your followers seem to trust you. And I gather they're pretty devoted to solving the murders. If madness is what it takes, and no one is truly in any jeopardy, I guess I can turn a blind eye."

"What took you so long to decide this? I'd almost given up on ever having the chance to speak to you again after you kept turning me away from the bakery."

"It's only been a week, Grant. One week since I found you in those woods," Colette stated matter of factly as she returned to the space beside him, taking a seat so she rested next to him once more. As she tucked her legs beneath her and placed her hands delicately on her lap, she took notice of his massive size again, his long-muscled limbs appearing so gangly and wide as they stretched out from where he sat. For a tall woman, Colette felt like a folded-up butterfly whenever she was in his presence, like she had yet to break out of her cocoon.

"One week in February. In Point Roberts, that's basically a lifetime."

"Perhaps it feels that way to you, but it was just another week—although it was a busy one."

"At the bakery?" Grant asked, trying to allow the conversation to take a more casual turn, even though they still had many pressing matters to discuss. He had to convince Colette to reconsider joining his fold. He could sense that in the week since he'd last spoken with her, she'd learned more about the Fifteen. He could smell it on her, the scents of certain secrets wafting out of her pores like spirits drifting across a graveyard. He couldn't see them, but he knew they were there.

"Well, yes, the bakery has been busy," Colette admitted, "but it's more than that. Theodore and I have learned some things. We broke into Emory's office yesterday and found something we think holds major significance."

"You what?" Grant asked, scarcely able to believe what Colette had delivered so casually, even though just moments ago he had predicted something crucial coming from her lips.

"Have you ever heard the name Jon Templeton?"

"Jon fucking Templeton," Grant said, unable to stifle a nervous chuckle. "It just so happens he came to my attention a week ago, the night you ran off. What about him?"

Colette told Grant what she and Theodore had discussed and discovered over the past two days, careful not to reveal all she knew, only offering the tidbits needed for Grant to comprehend what she and Theodore were planning to let him in on. She described Theodore's book in the vaguest of terms and told him what Theodore and Liza had begun and where she'd joined in on their escapade. Colette revealed how someone had threatened Liza on the telephone, and how Theodore had sought her out at Honey B's, which resulted in the book being stolen by Emory only for them to recover it again. And the receipts. Oh, the receipts.

It wasn't that she was baiting him, but the trail of breadcrumbs she scattered before his nose was anything but consistent. Her goal was not to lead Grant right into the witch's oven, because she wanted to pull more information from him than what she was willing to disclose. Nevertheless, the trail she wove through the forest would inevitably cause Hansel and Gretel to lose their way.

He had to earn her trust. It was not something she would give him freely.

"I had an inkling Emory discovered something he wasn't sharing," Grant exclaimed when Colette paused in the midst of her story. "I could sense it from his behavior at the vigil where we met. If it weren't for what I learned at BGS last week, I would have guessed he'd been keeping these receipts a secret for years. But no, these are newly in his hands, they reek like freshly executed roadkill."

"What a horrifying thought," Colette said, an audible swallowing sound humming down her throat as if to back up what she'd said.

"These are terrifying times, Colette. I feel there's no need to shy away from wherever my mind wanders," Grant replied, his hands suddenly sliding across the tops of his thighs. His palms had become sweaty. "We need to work together. These receipts are another piece of the puzzle. There's someone I want you to meet, a woman who came to BGS for the first time last week. She's the one who told me about Jon. Her name is Bianca, and from what she's told me—if she's to be believed—I think her story might lead us to justice."

"Does she think Jon could be a suspect?"

"I think you should hear it from Bianca herself. It's not the easiest story to retell, and I don't want to gloss over any of the important elements. Every piece appears to be key. But I will say that what she's told me about Jon Templeton links him to the Fifteen. Maybe even more than any of the other four suspects the Point Roberts police considered."

"So Jon looks guiltier than Robert Turner, Sean Jensen, Jason Dawkins, or Marcus O'Reilly?" Colette asked quickly, rattling off the names like secret codes found on the back of a cereal box she'd studied every morning as a child.

"You really know your stuff for someone who hasn't lived here long. I guess Theodore's a better teacher than I thought he'd be."

"Please don't speak down on Theodore," Colette retorted, the shell of her exterior hardening just as she had allowed herself to soften. Grant's personality was hard to read, constantly fluctuating back and forth. His presence was cryptic, yet it still commanded the room.

"My apologies," he replied, offering a sincere tone that Colette believed. "But to answer your question about the suspects simply: yes. As I'm sure you and Theodore discussed, the evidence linking those four to the crimes were all either coincidences, circumstantial, or the work of the real killer trying to place the blame on someone else. Robert and Sean were both boyfriends of the deceased, Jason was your friend Elsie's father, and Marcus O'Reilly was just a drifter who happened to be in the wrong place at the wrong time. There hasn't been a promising suspect since they were all cleared. And it—"

"But what about the anonymous tip someone called in about seeing Sean with the body at the beach?" Colette inquired.

"We've tried to figure that one out for years, but haven't been able to pin down exactly who called it in. Regardless of how anonymous the caller has remained, they were lying."

"How do you know they were lying?"

"Come to our meeting tomorrow and maybe you'll find out," Grant said, standing up and grabbing his coat, his colossal frame stretching out above where Colette sat, tucked in her cocoon.

"Don't do that," Colette pleaded, sensing he, too, was dropping a trail of breadcrumbs for her to follow. They both wanted this to go a certain way, their paths starting in the middle and spreading from the epicenter they'd agreed on. "I can give you something else if you at least give me that answer before you go. Something else we discovered in Emory's office."

"Something more important than the receipts?" Grant asked as he remained standing in front of the couch, his eyes shifting away from Colette to the window where a loud truck rumbled past on the street, it's headlights brightening the gray afternoon.

"The binders on Mallory and Elsie. We took them. They were empty."

"Those damn case files. He must have the real versions locked away. You're not missing much; I've read the one on my grandfather, and it was pretty useless. I suspect the others are too. Besides, Briar's Grove has all the information they contain. Hell, I bet even Theodore has those details," Grant went on, moving away from Colette in a direct fashion, stopping the discussion as he walked to her front door and put on his raincoat.

"Is there something about Theodore that bugs you?" Colette blurted out as she hurriedly got up from the sofa and moved to the door. She placed her back against it to block Grant's way, his complexion shadowed as he hovered above her. Her wings fluttered in dismay, the shell of her cocoon weakening but not yet ready to crack.

Grant sighed, his broad shoulders heaving upward before slackening beneath his coat, causing him to shrink ever so slightly.

"We don't get along." He kept his response brief. Grant knew the only way he was going to convince Colette to join the Briar's Grove Society was if he left her thirst unquenched, her dry throat begging for more. He moved again for the door.

"That answer isn't good enough," Colette argued, shifting her body so the doorknob was behind the small of her back.

"We don't get along because he doesn't like BGS. I've tried to get him to join so I can find out what he saw that night. He's the only person who's ever come in contact with the killer and lived to tell the tale. But the guy refuses to talk to me. He always gets mad, as if I'm gunning to be the main authority on the Fifteen and replace him as the head honcho on Point Roberts' detective throne. Now please, if you'll let me go, I have errands to attend to. Other people to speak with this afternoon."

"Like who?"

"Come to the meeting at midnight, and you can find out and talk to them too."

"Fine! I'll come!" Colette blurted out, a bit too enthusiastically. It had been her plan all along to agree to join BGS for their next rendezvous before Grant left her company, but she hadn't wanted to appear too willing. It wasn't every day you joined a cult that threw stones at robed people while cavorting around a bonfire in the woods.

"And to think, it only took us a little over an hour to get here. Let's be real, we both knew this was inevitable," Grant said with a smile, unable to hide the glee Colette's announcement had brought him.

"Well, I mean—" Colette began before her cell phone started vibrating on one of her end tables.

"Should I let you get that?" Grant asked.

She looked over at her phone shaking on the table, noticing whoever was calling had blocked their number.

"Yes, I . . . Yes, just wait one second," Colette replied, moving from the door and putting up a hand with a finger raised so Grant would know she wanted him to stay.

Colette swiped across the touch screen, picked up the phone, and placed it against her ear.

"Hello?"

"Colette Bernard. Grant Fisher. Numbers eighteen and nineteen. See you soon."

The warbled voice rattled through Colette's consciousness for just six seconds, but the memory of it would last her a lifetime.

The caller hung up before she was able to respond, the dull thrum of the dial tone ringing in her ear, a look of pure terror etching itself upon her perfectly symmetrical face.

"Who was it?" Grant asked.

"It appears we're next," Colette told him quietly as she set her phone back down.

Without offering any other explanation, she pushed past him, threw the door to her home open, and ran in her bare feet out into the rain, having finally made the decision to burst free of her cocoon.

Standing naked under a golden robe a few minutes past midnight on February 11, Colette Bernard was initiated into the Briar's Grove Society, not with rocks being thrown, but by the call of a crow.

Grant had promised Colette he'd make an exception and welcome her into BGS without any violence—it was the one condition she'd made him swear on once she returned from her barefoot jaunt in the rain—but he had no real plan on how to achieve such an undertaking. The initiation ritual was enforced for every member, and to allow Colette among them, to let her learn their secrets without any pain inflicted upon her skin, would likely make the other members feel violated.

Grant stumbled through his words at the beginning of the meeting as the fifteen others gathered there in golden cloaks stood around the blazing fire. The night sky was filled with the illuminated pinpricks of a thousand stars. For once, it wasn't raining.

The evergreens towering above them swayed in the light breeze, and Colette noticed how Grant's typically powerful voice wavered along the rhythm of the wind. He was nervous about how the others would react to him letting her be above the rules.

"Colette Bernard has decided to join us. In the past week since we last met, she has gained a great deal of knowledge that will help our cause. I hope you will welcome her as a fully fledged member of BGS."

Fourteen sets of eyes stared at Grant as he paused, every one of them waiting for him to say more, but he stayed silent.

Finally, the oldest member of BGS, Arthur, spoke up.

"Who's going to throw the rock at her, then?"

"We're not going to do that tonight," Grant told him.

At this, hushed voices harrumphed and sounded their unhappiness. Why was this tall, slender blonde woman from another country allowed in without enduring what the rest of them had to? Was it because Grant didn't want to scuff the frame of the woman he was so clearly lusting after?

"Why does she get a free pass?" Arthur asked.

"It's not that she—" Grant started before he was interrupted by a loud cawing sound, a swooshing movement pushing through the air against them, vibrating against the wind.

A large crow—bigger than Grant had ever seen—dove into the space above their circle, having emerged from somewhere in the darkness of the treetops, leaving its roost to make a theatrical presentation. Its wings flapped aggressively as it flew clockwise around the bonfire, its sizable body hovering in the air over their heads as if it were moving in slow motion. It passed over each of them before stopping above Colette.

While everyone else was frightened by the bird's appearance, Colette seemed unperturbed. She stood still as the crow cawed again and landed on her left shoulder, its sharp talons digging into the fabric of the gold robe Grant had given her.

Colette wasn't sure what was happening. She had never been a fan of birds, but somehow, she knew this crow's arrival would work in her favor. The creature was marking her, showing everyone present that she was special and worthy of being accepted into the Briar's Grove Society in an atypical fashion. She let the crow stay perched on her shoulder, even as the weight of it almost caused her erect posture to crumble. She stood tall.

The crow cawed a third time, the loudest shriek yet ringing from its throat, the noise having been harvested in the deepest chamber of its body. The bird wasn't hurting her, but its close proximity to Colette's face was freaking her out, even though she was trying to keep her expression straight laced. She wanted it to look like this had been part of the plan.

The woman Grant had introduced as Bianca at the start of the meeting looked at Colette then as if she were a specter, a sliver of a ghost that had once haunted her home. The look sent a shiver down Colette's back, causing goosebumps to texture her flesh.

Everyone stood transfixed, not sure how to react. A few more seconds passed and then the crow left Colette's shoulder, lifting its large body over the fire's blaze and returning to the trees. The bird's black color camouflaged it quickly, so no one was able to follow its path for long.

"And that's why Colette is allowed to join us without the ritual. As you can see . . . she's special," Grant told the others, not missing a beat.

Mother Nature had handed them just the kind of distraction they'd needed. It was a weird one—an unexplainable one—but it worked.

Colette didn't want to question what had just happened, accepting it as a quirk of Point Roberts' uncanny strangeness. She silently thanked the crow, realizing its movements had absolved her of being any less than the other members of BGS.

"So we're going to have an extra? A sixteenth member? I thought the whole point of this society was that each of us is paired with one victim," Bianca asked Grant.

"Well, yes, that was always my intention, but it appears something is shifting the balance this year. Colette and I have reason to believe the Point Roberts Slayer is preparing to be active again for the first time since 1989. Either that or we have a copycat on our hands. Someone who's threatening to add new victims to the count."

"Are you serious?" a woman with short brown hair shouted out in disbelief.

"Yes. I'm serious," Grant told the group. "But before we get carried away, I'd like us to begin by recounting the circumstances surrounding victims five, six, and seven."

The others looked perturbed at this. They wanted to dig into the new information Grant had dangled before them, not feeling it necessary to go over the murders at this time. But

Grant thought Colette and the other new members needed to hear about the terrible fates of the Fifteen directly from BGS. He didn't want Colette to learn more details about how his grandfather and Elsie Dawkins were killed just from Theodore's old book. She needed to hear about them here, in the woods, before the fire.

The Briar's Grove Society made the murders' varying clues and circumstances coagulate right in front of them. Together, they used the disproportionate threads of each killing to weave a web unlike any other, hoping that one day their guilty fly would be caught in the center of the trap they'd so expertly spun.

⁓

William Fisher, Grant's maternal grandfather, was found with his throat slit in a bathtub full of blood at his home on Cliff Road near the Canadian border on the penultimate evening of February 1987. He was the last victim to be killed that month, and there was almost a yearlong gap before the next crime occurred. This led many people to believe the murders in Point Roberts were over.

They were wrong.

The coroner ruled that the cause of death was a combination of drowning and loss of blood. It appeared the Slayer had slit William's throat from behind, and the bruises on his neck and shoulders suggested the attacker had then shoved him underwater to disorient him further. The knife marks on his neck were haphazard and splayed, making the coroner deduce the perpetrator had sliced William's throat repeatedly.

Grant's mother found the body. The sight of her mutilated father in the crimson bathtub rattled her so deeply that her entire personality changed from that day forward. She shifted from a carefree, lighthearted woman to someone full of anger, taking out her frustrations by drinking heavily—a problem that got worse as the years went by. She brought her husband into the depths of her despair, causing him so much stress and heartache that he turned to drugs to cope with his crumbling marriage. By the time Grant was five, the two of them often teamed up together against their son.

Because of his grandfather's murder, Grant never got to see the kind versions of his parents. He only got to know the broken ones.

The Point Roberts Slayer ruined his family and altered the course of his entire life.

***

After nearly a year without any murders, Point Roberts awoke from its relatively peaceful hibernation—all things considered—and was pushed back into a dreadful frenzy when Christopher Smith was poisoned.

On February 1, 1988, the high school senior was found unresponsive at the back of a school bus after an evening football game. The bus driver noticed his feet sticking into the aisle once all the other students had gotten off. When the driver approached the boy to see what he was doing, he found him unresponsive, his face a dull shade of blue.

Christopher's death might not have been linked to the Fifteen due to the unusual way his life had ended, except for one crucial piece of evidence.

The killer wanted everyone to know their spree was not quite finished.

A note was found sticking out of the side pocket in Christopher's backpack that sat in the seat beside him. It read:

Happy February, Point Roberts!
Meet victim number six.
I'm back.

A few days after Christopher was killed, Mayor Schultz decided to enforce a strict curfew. To many, it seemed pointless, but it was something, as the initial six victims had all been killed under the cover of night.

Everyone obeyed.

That was, at least, until the next victim, thirteen-year-old Elsie Dawkins, was murdered in the middle of the day.

Elsie had discovered something on the afternoon of February 9, 1988—something the Point Roberts Slayer didn't want anyone else to find out.

Shortly before she was killed, Elsie called her mother at work, asking her to come home.

Later, when interviewed by the police, Mrs. Dawkins recounted what the young girl had said, word for word.

"Please come home right away, Mom! I just learned something bad! Oh, Daddy is going to be so mad!"

With everything that had been going on, Elsie's mother assured her she'd return home right away, telling Elsie to stay inside and keep the doors locked.

When Mrs. Dawkins made it back to their house nearly an hour later, having had to cross the border twice on her commute from her office in Blaine, Washington, she heard a man sobbing loudly, the noise coming from their backyard. As she moved through their kitchen and stepped onto the back deck, she found her husband on his hands and knees. He was kneeling before a large evergreen; an embankment dropped off behind it and led down to the ocean.

When she recognized the gruesomeness of the scene before her, Mrs. Dawkins forced herself to be distracted by the serenity of the sea, knowing she would never again enjoy the ocean views from their home.

Elsie Dawkins was hanging from the tree, a thick noose around her neck, her small body twisted at a broken angle. The entrails of her tiny belly had been ripped out. The person who killed Elsie had decided a hanging wasn't enough to subject the young girl's body to. They'd wanted to shame her even further for what she'd discovered, for what she'd almost told her mother.

She'd been disemboweled.

As Mrs. Dawkins screamed and ran back into the house, searching for the telephone to call the police, the last thing her daughter said kept ringing in her ears: "Oh, Daddy is going to be so mad!"

This proclamation was what led investigators to consider Jason Dawkins as a suspect, and when his fingerprints were found all over the rope that strangled his daughter, they thought they'd finally found their man. They tried to convince themselves Elsie had discovered her daddy's secret double life as the Point Roberts Slayer, and that he'd killed her to protect it.

It turned out what he said about his fingerprints on the rope had been true: he'd just been trying to get his daughter down.

When Emory learned the details of Elsie's death, he knew a curfew wasn't enough. He had to do more. It was on this day that the idea of locking Point Roberts down sprang into his head, but it would be more than a year and eight additional murders before he decided to take such a drastic step.

By the time Emory's wife was killed, everyone—especially him—had reached a point of no return.

And so began the era of the town that skipped February.

⁀

When the three members of BGS who'd been assigned William Fisher, Christopher Smith, and Elsie Dawkins finished recounting their murders, Colette felt like she was going to be sick. The strength the crow had imbued her with earlier had left her; the horrors of what'd happened to these three victims, especially Elsie, haunted every corner of her mind. She listened as the others asked questions. They tried to gauge if anything had been uncovered that could help them find a new path to follow from these three murders, but nothing meaningful had.

At least not yet.

When the trail of questions dissipated, Grant shook off the sadness that had enshrouded him when the details of his grandfather's death were recounted by the fire. It was time to move on. He took this pause as his cue to loop back to the teaser he'd announced earlier, filling everyone in on what he and Colette had learned over the past week. He began by sharing news of the receipts Theodore had uncovered in Emory's office, and what he believed they could mean. He also mentioned Liza, the teenager he hadn't met, asking the others to keep their eyes peeled for her around town in the coming days. Grant wanted everyone to make notes of her movements if they saw her. Both she and Theodore were actively trying to find the killer. Whether they were members of the Briar's Grove Society or not, their actions still held weight. They were all in this together.

When Grant finished speaking, Bianca's shrill voice made itself known. There had been so much to cover from the past few days that Grant hadn't yet given her the chance to address the group. He'd asked Bianca to reveal everything she'd told him to the others, wanting the society to hear it from her.

"Liza and Theodore aren't here. I think we should focus on ourselves. And what we know."

"Yes, please, Bianca, tell them your story," Grant egged her on. "I appreciate your patience." Grant assumed she'd been dying to talk ever since the match was struck over an hour ago, creating the enlarged flame they were standing around, their bare bodies protected only by the golden cloaks and emanating heat.

"The receipts are crucial, but they're not the most important part. I've waited nearly thirty years to tell someone this."

"You mean everything you told me about Jon Templeton?" Grant asked.

"There's more."

"More?" Grant couldn't believe there were further details to her story. Bianca seemed ready to offer even more dramatic claims than what she'd already explained to Grant, dragging all of BGS into a vortex he feared would overwhelm everything.

"Yes. More. I know of another eyewitness who saw one of the murders take place. Someone other than Theodore Price. And they've never talked about it to anyone. Until now."

"Who is it?" Colette asked Bianca, whose wild amber eyes darted to her face as she asked the question.

"Me," Bianca said with a nervous giggle even though it wasn't funny in the slightest. I watched Jon Templeton kill my mother, Amelia Schultz, right in front of me. After he murdered her, he took me to the mainland, where I lived with him for the past twenty-eight years. I can tell you now without a doubt, he killed every member of the Fifteen."

"Are you fucking kidding me?" Grant asked exasperatedly. "Why didn't you tell me this before?"

"I had my reasons," Bianca said without elaborating further.

"Well, where is he then? Is he in Point Roberts? He's probably the one who made the threatening calls!" Colette said, spitting her words out as quickly as she could.

"Oh, no, he's not in Point Roberts. And he can't have been the one who called you. I know that for a fact," Bianca said before turning from Colette to look directly at Grant, her gaze burning into his soul. "Jon Templeton is dead."

CHAPTER NINE

GRANT & MAUDE

Flowers were blooming in Maude Oshiro's garden. Even though it was a balmy mid-February day in Point Roberts, Grant still found it odd that big white blossoms were already opening up, contrasting against the dark green leaves where they burst forth. There were no other colors present among the long-abandoned patches lining Maude's walkway, the careful hand her husband had once lent to the gardens having long since disappeared. Grant's eyes left the flowers as a breeze interrupted his daydream, his attention shifting back to the front porch where he sat, waiting for Maude to return home—her home that, for decades, she had never left.

Things were changing in Point Roberts, all around.

Grant was even more eager to speak with Maude now than he had been that first morning when he'd chased off those prepubescent boys who'd been terrorizing her. The conversation he'd wanted to have with her then had never taken place due to her insistence to let things rest. But this time Grant felt confident he could convince Maude there was much they needed to discuss, so many details to siphon through.

Since Maude wasn't home when he arrived, Grant was optimistic that something had changed since he'd last seen her, something that would make her willing to speak with him.

Grant was determined to talk with Maude about her son, Jon Templeton, and connect her with Bianca so she, too, could hear what Bianca had confessed. He hoped Maude could provide more insight into the damning claims Bianca had shared with the Briar's Grove Society.

Just as he was about to call it quits and head to Honey B's to pick up something to eat to quell his grumbling stomach, Grant noticed someone making their way up the steep staircase that led to the forsaken garden before the house. The woman had thick jet-black hair, which was cut into a chic bob and adorned with a glittering dragonfly pin, and her bright salmon-colored dress with gold pinstripes made her look taller than she was. Her attention was unfocused as she walked toward the house, like she was still longing for the path from which she'd come.

From this distance, Grant assumed the woman must be Maude's younger sister, her footsteps falling along the stone pathway delicately as she sauntered past the white blossoms. Their petals stretched out to greet her, grazing her arms like they needed her touch to release their nectar.

She acknowledged the flowers, looking down at them with a small smile as she moved closer to where Grant sat, finally looking at the house, her eyes landing on him.

"Oh my goodness!" the woman exclaimed in surprise, the aquamarine gloves on her hands rising to cover her mouth in half-suppressed shock. She let out a deep breath, her hands falling away as her demeanor changed, recognizing the man sitting on her front porch. A gentle laugh left her lips. "I wasn't expecting you, Mr. Fisher."

It was only when his last name left her mouth that Grant realized he was looking at the woman he'd been waiting for.

The last time he'd seen Maude Oshiro, she'd had long, scraggly gray hair, unkempt clothing that was two sizes too big, and not an ounce of makeup on. The Maude he'd met looked like she'd lived a life of sadness, the despair etched deeply across her features. This Maude—the woman before him now—looked like a completely different person. She was glamorous and well put together, with a confidence that showed she was ready to take on the world, no matter the cost.

This was the Maude he'd been waiting for. He just hadn't realized it until she arrived.

"I'm sorry for showing up again unannounced. I really need to talk to you, and I won't take no for an answer this time."

"I see," Maude said, taking the final steps up to her porch so she could place herself in closer proximity to Grant. He went to get up, but she put up a gloved hand in protest to signal that he should remain seated. The size of his frame had overwhelmed her that first day they'd met. She knew if he remained sitting, she could focus better on what he had to say. Maude took a seat on the top step, adjusting her dress before crossing her legs at her ankles.

"Where have you been?" Grant asked, breaking the silence since Maude had said nothing once she'd taken a seat on the steps in front of him.

Maude turned and grinned at him, her teeth staying hidden behind the bright color on her lips, but the sentiment appearing the same. "I decided it was time to leave my windows."

"Is everything alright?"

"Things are okay. For February in Point Roberts, anyway. As I'm sure you know, this month doesn't bring out the best in people, but for whatever reason, this one decided to bring out me," Maude responded.

"When did you first leave your house?"

"It was actually the day you stopped by."

"Was it because of something I said? I know you didn't want to talk about Jon then, but I thought maybe now we could—"

"I still don't want to talk about him," Maude admitted, the tone of her voice becoming stern. Even though her mood had been lifting since she'd found the courage to leave home, she was still nervous to talk about Jon with Grant, worried that discussing her son might only shatter the progress she'd made.

Maude wanted to continue walking past the flowers, dressed in her finest, pretending like she didn't have a care in the world, as if the murders that had ravaged her once delicate and beautiful life had never occurred. But she understood the blasé lifestyle she'd been living the past week was only temporary. She knew Grant would come back.

"Maybe we could just talk about Bianca, then, the woman I was trying to tell you about. Or perhaps you could even talk to her yourself . . . hear what she has to say."

"Bianca," Maude whispered aloud, before stating the name twice again, as if it were a prayer she had to repeat in penance. "Bianca. Bianca . . ."

She hadn't forgotten the name, not since the night Jon had last mentioned it and left her forever. Not since Grant had said it in her presence a week ago, causing it to echo inside her mind.

She didn't want to talk about Bianca, but talking *to* Bianca was a different situation altogether.

"She wants to talk to me?"

"She does. There are things she's claiming about Jon that you need to hear from her. I want to be honest, though, this isn't going to be an easy conversation. But it might bring you some answers, no matter how wild her claims may be." Grant spoke as kindly as he could, his speech unwavering as the deep vibrato of his voice sank like rocks into the quicksand of Maude's skin.

"Alright, I'll meet with her," Maude agreed, drumming up the strength to commit. "Where will the three of us be speaking?"

"Well, Bianca thought the two of you should have a private conversation. I won't sit with you, but I'll be nearby in case you want to leave."

"I don't feel comfortable meeting with this woman alone," Maude divulged, knowing she wanted Grant beside her whenever this dialogue took place. She was already dreading whatever it was Bianca wanted to talk to her about, knowing it would likely be nothing good—nothing that could fix the reality that she hadn't seen her son, Jon, in twenty-eight years. Grant had to be there as a mediator and a protector to shield her if anything went awry. She barely knew the young man, but for whatever reason, Maude inherently trusted him.

She told Grant her conditions and made him promise she would have some control over how the conversation took place. Grant didn't hesitate to accept her request. He would much rather be a direct part of the exchange with Bianca than stand a distance apart from it.

They agreed to meet the next day at Maple Beach. Once the time was set, Maude kindly excused herself. He wished her well, his legs lengthening upward as he excused himself from her porch and ambled away.

Instead of watching him go, Maude went inside, the fabric of her dress creating a swooshing noise as it unbunched now that she was moving again. She walked through her front door and latched it behind her.

In the entryway, she stood for a moment and stared at the white flowers she'd plucked from the garden earlier that morning and placed in a purple vase on her favorite end table. There hadn't been flowers in her garden for nearly thirty years, but now ample blossoms were pushing up from soil she'd thought only held death.

Against all odds, life was beginning to flourish again.

⌣

The following day, after twiddling her thumbs for hours in anticipation, Maude left her house on the hill and took the many steps down toward the coast. Feeling anxious, she walked gingerly toward the hamlet of cottages crammed close together near where the sea continuously hit land. Even though her makeover had brought back some confidence, Maude knew this conversation could change everything.

Not wanting to overdo it, Maude only put on a little bit of makeup, wearing a neutral-colored dress so she wouldn't attract too much attention. She couldn't resist putting on a necklace, though, a simple piece with a silver hummingbird hanging at its center. It had been a gift from Jon; he'd given it to her a few weeks before leaving her life forever.

This was the first time she'd ever worn it.

Maude navigated through the smattering of houses that sat closely together along the beach, each one only accessible by sandy footpaths that meandered between them. As she got close to her destination, with the smell of salt hanging heavily in the air, she couldn't help but hesitate, looking back to her house sitting on the hill. It had a bird's eye view of the entire neighborhood. If she had been at her windows, she could have seen herself, a pinprick of beige stranded in the maze that wiggled between the whitewashed cottages.

She had always felt different than everybody else. The inner apprehension she clung to scribbled over her fears, constantly bringing a sense of uneasiness to the forefront. When children had started calling her the Point Roberts Witch all those years ago, she had accepted it, assuming it was a title fitting for someone so cowardly, someone so small.

Maude shook her head in defiance then, not allowing her former weaknesses to seep back in. The weight of her past could no longer hold her down. She wouldn't let herself regress.

Not now.

Maple Beach began beneath her feet with a collection of sea-washed driftwood piled high in an unplanned heap. As she delicately crawled over the wood, Maude's thoughts pulled back to a memory she had made here with Jon, one she could never forget.

"Who brought this wood here? Why did they leave it?" he had asked one morning when they arrived at the beach together when he was ten years old.

"What on earth do you mean?"

"The wood, there's so much of it. Why did they dump it here?"

"My dear Jon, no one brought this wood here. People don't just leave piles of driftwood on the beach. Nature is the force that discards it here."

"For real?" His eyes had glistened then, opened wide. He had always been so innocent.

"The ocean is a powerful force, one I don't think anyone can truly fathom in its entirety," Maude had explained, trying to keep his sense of wonder intact.

That had been so long ago, a time when Maude had been much nimbler. It took her longer to climb over the driftwood now, but when she made her way to the other side of the pile, the soft sand allowed her feet to relieve some of the tension she'd been holding in her calves. She took off her moccasins, the cool textured granules getting stuck between her toes.

As she faced the sea for a moment to take it in, she noticed two figures down the beach about a hundred yards to her left.

Grant and Bianca. They were sitting on a colorful blanket, highlighted in bright yellow and red hues.

They had picked a spot close to the wall, the enormous steel divider that separated Point Roberts from Canada. The immense sheet of black metal towered behind them over thirty feet, serving as an unmissable backdrop, an uninvited fourth guest. This was the wall that ran along the entire north side of town, the only part of Point Roberts not bordered by water. The physical structure effectively made the town an island, especially in February. The wall even stretched out into the water, well past where the waves broke on the shore, almost daring anyone to try and swim around it. No one could ever truly relax at Maple Beach, not with the imposing structure hovering so dramatically right on its edge.

Maude didn't like getting close to the wall. No one did.

As she walked toward Grant and Bianca, the few others on the beach disappeared behind her, making her realize why they'd picked this spot to lay their blanket down.

It would give them privacy, as no one else would dare come this close to the wall. They could sit and have their conversation in seclusion, where no one could overhear them.

"Mrs. Oshiro, it's nice to meet you after all these years," Bianca said with sincerity, standing up to greet Maude as she arrived at the blanket. Bianca extended her hand, but Maude did not take it, instead sitting down in silence on the other side of Grant. The man effectively created another kind of wall between the two women.

"Well then, okay," Bianca muttered to herself, even though it was audible to the others. She retook her seat beside them, looking somewhat defeated.

For a few moments, Maude just looked at her, studying the features of the woman who claimed she knew what had happened to Jon. Bianca's wavy hair was pulled back in a messy bun, a few strands of it shaking in the wind that rolled off the water. Her nose was scrunched into a button, and light freckles were scattered over her high cheekbones. She was an unusual kind of pretty, her big amber eyes lined with so much white. Maude scrutinized every light wrinkle etched into her face as if each one had been caused by Jon. Times he'd made her laugh over a silly joke, times he'd made her angry over a stupid mistake, or times they'd both sat sternly in contemplation, having heated discussions over what they should do about the town they'd abandoned, the people they'd left behind.

"Should we get right to it?" Bianca asked, sensing Maude was not in the mood for any lighthearted introductions. They both knew what they were here for.

Information. Answers. Solutions.

Nothing more.

"What happened to Willow Mendez?" Maude shouted out, a little too urgently.

Grant—who had been silent up until this point, trying only to serve as a quiet witness—interrupted then, raising a hand in agitation.

"What does Willow Mendez have to do with this, Maude?" The expression on his face was one of annoyance. They had so many other things to talk about without delving into questions surrounding the death of the eighth member of the Fifteen.

"No, it's okay," Bianca answered, trying to calm Grant down by placing a delicate hand on his shoulders. The tension left his body.

He had to stick to his plan to be a quiet witness, only to interject if things got complicated.

"I don't know much about Willow Mendez, besides what everyone in town already knows about her," Bianca said.

"Well, please humor me, if you will," Maude responded, her words sounding less abrasive than they had earlier. She was trying to remain calm, but her insides were rattling.

"Willow Mendez was the eighth victim of the Fifteen," Bianca began. "She died on February 19 in '88. Both her wrists were slit and she bled out while lying in her bed. At first, the police ruled it a suicide. And while usually no one wants to accept suicide as the cause of death for a talented eighteen-year-old girl, at the time, the citizens of Point Roberts prayed that was exactly the case. They didn't want to add another murder to the tally.

"Earlier that morning, before she was found pale, dead, and bloodless in her queen-sized bed, Willow had received a letter telling her she'd been accepted to Yale. Willow had always been a brilliant girl, but she was troubled. She'd been going to therapy for depression. She had demons no one could justify. She was a pretty girl, with wealthy parents who loved her. She had a life her peers were jealous of. So even though her death was shocking, no one could say they were surprised she'd taken her life. For a few days, everyone forced themselves to believe what the police had ruled, even if there were doubts."

"Willow was a good friend of Jon's," Maude interjected. "When she was murdered—as we all know she was—that's when he started to change. He was convinced she hadn't killed herself. He knew she was a victim of that monster before anyone else did."

"Even though the Slayer purposely made Willow's death look like a suicide, they didn't like it when her death wasn't added to the victim list," Bianca added. "It was like they had regrets about how they'd decided to kill her. And so they contacted the police for the first time shortly thereafter, spinning the case on its head."

"You really don't know anything else about Willow?" Maude asked again, wanting to make sure Bianca wasn't hiding anything before they moved on.

"No, Maude, I'm afraid I don't."

The wind rustled more severely then, causing goosebumps to rise on Maude's flesh, like turtles pushing their shells up from beneath the water. For a moment she tried to pretend she was somewhere else, shrinking her consciousness into a white glowing orb that skipped across the shells, forming a bridge on her skin.

There was nowhere to go but into the future, the unknown abyss that never stops shifting.

"Some of what I know, I only found out recently from Bianca," Grant explained then, breaking his silence to keep the conversation moving. The sun sank farther down toward the horizon as he spoke. The partly cloudy sky allowed it to peak out intermittently, its golden rays only sometimes flashing against their silhouettes, causing long shadows to stretch across the short length of sand before slamming into the border wall.

"That's why I wanted you two to meet—so this knowledge could be shared. Bianca's told me her story, more than once now, in private and to the members of the Briar's Grove Society."

"The what?" Maude asked. She'd never heard of Grant's organization.

"I can explain Briar's Grove another time, we only have a little while before the sun sets. I don't think this is a conversation we want to have in the dark."

"I suppose you're right," Maude admitted. She wanted to see every line on Bianca's face when she heard what she had to say. She wanted to see her for who she was.

"Are you ready?" Bianca asked Maude as she rubbed her palms over the maroon khakis she was wearing, wiping off the ungainliness of what she was about to share.

"I've been ready for nearly three decades. Please tell me your story."

"I left Point Roberts the night my mother was murdered," Bianca began, her tone making it clear she had a lot to say. "It was one of the worst evenings of my life, but it was also the dawn of my liberation. I often wonder if my mother hadn't been the last victim of the Fifteen, if I'd still be locked inside the basement I grew up in, rotting away. She never would have let me leave her possession, not willingly.

"My mother was not well. But still, that doesn't mean I condone what happened to her. Her brutal murder alarmed me beyond measure, as it would any daughter whose mother was killed in such a way."

"Why did she lock you in the basement?" Maude interjected as a mild gust of wind blew off the beach, ruffling her hair. As she waited for Bianca to answer, she looked at Grant sitting between them. He remained silent as if he were a statue, only there to observe the story.

"Amelia, my mother, was unstable, chaotic, controlling, and her mood often went from love to anger with the flip of a switch. I'm sure she was bipolar, possibly even schizophrenic, but she was never diagnosed. My father, Emory, tried to hide her mental illness as if she were a prized porcelain doll on the top shelf of his china shop. He'd never let her come down from her elegant perch, even if she wanted to jump. He wasn't home much, and to be honest, I feel like I barely know the man. And it's not just because I haven't seen him in nearly thirty years. We never built much of a foundation.

"As a child, I had violent, debilitating seizures on a daily basis. When I was very young, my mother took me to see dozens of doctors, but none of them could stop me from shaking. We tried many different pills, therapies, and even alternative medicine to cure my epilepsy, but nothing worked. When I was four years old, my mother lost trust in everything and everyone and—wanting to protect me in her own messed-up way—decided to never let me leave the house again. Once she made that decision, I stayed locked in that house on the coast for thirteen years, with only a few brief escapes that didn't get me very far. It wasn't until Jon arrived that night, the very same night my mother was killed, that I finally broke out of my house—my prison—for good."

"Jon told me Toshi was your doctor before he was killed. Is that how Jon found out about you?" Maude had a million more questions about Bianca's illness, her mother's behavior, and why Emory had allowed his daughter to be locked up, but this question about her son was what bubbled to the surface. She hoped her inquiry would merge with the sea the three of them sat beside, creating tide pools that would uncover the mysteries she'd been wrestling with for nearly three decades in complete solitude.

Maude focused on Bianca's face, the woman's large eyes like two islands in the middle of an empty map, the coordinates unknown.

"Yes, Jon and I met after Dr. Oshiro's death. Your husband had started making house visits in '88. For a short while, he was the only one besides my parents who knew I existed."

"Toshi? My Toshi?"

"Yes," Bianca said. "I'm not sure why my mother changed her mind about letting a doctor come and see me after so much time, but for whatever reason, she let Dr. Oshiro in."

"I can't believe he hid this from me. I never even knew you—"

"It's probably for the best you didn't know, Maude. What would you have done?"

Maude sat in silence, not sure how to answer Bianca.

"Before Dr. Oshiro was killed, he told Jon about me, not wanting to be the only outsider who knew. Jon learned everything he needed to know about my condition. Your husband shared the details that were necessary for Jon to know, should the need ever arise for him to act in his place. And so, after Dr. Oshiro was killed, Jon took over.

"When Jon showed up, I could tell my mother wasn't thrilled with the situation. I overheard them arguing upstairs. Eventually, she came down with him and introduced him as Dr. Oshiro's son, who would be caring for me moving forward since Dr. Oshiro no longer had time to make house visits.

"You see, Dr. Oshiro had never told me about the murders that were taking place in Point Roberts, and my parents never divulged the information, worrying it would upset me too much and cause even more forceful seizures. But Jon was around the same age as me, and our relationship was different. Even though my mother forbade him, he eventually told me everything.

"When I learned about the murders, it was like the lights were being turned on for the very first time. Jon's honesty, his truth, his respect, and his gentle nature washed over me like warm honey, soothing and sweet. Jon was brave and kind, a calming presence in my life. For some reason, he felt a responsibility to care for me, an epileptic girl he had never met locked in a basement. It didn't take long for me to fall in love with him."

Bianca took a deep breath then as if her lungs were longing for Jon, missing his presence at her side. She knew this conversation was difficult for Maude to hear, but it was hard for her too.

"My Jon, he was always like that, putting himself last in line, caring for others before he ever thought about himself," Maude said.

Maude studied Grant's expression while digesting what had been said so far, feeling like she knew him better than she knew Bianca, when really, he was just as much of a stranger. His silence was quieter, more easily discernible. Grant was enthralled by Bianca and her tale, buying every morsel she placed on display, tasting each bite and swallowing it whole. He felt Bianca was the key to solving the mysteries around the Fifteen, the piece of the puzzle they'd always been missing.

While Bianca recounted her story, Maude couldn't help but be skeptical. Maude wanted justice for Toshi and the others as much as any citizen in Point Roberts did, but she couldn't shake the feeling that something was off. Bianca had glossed over so many details, jumping from one complicated subject to the next. There were so many elements to unpack, so many spaces to be filled in.

Bianca Schultz had always been such an enigma. Her name was the last one Jon had said aloud in Maude's presence, the last person they'd discussed. Once Jon was gone, she never told anyone how Jon claimed the Schultzes had a daughter they'd kept locked up. She added it to the long list of Point Roberts' secrets. Ever since, Maude had wondered who Bianca really was, and why she'd mattered so much to Jon. And now, here she was, sitting before Maude on a blanket at Maple Beach.

~

"I just want to know what happened the night Jon left me." Maude stated her words clearly, her tone balanced as golden light warmed her face, the sun emerging from behind a cloud and sinking closer to the horizon as the wind began to soften.

Night was coming.

"I understand," Bianca said, trying to sound sympathetic. "And before we dive deeper, I want to be honest—my memories from that night were hazy and mixed for many years. One of the side effects of my seizures was memory loss. Sometimes the memories came back, sometimes they didn't. The events that happened before and after a seizure were always the hardest to recover.

"That night in '89—the way I remembered it for a long time—was that Jon arrived to break me out of the basement for good. He didn't have to pull me from my mother's clutches as we'd planned. Instead, he had to tiptoe over the messy piles of blood he found spread all over the kitchen and dining room, being careful not to leave any footprints that would tie him to the crime. When he brought me up from the basement, I had a seizure as soon as I caught a glimpse of all that blood. He had to get me out of Point Roberts. It had already been bad enough, but now it was much worse.

"Jon tried to shield me from the blood, knowing it would likely trigger something dangerous. If it had been up to him, I wouldn't have learned my mother had been murdered at all. But I did find out. Still, that evening has always been blurred in my mind. It's only recently, since Jon's been gone, that the true events have started coming back to me."

"What do you mean 'since Jon's been gone'?" Maude asked, standing up without even realizing it, her small feet shuffling backward off the blanket and into the sand. She did not trust Bianca, and now, she wanted to get away from her.

"Maude, please sit back down," Grant asked gently, reaching out and motioning for her to rejoin them.

"I want to know the truth," Maude continued, ignoring Grant, slowly sauntering backward to the enormous wall, the vast dark shadow behind them. "Why did you come back? Why are you telling us this? I want to know where Jon is! I don't want any more backstory. Tell me where my son is, or I'm leaving!"

Bianca took a deep breath, exhaling audibly, emitting air that was visible in front of her mouth.

It was getting colder.

"Jon is dead."

Maude let out a horrific shriek, her voice evolving into something unknown and beast-like. The confirmation of her darkest fear pained her in such a primal way. Her insides felt like they were melting.

As Maude continued to blubber in uncensored despair, her feet shuffled backward like she was in a trance, the flat side of her tiny bottom hitting the wall before either Grant or Bianca could stop her.

"Move away from the wall immediately!" a loud booming voice shouted from loudspeakers overhead, the noise reverberating in Maude's ears as she startled. "Move away from the wall immediately, or you will be arrested!" the voice shouted again as Maude realized her backside was leaning up against the towering barrier. She'd been temporarily frozen in shock.

Before she was able to pull herself together, Grant jumped off the blanket. He grasped onto both of Maude's wrists, moving her away from the wall and picking her up in his arms without hesitation. The loud voice ceased as Grant put distance between them and the wall, keeping Maude cradled against his broad chest where she remained still. The warmth of his body against hers helped calm her down as she quietly cried, nuzzling against him.

They moved together as one, leaving the wall in their wake as they headed down to the water, where the sound of the sea could muffle the conversation Grant knew needed to continue. There was still so much to address. He wouldn't let shouting parlancers halt their conversation.

"Should I grab the blanket and follow you?" Bianca called from behind as Grant and Maude got closer to the shore.

"Leave the damn blanket!" Grant bellowed in annoyance.

The last thing they needed was to draw further attention to themselves; that's why they'd chosen to sit so close to the wall in the first place, so no one would come near them. That plan had backfired. They didn't need to leave the beach, but it would be stupid to remain by the wall, where parlancers were now surely listening.

When they reached the water, Grant looked down at Maude, who appeared so tiny cradled in his arms. "Are you alright?"

"I don't know," Maude whispered. "But I think it's okay if you put me down."

Grant did as she requested, planting Maude delicately on the sand so her feet stood parallel to his. Bianca arrived at their side, reaching the spot where Grant towered over Maude just as a wave lapped at their feet.

"I'm sorry for causing such a panic," Bianca said quietly. "I knew there'd be no easy way to tell you that."

Maude turned to face her, trying to scrutinize the look in Bianca's amber eyes. Unable to discern what Bianca's gaze conveyed, Maude shifted her attention to the sea, the water before them glowing iridescent as the sun made its final stretch to the end of what could be seen.

"Why didn't you tell me about Jon from the beginning? Why spring it on me in the middle of your story?" Maude asked, wanting to get as many details as she could, even if it pained her to hear them.

"I thought it was important for it to be in context. Jon's death is what made me come back."

"How did he die?" Maude asked.

"He had a heart attack a few months ago while going for a morning jog along the ocean not far from our beach house in Moclips. It was his favorite activity, his favorite time of day."

It was clear Bianca was trying to soften the blow, and while Maude could appreciate her empathy, coming to terms with the fact that Jon was gone—*really gone*—still burned just as much.

"Believe me, I miss him too," Bianca continued when Maude didn't respond. Grant stood alongside them, once again a silent witness. The wind had died down, but the sea still roiled repetitiously as they talked, uncaring whether or not they remained at its edge. "I know you've missed him, and he missed you too. He would have wanted you to know that. It wasn't easy for him to leave you like he did. He loved you. But please know that Jon had a good life. We lived together in a charming house along the sea in Moclips for nearly thirty years. He had a fulfilling life—I think—a good, simple life. He tried to forget Point Roberts and all the hellish things that happened here, but he never forgot you. I loved him desperately, and he loved me too. But I always knew the kind of love he had for you, his mother, could never be surpassed."

Hearing these proclamations did alleviate some of the tension reverberating in Maude's core, but the questions crashing inside the deepest chamber of her heart still raged on.

"If Jon loved me so much, why did he never contact me? I stayed in my house for years, hoping one day he would come home. Or even just call me, and yet he did nothing to ease my pain. No correspondence at all. He's dead now, but in a way, Jon has been dead to me since the moment he left."

The words Maude spoke replayed themselves in her ears, abandoning any discernable sound as they were pulled back into the waves for fish to swallow. Maude found herself aghast at what she'd said. She was angry and bitter, but in truth, she had never given up hope that Jon would one day come back to her.

"Jon thought it was too dangerous to come back here, or even contact you. He thought you were safer not knowing. I tried to convince him hundreds of times to let you know he was okay, but he always made up excuses. With the Slayer still at large, he didn't want to put you at risk. And when February 1990 came and no more murders happened, he felt justified in his reasoning. He was able to convince me we'd done the right thing..." Bianca trailed off then, noticeably shivering. The sun was almost gone. "Now, though, I have a different theory as to why Jon never wanted to come back here."

"And what is that?" Maude asked.

"Hey, maybe this is enough for today," Grant chimed in, turning to the two women beside him, knowing it would soon be dark. He was regretting having this meeting at Maple Beach. It had been a stupid idea to do this in public.

"No, I want to finish," Maude said sternly.

"Well, how about we go back to my place to—"

"No. We can do it here," Bianca interrupted. "There is no point in postponing this any longer."

"Alright, but it's going to—"

"Jon was protecting himself," Bianca said, cutting Grant off. "When he died, I found the receipts."

"Receipts?" Maude asked, confusion etched across her face.

Bianca explained the receipts to Maude then, the new piece of evidence that linked Jon to every victim of the Fifteen.

"I never thought Jon had anything to do with the murders until I found them. He'd hidden them for years at the bottom of a locked trunk I didn't have access to. When I discovered them after he died, I knew I had to come back here, even though I didn't want to. I felt it was my duty, that the receipts might lead to the answers we've been searching for."

"Where are these receipts now?" Maude wondered aloud.

"I gave them to my father, Emory. I left them with him anonymously. I don't want him to know I'm back. At least not yet."

"I don't like that man," Maude responded through gritted teeth.

"None of us do," Grant chimed in, turning to Bianca, who couldn't help but smirk at the proclamation. She'd never liked her father either.

"I thought he'd have the police dig back into the case at full force with this new evidence, or even publicize them since Jon is dead—but I was wrong. From what we've gathered, it seems they haven't even left his office. My father cares about no one but himself, and he clung onto those receipts like they were the holy grail. I thought time would have softened him, but power has gone to his head. For all I know, he'd rather the murders never be solved. I think he likes locking the town down every February. It gives him some sick sort of satisfaction. He doesn't want Point Roberts to know the truth, because he realizes that if the cases of the Fifteen are solved, the border will stay open. There'll be no more justifying these awful Februarys.

"So when it became clear my father wasn't going to do anything with the receipts, I needed another plan. I did some digging and discovered the Briar's Grove Society, deciding to attend their first gathering this month."

Maude's worst fears were coming true. Jon was dead, and it was becoming clear he might have had something to do with the murders of the Fifteen. But her son couldn't have been the killer. She didn't want to believe the possibility, even if the evidence pointed in that direction.

"We should go to the police," Maude spoke up, turning away from the ocean as the last stretch of golden light disappeared, the sun sinking below the depths. She stared at Bianca, trying to make herself sound forceful. Grant's tall, dark presence lingered beside them like he was a guard on duty, serving to protect the two women in his company. "I don't care if they're under Emory's spell, if he won't share the receipts with the detectives, I will, even though it pains me."

"Before we decide on that, there's more you should know," Bianca explained.

"I really think we should go somewhere else before you tell her more," Grant argued. "We can even go sit in my car and—"

"Remember how I said the memories from the night of my mother's death were muddled, how I couldn't recall exactly what happened?" Bianca continued, ignoring Grant as if he were no longer there. All her attention was focused on Maude. The two women now stood facing each other, the sea at their sides. They were mirrored silhouettes centered at a precipice, one side salt water, the other dry sand.

"Yes . . . ," Maude answered.

"Well, that night has been coming back to me in snippets ever since Jon died. At first, it was just little things, like coming up the basement stairs, getting into the car, seeing my house from outside as we pulled away, driving across the Canadian border, and stopping at a gas station once we were back in Washington. I thought coming back here might fill in the most important gaps that stayed out of reach.

"When I got back, I returned to that house, the place that had been my childhood prison. I stood in front of it for a while. The memories engulfed me in a flash, and what I recalled terrified me beyond measure."

"Which was?" Maude piped up when Bianca went silent. The suspense was unnecessary.

"Jon killed my mother."

"How can you be sure?" Maude interrupted, her voice devoid of any emotion.

"Up until recently, I'd always believed that when Jon arrived at the house that night, my mother had already been killed—that there was nothing he could have done to save her. My recollection of that night barely existed, so this version of events—what Jon told me later—was what I accepted as fact. But when my memories came back recently, I remembered my mother was standing there when we came up from the basement. She was alive. Jon had tied her up to a kitchen chair so he could liberate me, but she had broken free from her restraints and she attacked me just as we were about to leave. She tried to push me back down the stairs, not wanting me to leave the cell she'd kept me in. Just as she'd almost overtaken me, Jon stabbed her in the back. What happened next is still a blur, but I recall flashes of Jon cutting up my mother's body in the garage with a power saw, and the two of us dragging a trash bag full of her body parts to dispose of in the sea."

Maude gulped, afraid she might vomit at any moment, but then a thought crossed her mind, one she had to share right away.

"He was trying to protect you, to get you away from your mother. Even if he killed her, that doesn't mean he killed anyone else."

"As we were throwing what was left of my mother into the water, I asked him what we were going to do next. He started crying, dropping my mother's hand on the sand beside us, the last piece of what remained of her. The only piece of her body they ever found. Unabated, he made the proclamation, 'We have to get out of Point Roberts. We have to leave and never come back. I'm the Point Roberts Slayer. I killed them. All of them.' I said nothing in response. Instead, I took him by the hand and we walked off the beach. The man I loved, the man I spent my life with, was a serial killer. It took me coming back here to accept that.

"I think I blacked out his confession instantly. Maybe I would have even without the memory problems from my seizures. My mind processed his confession like it was an evil secret to hide from everyone, including myself. Crossing the border into Canada and pushing back into Washington was like drawing a curtain on that night and my previous life. I wanted to forget, and with my condition, it was too easy. After I left Point Roberts in 1989, I never had another seizure. I made myself believe that Jon's liberation had cured me."

"But why on earth did you go with him? If what you witnessed is true, why would you leave with Jon if he killed your mother?" Maude asked incredulously.

"I was desperate to get out of Point Roberts, no matter what it took. Jon was my only way out. I trusted him and soon forgot what actually happened, the account of that night being retold to me later from his made-up perspective, that my mother had been murdered before he'd arrived. For the last three decades, I thought it was just a coincidence that she became the last victim of the Fifteen the same night I escaped."

"I have to interrupt here," Grant said, moving from behind Bianca so he stood closer to the water, between the two women on the shore. "If what you're saying is true, and Jon Templeton is the murderer and he's dead, then who is making these calls and claiming there will be new victims? Colette and I have both been threatened, as has Theodore Price and that Liza girl."

"It has to be a copycat," Bianca replied. "They're not the original killer, regardless of whether or not these threats should be taken seriously."

"You've been threatened? When did this happen?" Maude interjected. She couldn't take any more bad news. Her heart pounded in her chest, beating at an unmeasurable rate.

"I think Grant's right, we should probably head indoors," Bianca went on. "There's just one last thing I wanted to tell you both. Something important."

"What could be more important than what you've already said?" Maude asked, exhausted.

"Jon and I had a daughter in 2000," Bianca answered. "He convinced me to give her up for adoption even though I didn't want to. He made me believe the murderer would come for us if they knew we had a child, that she'd be safer if she was unconnected to us, living a life free from the burdens of our past. As an adopted child himself, he assured me our daughter would have a beautiful life. Half-heartedly, I agreed."

"You mean to tell me I have a granddaughter?" Tears were streaming down Maude's face, hot tears that glistened in the fading light of dusk. Grant reached out to Maude and brought her in for a hug. It felt like the right thing to do.

As Bianca watched the unlikely duo embracing by the water—their sizes so disproportionate it was almost humorous—she continued, knowing they were still listening. "Yes, Maude, you do. I don't know much about her identity, but I know she's here, somewhere in Point Roberts, and I'm going to find her."

Without another word, the three of them rocked there in silence for a few pulsing beats, knowing it was time to leave the beach once and for all as the oncoming night finally snapped, swallowing them whole.

CHAPTER TEN

MAUDE & LIZA

On Valentine's Day, Liza was dressed entirely in red, walking down Benson Road through a thick layer of fog, barely able to see her feet in front of her. She'd left the trailer without a word, slipping out unnoticed so she wouldn't be barraged with questions. Her foster mother, Mary, had taken a sudden interest in Liza's whereabouts ever since she'd begun spending time with Theodore. When asked where she was headed each time she prepared to step out of the dingy, dust-covered home, Liza always had the same answer: the library.

This was not the truth, but since Liza and Theodore were primarily doing research, she considered the answer a simple white lie. Still, Liza felt guilty whenever she answered Mary's questions untruthfully. Pa had taught her better, and she was ashamed, knowing he would have been disappointed in her behavior—no matter her reasoning.

So instead of speaking another lie, she decided it was best if she didn't speak at all, exiting the front door a few minutes after seven o'clock, when the sun was just about to rise.

With the orange book tucked securely in her rucksack—having successfully begged Theodore to let her borrow it for a few days—Liza was walking toward Maude Oshiro's home.

Theodore didn't know she was going to see Maude. No one did.

Even though Liza and Theodore had been spending a great deal of time together—working their way through the book and using the receipts he and Colette had stolen from Emory to analyze if Jon Templeton could really be the Slayer—they didn't see each other every day.

Theodore had been trying to get Liza to meet Colette, but she kept resisting the introduction. Colette was his person, the other citizen of Point Roberts he'd decided to bring into their fold. Liza knew she would have to give way soon—to meet Colette Bernard and open up to her like she had with Theo—if they were ever to make any real progress. But she didn't feel ready, at least not until she'd found her own person.

Knowing Theodore was meeting with Colette in the afternoon, Liza had decided she'd use the day to take action. She had a feeling in her gut that if they were going to solve the killings, it would occur before the month was over, or it wouldn't occur at all.

And February was already halfway gone.

As she walked down Benson Road, the usually tall fir trees alongside her appeared only as thick dark trunks, disappearing into the bleached cotton-candy fog. It was as if every pine had been cut by an enormous ax a mere six feet from where their roots dug into the moist earth, not allowed to reach their full potential.

Liza hoped her bright red hoodie contrasted enough against the abridged evergreens, knowing if any car came by, it likely wouldn't see her until it was mere feet away. She walked on the left side of the street like Pa had taught her, being sure to face any car head on.

It was hard not to think of Pa on this holiday, as he had always baked a delicious heart-shaped cake for Liza every Valentine's. When she got home from school, she'd find him in his red blazer and crimson bow tie, making her smile as he served her as many slices as she wanted. It didn't matter how few cards she'd gotten from the other kids in her class, or how many boys had written awful remarks about her flaming hair inside the ones she did receive. She had Pa, and that was enough.

Since his death, she hadn't opened up to anyone until she met Theo. And now that she had him in her life, a man she really connected to, Liza yearned to find a female sage she could share the other part of her spirit with.

She had never been close to another woman.

Liza didn't know Maude Oshiro, but she hoped that would soon change. She felt drawn to her. Strongly. Inexplicably.

Theodore had instructed her to find her person, to open up to someone else and follow through with the agreement they'd made. Otherwise, how would they assemble a team diverse enough to solve Point Roberts' darkest mystery?

It wasn't long before a car appeared abruptly, far too close to where she walked, forcing Liza to throw herself into the brush. With no headlights on, the vehicle zoomed by without any regard for her existence, in no way acknowledging she'd been on the road. Watching the car disappear into the thick fog as quickly as it had emerged, Liza got up from the slick grass, wiping off the knees of her red corduroys that were now covered in mud.

She hoped Maude wouldn't judge the stains.

Continuing on, treading as far off the side of the road as possible without actually walking in the swamp-like ditch, Liza tried to regain her composure.

She felt uneasy on her feet.

It was hard not to be, when just days ago, someone on the telephone had threatened to kill her. And now Colette and a man named Grant Fisher had received a similar call too, according to Theo.

Who was making these calls? The disguised voice Liza had heard was so disfigured there was no way to know if it was a man or a woman. Ever since Theo and Colette had taken the receipts from Emory's office, Jon Templeton was their prime suspect, their only new lead. But apparently he was dead, and dead people couldn't make phone calls. They'd been doing everything they could to find out more about him.

The most intriguing thing Liza had learned so far was that he was Maude Oshiro's adopted son.

⁓

At the end of Benson Road, where she emerged from the thicket of trees, the fog still hovered in a heavy blanket, shrouding Liza in its embrace. The smell of the nearby sea came to her as she turned left onto Boundary Bay Road, heading toward Maple Beach. The houses grew larger and more frequent in number as she got closer to Point Roberts' northeast corner. A few more cars passed by, thankfully with their lights on—cautious of the fog that was so threateningly dense.

Getting close to her destination, Liza tried to recount what she knew about Maude, wanting to appear thoughtful and informed when she knocked on her door.

Just yesterday, Liza had discovered a photograph of a glamorous Asian woman hidden beneath another picture in the book's section on Toshi Oshiro. She recognized the woman immediately, even though the image depicted her thirty years younger than what she remembered.

The day before she met Theo, Liza had been running down the sidewalk near Maple Beach, the orange tome grasped firmly in her clutch, when she slammed into an older lady, knocking them both to the ground.

They had made intense eye contact, and as Liza began apologizing, expecting the stranger to scold her, the woman instead offered a few quiet words telling her it was okay, not blaming her for the collision.

Liza had not forgotten this kindness.

The woman she'd encountered that day was Maude Oshiro. The Point Roberts Witch.

The kids at her high school had often told stories about this terrifying and mythical creature, describing her as an old hag that never left her windows, continuously casting spells on the people of Point Roberts from her perch in the haunted A-frame that overlooked Maple Beach. The ones who'd been brave enough to climb the steps to the witch's lair had shared details of the woman's haggard features: her hair a mess of stringy gray knots, her face covered in warts, her attire a potato sack smudged with greasy smears.

The appearance of Maude Oshiro prior to her makeover on February 5 had been greatly exaggerated by the teenagers who talked about her, but it made no difference to Liza. She had only seen the swan transformed—an aged, more refined version of her previous self. The woman from the photograph in the book, living and breathing in the present day. Once Liza connected the dots and discovered Maude's identity, she knew she had to speak with her.

When she reached the bottom of the steps, Liza wasn't afraid to climb them, even though so many hooligans had warned her this path would lead to a cursed death.

She hadn't told Theo she was coming, because she wanted to wait until she had fulfilled her end of the bargain. He had Colette, and soon—hopefully—she would have Maude. While the idea of meeting Colette still frightened Liza, she felt no fear in meeting Maude. The woman was just like her: a discarded outcast no one wanted to take the time to understand.

She felt a strong kinship with Maude already, even though their previous interaction had lasted for a mere thirty seconds sprawled out on a wet sidewalk.

But Liza had noticed her favorite smell after they collided, and it had stayed with her: fresh rain seeping into the pores of the gray cement. It was an aroma unlike any other, and for whatever reason, it brought her bliss. Wet concrete.

She took it as a good sign.

The thought of this smell made her smile as she climbed Maude's stairs, one hand firmly grasping the shoulder strap of her bag while the other moved up the wobbly metal railing, pulling her higher.

As she took each step, Liza immersed herself further into the fog, reaching a point where she couldn't see her hand in front of her. Mildly panicking, Liza took a few deep breaths, trying to find her courage once more. She reconvinced herself those kids were wrong, that this wasn't a spell the witch had put in place to prevent intruders, but was instead a natural phenomenon that happened all the time near large bodies of water.

Her foot got stuck along a groove on a step that was half crumbling, tiny pebbles breaking away from beneath her as she shifted her balance to avoid tripping. Once Liza found her center of gravity, she continued to climb. Her head eventually burst through the fog, breaking out from the thick layer so that only wispy remnants of the ground-smothering cloud remained.

Liza ascended the final steps and reached a flattened path that wandered through an abundance of greenery, the dark A-frame appearing dramatically.

She had made it to Maude Oshiro's garden.

⌒

Taking in her surroundings, Liza appreciated the sight before her, where dozens of white blossoms caught her attention. Moving forward, the haze lessened, so by the time she reached Maude's front porch, it was gone. As Liza scaled the steps to the front door, she turned and looked over her shoulder, seeing only the garden and the first few stairs leading down and disappearing into the fog. The blanket of white hid the town below.

At that moment, Liza was safe on the hill, a world away from anyone who wished her harm. Acknowledging this and taking a few seconds in solitude, Liza counted to ten and then knocked on the large oak door in front of her.

She heard someone shuffling around inside, and in a few seconds, the door swung open, revealing Maude. The tiny woman looked surprised to see her.

"Hello, my name is Liza Jennings, and I was—"

Liza cut herself off when she noticed how upset Maude looked. She was wearing makeup, but it was smeared across her face, the mascara around her eyes running down her cheeks in dark streaks, as if she'd been crying for hours. She held an enormous clump of tissues in her closed fist, an oversized cardigan covering her floral dress. Her black hair was pulled back into large, diamond-covered clips, but many strands had broken free, creating thin, unintentional bangs that split her forehead into tiny segments.

"Oh. Oh. Oh—" Maude began, making only this one sound, thrice.

"I'm sorry, I must have come at a bad time. I should have called. I'm so sorry, Mrs. Oshiro. I should just—" Liza began profusely apologizing, her face flushing in embarrassment so it matched the shade of her red ensemble.

"It's okay, dear. You don't have to apologize. Excuse my awful face," Maude interrupted, trying to recover a sense of poise. It had been a hard couple of days for Maude, and she knew it showed.

Maude studied the teenager before her. The apprehension on the girl's face was apparent, but her expression still held a warm sense of grace. She recognized her from their run-in on the sidewalk, as the name Liza replayed in her head. She recalled Grant mentioning such a girl, but Maude hadn't put two and two together—until now.

Liza Jennings was on her doorstep. And she had a good guess why she'd come.

"I think we may have met previously, down there on the sidewalk. A few days ago?"

"Oh my goodness, yes. Again, I'm so sorry for that! I had just figured something out and was running and completely lost my—"

"My dear, you don't have to apologize. I'm sure you were in a hurry for a reason. What was that book you were carrying? It looked rather ungainly."

"Well, that book is why I've come to speak with you," Liza began, trying to regain her confidence as she slung the rucksack off her back and unzipped its large compartment. She pulled Theodore's book out and held it in front of Maude.

Maude stared down at the cover, the words *The Fifteen* glaring back up at her.

She covered her face with her hands, tears streaming from her eyes once again.

"Are you okay?" Liza asked her as she pulled the book away, even though it was obvious she wasn't. She was only upsetting the woman further.

"I've had a very rough couple of days," Maude explained, a look of pure melancholy etched across her features. She wanted to talk to Liza, to hear more about the book, but she was not in the right state of mind to do so. "Can you tell me—briefly—what you wanted to discuss?"

"Theodore Price created this book," Liza began, digging right into it, knowing she might not have much time. "It covers every member of the Fifteen and how they died. It's a treasure trove of information, theories, speculation, and evidence. Theo and I have been going through each of the murders and looking at them from new angles as new ideas develop. I was hoping to speak with you about your husband, and your son, Jon Templeton."

Maude could see the hunger in Liza's eyes, as if her well-being depended on finding out the answers the book could never contain. When looking at the girl, Maude saw a reflection of herself, the expression of an outsider who had hidden parts of herself away on purpose, too afraid to let anyone in after suffering a great loss. She didn't know Liza, but still, the teenager with frizzy red hair and the striking outfit appeared to her like a vision from the past, a crimson-shaded copy of a life she hadn't allowed herself to live.

"I'm going to be honest because I think we'll both benefit from it," Maude began, the tone of her voice kind yet more forceful than it had been up to this point. Liza latched onto every word. "Yesterday was hard. I heard things I didn't want to hear. I haven't been able to get any sleep. Frankly, I'm a mess."

"It's okay, I understand that must—" Liza started, trying to offer Maude some sympathy even though she had no idea what to say.

"Why don't you come back tomorrow? Would that be okay?" Maude interjected, knowing she didn't have the energy to stand in the doorway with Liza any longer. "I'm afraid I'm not ready for company now, and I want to have my faculties in order when we discuss this because I know it's important. If you'd like, I should be in a better place then. I could make us tea."

"That would be lovely, Mrs. Oshiro! With school being out, I can be free whenever you'll have me," Liza answered eagerly, thankful that Maude was willing to speak with her.

"Well, that's settled. I'll see you tomorrow, then, say 10:00 a.m.?"

"I'll be here! Goodbye for now," Liza said as she began walking away, not wanting to disturb the woman any further.

Maude said goodbye in return, too tired to close her door, instead standing in the open frame, watching Liza—dressed as if she were a Valentine's queen—walk through her garden and disappear down the front steps, slowly engulfed by fog until she was gone.

˜

The next morning, Liza sat cross-legged on the floor of Maude's dining room. Having only arrived a few minutes earlier, she'd been welcomed in by Maude—who looked much more put together—and guided to the large square pillows laid out on the dining room's slate floor, which surrounded a low circular table made from dark wood. With her bottom now pressed firmly against a pillow, Liza watched Maude take a seat on the floor across from her, the table between them decorated by an elaborate tea set that showcased an ornate floral pattern.

Liza had never been in a house like this—even Theodore's cottage didn't compare. Everywhere she looked, she saw pieces of Maude's identity. Her Japanese heritage was proudly on display, not only in the way she decorated the space but also in the way her home was constructed. The sliding doors Maude had pushed aside opened up the space to create one huge room, connecting the large windows at the front to the kitchen in the back. These sliding doors appeared throughout Maude's home, seemingly constructed of bright white paper, broken into dozens of tiny rectangles as thin wooden lines created perpendicular intersections across them. A few of the doors were painted with peaceful Japanese landscapes. Colorful tapestries, which depicted tiny men standing below waterfalls and climbing to the tops of strange-looking beanstalks, hung on the walls. There were bamboo shoots in large pots growing in corners, an impressive bonsai tree on the kitchen counter, and even a small bubbling fountain that churned water over black oval-shaped rocks into a large fish tank where koi swam among bright pieces of coral in a sunken cove.

Unlike the trailer Liza lived in with her foster parents, Maude's home—while very busy in a variety of titillating ways—was immaculate, as if every crevice had just been cleaned. It almost felt like a museum with displays to educate and entice, while still remaining balanced in a pleasing manner. This was the kind of home you'd never grow tired of—even if it was the only space you saw for thirty years.

The house on the hill had served Maude well, and now it shared its secrets with Liza, who was the first outsider to step inside since the day Jon left Maude decades ago.

"How do you like your tea?" Maude asked Liza, lifting the blue-and-white teapot from the table and pouring hot water into a matching teacup. "I wasn't sure if you would like matcha, so I decided to go with something simple, a nice Moroccan mint."

"I've never had tea before," Liza answered awkwardly.

"Never had tea? Oh my, that has to change," Maude said with a slight chuckle, trying to ease the girl's nerves. She could tell Liza was feeling a bit unsure now that they were alone together. The bravado Liza had showcased at Maude's doorstep the previous morning had slipped away.

This was uncharted territory.

Doing as she was instructed, Liza made her tea as Maude prepared her own. Once it was ready, a near silence hovered over them. The only noises to consecrate the occasion were the sounds of water babbling from the fish tank and the quiet clinking of cups against saucers as they prepared to bring the tea to their lips.

In this moment, Liza recognized that Maude was from a different world, an unknown realm of regality where drinking tea was not only a rite of passage, but a religion unto itself. She wanted to learn more about her.

"Were you born in Japan?" Liza asked as she set her teacup back on the table. The warmth of the liquid was still too hot, nearly burning her tongue and causing it to tingle.

"I was actually born right here in Washington. Not in Point Roberts, but along the shores of Lake Sammamish, near Seattle. I was the first member of my family born in the United States."

"I know Lake Sammamish," Liza responded, excited she was familiar with a place Maude was connected to. "My pa and I used to go for boat rides there. He had a friend who owned a house on the lake." Then, as if she'd forgotten her adoptive father was gone, her upbeat tone simmered down before she went on. "I'd give anything for Pa to still be here and have a day together there . . ."

"It's a lovely lake," Maude responded. "And I'm sorry your pa is no longer here. Did he pass?"

"Four years ago, when I was thirteen."

"I'm sorry to hear that. Losing a loved one is unbearable. I've lost people too," Maude said as gently as she could, wanting to ask more about Pa and what had happened to him, but trying not to pry. From the look in the young girl's eyes, which swelled in despair at the mention of the man who raised her, she could tell it was a delicate subject.

They were already going to discuss enough difficult topics as it was; adding in the details of another death of someone held so close—chronicling the pain brought about from his absence—would only make things more complicated.

"Yes . . ." Liza didn't know what else to say, sharing a look with Maude that allowed them both to acknowledge they should move on. "Have you been to Japan? Everything in your house is so beautiful, so authentic. You must have purchased some of these on your travels there?"

"Indeed, I've been many times. Most of what you see was brought back. You have a good eye."

"What's your favorite city there? I only know of Tokyo. Is it as huge as they say?"

"Even larger than what you imagine. It's a delightful monstrosity, like walking through a technicolor fantasy. At night, the metropolis is covered in pulsating lights, while an afternoon can consist of something as simple as a casual stroll through a green-and-pink garden. There are tall buildings that scratch the clouds, and trains that zoom faster than planes."

"It sounds magical," Liza said in awe, her expression one of wonder.

"It is a special place, but Tokyo is just a taste of Japan. My favorite place is Kyoto, the city of my ancestors, where both my parents and older siblings were born."

"What's it like?"

Maude's eyes lit up at the question, the excitement on her face apparent as she began to tell Liza about the city she loved most. "In Kyoto, you can walk to the top of a mountain while passing underneath thousands of enormous orange gates, taking steps up a path as you tunnel through the painted wooden arches. There are incredible gardens, sculpted from the remnants of a perfect dream, where greenery and flowers comingle in exaltation. There's a grand golden temple so unusual you'd think it was the best thing you'd ever seen, only for it to be surpassed by the pond it sits beside, its water so reflective the surface shows you more of who you are than any mirror ever could. It's a place where bamboo grows in a forest, stretching so high you can't see where it stops. Kyoto is unlike anywhere else I've ever been, unmatched in my heart."

"Wow, it sounds like a fairy tale," Liza said. "I hope I can go one day."

"You *must*."

"I've only been in Washington. Well, and Canada now, but that's just passing through," Liza admitted, her face flushing scarlet. Would Maude find her a simple child she couldn't relate to? How could she not, as someone who had visited exotic lands Liza could barely comprehend?

Liza adjusted her legs as she shifted her weight on the pillow, reaching out for her cup of tea to distract Maude from the red shade spreading across her features. As she took another sip, the liquid was still too hot, but she forced herself to gulp it down, the strong taste tattooing itself against her throat.

"You're young," Maude replied. "You have a whole life to travel."

"I guess so," Liza said as she set her tea down again. "But I'm still jealous. You've been all over Japan, and Theo has seen the entire world. Then there's me, stuck here, imprisoned in the Pacific Northwest."

"Have you gotten to know Mr. Price then?" Maude asked, seeking the opportunity to slip into the conversation they'd been barreling toward. "I'm intrigued to hear more about what you've discussed, and the different theories you've been working on from that book," Maude went on, nodding, her eyes focusing on the book she'd mentioned, which sat on the floor to the side of Liza's pillow.

Liza revealed the highlights of what she and Theodore had shared since she'd found the orange volume along Lily Point, starting with when she'd returned it to him and they'd begun reviewing each of the Fifteen's entries in the orange-colored tome. From Mallory Price to their most recent conversation about Willow Mendez. Liza told Maude all the details Theodore knew, things he had learned from his late husband, Bill, during his time as Point Roberts' sheriff, and clues he'd uncovered himself during his decades puzzling over the case.

After going over these bits of information, Liza's knowledge began to intersect with Maude's. The young girl's eyes grew wide as she recalled the threatening phone call she'd received—an altered, unidentifiable voice claiming she and Theodore would be the next two victims still rattling in her brain. Liza told Maude how Colette and Grant had received a call like that too, strengthening the idea that a copycat killer might be on the loose, or that the real killer had returned after a long hibernation.

At this point in Liza's recollections, Maude interrupted, feeling this was where they could start to work together, building something anew.

"I know Grant Fisher too," she said.

"Oh, you do?" Liza replied, somewhat surprised. "It's not that I know him myself. Actually, we haven't met."

"That's okay. I just thought you should know," Maude replied. She knew she could share what she'd experienced the past few days: from Grant finally convincing her to talk about Jon to the encounter at the beach that changed everything. Yet for whatever reason, her instincts told her to hold back. There would be an appropriate time to share these details, and this wasn't it. Maybe it was because she couldn't stop thinking about how the facial expressions Liza made when she got excited looked so similar to how Jon's once had. Maybe it was something else.

"That *is* good to know. Have you met Colette too?"

"I haven't met any new people for a long time, besides this month that is . . ." Maude trailed off. Now that her self-imposed exile was over, she felt more embarrassed than ever about what she'd made of her life. She had wasted so much of it.

Until just ten days ago, Maude had sat inside her house every single day of Liza's life—realizing this fact made her feel like a disgrace. She diverted her eyes to the slate floor, not able to look across the table any longer, her arms feeling too weak to pour any more tea.

"No worries, I was just curious. Theo wants each of us to pick someone. Another person to bring into our research group. He's decided on Colette—I haven't met her yet, either—which is why I was wondering if you had. I'd love to hear more about her from a perspective other than Theo's. He's been gushing about her. If he weren't gay, I'd think he had a crush on her."

"Oh my," Maude replied, a laugh pushing past her lips, forcing her to lift her eyes and take in the sight of the brave girl sitting on the floor across from her. It was the first time she had let someone into her house in so long, but Liza looked as if she had always been there.

"And well, I was thinking, " Liza continued, taking the delightful expression on Maude's face as a sign of encouragement to ask the question she'd been scared to. "I thought maybe you could be mine? My person."

"Oh, dear. That's so thoughtful of you to want to include little old me. You really think I'd be helpful?"

"I know you'd be."

"If it's important to you, of course I will. It's not like I have anything else to do," Maude said, smiling, her somber mood shifting into something different.

"Thank you!" Liza exclaimed enthusiastically. Without thinking, she leaned forward and reached across the table.

Brushing past the teapot and nearly knocking it over, Liza was undistracted by her clumsiness. She beckoned for Maude to place her hands in hers, and Maude obliged. Their skin touched for the first time, an odd sort of electricity binding their connection and creating a sensation unlike anything either of them had experienced.

"This group you and Theodore are forming, is it part of the Briar's Grove Society?" Maude asked, shifting the attention away from whatever spark had just ignited between them, not having the gumption to acknowledge it yet. There was something about Liza that made her feel as if they'd known each other their entire lives.

But they had only officially met yesterday.

"No, it's different. BGS is Grant's thing. I think it's part of the reason Theo doesn't trust him. I've tried to find out more about the group, but Theo doesn't like to talk about it. All I know is they hold their meetings in the woods, and for whatever reason, Theo thinks their methods are strange—unethical even."

"I see . . . ," Maude replied. Liza's explanations had piqued her interest further. Perhaps she would have to go to the next meeting.

The bubbling sound of water churning in the fish fountain gurgled in their ears. Liza took a large gulp of her tea, the temperature finally suitable for the liquid to comfortably slosh down into her stomach. She finished the cup in one very long sip and then placed it back on the table.

"Should we look through the book? I thought it might be nice to share it with you. We could pick up where Theo and I last left off. I think the next victim is James Turner."

"Let's," Maude agreed, standing up from her spot on the floor and moving to the other side of the table, taking a spot beside Liza. With the book between them, Liza used both hands to pry the chunky volume open. She flipped through the pages, passing by images of the victims in happier times, as well as photos of the crime scenes that displayed their mangled bodies, the days of their deaths.

"Ah, here it is. James Turner, victim number nine," Liza exclaimed as she reached a page nearly two-thirds of the way into the book.

⌒

James Turner—or Jamie, as he was affectionately known—was a popular drag queen who often performed in Vancouver. His drag persona, Regina Bell, was a vivacious character who adored glitter, rhinestones, and enormous blonde wigs that made her appear eight feet tall. Drag was a vehicle that allowed Jamie to express himself in ways he was unable to while presenting as a man. After putting on a full face, covering his eyebrows with glue, painting on feminine features, and contouring a new identity, he transformed.

Whereas Jamie was shy, soft-spoken, and demure, Regina was bubbly, loud, and full of energy. She was known to stomp across the bar at her gigs in Vancouver, kicking over the drinks of patrons who were too slow to move their cocktail glasses when they saw her coming. Her performances were so ridiculously fun that even first-timers didn't mind losing their beverages.

And the funny thing was, Jamie didn't even drink. He didn't need to take shots or imbibe alcohol to work his courage up whenever he performed.

He *became* Regina, and that transformation powered him through his routines, shifting his outward appearance into something that was more closely aligned with who he was inside.

On the evening of Saturday, February 20, 1988, Jamie had a gig in Vancouver. And while he usually spent the night at a friend's apartment in the city after his shows were over, on this night, he returned to Point Roberts. He had a consultation scheduled in Seattle that Sunday afternoon, and he wanted to get a good night's sleep in his own bed. He was meeting with a specialist to discuss the process of transitioning.

Jamie didn't want to pretend to be a man anymore. She wanted to be herself.

After crossing the border into Point Roberts around 3:00 a.m. on the twenty-first, having suffered an additional onslaught of questions from the border patrol since her appearance barely matched her ID, Jamie—as Regina—began the final stretch of her drive home.

She never made it.

At some point during the short drive between the border and her condo, someone intercepted Jamie and killed her in the most gruesome fashion.

Jamie's car was found abandoned in the middle of Greenwood Drive the next morning, the driver's door open, the keys still in the ignition.

Under the car, Jamie's body was found. She had been crushed to death.

The coroner would later discover she'd been run over more than ten times.

Someone had intercepted Jamie on her drive home and convinced her to get out of her car. Then they'd run her over with her own vehicle.

She was left on the street like an animal—the most beautiful, effervescent queen treated like she was a piece of roadkill.

***

"Lord above, I remember the morning they found Jamie's body. It was terrible. And the things people in town said about him. As if his death didn't matter as much because he liked to dress up like a woman. I will tell you, I scolded people in every corner of this town whenever I heard them speak against him," Maude told Liza as they finished going through the pages on Jamie Turner.

Recounting the horrible crime had fired Maude up, not only because of how upsetting it was—and how the people in Point Roberts had referred to the victim as a freaky hermaphrodite—but because after Jamie Turner's death, she knew what came next.

Toshi.

Before Liza had a chance to reply, Maude turned the last page covering Jamie and was presented with an image of her beloved husband.

"Oh, Toshi . . . how I miss you," Maude whispered as she stared down at his photograph, a professional image that had been taken for his pediatric practice the year he died. The look on his face was warm and approaching. When children saw it hanging up in the waiting room, it helped them feel unafraid of the man who would soon offer them care.

Maude flipped through the pages on Toshi, peering at the materials Theodore had collected on her husband's murder, scrutinizing them quickly without spending much time on any section. When she got to the pages that showed the police photos from that night, she abruptly shut the book.

"I'm sorry, but I can't look at those."

"I know it must be hard," Liza said as sympathetically as she could, taking the book and moving it behind her so it was no longer in Maude's line of sight. "Maybe we can just talk about it? I've already read about Toshi. If I'm honest, it's one of the reasons I wanted to talk to you. You were there, right after the killer struck. Besides Theo, you were the closest person to one of the murders."

"And what an unfortunate thing that was, to be so close," Maude demurred. "It was the worst day of my life. My husband died in my arms."

"Did you see anything? Did you get a glimpse of the killer?"

"If you've read Toshi's pages in the book, I'm sure you already know the answer to that."

"I know, but I thought—"

"I saw no one. It was dark. It was pouring rain. The only reason I went outside and found Toshi was because I heard the gunshot. My son, Jon, was working at Smith's Grocery Store, so I was home alone sitting in my chair reading some poetry when a loud cracking noise shook the house. Then I heard it again, followed by my husband's voice . . . screaming."

"Was he saying anything, or was it just a scream?" Liza interjected, unable to help herself.

Maude stared at her for a moment, her eyelids fluttering, not looking angry but also not looking pleased. It was impossible for her to look anything but upset while recounting this story.

"He may have said something, but I couldn't make it out. When I realized it was Toshi, I got up from my chair and ran outside, pushing through the garden as quickly as I could. Toshi was still yelling as I made my way to the stairs. The third and final crack rang out, and then he was silent. I jogged down the stairs and found him at the bottom, his white collared shirt stained in blood. He'd been on his way home from work, and someone had shot him. The first two bullets had missed, but the last one hit, and that was all it took. When I found him, he was still alive. I cradled him in my arms and began to cry, trying and failing to stay calm in the madness of the situation. Toshi spoke, urgently attempting to tell me something."

"What did he say?" Liza asked inquisitively. This part of the story was not in Theodore's book. If Maude had told anyone else previously, it wasn't recorded anywhere Liza was aware of.

"He kept saying, 'Tell Jon.' It was clear there was something in particular I was supposed to tell Jon, but the bullet had caused a lot of damage. As I held Toshi, trying to stop the blood from pouring out of him, he wasn't able to relay the message he was so desperate to share. He faded quickly. When it became apparent he wouldn't be able to deliver his message, I couldn't help but interrupt him. I told him to hold on and how much I loved him. When I said that, he was able to focus for a few seconds and tell me he loved me too—right before he left this world forever."

Tears dropped from Maude's eyes then, her nose suddenly clogged, her insides quivering as she began to shake ever so slightly.

Pain was never meant to be beautiful, but even in her distress, Liza found the sight of Maude empowering. She respected her bravery for sharing this story.

"I'm sorry. It's just . . . Even after all these years, it's still not easy to talk about."

"Of course, Mrs. Oshiro, I can't imagine. We don't have to discuss it anymore today, you've already shared so—"

"I never saw anyone. And none of the neighbors saw anyone either. Maybe if I had looked up from Toshi—maybe if I had paid more attention to our surroundings when I found him—I could have spotted the Slayer, I could have helped end this, but I didn't. All my focus was on him. And for that, I blame myself. If I had only thought more clearly, I could have saved five other lives."

"You can't blame yourself! And no one holds you accountable. You did what anyone would have done. You comforted your husband. You were there with him, and that's all that matters," Liza replied with wisdom beyond her years, moving closer to Maude and gently rubbing the older woman's back.

"It's hard for me to throw myself back into these terrible memories, but at the same time—looking at these photos and hearing how dedicated you and Theodore have been in trying to solve this—it makes me feel invigorated. We have to get to the bottom of this. Perhaps our little group could start by planning a time for the four of us to meet up?"

"That's an excellent idea!" Liza exclaimed, leaning forward even farther, bridging the gap completely as she embraced Maude in a hug.

Maude hugged Liza back. It was so nice to feel cared for by someone else. It had been so long.

"Do you think we could bring Grant into the fold?" Maude asked as their hug ended. "He's done a lot to bring me out of my shell, and I owe him for that. I think he has a lot of information we could use. And maybe it could help heal Theodore and Grant's rift."

"It's not a bad idea," Liza mused. "Can I ask Theo and get back to you? I want to say yes, but I think I should run it by him first. I can try my best to convince him. Maybe five is a better number anyway. Five people, fifteen murders to solve. It divides the work more evenly."

"I like the way you think, Liza," Maude said with a smile as an idea popped into her head. It was time to talk about what she'd been told on the beach two days earlier. "Do you know a woman named Bianca?"

As Liza's mouth opened to answer the question, the telephone in the kitchen rang, its shrill ringing overtaking the soft sounds of the bubbling fish fountain, killing the tranquility.

"I guess I ought to get that," Maude said, the question she'd asked Liza going unanswered.

Maude walked swiftly to the kitchen and picked up the phone from the receiver on the third ring. "Hello? Yes. Yes, this is Maude Oshiro. Who is this?"

Liza followed Maude into the kitchen, a strong hunch telling her this call would be an unwelcome one. From the look on Maude's face, it was clear she had no idea who she was talking to.

"Oh my! You should be ashamed of yourself for saying such—" Maude replied to the unknown caller as she noticed Liza beside her scribbling something down with a pen and paper. The deep, unrecognizable voice on the other side had ended the call, hanging up right after telling Maude she would soon be dead.

"They hung up on me," Maude told Liza as she placed the phone back on the counter.

"Was it a deep voice? Like someone talking through a disguiser?"

"Yes. Was that like the call you and Theodore got?"

"Exactly. What did they say?"

"A whole bunch of nonsense. So nasty! They said they were going to kill me. They even listed your names. Liza Jennings. Theodore Price. Colette Bernard. Grant Fisher. And then mine, Maude Oshiro: victim number twenty."

"I think Grant should be a part of our group like you suggested. Especially since whoever is making these calls thinks he's as big a part of this as any of us are," Liza said with intense sincerity. The pen still in her hand doodled around what she'd scribbled down, drawing Maude's attention to it.

"I think you're right. What did you write down?"

"The telephone number that came up on your caller ID," Liza replied, pointing to the blank digital screen where moments earlier a ten-digit number had been displayed. "I thought it'd be a good idea to write it down. My foster parents don't have caller ID, so we couldn't trace who called us. I thought they would have blocked the number, but nope, it was right in front of us."

"How smart! Do you think we can find where it came from?" Maude asked in earnest, ecstatic they might have a lead on tracking their threatening caller.

"We could try to google it at the library. See if anything comes up. That's all I can think of without involving the police."

"Yes, let's not involve them. The people of this town have given the mayor so much power, and he's used it to force the police to do his bidding. Why don't we google it here instead? I may be old, but I do have a computer."

"You do?" Liza asked in surprise. "Where is it?"

"Follow me."

Maude led Liza into a small study behind the kitchen, where an old, dust-covered Gateway computer sat beside a statue of a gilded cat on a desk. "I had it delivered to my doorstep fifteen years ago—taught myself how to use it. I don't get on it much anymore, but it still works."

Within a few minutes, Liza had pulled up an internet browser and typed the ten digits into the Google search bar. As she pushed the enter button, she and Maude held their breath.

A top hit was displayed in seconds—a perfect match.

"The Moon Hotel?" Maude asked, making sure she was reading what was displayed on the screen correctly, highlighted in electric lights.

"That's the hotel right on the water. Do you know it?"

"Yes, of course. It's just down—"

"Should we go there?" Liza interrupted.

"It could be dangerous. Whoever called us, they're probably there. Maybe we should—"

"Can you describe that woman you asked me about? Bianca?"

"What does Bianca have to do with this?" Maude asked, curious as to why Liza had brought the name up again, having almost forgotten she'd asked if Liza knew her.

"Can you please just tell me what she looks like? Trust me. I think it might help."

"Well, alright," Maude went on, a look of uncertainty in her eyes. "She has dark hair in soft, loose ringlets, almost like waves, with a pale complexion, amber-colored eyes, probably five seven or eight, and her nose is a tad peculiar, almost as if it's been pinched. She's kind of plain, but also pretty. She garners your attention. And when I met her, she was wearing interesting colors, almost bohemian."

"You described her perfectly," Liza said. "So . . . I don't know her. But I've seen her, a bunch of times. I think I even caught her following me once. But the reason I asked is because, well, I saw her yesterday morning coming out of that hotel. The Moon Hotel. And she saw me. We made eye contact. Do you think she might have anything to do with this? Is there a reason you asked about her?"

"Oh my goodness," Maude responded, not wanting to believe Bianca had anything to do with the call but feeling unsure enough to believe that she might have. With so much still unknown, she decided not to tell Liza about the accusations Bianca had made about Jon on the beach. "I guess we should go to the hotel. But we have to be careful. It'd probably be safer to wait a bit."

"When, then? Oh! We're going to solve this thing, I can feel it!" Liza said, her voice sounding higher with each word she spoke, unable to contain how anxious she was about the prospect of following clues. *Real* clues, the kind that led to answers.

"How about tomorrow morning? If you saw her leaving the hotel in the morning, maybe she'll be gone at the same time again," Maude surmised, a grin returning to her face as she fed off Liza's contagious energy. The young girl nodded to confirm their plan.

In the house on the hill, high above the adjacent beach, the Point Roberts Witch and the unwanted orphan discussed their next steps as one thing became clear to both of them: a dynamic duo had officially been formed.

In those ensuing moments, Liza and Maude felt confident they might catch the killer. The original. Or the copycat.

Perhaps they were looking for one and the same.

Parked near the trailer on Benson Road, Maude sat behind the wheel of her 1987 Ford Taurus the next morning waiting for Liza. It was the first time she'd driven a vehicle in almost thirty years. Her decision to have the local auto shop take the car for a quick spin around Point Roberts every few months during her three decades as a recluse had been worth it. The car still ran like a champ.

Once Liza hopped in the car, the drive to Front Street took just five minutes, as the trailer sat only about a mile and a half from the Moon Hotel. Maude and Liza could have walked there, but they needed the car to keep them more inconspicuous.

When they pulled up to the hotel, their attention was immediately drawn to the door of room number three.

This was Bianca's room. Liza had seen her come out of it on more than one occasion. She'd spotted her at the hotel as she sat at a nearby picnic table along the beach. The old hotel was just ten feet away from the sand, its location a perfect little walk from the nearby library.

Whenever Liza needed to take a break from her intense research on nicer days, she'd come over from the library and plopped down on the picnic table by the hotel. It was there she would eat the peanut butter and jelly sandwiches she'd pack for herself, soaking up the fresh saltwater air. She'd stare out at the water, becoming mesmerized by the continuous tides while remaining angry at them for imprisoning her. When she grew tired of the sea and the squawking gulls overhead, she'd turn her attention to those coming and going from the hotel, always noticing the interesting characters who emerged from their rented rooms.

Bianca—a woman who never went unnoticed—always caught Liza's attention. Primarily because Bianca always seemed to notice her too.

"Do you really think Bianca is making these calls?" Liza asked as Maude parked in the hotel's lot, picking a spot that sat far away from the building.

"I don't know, but it's the best lead we have from tracking the number and knowing Bianca's staying here. Maybe it's just a coincidence. But at the very least, I'd say she's a person of interest," Maude replied, deciding there and then that she would wait to tell Liza about her conversation with Bianca and Grant on the beach until they met up with Theodore and Colette. Those revelations were enough evidence on their own, a whole separate account that would take hours to sift through. She didn't want to overwhelm Liza. She wanted to protect her.

The two of them stared at the hotel, preparing to exit the vehicle.

It wasn't a large place, with only six ground floor rooms available, which guests entered directly from the parking lot. The large neon sign that showcased the hotel's name rested on the roof toward the right of the building, where the hotel office and front desk were located. The siding was painted in a pale-pink shade—which needed a fresh coat due to the many places where it had chipped off—and the bright turquoise guest room doors completed the beachy palette. Really, the place was a motel more than anything else, the name it had been given making it seem far more luxurious than it ever was. Its location right on the beach—with each room having a gorgeous direct view of sand and sea—made it the only hotel in Point Roberts that could boast such an amenity.

Before Maude and Liza even had a chance to get out of the car, the turquoise gateway to room number three opened, and the woman they were looking for emerged.

"Bianca," Liza whispered, like she had to be quiet, like there was a chance Maude wouldn't be the only one to hear her.

"Yes, that's her," Maude acknowledged, making it certain they were both thinking of the same person, seeing her together for the first time.

Bianca had a woolen poncho decorated in vibrant blocks of red, orange, and green draped around her shoulders. She clutched a large brassy key in her hand but didn't lock the door, leaving her room straightaway with a distracted look on her face. She abandoned the hotel in her wake, clearly with a destination in mind, and Liza and Maude watched her walk across the parking lot to the sidewalk along Gulf Road. She could be going anywhere. If you were in shape, you could easily walk from one location in Point Roberts to another no matter where you were. The walled-off peninsula was only five square miles.

Within a few minutes, she was entirely out of view. Turning back to her companion, Liza hatched an idea.

"Let's try to get inside."

"What?" Maude asked, feigning bewilderment.

"Oh, come on, Maude! You know that's what we were going to do if given the chance. She didn't even lock her door. If it didn't lock automatically, maybe we can find something in there—something to give us answers."

Without waiting for Maude to respond, Liza opened the car door and got out. Not wanting to be left alone, Maude followed, walking behind Liza toward the hotel room. The embellished gold "3" on the room's door shined like it was highlighted by an invisible sun on this overcast day.

Wasting no time, Liza, with Maude standing behind her, turned the doorknob to Bianca's room, the latch noisily unclicking as they gained access.

Once the door was shut behind them, Maude and Liza took in the scene. The room was an organized conglomeration of stacks of paper, binders piled high, photographs neatly sorted into grids taped to the walls, and countless manila folders in dingy gray boxes in every corner. It wasn't a mess—on the contrary, it seemed Bianca had spent a lot of time creating a system to ensure she knew where everything was. However, the number of documents in the small room was still overwhelming.

Where would they start?

"What on earth is she doing with all this stuff?" Maude exclaimed. "Where did she get it?"

"That's what we have to figure out," Liza replied. As her eyes scanned the walls covered in images, she recognized the faces of the Fifteen, making it apparent these materials had to do with their unsolved murders. Bianca was trying to solve the case too—or so it seemed. After drawing her attention back to the center of the room, taking a moment to decompress and find a place to start, Liza noticed a small journal-like notebook sitting on the freshly made bed. Its dark cover contrasted against the plain white duvet.

Liza picked up the notebook, opening to the first page where the words *Bianca's Diary* were scrawled in loopy letters, like the handwriting of a child.

"Look at this," Liza said to Maude, who approached the bedside and peered at the diary's title page. "Should we read it?"

"We've gone this far. I don't know why we'd stop now," Maude replied.

"I like the way you think," Liza said as she took a seat on the bed's edge and motioned for Maude to do the same.

Liza rested the diary on her lap and began to flip through its pages so she and Maude could review its contents simultaneously.

It took about two seconds for them to realize they'd hit the jackpot.

A very grisly, disturbing, harrowing jackpot.

On the pages of the diary, details of every murder were scribbled in the same handwriting found in the front. The victims, their ages, their occupations, the dates of the crimes, the causes of death, the locations the bodies were found, who found the bodies, which officers were first to the scenes, how the public reacted, and more were organized into fifteen different sections. But what was more revelatory were not the details Liza and Maude were already familiar with—the details anyone in Point Roberts was familiar with—but instead, the things that were written directly under each victim's name, before the details of the crimes were listed in succession.

This was nothing like Theodore's book.

The notes listed strange things about the victims: derogatory names, accusations, and reasons they deserved to be punished, or so Bianca's handwriting claimed.

> Mallory Price: traitor, slut, liar, can't be trusted
> Susan Kaiser: imbecile, two-faced bitch
> Brent Locke: faggot—obnoxiously flaming, prideful, sinner
> Jennifer Barnes: adulterer, cheater—selfish harlot with bad hair

And on it went for each of the Fifteen.

This was not a diary. It was a tool used to select victims, to pick out which fifteen people would die in terrible infamy. These notes showed how the Point Roberts Slayer had tried to justify their reasons for murdering innocent people.

"Are you seeing this?" Liza asked. "These terrible things, it's like she hated every—"

"And she tried to blame this on my son! She told me down on the beach she watched Jon kill her mother, that he admitted to every murder before they left together. The nerve of her to try and pin this on him!" Maude shouted in a flustered tangent, spilling out the details she had meant to keep from Liza for the time being.

"What?" Liza exclaimed. Frazzled, upset, and bogged down by this frightening information, Liza stood up, needing to put a bit of space between her and Maude.

Were they in the room of a killer?

When she stood up, the diary fell from her lap and landed on the floor, a collection of photographs they hadn't noticed before sliding out from the back.

Liza leaned down to collect the diary, picking up the five photographs in alarm. Her own face looked back at her from each one.

"What the fuck?!" Liza cried out, hot tears swelling in her eyes.

She had never been more terrified.

One of the photographs was her first-grade photo, her red hair pulled into bushy pigtails. Another was of her and Pa in front of their house in Bellingham, holding a gigantic fish they'd caught. While the remaining ones were more recent, taken in Point Roberts from a distance, but zoomed in. Liza sitting with her head down staring into a book at the library. Liza from behind, sitting at the picnic table beside the Moon Hotel. Liza walking down a path, captured through the spaces between the trees on her way to Lily Point.

Maude saw the photos Liza was shuffling through and realized they needed to get out of the hotel room as soon as possible. She'd been so stupid to put herself and Liza in danger like this.

"Liza, listen, we have to get out of—" Maude began, grabbing Liza gently by the wrist to try to get her to focus even though the young girl's eyes were still glaring at the photos she held in her hand, the diary clutched to her side in the other.

Laughter suddenly rang out from the other side of the hotel room door, a soft chuckle paired with a high-pitched squeal. Liza and Maude looked at each other, unable to say anything, unable to move.

The door opened, revealing Bianca before them, whose face quickly erased all sense of laughter and painted itself in shock, completely surprised to find Liza and Maude standing there. She glided into the room without saying anything, and an immense man followed behind her, nearly having to turn sideways to fit through the narrow doorframe. His earlier squeal echoed around them as he, too, was stunned into silence upon finding two intruders in his daughter's room.

Emory Schultz.

"What's going on here?" Even though the pitch of his voice was so ridiculous, it was laced with agitation, shaking Liza and Maude to their very cores.

"Who are you?" Liza shouted back, pointing at Bianca as she shifted the photographs and diary into one hand, lifting them up. "And what is this?"

"Oh, Liza. I'm so sorry. I never dreamed it would go like this. I know this looks bad. But you have to trust me that—"

"I said, who are you? Is your name even Bianca Schultz?" Liza persisted, not allowing Bianca to finish.

"Liza . . . I'm your mother. And this is your grandfather."

All the energy was sucked out of the room like a vacuum had been switched on, the photographs on the wall trembling as their taped backs clung on for dear life. Even Emory looked stunned.

Liza said nothing. Her face turned ghost white, nearly translucent.

Bianca stepped forward, extending her arms, trying to hug her daughter for the first time.

"Don't touch me!" Liza screamed, swatting Bianca away.

Bianca looked heartbroken, but she retreated and turned her attention to Maude. "Why did you bring her here? Did you figure out she's the daughter Jon and I had to give up?"

At that moment, before Maude could respond, something clicked in Liza's mind. She couldn't explain why, but somehow she knew what Bianca claimed was true. She was her mother. And if she was, that meant the old Asian lady who stood beside her in defiance—unshaking, powerful—was more than just her friend.

She was her grandmother. Adopted grandmother, but family nonetheless.

Liza questioned nothing more and hugged Maude fiercely, as if the connection between them needed to be solidified further as it evolved to new heights.

"Let's get the hell out of here," Liza whispered in Maude's ear before she pulled back from the embrace.

"Whatever you say, kiddo," Maude replied, offering a sense of humor through the confusion and despair.

Hand in hand, Maude and Liza pushed by Bianca and Emory, ignoring all their pleas and offers of reconciliation. They shifted their weight to create a free path past the mayor and his mysterious, murderous daughter, who now quivered in either sadness or fear. With the diary and photographs still clutched in Liza's free hand, they moved quickly to the Taurus in the parking lot as one.

They would answer no more questions.

From now on, they would be the ones asking the questions.

Together.

PART III

MOTHER, MAY I?

CHAPTER ELEVEN

LIZA, COLETTE & MAUDE

Lost in thought, Colette moved back and forth among the one-of-a-kind artifacts in Theodore's cottage, studying the materials from which they were made. She was alone, in a house that was not her own.

When she'd arrived five minutes previously, she'd expected to greet Theodore at his door. Instead, she'd found a note taped to the front of it on this cold, misty morning.

Theodore had called a meeting at his place, one which he'd intended to lead. Yet unforeseen circumstances had arisen, forcing him to abandon the plan. In his absence, he'd left instructions for Colette to take over as his second-in-command.

While admiring a collection of wooden llamas painted in bright colors, their curved backs carrying bunched-up collections of yarn as if they were important parcels, Colette tried to regain her composure. She knew Liza and Maude were due to arrive any moment, and with Theodore gone, she would be meeting these two for the first time on her own.

From what Theodore had told her on the phone last night, Mrs. Oshiro and the teenage girl had discovered a bombshell. Something that could finally break the cases of the Fifteen wide open.

But now Theodore was at the Point Roberts Clinic, the brief note he'd left scant on the details, only mentioning that he feared he'd developed pneumonia and that *under no circumstances* was she or anyone else to visit him. His note instructed her to focus on the important matters—the revelations Liza and Maude would soon be here to discuss—things he claimed took precedence over his health.

She was angry with herself, as she'd known Theodore hadn't been feeling well the past few days. They'd spent long hours digging through the leads that had come about from the receipts they'd snatched from Emory's office. All the while, Theodore's coughs had been growing thicker, with the mucousy noise of phlegm rising from his throat continuously getting worse. He mentioned having chest pains, and while Colette urged him to see a doctor yesterday, she regretted not taking him there herself. He was HIV positive, after all, a fact Theodore had just confided to her in recent days.

She feared Theodore had become too invested in the case, clinging onto the new developments like a man hanging from the edge of a cliff, refusing to be brought back to solid ground even though she was there to help pull him up. He was a stubborn man. He'd rather hold on until his fingers were pried loose. And now because of this, Theodore was going to be absent when they uncovered the truth.

Jon Templeton. Bianca Schultz.

Everything circled back to them.

They had eyed Jon as their prime suspect. It was evident he was linked to the murders. Whether he was the perpetrator, an accomplice, or an unwilling bystander, he knew something. But he was dead, unable to make threatening phone calls from the grave. Or so Bianca claimed.

With the discovery Liza and Maude had made in Bianca's hotel room the previous day—escaping with her diary, which suggested she'd committed the crimes—a new direction had been found.

It was why Theodore had called the meeting in the first place. The four of them needed to join forces and work as a team. It would merge their multiple threads of communication into a single cord, eliminating the possibility of losing crucial clues in the mix. When they spoke last night, Theodore had even mentioned the idea of bringing Grant into their fold at Liza's suggestion, a decision he was not taking lightly. They were supposed to discuss this in their first meeting, but now Colette feared that without Theodore present, they'd be unable to make the ruling. He was the one who needed to be convinced Grant was worthy of their attention.

If they were ever going to figure this out, it would be because of their five distinct perspectives, cooperatively forging into one entity to create something more effective than researching the cases on their own.

As Colette left the table of llamas behind to find something else to focus her attention on, she heard a vehicle pulling into Theodore's driveway. Moving to the window, she looked past Theodore's drooping plants—reminding herself to water them soon—and saw an old Taurus driven by a tiny woman whose head barely reached above the steering wheel. Sitting in the passenger seat was a young girl with fiery red hair and a bright yellow raincoat. As they pulled closer and parked outside the cottage, Colette peered at them through the window, the layers of glass both parties were behind creating a kind of translucent sandwich where the mist hung in the open air between them, preventing the connection from being formalized.

Liza looked up and saw Colette standing inside at the window, the blonde woman bringing a closed-mouth smile to her lips, raising a hand slowly in greeting.

Liza waved back, unsmiling.

Colette noticed Liza's curls were hazardously tangled, like she hadn't brushed her hair in weeks. Even from this distance, the young girl had a powerful aura about her, but from the look on her face, Colette could sense that it was thrashing in dismay.

Liza had not slept well. Really, she had not slept at all.

A strange woman was claiming to be her mother.

And that woman was a murderer.

Colette moved away from the large window, leaving the thirsty houseplants behind as she stepped outside, greeting Liza and Maude with a welcoming hello as they exited the vehicle. The morning mist was stagnant, as if each drop of moisture was suspended above the ground and the three women had to push past the globules of water to forge a path through so they could come together.

"Where's Theo?" Liza asked, noticing he hadn't emerged from the purple cottage. If he was home, he wouldn't wait to greet them. Too much was on the line to move slowly.

Something was wrong.

"Theodore's at the clinic. When I got here just a little bit ago, I found a—"

"The clinic?" Liza asked in shock. "What happened? Is he okay? Did someone come after him? What are we still doing here?" One question after another spilled from Liza, her body tingling in despair as she feared she was about to lose another person close to her. Without waiting for a response from Colette, she moved back to Maude's car; the rucksack slung over her shoulder shifted from side to side with her quick movements. She had to go see Theodore, wherever he was.

"He thinks he has pneumonia. He's been showing symptoms the past few days. His note was written before he left, so I'm not sure what he's found out since he arrived at the clinic," Colette began, trying not to cause Liza any more distress, while still maintaining a firm tone. She looked at Maude who stood before the front porch, saying nothing, merely watching the others who dominated the scene. "Since he's HIV positive, he's more susceptible to things like this. I think he's been putting too much stress on himself with the—"

"He's what?" Liza asked dubiously, releasing the car's door handle and coming back to face Colette. She had not known about Theodore's status. He hadn't confided this unfortunate reality to her, fearing it would be too much to share with someone so young. He was afraid she would look at him differently if she knew the truth. The successful author who had traveled the world would transform in her perspective into something unwanted: an old man with an incurable disease.

Theodore had been wrong to keep this piece of himself from Liza. She already cared for him too much to let something shift her view of him. He'd believed in her from the first day she arrived on his doorstep, and she believed in him.

"I'm sorry. I thought you knew," Colette admitted as she tried to regain control of the situation. This introduction was already veering off the rails. Theodore had entrusted her to lead the conversation in his absence, and so far it wasn't going well, as their shoes imprinted deeper into the moist grass along the driveway. She knew he wouldn't want them to focus on his ill health. They had to get back to the case. "Either way, Theodore was explicit that he doesn't want us to visit him. His note said we need to come up with a course of action. We can't delay."

"I don't care what his note says! I want to see him!" Liza argued, her volume escalating as she got more upset. "Is he really sick? You don't think he's dying . . . do you?" Her eyes glazed over then as she turned away from Colette, looking to Maude for comfort, even though it was clear she knew even less than Liza did.

"I'm sure it's going to be okay dear," Maude responded as she placed her arm around Liza's shoulder, trying to console her. "If Colette says Theodore doesn't want us to visit him, we don't want to show up and upset him further, especially if he's not feeling well. I think we should go inside and discuss the diary."

Liza reached up and grasped the hand that Maude had rested on her shoulder, not wanting to accept her reasoning but swallowing it down in thick gulps nevertheless. If Maude agreed with Colette, she would have to admit defeat.

Besides, she didn't even know where the clinic was, and without Maude's car, she had no way to get there quickly.

"Please come in," Colette said, motioning for the two visitors to join her inside Theodore's home.

Begrudgingly, Liza followed Colette into the cottage, staring at the back of the woman's blonde head so intently that she felt like the look of concern she'd seen on her face earlier had shifted 180 degrees, etching itself into her neat updo.

Even after such a brief introduction, Colette's intense beauty intimidated her. She was so well put together. Her hair was immaculately styled, her skin unblemished, the silk blouse she wore without a single wrinkle. The woman's French accent made her sound more intelligent, her statuesque frame towering above Liza as if she were a fashion model plucked straight out of a catalog.

Meanwhile, Liza knew she looked a mess. Her hair was disheveled and her shoes were covered in mud. Her raincoat was far past its prime, full of holes, and her face looked like the surface of Mars, having broken out from the stress of the past few days. Every time she and Colette made eye contact, she felt herself shrinking, as if her body were collapsing in on itself like a collection of Russian nesting dolls.

Once they were inside and Colette shut the door behind them, the air became dry, as if the molecules of condensation they'd left behind had been abandoned without cause.

Liza noticed Theodore's yellow rain boots sitting next to the front door, and this pained her further. Theodore went everywhere in those boots. If he'd left without them, was he planning on ever coming back?

"What a charming cottage," Maude said, breaking the tension as she admired Theodore's décor for the first time. "It's so eclectic and colorful."

"He certainly has a unique sense of style," Colette replied warmly, trying to turn her first interaction with Maude and Liza into a more pleasant one, even if it was just for a few moments. She knew there would be difficult discussions ahead. "Would either of you like anything to drink? Theodore's note said to make ourselves at home."

"Do you think he has any tea?" Liza asked, looking at Maude with a small smirk. Ever since the two of them had enjoyed hot tea together, Liza found herself craving it.

"Oh, I'm sure he does," Colette said, heading to the kitchen to prepare some.

As Colette boiled water and pulled out three clean mugs and an assortment of tea bags, Liza placed her rucksack on the floor, removed Theodore's orange book and Bianca's small diary, and put the two items on the dining room table side by side. Before sitting down, she stared at the books for a few seconds, unsure of how they should begin.

Without thinking—pushing any doubts aside as to how she would be viewed by the woman she'd been so hesitant to meet—she started to speak, filling Colette in on what had transpired in the past twenty-four hours.

She began by explaining that since she and Maude left the Moon Hotel, they hadn't yet reopened the diary, afraid of what they'd find. She told Colette of Bianca's claim of motherhood and how the comfort of Maude's presence had lessened the blow of this revelation. She'd felt a connection with Maude from the start—not too unlike the one she'd formed with Theodore—and now their relationship was even stronger since finding out Maude was her grandmother, regardless of whether or not they were related by blood. Maude had adopted Jon as her own, and if what Bianca was claiming was true, Jon Templeton was her father.

At this point in her monologue, Liza sat down at Theodore's dining room table, her hands grasping the diary but not opening it. Maude took a seat beside her as Colette brought the tea over and joined them. Liza continued her story, glancing up at Colette for the first time since she'd begun the tale, the look she found on her face one of affection.

Colette saw Liza for who she was—a brave young girl with a powerful spark—and her eyes welcomed her in. Liza's defenses melted just a little as she realized Colette was not one to judge a person by their appearance, instead weighing their quality by the strength of their character.

Liza explained how she and Maude had driven back to Maple Beach after leaving the hotel, discussing everything as they sat in the Taurus for two hours while gazing out at the Salish Sea, transfixed by the tide that was still coming in and lapping against the sand. They were too shocked to go inside.

Eventually, though, their grumbling stomachs led them up the hill to Maude's house, where she prepared onion bagels with smoked salmon and cream cheese. Over dinner they debated whether it was time to finally call the police. Ever since Theodore's husband had retired as sheriff and been replaced by a smarmy man with a unibrow named Lionel, he and the remaining officers had been tucked tightly into Emory's back pocket, afraid to go against him. The people in Point Roberts had voted for nearly all of Emory's resolutions over the years, including giving him unchecked power and control of the entire police force. And now that it appeared Emory and Bianca were in cahoots, anything the cops were told would be shared with the mayor. No, the police would only hinder their efforts to find long-sought justice for the Fifteen. They hadn't solved the murders for thirty years, who was to say that would change now?

The decision they'd arrived at instead involved a call to Theodore, the man Liza trusted more than any other on the locked-down peninsula. He would know what to do.

He hadn't answered right away, Liza's call only getting through to him well after the sun had set. After Liza explained everything, having to pause a few times as Theodore gasped through coughing fits, he told her to stay with Maude for the night and for both of them to come over with the diary the next morning. Liza worried that her foster mother would get upset if she didn't come home, but she didn't want to leave Maude's side, accepting whatever consequences would come. Theodore said he'd invite Colette too, but when Liza insisted Grant should also be involved, Theodore was unwilling to agree, instead saying they could decide on it once they were together. They'd planned to discuss what they were going to do about Bianca. And now they were doing it without him.

Their separate experiences now connected, Liza took a long pause, allowing either of the two women to speak.

"Can anything Bianca says be trusted?" Maude asked. She was already convinced Bianca was a liar. It was the question on everyone's lips.

"I've had a strange inkling about her—this self-proclaimed daughter of Emory Schultz—ever since she introduced herself in the woods during the Briar's Grove Society's most recent meeting," Colette said, confirming Liza's suspicions.

Liza didn't know what to think. Bianca had already revealed so much to the other two women, both in the woods and on the beach. The only new statement Liza had from Bianca was the one she'd made about being her mother. And what a claim it was.

She longed for Theodore's presence, wondering what he'd have to say at this junction. After all, he'd been the only one to see the Slayer, hidden in their strange disguise. Could Bianca have matched the shape of the figure who slaughtered his sister?

Liza was tempted to invite Grant over, yearning for more opinions. Both Colette and Maude had gotten to know the man she still hadn't met, and from what she'd heard, Grant was someone who knew a great deal about the Fifteen. Perhaps he could make sense of Bianca's madness. But she knew this would be disrespectful to Theodore's wishes. With him at the clinic, the last thing she wanted to do was rub any salt into his wounds.

No men would join this day's agenda.

Three women, each representing a different generation, would be all that was required.

Their collected bravado would be more than enough.

~

"I thought we could check out the entries in the diary together," Liza suggested. "We've been going through each murder in Theo's book, but now that we have Bianca's diary, we should probably use it instead . . . right?"

Colette and Maude nodded in agreement.

"Let's continue where I last left off, which I think would take us to number eleven: Diane Wertburger. The first murder of February 1989," Liza said as her fingers delicately opened the diary as if she was trying to touch it as little as possible.

The other women watched while sitting on either side of Liza as she flipped through a handful of pages until she arrived at her desired location, releasing a deep sigh as she looked down.

This was not going to be easy.

"God almighty," Maude exclaimed as she craned her neck to read the words scrawled underneath Diane's name. None of them were pleasant attributions.

Violent. Selfish. Chaotic.
Not fit for motherhood.

"Why did Bianca hate these people so much?" Colette asked as she read the words written on the page.

"Look here," Liza pointed, showing Maude and Colette the smaller words in pencil above those etched in black pen.

"Reasons for selection," Maude read. "You think she was justifying why she killed Diane?"

"It sure seems like it. These are just like the other descriptions we found on earlier pages. But look, there's more," Liza went on as her eyes followed the arrow that led from *Reasons for selection* further down the page to a short paragraph.

"*Diane Wertburger regularly beats her nine-year-old daughter, Alice. Alice is an innocent, sweet girl with honey-blonde hair who wouldn't hurt a fly. Many people in Point Roberts have witnessed Diane smacking her daughter in public, whether at the grocery store or the post office. Alice's teacher has noticed bruises on her arms on more than one occasion, and recently, bruises have even started to appear on her face and neck. Diane is to blame. She must be stopped. She must be informed of the correct way a mother should treat a daughter: with unconditional love. And then she must expire.*"

"*Mon dieu,*" Colette exclaimed in French as Liza finished reading the paragraph. "This is dark."

"Wait a second," Maude interjected. "How would Bianca know about Diane beating her daughter in public? Wasn't she locked up in her basement during the years the murders took place?"

"So she claims," Colette replied. "But maybe hiding in that basement was her own decision. If no one knew she existed, no one could suspect her."

"That's a good point," Liza said. "I still have a feeling something is off, though. If Bianca killed these people like this diary makes it seem, she would have been around my age at the time. As she appears now, she doesn't look like a particularly strong woman. I imagine that back then she was even weaker. How could she have overpowered so many people?"

"The element of surprise?" Maude proposed. "Not to mention she usually had a weapon in her possession."

"I guess so . . . ," Liza said.

"And that part about mothers needing to treat their daughters with unconditional love. It again shows Bianca is likely lying about being locked up by her mother for years. Because if she had been, why would she write that?" Colette asked.

"It doesn't make sense," Maude agreed.

"Well, maybe we should keep reading to see if any of these other notes help make sense of this," Liza said, holding the diary open with one hand as she used the other to tuck the loose strands of hair that had fallen in front of her face back behind her ears. "This next page is about what actually happened. Maybe we can compare it to what's in Theo's book, to figure out if this diary has details the public doesn't know."

"That's a great idea!" Colette exclaimed as Liza slid the orange volume over to her. She pried the cover open and flipped to Theodore's account on what happened to Diane Wertburger.

A loud pattering began striking the roof of the cottage, causing all three to look up from where they sat in mild alarm. Their attention turned to the large window leading out to the woods that surrounded Theodore's home. The mist from earlier had transformed into a heavy rain. Large pellets of moisture were dropping hastily, hitting the window at an angle as the wind pushed them down destructive paths.

A storm was coming.

"I didn't think it was supposed to rain like this today. The forecast on the radio said—"

"You can't trust the forecast, dear," Maude interrupted, telling Liza that Point Roberts' weatherman was notoriously unreliable. "It changes all the time. There's a chill in the air, and from what I surmise, it's only going to get colder as that rain comes down."

"You think so?" Colette asked.

"I guess we'll see," Liza replied as she turned away from the window and focused back on the diary in front of her. "Where were we?"

"Diane Wertburger was killed on the morning of February 4, 1989," Colette began, reading from Theodore's book. "Her body was found along the trail near Lily Point. She had been struck with a large blunt object at the back of her head. The autopsy report concluded this blow had knocked her unconscious, but it hadn't killed her. Instead, whoever attacked Diane had beaten her senseless, hitting her in the face repeatedly with the same blunt object, kicking her in the stomach, back, and ribs as she lay on the ground. She didn't die quickly. Instead, the multitude of injuries combined, a broken nose, fractured ribs, bleeding of the brain, and a collapsed lung, killed her. Whoever murdered Diane Wertburger wanted to do as much damage to her body as possible.

"Diane was an avid runner. She ran the same time each morning. Police suspected whoever killed her knew she would be at this part of the trail at this specific time. They were waiting for her. The blunt object used was not left at the crime scene, but the forensics indicated the object was metal due to the trace evidence and shape of the gashes on Diane's head and face."

"You guys . . . look at this," Liza interrupted, turning the diary around and pushing it toward the center of the table so the others could see what she was pointing at.

There in the diary, on the page after the first spread about Diane, was a black-and-white photograph of a trophy. It was a silver trophy with a wooden base, the metal part of the award fashioned into the shape of a five-pointed star. The wooden base's nameplate read: "Amelia Schultz: Second Place, Women's Liftathon, Point Roberts, WA, 1983."

"I think we just found the murder weapon," Liza said as the other women stared at the photograph in disbelief.

The call of Theodore's cuckoo clock abruptly cawed then, breaking the tension as the miniature bird pushed out of its house and into the cottage, surprising the ladies who were gathered there. It was not the kind of sound one could get used to, even if it came on the hour, every hour.

"This is too fucking much," Colette exclaimed as she stood up from the table and moved back to Theodore's large window, once again focusing her attention on his side table covered in llamas, reaching out to trace her fingers down their necks, as if petting them. "I don't know how much more I can handle. It's bad enough with Theodore at the clinic, but finding the killer—even though it's what we've been striving for—it's a lot."

"And to think, this woman claims to be my mother," Liza replied, standing up as well, Maude joining suit as they both moved across the room closer to where Colette stood by Theodore's thirsty houseplants. Their gazes drifted to the view outside, where the giant green ferns in front of the cottage swayed in the wind, each drop of rain hitting their leaves like miniature catastrophes.

"I'm sorry," Colette said, trying to calm herself down. "I can't imagine how you're feeling right now, Liza."

"It's okay. I mean, we don't know *for sure* she's my mother."

"I think she is telling the truth about that," Maude replied.

"What makes you say that?" Colette asked.

"Well," Maude began, turning to look at Liza. "Ever since I met you, I've felt a pang of familiarity, as if we'd met in a past life. Something in your eyes or the way we connected made me feel as if I knew you. It was only when Bianca said you were her daughter—the child she had with Jon, no less—that I realized why I felt this way. You look so much like him."

"I do?" Liza asked, drinking in every word Maude said, as if she'd been drowning in the ocean all her life but was now buoyed up with this perspective, floating atop an abundance of salt.

"You do. I haven't seen Jon in so long, and to be honest, I haven't looked at a photo of him in nearly ten years. It's too hard. He exists mostly in my memory. But now, a part of him is here before me," Maude continued, her eyes glazing over as the weight of her statements began to bear down on her.

"Oh, Maude," Liza whispered as she reached out and embraced her.

As Colette watched the interaction, her heart warmed and her earlier anxiety began slipping away. An idea came to mind—something unexpected, but a proposal she needed to share. Once Liza and Maude released one another, she spoke her mind.

"I think delving through these terrible murders and being trapped on the peninsula has started to take its toll. This has been so ridiculously stressful for all of us. When was the last time we did something fun? I think we could use a break. If we're going to close this decades-old cold case once and for all, we need to be strong enough to do so. To get there, I think we should be in a better state of mind. And right now, I don't feel I am."

"What are you suggesting?" Liza asked.

"I just want one day where we can put this on the back burner. Point Roberts is locked down. If Bianca is the killer, we know she's on the peninsula. She's not going anywhere. And I don't want Theodore to be stuck at the clinic when the murderer is finally found. He deserves to be a part of this."

"I think you're right," Maude said.

"Why don't you both come over to Honey B's tomorrow, after hours? Once I shut the bakery down for the day, we could hang out there and bake Theodore a cake. And *not* talk about the Fifteen. Instead, we could get to know one another, and have some girl time. Maybe even pop open a bottle of wine? Don't you think we deserve that?"

Liza looked to Maude, unsure of how to reply. She wanted to agree with Colette and let the case go for a day and have some fun, but they were so close to solving everything. It would be difficult for her to pump the brakes at this crucial juncture.

She didn't know what she wanted.

It was as if half of her was ocean. And half of her was sky.

In her hesitation, she said nothing, instead allowing Maude to decide for her.

"That might be just the kind of thing we need. I know I've cried so much the past few days, I feel like my eyes are about to fall out of my face. It'd be nice to focus on something else for a day. Liza, what do you think?"

Liza nodded in agreement, letting the other two women guide her decision as emotional exhaustion took over. The horizon of her being—where dark-blue seas and azure heavens crashed together—was stretched to the ends of the earth.

Unseen.

Agreeing to a carefree evening was not the hard part. Instead, admitting to herself that she liked Colette—when she had fully expected to be threatened by the other major player in Theodore's life—was the more difficult pill to swallow.

As Liza looked at Colette, who'd begun proposing other suggestions for the following day, she sucked on the unexpected sweetness she'd found.

Tomorrow, she would allow herself to have fun for the first time in what felt like months. She would force herself to temporarily forget about the murders and enjoy some time with these two women who had already inspired such gumption within her since they'd met.

She would help bake a cake.

And for the very first time, she would drink wine.

⌒

As Colette flipped the red plastic sign on the glass door of Honey B's from Open to Closed, she noticed tiny white pinpricks falling from the sky, as if the clouds were disintegrating into smaller particles. Watching in amazement, her gaze lingered outside as she stood at the door, but she eventually pulled her attention away and returned to the bakery's counter where Liza and Maude were waiting, having just arrived.

"I knew this was going to happen before the weatherman did!" Maude exclaimed, taking off her long woolen coat and draping it over one of the turquoise stools where she and Liza had parked themselves. "There's been such a chill in the air ever since yesterday. Let's be glad it wasn't cold enough to snow when it was pouring at Theodore's. We'd have inches!"

"We may still get a few tonight," Liza interjected as she pulled off a knitted purple beanie and placed it on the counter, her curly locks doubling in size as they were released.

Colette moved behind the counter and beckoned the others to join her at the large wooden island where she'd laid out ingredients for Theodore's cake. "You said you're pretty sure Theodore likes carrot cake, right Liza?"

"For sure! He had a big one in his fridge he'd bought from the grocery store and told me it was his favorite. He mentioned that one was a bit too dry, though."

"Well, we'll have to make sure this one is moist enough for his palette," Colette said as she scanned the island, ensuring she had all the necessary ingredients.

"Have you heard from him?" Liza asked.

"I haven't," Colette said. "I even tried calling the clinic. They confirmed he was there—and in stable condition—but they said he didn't want to talk."

"Poor Theodore, he must really be having a go of it," Maude replied.

"I do think he's having a hard time. All the more reason to bake him a cake!" Colette said, trying to turn their attention away from the sad subject of Theodore's illness. "I thought we could work together and split up the tasks? Liza, maybe you could grate the carrots? And Maude, you could work on the cream cheese frosting?"

Liza and Maude obliged, offering their help with the proposed tasks as Colette gave them the necessary ingredients and tools to get started.

"And I'll work on mixing up the cake batter," Colette said as she pulled a few yellow aprons off a nearby hook, tying one on and handing two over to Liza and Maude. "I've made this cake dozens of times alone, but it's so nice to have assistance! I love baking with others. It reminds me of making cakes with my mother back in Quebec."

"I don't think I've ever baked a cake," Liza admitted as she tied her apron on and started rinsing the skinny orange carrots in the gigantic sink.

"Well, I'm glad Colette and I can be with you to check that item off your bucket list," Maude said with a smile.

"Should we listen to some music?" Colette asked.

"That'd be nice," Maude answered.

"Any requests?"

"I love eighties music," Liza said.

"Oh, me too," Colette replied. "Such a great decade."

Maude looked up at Colette then, her eyes conveying an emotion only someone who had lost a loved one in Point Roberts could understand.

"Oh my goodness. Well, I just meant the decade itself . . . not what happened *here* during the eighties, of course. I've already put my foot in my mouth," Colette said, her words tripping over themselves.

"It's fine, dear. I know that's not what you meant," Maude said, reassuring her. "We could start with something by Wham! I always loved that go-go song."

Colette nodded and went back to the bakery's stereo to plug her phone into the control system, queuing up "Wake Me Up Before You Go-Go" to be followed by a playlist full of upbeat eighties hits.

The music started in earnest, and Colette turned it up louder than it would typically be when customers were in the bakery, still keeping it at a respectable level so the ladies could hear one another. She strutted out from the back room, turning her feet at odd angles with each step she took, like a duck, her hips swaying and head bobbing to the sound of George Michael's voice.

"Oh, isn't this fun?" she asked rhetorically as they got to work, the snowflakes outside doubling in size as a white coat began to stick to the ground.

Honey B's had been placed inside the middle of a snow globe.

⌒

For the next half hour, Maude, Colette, and Liza became so intensely focused on their respective tasks that the music swelled and took up every inch of the bakery, forcing out any space where a conversation could take hold. As they progressed closer to completing their jobs, Colette spoke up, offering an idea she thought would help spur a conversation excluding any reference to the Fifteen, while the stereo started to play "Love Is a Battlefield" by Pat Benatar.

"You know what I was thinking about the other day? How original stories are such an important part of the human condition. There are so many reboots and rehashes nowadays. Studios and entertainment bigwigs never want to take a chance on anything new. But when they do—and when it's good—witnessing a new story for the first time . . . well, I find it rather incomparable."

"What do you mean?" Liza asked as she brought Colette her bowl full of grated carrots. Colette thanked her as she whisked a second egg and a drop of vanilla into the batter, mixing the carrots in and stirring it all together.

"Well, for instance, have you gone to see *La La Land* yet?"

"I adored it," Maude replied.

"How did you see it?" Liza asked in surprise.

"It was the first thing I saw at the cinema when I left my house. I'd read so many rave reviews about it in the paper. I figured it would be the perfect reintroduction to the theater," Maude said.

"It really was great. Of course, it's inspired by other things, including a French film from the sixties, *Les Parapluies de Cherbourg*," Colette continued, "but it was still a story all its own. The songs, the acting, the cinematography . . . the ending. Well, I don't want to spoil it if you haven't—"

"I've seen it too," Liza said.

"Oh, good," Colette went on. "I'll never forget what it felt like the first time I saw it back in December. I'd gone to the theater alone after a particularly stressful day here when everything was going wrong. I was questioning so many things, and second-guessing my decision to move here to open Honey B's, even though having my own bakery has always been my dream. *La La Land* made me feel like it would be worth it, even if things weren't going to be easy, or end up how I'd expected them to."

"How so?" Maude asked.

"Well, remember that scene where Emma Stone's character has given up after her one-woman show is a bust and she's gone back home to her parents? Ryan Gosling's character follows her there and they have a conversation out on the street. She talks about how hard it is to continue following your dream year after year when you're getting nowhere and it feels like no one believes in you. Sure, you can always believe in yourself, but when you've reached that breaking point, just as she had, sometimes it doesn't feel worth it anymore.

"That scene hit me hard. I cried as she spoke. Because I'd almost decided to pack my bags and give up on Honey B's at that point. It had been so much harder than I'd expected it to be, but that scene made me refocus on this dream," Colette said as she lifted her arms at her sides, indicating her bakery was the goal she'd always longed to make a reality.

"Hearing her give that impassioned monologue lit a fire under my ass. Ryan Gosling's character is there to encourage her in the movie, but I realized I could encourage myself. My ex-boyfriend, Victor, who I left in Montréal, had never built me up like that. Sometimes I wonder if he ever really loved me.

"In the movie, they're there for each other during the most crucial parts of their lives. They shape each other so much, and yet they don't end up together. Most Hollywood movies don't take that chance. Most films wrap everything up neatly. Not *La La Land*. It shows that the ending you expect is not always the one you get.

"The movie made it clear to me that some people are only meant to be in certain chapters of our lives—to make their impressions and move on. As I sat there in the theater and the credits rolled, crying again after the final montage where Emma and Ryan dance across the screen to that gorgeous score, I made two decisions. One: I was going to let go of every last piece of Victor, once and for all. We'd already been broken up for a while, but I still found myself thinking about him often, and I couldn't keep going on like that. And two: I was going to start believing more in myself and in Honey B's and make this bakery a success no matter what."

"Wow," Liza said, in awe of Colette's story. This dazzling woman had been stirring cake batter in a mesmerizing fashion while she spoke, her spoon following the path of a figure eight.

"I guess that's what I mean when I say original works of art are so important. A rerun of *Friends* isn't going to make you feel that way. The fifth reboot of *Ghostbusters* or a prequel to Harry Potter isn't going to force you to make the hard decisions. There's something special about the very first time you experience a story."

"I think you're right, Colette. The first time is magical, especially when it's so profound," Maude said.

"Reminds me of the first time Pa and I went up in his seaplane," Liza said as Colette began pouring the finished batter into the large baking pan she'd greased and placed on the counter earlier.

"What was that like?" Maude asked while she finished mixing up her bowl of frosting and placed it next to the pan Colette had just filled.

"It was scary, to be honest. I'd never been in a plane before, and he'd just gotten his pilot's license. I went up with him the first time he flew on his own, and I sure as hell didn't know how to take over if anything went wrong."

"How old were you?" Colette asked as she opened up the large preheated oven and popped the cake in.

"Twelve."

"So five years ago?" Colette asked. She spoke again before waiting for an answer. "Sorry to interrupt, but we have about forty minutes until the cake is ready. Should we move over to the booths? Pop open a bottle of wine?"

"Yes and yes," Liza replied enthusiastically.

"Have you ever had wine?" Colette asked.

"No, I haven't, but if it's okay with the two of you, I'd like to change that."

Colette looked to Maude, who grinned and shrugged.

"Why don't you grab us three glasses in that cabinet over there?" Colette requested, indicating Liza would be able to drink with them.

Liza pulled out three glasses and placed them on the counter, and Colette filled them up with white wine. They each grabbed a glass and moved to a yellow booth next to the windows as the stereo played "Time After Time" by Cyndi Lauper.

"Wow! It's really snowing out there!" Liza exclaimed as she watched the snowflakes fall, the early evening hour growing darker with each passing minute as the blanket of white congregating on the ground grew brighter.

"We might get snowed in," Maude joked.

"Um, but actually . . ." Liza laughed in response.

"So flying with your pa," Colette interjected, circling back to the story Liza had been telling before she'd suggested they move to a booth. "What was that like?"

"It was thrilling," Liza replied, taking her first small sip of wine and scrunching her face in surprise at the taste. She'd expected something more like grape juice. Colette and Maude noticed her expression but said nothing, not wanting to interrupt again. "We took off from Lake Whatcom in Bellingham. I'd lived there my entire life with Pa. We'd hiked through those forests, along Puget Sound collecting rocks, and to the tops of nearby mountains for epic views. But getting up in the sky, seeing everything from a bird's-eye view, that was such an incredible feeling. It shifted my perspective. I felt so alive when we were up in the sky—like I was seeing everything from heaven. I could see the entire city, the mountains, and more of the water than I'd ever seen before, all on one massive canvas. It didn't feel real."

"That sounds like such a special memory with your pa," Maude said as she lovingly put her hand on Liza's shoulder.

"It really was. I went from being terrified when we took off to being so in love with the experience that I didn't ever want to come down. I wished Pa and I could stay up there forever. It's one of my favorite memories with him."

～

The smell of carrot cake wafted through the air as the three sipped their wine and shared more memories while enjoying iconic eighties jams. Liza and Colette exchanged a few more stories, but Maude remained mostly quiet until Liza asked her to share something.

"Well, I'd be happy to, it's just that I don't have any memorable events from the past thirty years. Nothing good anyway," Maude admitted before taking a big swig of her wine, her glass now empty as she set it down on the booth's table. Colette quickly got up and retrieved a new bottle from the counter, giving her a refill. "Thank you, Colette," Maude said as she took another sip, thinking. "I suppose I could tell you about the last time Toshi, Jon, and I went on a trip. It was the August before Toshi was killed. We went down to Crater Lake National Park in Oregon. Would you like to hear about that?"

"Of course we would," Liza said, hungry for any story that featured the man Bianca claimed was her father.

"The drive down was long but pleasant, and sunny the whole way. Southern Oregon feels different from the rest of the state—there are still forests, but it's more barren. Before long we got to the park, cresting over a ridge that leads to a cliff that drops off to the lake below. *Wow.* Let me say, it's better than any magician's reveal. That sparkling blue lake is the brightest, clearest thing you've ever seen. I never knew water could be so magnificently colored.

"Our first night, we hiked up to Watchman Peak to drink in the view. We could see the whole lake from that spot, with an astounding vista of Wizard Island right in front of us. I remember Jon saying it was the most beautiful thing he'd ever seen," Maude said before pausing and taking a deep breath, the loss of her son and husband still so painful to bear.

"We stayed up there for a while and watched the sunset together, the colors of the lake and the surrounding mountains shifting in the clear sky, painting themselves upon me as I tried to firmly imprint that moment in my mind forever. I sat on some rocks with Toshi to my left and Jon to my right, my arms around them, our entire family so present in that moment . . . connected. If I could only keep one memory from my entire life, it would be that one. There with them, taking in that view, I was so very much alive."

"That's so lovely, Maude," Colette said.

"It really was, dear. And you know, I think it's important what they say," Maude continued as she lifted her glass and held it out, motioning for Liza and Colette to cheers with her, which they gladly did. "Trying to be happy every day in those in-between moments, on those average mornings waking up in our own beds, getting ready for work, accepting the monotony of our schedules . . . yes, we need to be happy there. Because life is built from the ground up with those moments. But I'll be damned if I ever let go of the highlights. The extraordinary moments, the instances where the small hairs stand up on the back of our necks, those memories matter *so much*. Whether it's seeing a spectacular film for the very first time, or flying in a plane piloted by someone we love, or sitting at the edge of the deepest, darkest, bluest lake with your family—gosh darn it—I'd argue the highlights are how a life is truly measured."

"Here, here!" Liza exclaimed as she lifted her glass to her lips and took another mouthful, finishing her first glass, clearly becoming tipsy.

At this point in the evening, as Honey B's became a warm, glowing orb in the center of the snowy night, the oven timer went off, signaling Colette to check the cake. As they got up from the booth to see if it was ready, one song ended and another began: Billy Idol's "Dancing with Myself."

"Oh my God! I love this song!" Liza yelled, placing her empty wine glass on a nearby table as she began to gyrate in the middle of the bakery, her feet placed firmly together as she wiggled her lower body back and forth while shaking her head. She looked ridiculous, but she didn't care. For the first time since the beginning of February, she'd forgotten about the Fifteen. She continued to dance in excess, her movements exaggerated and uncontrolled.

"Come on, listen to Billy! You've got to join me!" Liza begged.

Colette and Maude looked at each other, unable to wipe the grins from their faces as they set their glasses down and joined Liza for the length of the song.

The cake could wait.

As they danced in the middle of the bakery—their hips jiving to the beat, their hands balled into fists, which they shook like invisible maracas—Colette was happy. This was exactly the kind of evening she'd had in mind.

"Maude! You have such great moves!" Liza said excitedly, watching the older woman shake it to the classic song as if she'd been dancing to it all her life.

"I may have gotten down on the dance floor a time or two in my day," Maude replied as they sang along to the lyrics, continuing to soak up every ounce of this carefree release.

When the song ended, they left the middle of the bakery with lifted spirits, grabbing their empty wine glasses and heading over to the oven, where Colette checked the cake, decided it was done, pulled it out, and let it cool on the counter while she topped up everyone's glass with more Riesling.

"So . . . what do you say we have a sleepover?"

"Tonight?" Liza asked.

"Yes, tonight. Maude, you've probably had too much to drink to drive home. Plus, that snow is coming down out there, and we all know the roads won't be plowed. It's really for the best. For your safety."

"A sleepover? *In the bakery?*" Liza asked, acting like she was shocked by the suggestion.

"Sure, why not? I have some blankets in the back room, and the booths along the wall are pretty comfy. We could make a night of it. Tomorrow's Sunday, so we open later anyway."

"Let's do it," Maude answered. "I don't want to drive on those roads. Besides, this is the most fun I've had in decades. Why put an end to it? Can I ice the cake?"

"Hooray! I'm glad to hear it. Let's give the cake some more time to cool. Then you can have at it, Maude. I'll get the blankets. Liza, call your foster mother to let her know you're snowed in and staying overnight."

Before long, Maude was icing Theodore's cake, using her knife like a wand as she spread the white cream frosting in a haphazard manner that somehow still made the cake turn out beautifully. Colette and Liza returned to the dance floor to groove to more eighties tunes together until their legs were worn out. Then they joined Maude back in the kitchen, and Colette prepared some sandwiches on her famous baguettes for a late dinner. The night wore on, and as they continued to talk and drink, the three ladies found an even deeper level of intimacy.

By ten o'clock, having chatted and danced their hearts out, Colette turned the music off and they cuddled up with blankets in the plush yellow booths. They drifted off to sleep as the snow continued to accumulate, their dreams littered with the meaningful recollections they had spoken of so fondly, filtered through the lens of a warm wine high.

In the morning, they were awakened brusquely with a pounding knock at the locked entrance to Honey B's, which, paired with their hangovers, caused an unpleasant buzzing sensation to bounce around in each of their heads.

Bianca Schultz was at the door.

―〜―

"What are you doing here? Go away!" Colette yelled at the closed door, getting up from the booth where she'd been in the throes of a deep slumber. As she sprang into action, she could hear Liza and Maude stirring.

Bianca stared at her through the glass door, a look of desperation on her face. Her darkened silhouette was surrounded by bright white snow on the ground, the morning sun's glow already melting what had accumulated.

"I want to try and explain myself. Things have gone off the rails. I want to speak with Maude and my daughter. This is not what it seems."

"We don't want to talk to you," Colette responded, standing right before the door now, so the only thing separating her from Bianca was the single pane of glass, utterly transparent.

"That's not entirely true," Liza said from behind Colette, rising from the booth and slinking up to the point of confrontation.

"Liza?" Colette asked in a state of surprise.

"I mean, she has a lot to explain, doesn't she?" Liza asked, looking to Colette as Maude also sauntered up beside them. Three ladies stood inside Honey B's, while one remained banished out in the cold.

"I know I do," Bianca interjected, answering the question before Colette or Maude had the chance to. Even though she was outside and the door was firmly locked, her words came in crystal clear. "I want to tell you about the diary you took, Liza. It's important I give you the whole story, the *real* story this time. No more lies. No more misdirection," Bianca went on solemnly as Liza looked into her eyes, trying to gauge if the woman was sincere. "You're my daughter. It's important you know what happened."

Bianca was hard to read, but Liza's gut told her she was being truthful. She wanted to trust her, even though there were so many red flags in every direction she looked.

If they wanted to get to the bottom of what happened to the Fifteen, they needed to listen to Bianca. They had to let her tell her story and explain what the diary was about. It was the next logical step, regardless of whether or not it was a trap.

Liza decided to throw caution to the wind.

"I think we should listen to her," Liza suggested to Colette and Maude.

"I've listened to her before, Liza, and all she did was lie," Maude said.

"Liza, I don't know if this is a good idea. Maybe we should check in with Theodore or Grant before we make any decisions," Colette argued.

"No, we don't need the men," Liza persisted.

"If you'd like to hear the truth, come with me to the Moon Hotel," Bianca said. This offering was her last request as she turned away, retreating down the sidewalk to head back toward the small hotel along the sea.

"We have to go," Liza said, not waiting for a response but instead finding her raincoat, throwing it on, and lacing up her boots. She was going one way or another.

"Well, we can't let her go alone," Maude said.

"Of course we can't," Colette replied with a heavy sigh as she took a second to emotionally prepare herself for whatever was to come. She bundled up in her golden shawl, grabbed her jacket, and slipped her boots on as Maude also got ready to brace the cold. When all three of them were ready, Colette unlocked the front door of the bakery and they stepped out into the brisk morning air.

As they walked to the Moon Hotel, Bianca was just in sight ahead of them, far enough away that they weren't in the same spheres of influence, but close enough to watch her every step. The glittering sun above slowly dragged itself across the pastel-blue sky. Its rays persisted upon the layer of snow that had fallen the night before, melting it into rivulets that pooled in the cracks of the sidewalk.

Snow had come to Point Roberts, but just as quickly as it had arrived, it began to disappear.

Liza delighted in the rays of sunshine streaking across her face, all the while staring at the back of Bianca's head in the distance before them. The woman who claimed she was her mother. The woman who Maude truly believed was her mother.

This morning, she would have the opportunity to decide for herself.

When they got to the hotel, Bianca was waiting in front of the door to her room. The oversized navy-blue cardigan she was wearing contrasted dramatically against the brightly painted portal to room number three.

Liza stopped at the edge of the parking lot when she saw Bianca standing there, her attention pulled to the gulls squawking overhead, zooming around in zigzagging patterns as they made their way to the water.

A part of her wanted to run to the beach to escape this, to start swimming, to get the hell out of Point Roberts.

But the other part, the cornerstone of who she was, pulled her toward the hotel where answers awaited them.

"Are you sure you want to do this?" Maude asked.

"No. But I know we need to," Liza responded before she started walking forward again. Maude and Liza followed after her in single file, heading toward Bianca's room.

Bianca unlocked the door and welcomed them in.

The room looked just as it had the other day; the stacks of paper, binders sorted into neat little rows, and photographs taped to the walls had not moved since Liza and Maude had first discovered them. As Bianca asked the ladies to take a seat on the bed, Colette took in the scene for the first time, trying to read the handwriting etched across the boxes piled atop one another. There was barely a path to walk through the room, let alone anywhere to sit.

The bed where they placed themselves was the only real option, that and the single desk chair Bianca was now wrestling free from behind a stack of crusty boxes. Once she'd wrangled it loose, she placed it a few feet from the edge of the queen mattress, facing them directly. The morning sunlight continued its dominance of the day, shining through the window, filtering in past the dingy curtains, and highlighting the edges of Bianca's dark hair. The effect made a kind of golden lining around her head, creating a much-undeserved halo.

"I'm not one to beat around the bush, so I figure we'll just get right to it?" Bianca asked.

"Please," Liza answered quickly.

"Alright. Well, where do I start? There's so much to share."

"Why don't you start at the beginning? Tell us everything we need to know to make sense of this," Colette recommended.

"Very well. I think it makes sense to start with you, Liza . . . how you came to be."

Liza gulped, audibly, but none of the other women knew how to acknowledge it, so they didn't.

Bianca began her story.

"After Jon and I left Point Roberts in 1989, we moved to a small beach town called Moclips on the Pacific Coast. We tried to start fresh, living a simple, happy life. My seizures stopped completely once we left. We didn't know why, but it was a welcome development, so we didn't question it. With my health stabilized, I tried to forget about being locked in that basement and what happened when Jon broke me out. As I explained to you before, Maude, and as I'm sure you've told Liza and Colette, my memories from that night were muddled. Either way, I knew my mother was dead—and to be quite frank—I didn't really care who killed her. I was just happy to be free.

"For the next eleven years, Jon and I lived in peace on the beach. We got married in the spring of 1990. There were no guests, but I didn't mind. I loved him, and he was good to me. I was happy, truly happy for the first time in my life. Jon bought me a puppy that summer, an adorable corgi I named Toby, who became my trusted sidekick for the next decade. Jon started working at a hardware store and quickly became the manager. I started crafting, finding solace in creating weaves with colorful yarn on a large wooden loom Jon built for me. Together, we cooked delicious meals, danced to records by candlelight, read poetry to one another as the sun set before our eyes, and went for long walks on the beach. After enduring such a terrible prologue to my existence, I selfishly reveled in this newfound idyllic life. I tried to erase Point Roberts and the pain I experienced here from my mind. I realize now that that was a mistake. There were things I knew that could have solved this case so much sooner. But I didn't want to think about them, so I repressed the realities I knew. I used my blackouts as a convenient excuse to tell myself that what I thought I'd seen—what I thought I knew—I actually hadn't.

"And then the year 2000 came around and I had one very life-changing day. In the morning, I found Toby had died in his sleep, and that same evening, I found out I was pregnant . . . with you," Bianca said, a warm smile coming to her face as she looked longingly at Liza.

Liza tried as hard as she could not to react. She didn't want to offer up any part of herself.

"It was a surprise, finding out I was pregnant. Jon and I hadn't planned for a baby. We took measures to prevent ever having one. I took birth control regularly and he always wore condoms. It wasn't that we didn't want a child. It was just that . . . well, we didn't think it was safe to have one.

"For one thing, what if the baby inherited my unexplainable affliction? I didn't want a child to suffer through the seizures and health issues I'd dealt with as a kid. And then there was the baggage that came with the murders, Point Roberts, and our escape. Jon convinced me that if we had a child, we would put it in danger merely by being its parents. He reminded me how fifteen people were murdered in Point Roberts, and how the killer had never been caught. The last victim had been my mother, while I was in the house no less. He made me believe the Point Roberts Slayer was still out there, and that at any moment, they could come for us.

"And so when you were born, Liza, we gave you up for adoption. I didn't want to do it. It barely made sense to me *why* I was doing it, but I trusted my husband, and he assured me it was for the best. As an adopted child himself, he made me believe that you would have a better life, just as he had with the Oshiros. A life without complications, a life without having to deal with our history. We were able to meet with prospective parents who wanted to adopt you, and when I met your pa, well, I knew he would be right for you. He was one of the kindest, most endearing, and fascinating men I'd ever met. Once we decided he would raise you, I felt at peace with the decision, no matter how hard it was."

"But what about my life *after* Pa?" Liza interjected. "Sure, the first thirteen years of my life with him were great, but since he died, it's been anything but."

"Well, I had no way of foreseeing Pa's death. And I'm terribly sorry that you lost him, he was a wonderful—"

"Your sympathies aren't going to bring him back!" Liza shouted, not letting Bianca finish. It was clear this story had run a number on her. "Maybe if my real parents had raised me, maybe if you and Jon hadn't been such cowards, we could have lived happily ever after on the beach! But no, instead, the story has turned out quite differently, hasn't it? And now we're all stuck in this god-awful town with the Slayer still on the loose, threatening to kill me and my friends!"

As Liza was yelling, she stood up from the bed, hovering over Bianca as she released her frustrations. Now that she had stopped talking, she felt like she might float away, like hot air rising and getting trapped against the hotel room's stained ceiling.

Colette and Maude both reached out, gently grasping the back of Liza's arms and guiding her to the bed to retake her seat. They didn't want this to escalate any more than it already had.

"Down on the beach, you never said anything about Liza being your daughter. You said you knew she was here, but that you didn't know her identity," Maude said to Bianca. "That was a lie. What else have you lied about?"

"I said that because I wanted to approach Liza on my terms, to talk to her before anyone else did. As her mother, I thought I had that right. Through the adoption agency, I was able to track her, and I've been watching her since I came to Point Roberts. I was working up the courage to approach her. Unfortunately, the two of you arrived here before I'd gotten that far."

"All that stuff you told Grant and me and the other members of BGS about being locked up in your mother's basement and your seizures?" Colette asked. "You're saying that was all true?"

"Yes, that was the truth," Bianca replied. "I've only lied about two things. The first being that I didn't know the identity of my daughter. The second being what happened the night Jon and I escaped—the night my mother died."

Maude paused the conversation here, raising her hand in a subdued rage. "You told me Jon killed your mother! You said he killed everyone!" The tone of her voice was icy but controlled.

"I'm sorry, Maude. I know it was a terrible thing to do, but I swear it was for a reason. The truth is, Jon never said anything about killing any of the fourteen victims before my mother, and when he came to rescue me, her blood was already spread across our kitchen walls, her body nowhere to be found. I was convinced we were being listened to out there on the beach. That's why I lied. And with the parlancers having such sneaky methods to catch anyone discussing the murders, I thought they'd be listening in. I thought my father, Emory, might have even planted a device on you or Grant to record us. I know now you haven't been compromised.

"When we spoke on the beach, I thought the person who killed the Fourteen was still at large, and for the first time in a long time, I believed they were in Point Roberts. I was trying to coax them out with my lies. To give them a false sense of confidence. I thought whoever was threatening the five of you was the real killer, not a copycat. I convinced myself that the Point Roberts Slayer had finally awoken from their slumber and was ready to add to their tally.

"I know you've been looking through the diary. I know it has my name in it. But it's not mine. I haven't killed anyone, so you can get that out of your minds now. I never wrote any of the things inside it. I just read through it for the first time the day before you took it from me."

"Where did it come from then? Why does it have your name in it?" Colette asked.

"I'll get to that, but first I think you should know why—"

"Why did you say 'the fourteen'?" Liza asked. "When you said you thought whoever killed everyone was still out there, you said 'fourteen'—like that's the total number of victims, when of course you know there were fifteen."

"You're observant Liza, just like your father was," Bianca replied, referring to a trait of Jon's while avoiding clarifying what Liza had just noticed. "I'll get to that too. I promise."

With those two words coming from her mother's lips, Liza sensed a twinge of something unfamiliar take over her body, an emotion she hadn't yet felt toward Bianca: sympathy.

"This has all come to a head this particular February because of Jon's passing in November—of natural causes no less. After his funeral in Moclips, I went through some of his old belongings. That's when I found the receipts."

"The receipts from Emory's office?" Colette asked.

"The very ones. Since I know you've seen them, I won't go into the details of what they show. But let's just say, when I discovered them, when I saw before my very eyes that Jon had a direct link to each of the fifteen victims the week they were killed, I doubted everything I knew. I wondered if maybe Jon had been the killer all along. That's why I came back. To find answers. To find out if those receipts meant anything. After studying them as much as I could, I passed them along to my father anonymously, hoping he would look into them and share them with the police. But he held on to them. So, losing patience, I decided to confront him the other day, to get to the bottom of it. When you saw us together, it was right after our second meeting, our first having happened the day before."

"Yeah, the two of you were laughing together, having a great ol' time," Liza said.

"It looked like you were in cahoots," Maude added.

"Well, let's just say our second meeting went better than the first," Bianca said. "We hadn't seen each other in almost thirty years. I wasn't sure if he knew I was still alive. He never filed a missing person's report when I disappeared. I didn't know what he'd do when he saw me. But still, I succumbed to the pull of wanting to see my father again, regardless of how complicated our relationship was. He's the only parent I have left. I know he's a difficult man. You probably don't like him, hell, I don't like him—not after what he let my mother do to me and what he's kept secret—but still . . . I'm open to giving him a second chance."

"I doubt he deserves it," Colette muttered quietly.

"Maybe you're right, but it's because of him I finally know the truth."

"And what is the truth?" Liza asked.

"If only the truth had been simple to find. With all the blackouts my condition caused the first seventeen years of my life, it's likely I'll never recover some of the memories I should have—memories that could have brought the truth much sooner. When I came back, I wanted to clear Jon's name, or find out if he really was involved.

"My father assured me Jon wasn't the murderer by sending me these files, all these photographs and boxes. They arrived here after our first meeting, after I told him why I came back. They're copies of everything the police have on the murders. None of the crime scene evidence points to Jon. The receipts are the only thing that does, but my father told me they're a misdirect. Some are even fakes—created by the Point Roberts Slayer to frame Jon. They just never had the chance to deliver them to the police back in '89. Instead, Jon found them and confiscated them. That's why he had them in his possession, why I found them after he died.

"The missing piece of the puzzle is the evidence my father has had in his possession this entire time. The diary. He's known since 1989 who killed those people, if not earlier. But he hasn't revealed it, because he's been protecting himself and his grip on power. The diary came with these files. It wasn't in my possession for very long. So if it seems my story has changed since we last spoke, Maude, it's because my understanding of the entire case has."

"Can we just get to it already?" Liza asked, growing impatient.

"We're close," Bianca said.

"Come on, Liza, you know details are important," Maude interjected. Every ounce of Bianca's story had put her under a spell.

"I think Maude's right," Colette added, turning to Liza beside her, trying to encourage patience in the teenager who looked like she was ready to crawl out of her skin and throw it on the hotel room's dirty brown carpet.

"Alright. I'll listen. I just feel like I'm stuck at the top of the first drop of a roller coaster," Liza pleaded.

"How much do you know about Judy Dennison?" Bianca asked.

"Victim number twelve," was all Liza responded with.

"That's right. She was a large woman, well known around town, kind, endearing even, but, well, as it claims in the diary, she was rather gluttonous," Bianca said. "She ate out often, and while folks liked her, people also couldn't help but stare whenever she ate in public. It was as if she had been starved for years prior to each meal. The murderer, the person who killed her by stabbing her in the throat with that huge serving fork, took offense to this. I remember exactly what it says in the diary on

Judy's page. I'll never forget those words, because when I read them, I realized once and for all who the Slayer was. When I opened up the diary for the first time, Judy's page was the one I landed on. You see, my father didn't reveal to me what he's known. Instead, he instructed me to read the diary to figure it out for myself. He knew the identity of the killer would quickly become apparent to me.

"On Judy's page it says: *Gluttonous, a pig, unwilling to share, ate the whole box of my white-frosted cran-grape doughnuts at the Pinecrest Bake Sale before anyone else had the chance to enjoy them.*"

"Someone who liked making jelly doughnuts?" Liza asked, thinking about the peculiarity of her question and wondering if it was really going to lead to the identity of the killer.

"Indeed. You see, the diary was meant to be mine, that's why my name is in the front. But it's not my handwriting where *Bianca's Diary* is written. It's my mother's. It's her handwriting throughout the diary. I don't know why she decided to turn it into her horrific manifesto after writing my name in it, but she did. I never saw the diary until a few days ago when my father gave it to me.

"My mother, Amelia Schultz, was a very sick woman. I think that fact has already been made clear since she imprisoned me in our basement for over a decade. But what makes it even more evident is what she wrote in the diary about the fourteen people she killed. I've been able to corroborate everything she wrote in this primary source with the evidence in these files surrounding us, which backs up this conclusion precisely.

"Amelia Schultz, my mother, killed fourteen people in Point Roberts between the years 1987 and 1989. I just have one remaining question to find the answer to."

"And what the fuck is that?" Liza asked exasperatedly, unable to sugarcoat her language after this incredible revelation.

"Well, Amelia Schultz is dead. So the question now is . . . who killed *her*?"

CHAPTER TWELVE

LIZA, THEODORE & GRANT

Having spent the past three days in the Point Roberts Clinic, Theodore felt incredibly guilty for leaving Liza and Colette behind. He'd abandoned Maude too. A woman he had yet to meet. He'd had no desire to desert the case, but his ailing health had forced him to. They were so close to solving the murders of the Fifteen, and Theodore was lying in bed, his lungs heaving.

He was paralyzed.

With fear or with hope, that remained unknown.

Granted, he was feeling better. He was getting the pneumonia under control, and his discharge papers were on their way. The doctor who'd cared for him had been patient and kind, making the situation far more pleasant than it should have been. It didn't hurt that the doctor was also a very handsome young man.

The Point Roberts Clinic wasn't a real hospital. Instead, it was a makeshift care center that operated out of an old warehouse, only open in February. There wasn't a hospital in town, and with the border closed for the month, the clinic opened so the ill had somewhere to go.

It was rather strange for Theodore to be lying in a bed—hooked up to an IV and surrounded by machines monitoring his heart rate—in the same place his father had once worked packing frozen seafood to be shipped across the country. If his gaze didn't wander upward, it looked like any regular hospital. But if his eyes moved toward where the ceiling should be, ten or so feet above him, he found it wasn't there. In its place, an open abyss greeted him, where steel beams and rusted trestles joined together to support the warehouse roof some forty to fifty feet above where he lay.

There was no lid to the petri dish he'd been percolating in during his stay, the heights of where his attention could rise up almost limitless. Until he reached the roof, a different kind of container.

It was time to get out of this place.

A knock on the door sounded, and Dr. Epstein entered immediately after, as he never actually waited for Theodore to answer before coming in.

"Alright Theodore, so as I said, you're healthy enough to leave now, since you've made it clear you want to," Dr. Epstein said as he walked over and stood to the side of Theodore's bed, handing him a few papers on a clipboard to sign. Theodore pushed his body into action, sitting up and forcing his heavy legs to swing over the side of the bed so he could face the doctor.

Dr. Epstein had a warm expression on his face, his sandy-brown hair in a perfect swoop atop his bold, symmetrical features. His bright green eyes pierced Theodore sympathetically as he aimed to convey both care and concern. If Theodore had been twenty years younger, he might have even given the doctor his number, as he had an inkling his caretaker had been flirting with him these past few days.

Then again, maybe Dr. Epstein was just bored. Theodore was the only patient at the clinic who'd been staying overnight.

Besides, Theodore wasn't even sure Dr. Epstein was gay. And he was too full of shame to act on his attraction, regardless of their age difference. The boldness of his youth had vanished long ago.

His love life had died with Bill.

"To be more cautious, it'd be good for you to stay another day or two, but of course, if you want to go, you can go," Dr. Epstein said as Theodore signed the bottom of each page where giant red *X*'s indicated the spots to scribble his name.

"I think it's time, Dr. Epstein. There's a lot I need to attend to."

"Please, now that you're about to leave, call me Henry."

Theodore looked up at the doctor at his request, having signed next to the final *X*. As he handed the clipboard back, he found a nervous look on Dr. Epstein's face.

This was the first time he'd seen him look this way. Theodore had come to understand his expressions over the past few days, as his Roman nose, high cheekbones, and square jaw had been the only thing of interest to look at.

"Alright, then. Thank you, Henry. For everything," Theodore said as he stood up, preparing to leave.

"You're welcome, Theodore. But before you go, I have some news to share. And I think it's probably best if you're sitting when you hear it."

"What?" Theodore asked, sitting down from the surprise of Henry's precursory statement alone. What kind of news could the doctor have that would make him need to brace himself?

"I've had some tests run while you've been at the clinic. And I've discovered something that may come as a shock to you based on our earlier conversations about your health history."

"And that would be?" Theodore asked, already feeling impatient.

"You're not HIV positive."

"What?" Theodore was sure he had misheard. "What did you say?"

"You don't have HIV, Theodore. I ran the test three times. I'm certain of it."

"But how can that be? I've been HIV positive for more than two decades. My husband, Bill, died of AIDS recently. There's got to be some mistake." Theodore felt as if his body had liquified. His nerves no longer existed. He couldn't feel anything.

"When you came in, you told me you were HIV positive—that you'd tested positive for the virus in 1992—but that you hadn't been on any antiviral treatment. I found that peculiar right away. If you hadn't been treating the disease for twenty-five years, you'd have been dead years ago."

"But I—"

"I sent your blood to the lab and the results came back negative. Because of your claim, I even had the lab use two different kinds of tests, both of which are highly accurate. Each test gave us the same result: negative."

"You're saying that—"

Henry interrupted Theodore again. "When was the last time you had sex with your husband before he passed?"

"What has that got to do with anything?"

"Well, you said your husband died of AIDS, so I want to rule out the possibility that you were infected recently, as there is—"

"The last time Bill and I had sex was in 2015," Theodore said dryly. "He was so weak the last year of his life. The last two years together, the most we ever did was cuddle. And kiss." The weight of this new reality wrapped around him like a soaked towel in the middle of a hurricane.

He was suddenly very cold. His teeth began to chatter. His insides thrashed.

How could I have been so stupid?

He'd made assumptions about his life. He'd accepted his fate. He'd filed away his grievances and powered forward even though he remained angry.

How could I have been so wrong?

"Well then, if it's been that long since you and Bill had any sexual contact, and if you haven't had unprotected sex with anyone else, I can say with certainty you're negative. It would have shown up on the tests otherwise. Your pneumonia wasn't caused by HIV. If anything, it's due to the stress you've been putting yourself under. That and our typical February weather."

"Damn the weather," Theodore whispered. He didn't know what else to say. He avoided looking up at Henry. He was so embarrassed; it overpowered his urge to feel relieved. He stood up again, wanting to escape even more than before, and headed toward the door.

"Can I ask why you were so sure you were positive?"

Theodore turned back to face Henry, trying to think of the most accurate way to answer the question. "Well"—he sighed—"Bill was positive, and we had a lot of sex, unprotected sex, so I assumed I was too. I thought I'd been the one to give it to him. I'd been much more promiscuous than Bill ever was before we got together. And I mean, I'm not a complete idiot, like I told you, I got tested back in '92. At the same time Bill did. We went together. Both of our results were positive, so there was my proof. I never thought to question it."

"You must have gotten a false positive," Henry explained as he took a seat on the now-empty bed. His striking face wrinkled in contemplation as he completed the final move in this dance with Theodore, placing himself in the spot where his patient had once been. "That can happen. And you never followed up after the test to confirm your results? You were never treated?"

"I was afraid to put those drugs in my body. I planned to let nature take its course. I just wanted to forget about it and move on. Besides, I've never been a fan of doctors—no offense—so I never saw one unless absolutely necessary. Whenever my time was up, it would come. I didn't think I could do much to stop it."

"And Bill?"

"Bill took the medicine," Theodore admitted. "And he hated that I didn't. We fought about it for a while, but eventually, he let it go."

"Did you ever wonder why you weren't getting sick?" Henry asked.

"I guess I was too worried about Bill to think much of myself. I'd accepted my fate and put it at the back of my mind. I feel like an imbecile now."

"You shouldn't be too hard on yourself. If anything, take it as a new lease on life."

"I'll try that. Thank you, Henry. Now, if you'll excuse me, I think I need some fresh air."

"Of course. I hope you continue feeling better," Henry said as Theodore dashed out the door, a draft pushing down from the exposed rafters and propelling him forward. He began running through the clinic hall, hurriedly grabbing his belongings from the nurse at the front desk before bounding outside into the brisk winter air.

Looking around at the towering evergreens lining either side of the clinic, he silently praised the fact that it wasn't raining. Puffy gray clouds assembled in pairs, with splotches of somber blue showing through. The last thing his lungs needed was a wet day. He couldn't allow himself to get sick again. If this experience had taught him anything, it was that he needed to take better care of himself.

～

Utterly gobsmacked, Theodore trotted over to where his car was parked, unlocking the vehicle and sinking into the driver's seat. Before starting the engine, he pulled his cell phone out of the plastic bag the nurse had given him and powered the device on.

It quickly lit up with notifications.

He had fifteen voicemails.

One was from the funeral home—*Have they finally found Bill's ashes?*

Four were from Colette.

Ten were from Liza.

Theodore had decided to ignore his phone while in the clinic, just as he had decided to tell Colette he didn't want any visitors.

He knew it was a selfish act. The others would be seeking his guidance at this crucial juncture, but he wouldn't be of any use unless he got better. To do that, he needed to rest. And so he'd shut himself off from everything but his own thoughts for the past three days.

He'd subsisted on his thoughts and Dr. Epstein's smile alone.

He hoped that in his absence, Liza and Colette had paired together to form a more powerful team than the one he'd left behind.

They'd been worried about meeting each other. If Theodore had been present during their introduction, he feared it wouldn't have gone well. Their strong separate connections to him might have gotten in the way of a direct link between the two of them. But in his absence, they would have had a better chance to mesh, the tendrils of who they were linking together into a new kind of bond.

Theodore skipped past all the voicemails but the most recent one.

It was from Liza, recorded just an hour ago. He put the phone on speaker, pushed play, set it on his dash, and placed his forehead on the steering wheel, listening to the young girl talk. Her voice came through so clearly it was like she was sitting in the car next to him.

"Hi, Theo. It's me again. I'm still just sitting in my room. I don't have anything to do. Colette and Maude are with Bianca. Bianca's convinced them it's too dangerous for me to be around as they try to wrap up the loose ends. So they gave me this job. To wait for you. To be here when you get out. God, I hope you're almost out. I don't know if I can bear this much longer. I'm trying really hard to respect your wishes, but my impulses may take over soon if I don't hear from you. Can you please call me as soon as you get this? I want to know you're okay. And I have an idea. But I want your blessing before I do anything. Please call me. We have so much to talk about. You've missed a lot. And I know those other voicemails I left you probably make no sense. But we're *so* close. We almost have this solved. And I want you to be here with us when we finally crack this open and tell everyone what happened. Point Roberts deserves the truth. And that truth never would have been discovered if it wasn't for you. You brought us together."

The voicemail abruptly ended there.

Theodore raised his head and picked up his phone. His finger lingered over the call back button, nearly pushing it before hesitating.

He still needed time.

He knew he needed to reach out to Liza as soon as possible, but he also needed to digest the news he'd just received. The news that he was a perfectly healthy fifty-four-year-old man.

One recovering from pneumonia no less, but that was an affliction that would pass.

He never thought he'd make it past sixty.

And now? He could live to be a hundred. It almost felt like he could live forever.

He'd been preparing to be reunited with Bill.

He'd been ready to see Mallory. For thirty years he'd wanted to see Mallory again. Now, he would have to wait a bit longer.

There was still so much to do before he was done.

As shock firmly took him over, he placed the phone down on the passenger's seat and convinced himself it would be best for everyone, especially Liza, if he took a day to process this. He wanted to have a sound state of mind when he came back to her.

Driving home in silence, Theodore noticed the day's morning sun rising above the trees and pulsing in through the car windows, highlighting his skin in a titillating glow. Steering as if drunk, Theodore made it home in ten minutes, exiting his car and stumbling into his cottage on autopilot.

The ladies had cleaned up after themselves, but it was still apparent his home had welcomed visitors in his absence. The space felt lived in, appreciated, safe.

His plants along the large window looked perky. He touched the soil in one of the terracotta pots, the moist dirt lingering on his fingertips.

Colette had watered them.

Heading to his bookshelf, Theodore brushed off his hands on the front of his trousers and pulled down a photo album that held pictures from his and Bill's trip to Greece in 1992. The trip that had come right before they got tested. The trip before everything changed.

He took the album over to his maroon armchair, plopping down into it and sinking in. He turned the pages open at random, landing somewhere in the middle, where an image of him and Bill in Santorini looked back at him. In the photo, his arm was draped around Bill's shoulder, bright smiles on their faces as they were bathed in light, not unlike the light of this very morning. Behind where they stood, the white walls and blue roofs of Santorini's enigmatic villas plunged toward the coast.

It was a magical land, and at his side, there had once been a magical man.

He cried then, as his thoughts wandered back to the night that followed the day pictured, a night when he and Bill had made rapturous love in a four-poster bed. The doors to their balcony were wide open; the delightful essence of the Grecian air covered them, and the smell of salt sank into their skin as sweat dripped down their foreheads. Their lower limbs were entangled as they stared at one another, their connection unwavering.

"I wish this could last," Theodore had whispered to Bill, still somewhat out of breath. "These moments, these places, this feeling. I wish it wouldn't fade. I wish we could stay here forever."

Bill's eyes had glistened as if he knew a secret Theodore would never understand. He lifted his hand and gently caressed his lover's face. Even though he knew Theodore wouldn't quite get what he meant, he proclaimed the message of his heart.

"Some things last."

It was just three words, and even though it could have been in reference to many things, it lodged itself deep inside Theodore, getting stuck somewhere between his bones and tissue, not far from the essential parts of what allowed him to live.

Even though Bill was gone, Theodore's memories with him were too strong to ever fade.

Bill hadn't been a victim of the Fifteen, but he'd been a victim of a monster nevertheless, a terrible disease with no cure. His time as the sheriff of Point Roberts hadn't been easy on him, and Theodore feared the stressors of the cold case had coupled together with his illness to bring him swiftly to his end.

Theodore—the man left behind—contemplated what it all meant.

Yes, some things were meant to last. But the unsolved murders of the Fifteen were not those kinds of things, Theodore told himself.

This mystery that had always haunted him—Theodore swallowed it now like it was the disgusting medicine he thought he'd always needed but had never taken. He stared down at the photo of his lover and promised Bill one thing: the cases of the Fifteen would soon come to an end.

***

Mary, Liza's foster mother, had gone to visit her friend across town, leaving Liza home alone for the first time in days. Her foster father, Herb, was always absent during the weekdays, working at the sewage plant near the border. Even though the town was closed off and many local businesses were shuttered, offering some of Point Roberts' citizens a monthlong sabbatical, the same did not apply to Herb. No matter what happened, people never stopped shitting.

Lying on her bed, Liza had her back firmly pressed against the lumpy mattress as she stared at her bedroom ceiling, large brown water stains showing up on the textured white paint job as if they were dirty planets orbiting a forgotten sky. Theodore's book was clutched against her chest, her deep breaths causing it to rise and fall with every exasperated exhalation she made.

Liza was in limbo. Stuck waiting for an assignment that might never come. She hated this juncture. They had finally uncovered the identity of the Point Roberts Slayer, and while the other three women were working on wrapping up the case before making their findings public, she was stuck in her bedroom on Benson Road, waiting for Theo.

When she'd woken up that morning, she'd told herself these would be the last few hours of purgatory, giving Theo until noon *and noon only* to make contact. If he didn't, she was going to Grant's cabin.

Otherwise, she feared she'd go mad.

After Bianca's revelation that her mother, Liza's *grandmother*, had murdered fourteen people in cold blood, the careening vehicle they'd been strapped into had come to a screeching halt. Liza's seatbelt had snapped as she was ejected from the automobile, the others telling her she'd be okay as they left her on the side of the street and drove on into the unknown.

She hadn't wanted to come back to Benson Road. No matter how much she missed Theodore, she was not happy with the cards she'd been dealt.

Colette and Maude were still with Bianca at the hotel, going through the stacks of files piled high in each corner. The women knew they needed to build a foolproof case. They had evidence proving Amelia had killed people, but what they didn't have, what they didn't understand yet, was a motive. And until they had some idea why a wealthy middle-aged woman had killed fourteen people—fourteen specific people in completely random ways—they were worried about presenting their findings. They would be wrenching the lid off a jar of molded decay that had been baking in the sun for three decades.

When their findings went public, it was likely Point Roberts would tear itself apart.

Especially if they presented their other suspicion: that Emory had killed his wife, Amelia, and that for the past thirty years, Point Roberts had been locked down not to protect the citizens from a serial killer still at large but to hide the devilish secrets of a family unhinged. This was the story of an evil mayor hungry for power and the return of a daughter who'd long been forgotten.

It had been Bianca's suggestion that Liza go home, convincing Colette and Maude it was too dangerous to allow a teenager to continue with what they were aiming to accomplish. Bianca feared her father might learn of the new course she'd taken with the investigation, and she didn't want her daughter present for the fallout.

Liza didn't see it that way though. She was *not* a child. She was a young woman who deserved to be there, tying up the last remaining strings to secure a package she'd always planned to send from the very beginning. It wasn't right that she was being excluded now.

Instead, the job of waiting for Theodore had been assigned to her, a job that was about to end, as the forty-eight-hour mark they'd agreed on was about to expire.

⌒

Fully dressed and with her yellow raincoat wrapped around her waist, Liza tried to keep her eyes closed as she continued lying on her bed, her thoughts buzzing erratically while she aimed to suppress them. She practiced meditating, bringing herself a sense of calm as she felt the weight of her body imprinting upon the mattress, the tingles of her nerves and frustrations rattling down to her fingers, her toes pulling inward and then stretching out inside her still-damp shoes.

An hour to go.

A half.

Ten minutes till noon.

Just as her bedside alarm clock was about to alert her of midday's arrival, another sound interrupted the fray, bringing Liza upward as she peered past her ratty white curtains to see a car pulling into the trailer's driveway.

Theodore's Subaru.

Without thinking, Liza threw the orange book down on her bed and bounded out of the room, ran down the hallway, and burst outside to greet Theodore, arriving at the driver's door before he had a chance to step out. Impatient and excited, Liza ripped his door open, throwing herself into his arms where he sat behind the wheel, hugging him tightly as her body angled itself in half to secure the embrace.

"Theo! Oh, how I've missed you!"

"Liza, I—" Theodore began.

"Are you alright?" Liza asked, her arms still wrapped fiercely around his midsection.

"I'm going to be fine," Theo said; his body almost shrank away from the hug due to the surprise of its strength, but then he fell into the rhythm of it, his muscles slackening as he realized how sincere this display of affection was. "I've missed you too."

He allowed himself to be vulnerable.

"Now, if you'll let me, I can get out of the car, and we can talk," Theodore said, half laughing. "I listened to all your voicemails this morning."

"Oh, right . . . sorry about that," Liza said, apologizing both for her incessant calls and the strength of her grip as she released him, taking a few steps back. Standing in the driveway, she stared at Theodore as he unbuckled himself and got out of the car, his tall stature stretching out before her as she noticed how skinny he looked, even thinner than usual. "Is the pneumonia better? You look like you've lost weight. Why don't we get in the car and go find somewhere to sit? I feel like you should be taking it easy. There's a spot in the woods not far from here that has a bench along one of those trails that no one ever uses; it's private enough, and we could talk about what's happened since we last—"

"No," Theodore interrupted, causing Liza's word vomit to meet an abrupt end. He knew her well enough now to realize her ideas would keep spinning outward, aloud, until he interjected, shifting her perspective in another direction. "We shouldn't talk about this outside. It's not safe. Even though you don't see them, the parlancers are everywhere, monitoring what we discuss. I don't want us to get in trouble. This is too important. We should go inside. Are you home alone?"

"Mary said she won't be back until three or so, but I—"

"Say no more," Theodore said as he left the side of the car and headed toward the trailer. He opened the front door, which squeaked as he walked inside.

"Wait!" Liza yelled, unfreezing herself and moving into action, jogging after Theodore and bounding up the front steps to head back inside.

Liza kicked past the unruly pile of muddy boots gathered at the door and looked around to see where Theodore had gone. He'd somehow already disappeared into another room.

"Theo?"

"I'm back here," his voice called out gently, the tenor of his voice gliding out from her bedroom.

Liza followed the sound, walking back to her room past the awful acrylic paintings of tabby cats Mary had hung over the wood-paneled walls in the hallway. She knew their forthcoming conversation was going to be a turning point. One of those moments in life where you get a flash of déjà vu that wrings your insides out. As if, for a split second, you're drowning. As if, for a mere moment, you know the day you're going to die.

She found Theodore sitting on the edge of her bed, the fluffy magenta duvet Mary had picked out for her looking extra ridiculous as Theodore's outfit of dark navy contrasted against it. The last time he'd come to the trailer, she'd purposely not let him see her room. Compared to Theodore's cottage covered in beautiful artifacts from around the world, the place where she slept was an embarrassment.

He had picked up his orange tome and was tracing the cursive scrawl on the front with his fingers, his attention focused on his actions, but his words concentrated somewhere else entirely as he spoke without looking at Liza.

"Yesterday, right before I left the clinic, I found out I'm HIV negative. For the past two and a half decades, I was convinced I was barreling straight toward the end, only to have the script flipped, to be given a new lease on life. Sure, I have pneumonia, but it's far better than when I checked myself in. I'm going to be okay."

"You mean that . . . The doctor told you . . . How did this . . . I don't . . . ," Liza began four sentences, unable to finish one.

Theodore looked up at Liza and patted the spot on the bed next to him, wordlessly asking her to join him. She did so, and as they sat side by side, the pink daffodils painted on her headboard perked up just a bit from their previously droopy states, wanting to listen.

Explaining the mistakes that had brought him to his false conclusions, Theodore revealed to Liza how he'd been so wrong. He was ashamed of how irrationally he'd believed his untruths. Liza welcomed his story without judgment, the humiliation she felt for the bedroom she was forced to reside in slipping away as they both bared the discomforts of this intangible life.

When Theodore finished his explanations, Liza wanted to ask him why he'd never told her of his misdiagnosed status in the first place. But now that it was null and void, she decided not to press the issue, allowing the scab to cover the self-inflicted wound a millimeter more. She was glad he'd taken a day to process this surprising news, because now they had to dive back into what had transpired since he'd been gone.

Adding to the details of the voicemails he'd already listened to, Liza filled Theodore in on everything he'd missed, bringing their paths together so they stood at the same intersection, waiting for the light to change.

"But Amelia Schultz is dead. If she's the Slayer, what kind of justice can we bring to the victims and their families?" Theodore asked as Liza concluded relaying the new discoveries.

"We can bring them the truth."

"I suppose, but what would her motive have been? Why would she have killed Mallory? I never dreamed the killer I saw in that mask could have been a woman. Then again, I never met Amelia. I never thought of her as anything other than a victim . . ."

"Some victims deserve to die."

"Liza!" Theodore said, raising his voice at the sheer candor of her statement.

"I'm sorry, I didn't mean . . . You know what I mean."

"Of course, but still you shouldn't . . . Do you really think Bianca can be trusted? The fact that she's your mother boggles my mind. I want to talk to her, to hear from her myself."

"We can't talk to her yet. Colette and Maude gave me strict instructions on what we're supposed to do as they work with Bianca to try and figure out Amelia's motives by poring through those files. They have the diary, the notes in Amelia's handwriting that link her directly to the victims, the reasons she used to try and justify killing them."

"What does it say about Mallory?" Theodore asked.

"You should probably read that for yourself. I don't want to bungle anything by trying to recall what's there. Besides, I don't think I can repeat what—"

"Okay, okay," Theodore said, realizing his request was too much. "I just wish Amelia were still alive so we could question her. No matter what evidence they find, we'll never know the whole story."

"That may be true, but I have this feeling we're going to uncover more. She was obviously crazy, but I think there's more to it than that. And eventually, when we figure it out, we'll have to talk to Emory."

"That bastard," Theodore uttered in disgust, "I always knew he was hiding something. I believe your theory—that he figured out Amelia was the Slayer. It makes sense, right? He murdered her back in '89, killing her for her crimes. Closing down this town every February was nothing more than a scam to cover his ass."

"That may be the case, but we can't confront him until Colette and Maude give us the go-ahead. You know how impatient I am. I almost died waiting for you, but I think staying in our lane will help us, no matter how hard it is. We have a role here, and I promised them I'd stick to it. My job was to wait for you, and now that you've shown up, it's time for the next step on our agenda."

"And what's that?" Theodore asked, already unsure of the plan before he'd even heard it.

"We have to talk to Grant Fisher. He deserves to know about this. He's as big a part as any of us. Colette told me where he lives and said as soon as you came back, we're supposed to go find him. To tell him what we know now, that—"

Theodore started to cough then, his lungs heaving as his throat seized, the deepness of the noise rising from his core and layering the dust-covered room in the reverberations of an unexpected echo. Once he started coughing, he couldn't stop.

Liza sat there, unsure what to do, her eyes wavering back and forth until his hacking repetitions were replaced with deep, quivering breaths.

"Are you okay?"

"I'm fine. I think the pneumonia is—"

"You're still sick," Liza said, stating the obvious.

"Yes, but I'm okay. I'm getting better. So . . . Grant Fisher. Okay. I don't like it, but okay. Should we head there now?" Theodore asked, pushing on through the burning pain he felt in his lungs.

"No," Liza replied.

"What? I thought you just said that we're supposed to go see him?"

"We are. But you're sick. You should be in bed. You should probably still be at that clinic, even though I'm glad you're not. It will have to wait till tomorrow."

"Tomorrow?" Theodore asked, the weight of impatience shifting off Liza's shoulders and onto his own.

"If there's one thing I've learned since living in Point Roberts, it's that nothing important ever happens until the next day. Everything moves like molasses here. You need more time to recover; even though I kind of hate the idea, I know it's the right one."

"Tomorrow. Okay," Theodore replied, accepting Liza's reasoning. "And what do we do in the meantime?"

"You go home and rest. Get yourself better. Drink tea. And I'll return to what I was doing before you got here."

"And what was that?"

"Waiting. I'll sit here. And wait. I hate it, but I have to admit, I think I've gotten quite good at it," Liza explained with a sheepish grin. Waiting wasn't as hard when she knew what would come next.

Tomorrow, she would meet Grant Fisher, the only other person in Point Roberts she cared to know.

⌒

Theodore parked his car on the side of the road at the end of Grant's unpaved driveway, not wanting to drive directly up to his cabin unannounced. He and Liza got out of the vehicle together, emerging at the bend in the road where the street turned a full ninety degrees, one direction leading along the border wall to the east, the other moving along a tall line of trees strung out against the coast, moving south.

Liza grinned as sunlight bathed her face in a warm glow. She was happy to greet a pleasant morning where the clouds were absent, running late for their regular arrival. She'd never been to this part of Point Roberts where the northwest corner of the peninsula jutted up against both wall and sea. It was the mirror opposite of where Maude lived. But whereas Maple Beach had a smattering of houses near one another, Grant's crook of Point Roberts was quite the opposite. The only things that congregated here were tall evergreens.

"You're sure this is the right spot?" Theodore asked.

"Yeah, this is it," Liza replied as she spotted a red mailbox at the end of the driveway with 1901 displayed in silver numerals. She'd confirmed Grant's address with Colette yesterday afternoon when she'd called her to update the women at the hotel about Theodore's reappearance.

Liza began walking down the driveway as Theodore followed after her, their boots squishing in the moist dirt. The rain from last night had yet to fully sink into the ground.

The farther they moved into the woods, the more Liza felt she was stuck between two worlds, the sun and the shadows both fighting for dominance. While the clear sky was sure to prevail until precipitation returned in full force, the trees tried to trick her into believing otherwise. Their tall, elongated bodies blocked out the sun, so that repetitious lines of darkness caused the morning's brilliance to fade in and out in flashes.

Excited to meet Grant and bring him into their fold, Liza tried to keep her focus on the log cabin poking out from behind the wide trunks in front of her, but the ocean to her left continuously sought her attention. Twittering birds clamored in the overstory, and gentle waves lapped at the coast she could only spot glimpses of. Grant's driveway was elevated nearly forty feet above the beach, the tree line a natural wall above it. This layer of foliage was just thick enough to create a barrier, while still allowing visitors to peer through it, the gaps permeating the swathe with views of bleached driftwood discarded in horizontal fashions. It was as if the trees still rooted in the ground wanted Liza to pay her respects to their fallen brethren down on the beach, like they were a collective no matter if they were dead or alive.

"This town is so weird," Liza said aloud, talking to herself. She was distracted by this new part of the peninsula, momentarily forgetting Theodore was right behind her, until he grunted in agreement. "Where else can you walk along the sea as you approach a cabin in the woods that's smack up against an international border?"

"Probably not many places," Theodore answered, not sounding amused.

A bright flash of red caught Liza's eye among the trees, stopping her in her tracks.

Theodore slammed into her back.

"Ouch!" Liza cried.

"Sorry, I was looking at the—"

"Hello?" a deep voice called out from behind the red stretch of fabric that hung perpendicular between two trees, appearing as if a giant had taken a paintbrush and colored the woods with alien blood.

Liza and Theodore stood side by side as they watched a head emerge from behind the red, realizing they were looking at a large hammock tied up between the trees as Grant's face came into focus.

"What are you doing here?" Grant asked as he swiveled his body up, moving his feet out of the hammock where they'd been nestled and placing them onto the forest floor he'd been hanging above.

He returned to solid ground, his frame stretching upward as his full height was put on display. He slowly approached them.

"Wow," Liza exclaimed, as always, unable to censor herself. No one had told her Grant looked like a professional basketball player. He had to be almost seven feet tall. "Uh, sorry to surprise you like this," she went on. "We're friends of Colette and Maude. Well, actually, Colette is a friend. Maude is my grandmother. I don't know if you know that. That's part of the reason we're here. To fill you in. They gave us your address and told us it'd be okay if we stopped by to talk to you. We have news about the Fifteen."

Grant's stern expression softened at the mention of Colette and Maude. He trusted those women, enough to let two intruders they'd sent arrive unannounced, interrupting a moment of relaxing solitude, no less. "I see. Well, I'm Grant Fisher, and this is my little corner of the world. If you're friends with Colette and Maude, I'm happy to talk to you."

"Oh, wonderful," Liza exclaimed as she reached out her hand and introduced herself. "I'm Liza Jennings. It's great to finally meet you! I've heard a lot about you."

"Ah, Liza, yes. I've heard rumblings of you as well, your reputation precedes you," Grant said with a smile, his friendliness putting Liza at ease, even if only for a moment before an awkward silence took over. Gulls swooped between the trees as they urged the smaller tweeting birds of the forest to cease their shouting—the feathered creatures of the ocean were arguing with those of the woods.

Grant and Theodore stared at each other. Liza was an interruption between them, making her feel like she was in the wrong place at the wrong time.

She waited for one of them to say something, anything, but neither spoke. Grant's expression furrowed in apprehension. It was obvious he recognized Theodore.

After a few thrumming beats, the squawks of the birds rose to a rambunctious cacophony, the robins in the trees screaming back at the gulls and drowning them out. Theodore pulled his attention away from Grant, looking like he had teleported to the spot against his will.

"And this is Theodore Price," Liza finally said, nudging Theodore toward Grant, unable to allow the pause to linger any longer.

"Hello, Grant," Theodore replied, not extending his hand. "It's been a while."

"Indeed it has," Grant said, his body stiffening, somehow growing taller at that moment as if to show his dominance, becoming more prominent than the trees he stood before.

It was clear these two men had a history. A complicated history with more layers than an onion a mile thick.

Whether she liked it or not, Liza was here to moderate.

"Anyways," Liza spoke again, wanting to move on. "Has Bianca spoken to you at all these past few days? Colette and Maude told me you've had a lot of conversations with her this month."

"I haven't spoken with Bianca since I was with her and Maude on Maple Beach. She hasn't been returning my calls, and she didn't come to the last BGS meeting. Frankly, I don't know what's been going on, so I'm glad you're here. Colette texted me a few times, but she was speaking in riddles. I guess what she wanted to tell me was too important to include in a message, and she's been too tied up to get together."

"I'm sorry, I'm sure that wasn't intentional. We've wanted to include you, it's just that there's been so much going on, and we got kind of sidetracked. But we've been thinking about you, wanting to fill you in."

"Well, I appreciate that," Grant replied. "And where are Colette and Maude now? I'm guessing they're still occupied if they sent you two?"

"They're with Bianca at the Moon Hotel. Theo and I talked to Colette this morning before driving over here. We've learned the identity of the Slayer—of victims one through fourteen anyways. We know the *how*, but we're still trying to figure out the *why*. Colette wouldn't say much over the phone. The plan is to meet up once they have evidence on what happened to victim number fifteen. My other grandmother. She's the Point Roberts Slayer. But then, before she got caught, she got herself killed."

"What the fuck?" Grant whispered, shocked at the news that had just spurted out of Liza's mouth like she was reading it from a teleprompter. How was this teenage girl talking about this so calmly? She'd just given him the answers to everything he'd been struggling to solve for the past four years.

"We need to go inside," Theodore said, exhaling in agitation. "We can't talk out here like this. I've told you before, Liza, the parlancers could be listening in. We're too close to the wall."

"I haven't seen a parlancer in days," Grant replied, "but you're right. We don't want them listening, especially if we're still trying to figure this out. Follow me."

Grant left the spot before them, twisting his torso as his long legs traipsed toward his log cabin, which rested at the end of the driveway. Their destination.

Liza and Theodore followed Grant up the creaking porch steps where he welcomed them in, holding his cabin door open. Liza moved quickly, entering the cozy living room as she took in the space. A friendly orange tabby cat pounced off a pile of dirty laundry to greet her, and his small fluffy body began rubbing itself against her legs, purring in exaltation.

Theodore hesitated in the doorway, half his body in, half his body out.

"Binx doesn't bite," Grant said, looking down at the older man whose gaze was focused straight ahead, trying to ignore the fact that Grant was holding the door open for him.

"I'm not afraid of cats," Theodore grumbled.

"Well then, you shouldn't be afraid of me either. We're on the same team, Theodore. We always have been, regardless of whether you've felt that way."

Theodore looked at Grant, nodding slightly as his fierce gray-blue eyes penetrated the younger man. He'd always thought of Grant Fisher as his competition, the only other person in Point Roberts who had the guts and gusto to figure out what the hell had happened to the Fifteen before he did.

Maybe it was time to stop feeling threatened.

"I'm sorry. I guess you're right," Theodore said, trying to infuse his words with as little emotion as possible. He was forging a truce with Grant, speaking little but saying a lot. This man was not his enemy. He never had been. And so he began to put their past behind them, walking into the cabin, ready to try and work together.

Four officially ticked to five, the number it was always destined to be.

And at this threshold, Amelia Schultz's ghost pulsated above its nonexistent grave, the birds outside communicating a warning as their beady eyes watched the cabin door close.

Time barreled forward as the dead woman swallowed the news, devouring the warning only she could have understood.

Birdspeak, awakening the beast.

꩜

Grant asked Liza and Theodore to make themselves comfortable on the couch by the fireplace as he filled up a pitcher with water in the kitchen. He brought over the pitcher and three glasses, set them on his large wooden coffee table, which had legs showcasing lions with screaming faces, and poured water into each glass.

As she got situated on the couch, Liza noticed a large golden robe draped over the chair next to where she and Theodore sat, the fabric bold and bright, its oversized hood folded many times onto itself, creating numerous layers. The bottom of the robe was covered in mud and collected in a pool on the floor—contrasting against the maroon rug covered in a paisley pattern. The mud on the robe showed up as both flecks and smudges, like it had been dragged through the forest in a storm.

Grant started a fire, quickly getting one going without a struggle. Once he turned around from the fireplace, he realized the robe had captured Liza's attention, so he picked it up and moved it to a hook near the front door.

"What's the robe for?" she asked.

"We wear them at our meetings."

"Meetings?"

"For the Briar's Grove Society," Grant replied. "Our next meeting is tomorrow, so I was trying to spread it out to dry. It still feels a bit damp from the last time I wore it."

"Ah, of course. *The meetings.* Colette mentioned she went to one. It sounds like quite the organization," Liza said, a playfulness in her tone.

"It's a cult," Theodore interjected, momentarily letting his emotions take over even though he was trying to swallow his pride and move forward as a team player.

Grant looked at Theodore as he took a seat in the empty chair, his body plopping down with a pop as the chair's cold material suctioned against his warm skin. Before Grant could protest Theodore's claim, his cat reappeared from wherever he had run to once he'd left Liza's legs, and clambered into his lap—a space Grant happily reserved for Binx whenever possible.

"It's not a cult and you know it," Grant argued. "Our only goal is to solve the murders of the Fifteen. The same goal you've been working on."

"Alright," Liza spoke up, trying to ease the tension before they fully regressed. "We're never going to get anywhere unless you two clear the air and make amends. Then we'll dig into the case."

"I don't think we need to talk about it," Theodore said dryly.

"That's bullshit," Liza responded, turning away from Grant as she reached out and grabbed Theodore's arm, her touch in contradiction to the tone of her voice. She hadn't meant to yell at her friend. Still, she knew Theodore was a stubborn man. "Sorry, I don't know what the situation is between you two, but it's clear there is one. I think I deserve to know why."

"I always wanted Theodore to join the Briar's Grove Society. Since its inception," Grant began, taking the lead and answering Liza's questions before she asked them. "He was the first person I went to four years ago when I started the group. He was the main person I wanted by my side. Everyone in Point Roberts knows Theodore's an expert on the murders. He's been researching the Fifteen for decades as the subject of his second book. He's the only person who definitively saw the killer, masked or unmasked."

Grant talked about Theodore like he wasn't in the room, the space Liza occupied on the couch between them serving as a buffer, while the fire danced in the hearth. Liza pulled her raincoat off as the room began heating up, her throat starting to feel sticky as she listened. She reached down to the coffee table to grab the glass of water Grant had poured for her, needing something to occupy her fidgeting fingers, and took a heavy gulp, trying to act natural even though she felt awkward stuck in the middle.

Liza began to conclude that these men didn't actually dislike each other. It was more that neither of them felt acknowledged by the other. They both wanted to be the leading authority in the game. Both of their prides had swelled too large to make space for the other's opinion.

"But Theodore shrugged me off. When I went to him, at the beginning, he told me forming a society to discuss the Fifteen was a waste of time. He acted like he knew everything there was to know about the murders and that random citizens of Point Roberts would have nothing to add to the mix. He essentially told me my idea was terrible."

"I don't think I was that harsh," Theodore retorted, his voice hushed as if he was trying to recall how pointed his tone had been at the time.

"You were. You almost made me give up. But I was inspired. I had the time, and I convinced myself that maybe you just didn't want any competition. That you told me not to work on the cases because you wanted to save all the revelations for your book. Sure, you wanted the murders solved, but you wanted to be the one to solve them, or you didn't want them solved at all."

"That's ridiculous!" Theodore cried out, standing up with his fists clenched at his sides, trying to assert some power over the conversation even though in his current state of recovery, he appeared rather frail. At the outburst, Grant's cat dove off his lap. A heavy cough rose inside Theodore's throat, bursting into the room as he covered his mouth, trying to get a better hold of himself.

"Theodore, sit down," Liza said. It was a directive, not a request. She reached out to him again and guided him back to the couch. "You know you're still sick. It's not worth getting yourself worked up."

"I'm sorry," Theodore apologized, even though it wasn't clear if he really was.

"Let Grant talk, I want to hear his side of things. Then it can be your turn."

"Alright..."

"I ended up starting the organization anyway," Grant continued, acting as if the interruption had never happened. "There were other people in Point Roberts like me, people who felt helpless. They wanted to work together, to see if we could poke any leads loose. And once we started in February 2014, it didn't take long before we started to discover new things. Word got around Point Roberts, and I think some of the folks in town started to view me as the new authority. An alternative to the be-all and end-all knowledge Theodore claimed to have."

"Sure, you figured out some things, but you never got to the truth, the real truth," Theodore said. "It took Liza getting involved, and Colette, and Maude, before we figured anything out."

"I don't think I can take that much credit. It was because of your book, Theo... You know so much," Liza added. "All of us played a part. If Bianca had never come along, we'd still be circling the clues, unable to see where they pointed."

"Maybe you're right. It's hard for me to admit when I'm wrong, but I'm trying to be better about it," Theodore replied. He took a sip of water and leaned back into the couch, his body slackening as he took a deep breath. "Before he died, Bill asked me to stop being so stubborn. He always thought your group was a great idea, Grant. He told me I should join. At one point, I even considered it, but too much time had passed, and by then, it would have been weird for me to suddenly appear."

"It wouldn't have been weird," Grant said. "We would have welcomed you in."

The dialogue between them opened then, Liza becoming a witness to the significant reparations taking place.

"I heard rumblings about your methods. The robes, the stones, the fires in the woods in the middle of the night. It all seemed like a distraction, like you were up to something else, trying to call out spirits in the dark like a bunch of banshees, screaming and dancing among the trees. I couldn't get myself to support that kind of behavior, let alone be a part of it."

"You know only the outer layers of what BGS is about. The facade hides a more compelling truth, I think," Grant said, wondering how Theodore knew what he did. Had he intercepted a member of BGS and gotten them to spill details about their meetings? Before he could ask, Theodore answered on his own.

"Last year, after I turned down the Netflix producers for the third time, they asked me if I thought you'd be interested in taking part in the documentary. That's when I decided to go into the woods after one of your members invited me and told me the time and place. I watched your initiation ritual from a hidden spot in the distance. Far enough away that you wouldn't notice me, but close enough that I could see you. All of you."

"And robed people in the woods throwing stones at each other was too much for you?" Grant said, half laughing at the absurdity of his actions but forcing himself to stay composed. He tried not to show any of his true persona to Theodore, a man who had rebuked him for so long.

"I think it's too much for anyone," Theodore said without hesitation.

"Is it too much if it helped lead us to the killer, though?" Liza asked, posing an important question.

"Did it?"

"We only found Bianca because she came to a meeting," Grant answered, putting everything in perspective. "Who knows how this would have played out if BGS didn't exist."

"I guess that's a valid point," Theodore said, sitting up again, his chest puffing outward as he winced, his lungs still fighting against him whenever he tried to maintain normal posture. He needed to get his shit together, to accept he'd been wrong. "To tell you the truth, once your group got going, I started to get jealous of the attention you were receiving. And yeah, I wanted to be the one to figure it out. I've been working on solving these damn murders for what feels like my entire life. When I was young, all I wanted to do was write novels, to tell fictional stories that inspired people. Instead, after my first book, I've been stuck in a quagmire I can't get out of, writing this damn account on the Fifteen. It's the story that never ends. I've scrapped so much material over the years. I haven't even worked on it since 2015. My publisher's basically given up on me."

"Well, think of it this way, Theo," Liza began. "Hopefully, by the end of the month, there will be a definitive end to this awful story. And what better time to dive back into your book than when you can reveal the twists and turns and answers everyone's been waiting for?"

"Yeah . . . ," Theodore responded. He didn't know what else to say.

"So now that you've both explained this situation, can you make up for good? No more jabs, no more rude remarks. Let's put this behind us and admit there's no point in thinking your methods are above the other's. That doesn't matter now. We're in this together," Liza said, working as a miniature mediator between two powerful men, trying to forge a lasting connection.

"Alright, agreed," Grant conceded.

"Yeah, okay," Theodore said, following suit.

"Wonderful!" Liza exclaimed, feeling exuberant. When she'd woken up that morning knowing they were coming to Grant's, she hadn't realized how much of a peacekeeper she'd need to be. And even though it hadn't been fun, she was satisfied with the results. "Now that that's done, Grant, we've got to fill you in on what you missed."

Quite like she'd done with Theodore the day before, Liza recounted what they'd uncovered the past few days, telling Grant about the revelations Bianca had given them, including the surprising fact that she was her mother. As she talked, Grant listened carefully, with Theodore chiming in to fill in some of the details Liza left out. The narrative covered Maude and Liza meeting and finding the diary in the hotel room. They discussed the Schultz family tree, Bianca's lies, Colette and Maude's mission to figure out what happened to Amelia, and what they were going to do next.

When he was brought up to speed, Grant shot off questions without hesitation, asking things Liza hadn't thought about, his queries constructed with the expertise of a professional reporter.

"Why did Bianca leave so much of this out when we talked? Why did she lie? She made this so much more complicated than it needed to be."

"There's no simple answer. I think her memories are like abstract paintings. They only make sense if you look at them a certain way," Liza replied, not sure how else to explain her mother's madness.

"If Colette and Maude are trying to prove Emory killed Amelia—I believe it wholeheartedly. I don't even need evidence. That fucker is evil," Grant said through gritted teeth, his hands grasping the armrests of his chair tightly. "If we get him to confess, I bet he can reveal why his wife killed the others. The two of you need to come to BGS tomorrow," Grant suggested. They were trapped in a stalemate, and this was the only move available. "We're covering the murders of Eddie Wayne and Alan Henry. And if this is all true, they were the last two victims Amelia Schultz killed before she was killed herself.

Maybe their deaths hold clues to how this ended. They might be the most important cases to scrutinize."

"I'm totally down! As long as I get to wear the official garb," Liza said ecstatically, already dreaming about how cool she would look in one of Grant's golden robes.

"I have some extra robes, sure," Grant said with a laugh, a smile cracking over his face.

"Theo, does that work for you?" Liza asked her partner.

"I have nothing better to do," Theodore said as Liza looked at him, playfully rolling her eyes as she listened to his sassy response.

"I guess that settles it," Grant said, getting up from his chair and heading to the hall closet next to the kitchen, pulling out two golden robes and bringing them to his visitors who both stood up to accept them.

"Do these things only come in one size?" Liza asked, realizing how much fabric she was holding. "This is going to be huge on me."

"That's kind of the point," Grant replied. "The more mud you get on it, the better."

"Okay . . . but just to be clear," Theodore spoke up, "I am not going to allow people to throw stones at me."

"We can make an exception. You'll be special inductees. That's the beauty of BGS," Grant said. "I'm the leader, so I can make up the rules as we go."

"Thank God," Liza exhaled, happy that Theodore had made this demand. She didn't want to be pelted with stones either.

Grant told them where to be the next evening as they said their goodbyes and thanked him for welcoming them in. Theodore extended his hand to solidify their partnership as Grant opened the door to let them back outside.

Firmly taking Theodore's hand, Grant shook it with sincerity, looking into the deep gray-blue eyes of a man he had always secretly admired.

"Thank you," Grant said, knowing that none of this had been easy for Theodore.

"Thank you," Theodore replied, regurgitating the same two words.

After saying goodbye, Liza and Theodore walked down the driveway, getting a bit of distance between them and the cabin before Liza spoke, talking over the birds who were still tweeting incessantly.

"Was that really so hard?"

"Harder than you'll ever know," Theodore answered. He had never been one to swallow his pride. But the tide was turning, and things were changing. He knew he had to change too, or he'd be left behind. And so he'd taken a big gulp, opening wide, allowing himself to imbibe anew, drinking down the depths of the sea.

The next evening, darkness dropped on Point Roberts like a curtain, presenting no segue of dusk. One moment Liza was sitting at her bedroom window watching a deer gallop through the field alongside the trailer in the afternoon light and then, in a flash, it was pitch black, the animal having disappeared from sight.

At ten o'clock, Theodore's car arrived on Benson Road, slowly pulling over onto the berm, not turning into the driveway, as Liza had requested. Mary and Herb were already fast asleep in their La-Z-Boys with the TV blaring, the voices of Fox News anchors shouting in alarm, providing a buffer for Liza as she made her quiet escape.

After hopping into the car and gently closing the passenger door, Liza threw her gold robe into the backseat next to where Theodore's was crumpled. It was the only thing she'd brought.

"Are you sure you want to do this?" Theodore asked, looking hesitant behind the wheel.

"Theo, we're not chickening out," Liza replied, sounding a bit irritated.

"Okay, okay," Theodore agreed as he began driving to the woods behind the elementary school, where BGS held their meetings.

When they arrived at the school, they parked and exited the vehicle. Liza looked up to the sky as a steady drizzle began, hitting her face with drops. The rain was coming down hard enough that she couldn't ignore it, but gentle enough that she knew the trees would shield them from its full force.

"Should we put these on now?" Liza asked Theodore as she pulled her robe from the backseat.

"I suppose so," Theodore answered begrudgingly, tossing the robe over his head and pulling it down, the gold fabric flowing out and hitting the ground with a soft thud. His feet were completely covered. "It's huge."

"They're supposed to be, it's part of the aesthetic," Liza said as she put hers on too, swimming in the robe as if it had been made for someone three times her size. "You know, I think we're supposed to be naked under these."

"We're not getting naked," Theodore said with a growl. "Come on, let's get this over with." Theodore began walking away from the car and into the woods, producing a short, hacking cough as he went. He used his cell phone as a flashlight to follow a mild compression in the forest floor where other footprints were visible. Theodore knew this was the path to follow, the one that would lead to the BGS members gathered around their fire.

They always had a fire.

The wind picked up as Liza followed Theo, the needles of the evergreens overhead quaking as they flicked raindrops off their tiny sheaths, no longer wishing to cling onto the moisture that kept falling.

After walking through the trees for ten minutes, Theodore and Liza arrived at a small clearing where multiple figures clad in identical golden robes circled a bonfire, its flame illuminating the scene in a haunting half-light.

"Ah, there they are! Please join us!" Grant called out. Liza spotted him by following the sound of his deep voice. He stood on the north side of the circle next to the fire, facing them, on the lookout.

Theodore and Liza walked up to the group, the others widening their circumference to make room. They took spots side by side directly across from Grant, the crackling fire centered in the middle. As Liza looked around to see if she knew anyone in attendance, she noticed everyone had their hoods up. Since her hair was getting drenched by the rain now that the trees no longer protected them, she decided to do the same, signaling to the group that she wished to align with them.

"Welcome Liza and Theodore, and thank you for coming," Grant began. "These two are attending this evening as special recruits to the Briar's Grove Society. They have a great deal of knowledge on the Fifteen and were kind enough to share some of their new theories with me. I thought it would be beneficial if they joined tonight, as we discuss the murders of Eddie Wayne and Alan Henry."

"What made you decide to join after all this time, Theodore?" an older man asked, sounding agitated. "We know Grant's been trying to get you to join since the beginning."

Theodore recognized the man as Arthur Smith. He owned the grocery store in town. Theodore didn't know Arthur, not really, but from the way the older man was looking at him, he made it seem as if they knew each other intimately. He'd bagged Theodore's groceries for years, yet they'd only ever exchanged simple pleasantries.

"Things have changed," Theodore replied, trying to keep his answer vague. "And I've realized it's worth trying to work together—all of us—to solve these murders once and for all, to get the evidence we need. We each have separate pieces. Maybe united, we can put it together."

"Well, I think I can speak for everyone when I say I'm surprised you're here," Arthur admitted. "When Grant told us you were coming, none of us thought you'd actually show. I always got the sense you thought you were better than us."

"I'm not—" Theodore started to reply, but Grant raised his hand to interject.

"That's enough, Arthur. Let's make our guests feel welcome. We're not going to get into all this. I want this meeting to be a simple one, a way for Liza and Theodore to ease in. We're not throwing stones, not physically, not metaphorically. We're here to talk about Eddie and Alan. Nothing more. And in this rain, I'm sure you'd all be fine with a shorter meeting."

"You can say that again," a plump woman next to Liza said with a snicker.

Grant had decided not to tell the other members of BGS that they'd discovered evidence linking Amelia to the murders. At least not yet. Not when Colette, Maude, and Bianca were still finalizing their case. He trusted the others, but it wasn't worth risking the information slipping out to the general public before it was ready. They'd find out soon enough, but not until everything was signed, sealed, and delivered. He wanted the thirty-year-old cold case closed at all costs, and if he had to hold back intel from those he'd been working with for years to solve this damn thing, he'd do it, no matter how uncomfortable it made him feel. Grant instead tried to focus his energy on the newcomers to his society, taking special notice of Theodore, who suddenly looked alarmed.

Theodore felt his phone vibrating in his jeans pocket, but couldn't get to it easily without drawing unwanted attention to himself. Whoever it was, they would have to wait. He turned to look at Liza beside him as the phone's buzzing finally ceased. She was beaming.

Even though not much had happened since they'd arrived, Liza was already hypnotized by the Briar's Grove Society. There was an electric energy in the air, a collective force of unique souls gathered together in the darkened woods, working together toward a singular goal. Her gaze kept spinning around the circle as she admired everyone in their gold robes, the firelight dancing across their faces as she studied each of them. She wanted to remember their features, every person in attendance appearing like a magician to her, each one offering a special power that would add to the list of necessary spells they'd need to bring justice to Point Roberts.

She was partaking in something pivotal, like a scene in a thrilling movie where the climax was just about to occur. As the precipitation picked up and pelted them harder, Liza had never felt so peculiar and so enthralled at the same time. No amount of rain could ruin this parade.

Theodore, on the other hand, was unimpressed. Grant's society appeared just as he'd always perceived it: gimmicky and full of unnecessary theatrics. Why couldn't they have met in someone's house, dry and in their regular clothing? He didn't agree with Grant's methods, but he was willing to listen. That's why he'd come, after all.

At this junction, Grant nodded at a wiry man with an extraordinarily large nose who took a step forward and began to recount the murder of Eddie Wayne. Theodore tried to tune out his doubts and listened intently to the group's take on victim number thirteen.

"Eddie Wayne was an outsider. Unlike the rest of the Fifteen, he wasn't from Point Roberts. In this small community, that alone made him stick out like a sore thumb. He had a sense of confidence about him. A city slicker from Seattle, you noticed Eddie. He was a handsome, well-mannered fellow with a quick wit and a whole lot of questions for anyone who would answer them. The KIRO news station sent him up here as their field reporter to cover the murders. This being the third February in a row where people were getting killed, the Seattle station decided to keep someone up here for the whole month. Staying in town and not having to deal with the border crossings allowed them to be first on the scene if any more victims turned up.

"Eddie jumped at the chance to cover the story, whereas many other reporters had been hesitant to do so, worried for their safety. But Eddie was young and passionate and felt he had a lot to prove. He thought covering the Point Roberts murders could be his big break.

"Instead, his eagerness ended his life. Eddie was found with his throat slit, his arms and legs tied to a chair, and his mouth stuffed with a towel on the McMann property where their new house was under construction at the end of Island View Lane. The contractors found him in the morning, showing up to work and making the horrific discovery of Eddie on that chair in the middle of what would have been the McMann's formal dining room. Construction was halted indefinitely. The half-built house became a crime scene, but even once the police cleared it, the house was never finished. When Olivia McMann learned a man had been brutally killed in what was to be her new summer mansion, where she'd hoped to escape the busyness of Vancouver, she told her husband to abandon the project. They knocked down what progress had been made. The plot's still empty now. No one's ever built there.

"The point of Eddie's murder seemed rather clear. He was asking too many questions. He was asking the *right* questions. Someone wanted to shut him up before he got too close to the truth. Before he figured it out."

The wiry man stopped speaking then, lifting both of his arms at his sides, making a dramatic circular motion with them as his robe's sleeve swooshed and he brought his hands together in front of him like he was about to say a prayer. His eyes darted back and forth around the group, lingering on Liza for a beat longer than the rest.

A shiver went down her spine. Before Liza could speak up, wanting to ask questions about what happened to Eddie, the plump woman beside her stepped forward. From the silence that lingered, it was clear the other members of BGS knew what was going to come next. The woman was ready to share more of the story as rain fell on them from the pitch-black sky.

"Alan Henry decided to run against Emory Schultz for mayor in 1989. The first challenger Emory had had since he took office. Alan was well liked in town, a retired high school teacher who'd been beloved by his students, many who still lived here and were sure to support him. Alan ran on a platform of safety, promising the terrified citizens of Point Roberts that he would bring an end to the madness and murders. He guaranteed an improved police force, tougher security at the border, and curfews until we had a February in which no one was killed.

"He also offered other ideas to spruce up Point Roberts, ways to entice investment. He wanted to make sure his campaign focused on some positive things and wasn't just all about the killings. He was the first person who had the idea to refurbish the marina and build the picnic structures at Lighthouse Marine Park. He wanted Point Roberts to be a better version of itself.

"The election was set for March, but Alan never made it to election day, which is a real shame, as I'm sure he would have won. I know I was going to vote for him. Toward the end of that February in '89, his lifeless body was found tied to a ship at the marina, bobbing in the water alongside the boat's hull like an inflatable buoy. He'd been drugged, strangled, and drowned. The coroner was never able to figure out which of the three killed him. Most likely, it was a combination.

"No one else has ever challenged Emory for the mayorship. And I think it's because the last person who did got murdered for it."

The woman stepped back then, returning to her spot in the circle. Liza looked over at her, hoping to catch her eye, but she was peering intensely forward. Instead, Liza turned to her other side and caught Theodore's concerned gaze, the light from the fire wavering across his features in a shifting amber glow.

"What a lovely story," another woman's voice bellowed, emerging from somewhere in the trees behind where those dressed in gold robes were circled. The group's attention turned to discover where the voice had come from, everyone looking at each other, confused when the newcomer was not immediately found.

Two figures emerged from the woods then, joining the edge of the gathering so the others could see them, their appearances equally odd and terrifying. The taller figure was dressed in a large red cloak the color of blood, a white mask on their face with hollowed out black eyes and an elongated beak where their nose should be. This taller figure stood with their arms crossed before them, their hands hidden in billowy sleeves as they leered over the scene like a voyeur. The other person was also similarly masked, but instead of a white beak, they had pointy white ears that poked up at the top of their head, a forest green cloak making it so they almost completely blended in with the trees. This figure was shorter in stature and clearly rotund.

"We're here to change the way this ends," the woman's voice spoke out again, identifiably coming from the figure in the red getup.

Liza and Theodore were visibly shaken. Taking in both the sight and sound of these creatures had caused simultaneous revelations for them—albeit for different reasons.

Theodore recognized the costume of the figure clad in red. It was the exact same outfit the murderer had worn when they'd killed Mallory in front of him. He could never have forgotten that outfit. It had haunted his dreams for decades.

And Liza had recognized the voice of the woman who spoke, only able to place it the second time she heard it, parts of her memories clicking together as she found forgotten breadcrumbs she'd left behind weeks ago.

The masked figures pulled out guns, one aiming at Liza and the other aiming at Theodore, who were standing on the edge of the circle closest to the assailants. The plump woman beside Liza screamed shrilly, not pleased with her location so close to the intruders' targets.

"Who are you?" Grant shouted as he began to move closer to where the confrontation was unfolding, trying to regain some control over the clash.

"Don't step any closer, Mr. Fisher," the woman said from behind her mask, "or I'll have to shoot one of your friends here. And wouldn't that be sad."

Grant stopped dead in his tracks. If Liza or Theodore were killed, he would never forgive himself. He was the reason they were here.

"We're here to give you new information on the Fifteen, as I know that's the whole purpose of your little club," the woman in red continued, silliness lacing her voice like she was a stand-up comedian performing at a bar. "Because frankly, you're all a bunch of imbeciles for not figuring this out. Granted, I suppose I'm glad you didn't, but still, there were *so* many clues."

"What do you want?" Liza asked, clenching her teeth as she spoke so that her rattled nerves wouldn't be delivered with her words.

"Well, to be honest . . . *you*, dear," the woman said as her mute henchman lunged forward and grabbed Liza, latching onto her arms and tugging her backward, away from the group. Theodore tried to pull Liza back, but the stout figure in green kicked him in the shins, then cocked their pistol and aimed it directly at Theodore's forehead. Theodore began to cough uncontrollably.

"I don't think that's a good idea, Theodore," a voice said from behind the green figure's mask. A voice Theodore could place anywhere.

"Emory fucking Schultz," Theodore whispered as he cleared his throat, slowly taking two steps back.

"I guess we don't need these anymore," the figure in red said as she turned to her accomplice. Liza was now sandwiched between them, a terrified look on her face. Liza wasn't sure what to do. Should she try to pull away and run? Should she stay put?

She didn't want to die.

So she did nothing, instead watching her captors rip off their masks and discard them on the forest floor.

The man in green was, of course, Emory Schultz.

The woman in red was, somehow, victim number fifteen: the Point Roberts Slayer.

His wife, Amelia.

Back from the dead.

"How in the hell?" Theodore said in shock, utterly exasperated that Amelia Schultz was alive and standing before him.

"Yes, Theodore. It's me," Amelia said, pushing her free arm forward from her sleeve and waving a fleshy stump back and forth in his direction, showing the gruesome scar where her hand had been haphazardly cut off. "The reason you people never found my body was because there wasn't one to find. But more on that later, I think it's time we take young Liza here and get going, Emory."

A loud crack of thunder erupted then, causing everyone—even Amelia and Emory—to jump in surprise.

It never thundered in the Pacific Northwest.

"Wait!" a voice screamed from somewhere deeper in the woods. Multiple footsteps running toward the gathering came into focus as the rain pelted all those standing glued to their spots, paralyzed with fear and apprehension.

Within seconds, Colette and Bianca appeared, bursting forth from the trees, covered in mud, their hair slick and disheveled, two varying looks of dread on their faces as they registered the scene; the exact thing they'd come to warn BGS about was already transpiring.

They were too late.

"Amelia Schultz isn't dead!" Colette yelled, stating the obvious, but still needing to say it since she'd been holding it on her tongue since the moment they'd discovered as much just twenty minutes ago at the Moon Hotel.

"Thank you for that, Colette," Amelia said with a devilish smile. "I wondered if you'd ever figure that out with that mountain of evidence you've been poring over."

"You, you, what, what are you—" Bianca began to stutter; the core of her shook to be standing before her murderous mother. The mother everyone believed had been chopped up into pieces three decades ago.

"My dear Bianca, has it really been almost thirty years?" Amelia asked, moving away from Liza and looking at Emory to make sure he had a good hold on her. She jammed her gun into Bianca's side, causing her to wince in pain.

Bianca glared up at her mother, saying nothing.

Colette faltered, moving away from the clash, Bianca was frozen, and everyone else remained at their original spots around the fire. It was as if a foul play were unfolding onstage and only the principal actors in the scene could move.

Amelia pushed her gun into Bianca's back, urging her to move forward, farther away from where Colette now stood, and closer to where her father, Emory, held on to Liza. "I think we'll take you too," Amelia said.

The two villains now had one prisoner apiece.

Thunder boomed again, lightning momentarily causing the sky to flash white as it cracked overhead and struck a tree on the edge of the woods. A large branch fell and landed in the middle of the bonfire, a few members of BGS having to dodge it as the flame swelled in size.

Chaos ensued.

The rain that had never let up during the gathering was now coming down in buckets, the already saturated forest floor turning into a shallow sea.

The bonfire ate the rogue branch, swallowing it like delicious fuel as those in gold robes huddled together on one side of it, separate from where Liza and Bianca were held. Colette moved alongside the group, joining Grant and Theodore, who were standing in front of the other members of BGS, wavering in uncertainty, unsure what to do.

"Let's get the hell out of here," Amelia said to Emory, before shouting, "Don't follow us, or these two die!" to the rest of the group, who flittered in dismay like gnats against the ever-growing flame.

Amelia and Emory ordered Liza and Bianca to start walking forward, out of the forest, pushing them to move with the guns nuzzled in the smalls of their backs.

Liza looked at Bianca beside her, wanting to say something but having no understanding of what words even were anymore.

Instead, she thought back to the moment when it had all clicked—when Amelia and Emory first arrived at the meeting—when she'd realized where she'd heard this terrible woman's voice before.

To confirm her suspicion, she turned around ever so slightly as they trudged out of the woods, her drenched robe feeling so much heavier. She just wanted one more look at Amelia—her grandmother, the murderer, the monster—to be sure her conclusion was correct.

The same face looked back at her, the same face she'd figured it out to be.

Amelia Schultz was the woman who had been down on the beach. The woman who had pounced upon Liza at Lily Point right after she'd found Theodore's orange book. The woman who'd yelled and clamored at her as Liza made her escape, enraged that Liza was running away even though she'd been the one who'd startled her in such an unfriendly way.

Liza had met the Point Roberts Slayer on the first day of February.

PART IV

AMONG THE DEAD

CHAPTER THIRTEEN

THEODORE, COLETTE, GRANT & MAUDE

We can only perceive this world one way: locked inside the bodies we were born into.

Perspective is a creature that can never shed its skin.

No matter what we do, we can't experience the world from any other viewpoint besides the one we were assigned at birth.

You can never know what it means to be someone else.

We only live our lives as a single entity, with one identity. Yet sometimes, it takes a group of various perspectives aligned together to solve a dark and confusing mystery. To find a missing girl and her mother. To bring a murderer to justice.

Sometimes, you need more than one.

THEODORE

In the aftermath of Liza and Bianca's capture, I momentarily lost myself. Seeing Amelia Schultz in that same getup rattled me to my core, bringing back haunting memories of Mallory's murder, while my lingering pneumonia caused a burning sensation in my chest. At first, I was paralyzed with fear, but it wasn't long before a fury bubbled up inside me, ready to burst out as the storm raged on in the woods.

But before I could act, they were gone.

We didn't follow them, not wanting to put anyone in further danger.

We had to regroup.

The Briar's Grove Society disbanded. Everyone ran through the trees and back to their cars, hoping lightning wouldn't strike again and cause more branches to crash down.

I spoke hurriedly with Colette and Grant before we left, agreeing to meet at Honey B's to figure out what we'd do next.

We talked through the night at the bakery, trying to figure out how to get Liza back.

By the time 4:00 a.m. hit, the three of us had decided to go home to get some shut-eye and return later in the morning. Colette assured me Maude would also be in attendance when we came back. There was no gain in having someone stay behind at the hotel anymore. Whatever was in those files didn't matter now that Liza and Bianca had been taken.

We had to find them, and fast. And to do so, all four of us needed to work together.

When I arrived back at Honey B's later that morning after getting a few hours of restless sleep, I found a handwritten sign taped on the inside of the glass door. In thick black sharpie, four words were scrawled: *Closed until further notice.*

I tried to open the door, but it was locked. I knocked instead, causing a small Asian woman sitting in one of the booths near the front counter to rise to her feet. She shuffled forward, unlocking the door to let me in.

"Theodore, I'm so glad to finally meet you, even under these terrible circumstances," she said.

Maude Oshiro was standing before me.

Rumors of the Point Roberts Witch had been around ever since Maude locked herself up in her brown A-frame and never again stepped foot outside, instead examining the citizens of Maple Beach with a watchful, unwavering eye. I'd heard rumblings of kids bothering her, of the frightful appearance she displayed when they were bold enough to get close.

When he was alive, Bill had even intervened on a few occasions, chasing troublesome teens off Maude's property. He'd gotten a look at Maude himself one of those times, telling me later about the haggard, disheveled woman he saw looking back at him through the glass, emotionless. He felt pity for her. Her life had become a soft, saddened shell.

What Bill had described and what I'd heard over the years did not prepare me for meeting Maude in the flesh. Standing before me was not a witch, or an old woman withering away in despair, but instead a figure of distinction. Her sleek jet-black hair was styled in a chic bob, her fuchsia pants perfectly tailored and fitted and paired with a white linen blouse. She was beautiful, poised, powerful.

"It's nice to meet you too, Maude," I said as I leaned down to hug her, the smell of peonies emanating off her skin as we connected.

"I'm glad you're here," she said as I pulled away, our eyes locking and registering the lines etched into each other's faces. We'd both lost loved ones before we were ready to let them go, this unspoken truth allowing us to bond right from the start.

"Ah, Theodore!" Colette said as she came from behind the counter to join us, holding a plate of pastries in her hands. "I keep forgetting you two haven't met yet. It's about damn time!"

"Indeed it is," Maude added. "Should we take a seat?"

"Yes, of course. Would anyone like some coffee?" Colette asked. "The bakery might be closed, but I'm happy to make some."

"I could definitely use some," I replied as I followed Maude back to the booth she'd been sitting in when I arrived. "A cinnamon roll sounds nice too."

"Please, help yourself," Colette said as she placed the plate of pastries in the center of the table. She went to the counter and came back shortly with a fresh pot of coffee and a few mugs.

"Should we—" she began after setting them down, a knock at the door interrupting her as we turned to see Grant standing outside.

"Coming!" Colette shouted as she went to welcome Grant in. I watched as Colette relocked the door before rejoining us. She noticed my look of apprehension as she returned. "What? We can't be too careful. There's a killer on the loose."

"I guess you're right," I admitted, taking a bite of the huge cinnamon roll I'd just picked up, washing it down with hot black coffee that would, hopefully, help wake me up.

"Where do we begin?" Maude asked. "I'm at a loss. As if Amelia being alive wasn't bad enough, we've lost Liza and Bianca on top of it."

"We haven't lost them. They're just missing," Grant added, trying to temper the situation before it became grimmer.

"I shouldn't have stayed at the hotel. I should have come with you, Colette," Maude said, sounding guilty.

"We agreed it made sense for you to stay back, Maude. Your coming to BGS wouldn't have changed anything. It just would have put you in danger too," Colette reasoned.

"We can't go back," I said after swallowing my last bite of cinnamon roll. I had engulfed the whole thing in two minutes flat. "We can only move forward."

"So what do you propose?" Grant asked, a placid look on his face. I turned my attention to the two women, trying to gauge where to go from here. Their brows furrowed in anticipation, looking to me for leadership. For direction. For a plan. When they realized I didn't have one, Colette spoke instead.

"When I woke up, I called Liza's foster parents. I spoke with the woman, Mary Retton, and told her Liza had been taken," Colette shared. "She didn't sound too worried about it—even when I said Amelia Schultz had kidnapped her—but promised me she'd call me if she saw any sign of her."

"Not worried? Even when you mentioned Amelia?" Maude found this hard to believe.

"How did you realize Amelia was still alive?" I asked, trying to take a step back. "You found out before you saw her at BGS, right?"

Colette and Maude glanced at each other across the table to see who wanted to respond.

"We found a postcard addressed to Emory," Colette began. "It was at the bottom of one of the boxes, stuck to the back of a manila folder. The stamp had some residue on it, making it sticky. Every other document Emory gave us was in a folder, except for this postcard. I don't think it was meant to be seen."

"What did it say?" Grant asked.

"It said, *I'm coming back.* Nothing more, nothing less," Maude went on, picking up where Colette left off. "Amelia didn't sign her name, but poring over the diary has made us very familiar with her handwriting. It's quite distinctive. And why else not write your name on a postcard? Unless everyone thinks you're dead."

"But how did you know it meant she was alive?" I asked, trying to figure out how the details led us here as I took another swig of coffee.

"It was dated January 24 of this year," Colette continued. "The postcard depicted an icy scene in the Yukon. It seems she's been hiding in Canada these past three decades. And if she had to tell Emory she was coming back, he's known she was alive all this time."

"That son of a bitch," I exclaimed, the words coming quickly. Any chance I had to curse Emory was one I'd accept.

"Wow," Grant said.

"Wow, indeed," Maude echoed. "So what do we do? How do we find them? I'll never forgive myself if something happens to Liza."

"It's my fault she was kidnapped in the first place. You have no one to blame but me," Grant said with a heavy sigh.

"Don't be ridiculous." I urged him to lift his head back up, which had drooped down in shameful submission.

"If it weren't for me, you and Liza never would have come to the meeting. And Liza would still be with us," Grant replied.

"You can't think like that," Colette said from her spot in the booth next to me, reaching out and taking Grant's large hands in hers, the color of her porcelain skin contrasting against his. "Like Theodore said, we have to move forward. We can't think about what could have been done differently. We have to focus on what comes next."

"I know we've all connected with Liza. She's a smart young woman. Resourceful. Gutsy. Kind. Even in these dire circumstances, I'm holding out hope she'll be okay," I told the others.

"She's the glue holding the five of us together," Maude went on, adding to my words. "Is it time to call the police? Maybe they can help us get her back."

"I still don't trust them," I replied. "Ever since Bill left the station, they've been corrupted. They've been in bed with Emory, and now that we know he's even worse than we feared, who knows if they'd even be helpful."

I wished more than anything that Bill were still with us. My husband had been a damn good sheriff, the most brilliant investigator Point Roberts had ever seen. I always thought he'd be the one to solve the case, even with all the dead ends.

He just didn't have the right evidence. The right clues.

Emory had been working against him and the interests of the entire town. Who knew what the mayor had covered up? All this time, he'd been protecting his insane wife at the expense of his citizens.

Another thought crossed my mind then as memories of Bill flooded my brain. A tidbit of light that I thought could help lift everyone's spirits in this time of darkness.

"I'm okay by the way," I began, turning my attention especially to Colette beside me.

"Oh, Theodore, I'm sorry for not asking! With everything that happened last night, I got so caught up and—" she began.

"It's fine. Each morning I've been feeling better. I found out I'm fine. Like, *completely* fine. I don't have HIV."

"What?" Colette asked, a hand covering her mouth in surprise.

"The doctor ran the tests. I've been under the wrong assumption all these years. Apparently, I got a false positive and never got rechecked. It's embarrassing, to say the least, but—"

Colette burst forward and pulled me in, hugging me close as she cried out, a noise of stifled half anguish–half jubilation spreading across the quiet bakery. "That's the best news I've heard all year!"

I leaned into the hug, letting the warmth of Colette's kind embrace soothe me for the few seconds it lasted. I knew that when we pulled back from one another, we'd have to forge ahead into the unknown.

When we let go and readjusted our positions in the booth, Maude and Grant also offered me their happiness at this unexpected news. I assumed Maude had been made aware of my confused condition in my absence, but I wasn't sure if any of this made sense to Grant. But then, it didn't matter anymore.

I was fine.

"Needless to say, I'm ready to start searching this damn peninsula, and I don't have any afflictions to hold me back. If you hear me cough, please don't be alarmed. It's just a cough," I added, trying to make the situation lighter.

"Where should we start?" Maude asked.

"Maybe Emory's office?" Colette suggested.

"I tried stopping there on my way back over here," Grant admitted. "I couldn't get into the building. The whole thing's on lockdown. Two armed police officers are guarding the front doors. And there's one officer blocking each of the two back entrances."

"Meanwhile, everyone else in Point Roberts who wasn't at last night's meeting has no idea any of this is going on," I replied. "We have a duty to solve this. To find Liza and Bianca, and to make sure those two wretches spend the rest of their lives rotting in prison."

"Why don't we start with each of the four corners? And then work our way into the center?" Colette asked.

"I like that idea," Grant agreed.

"They'll want to be close to the water, to have some way to get out of town," Colette continued. "I don't think getting past the wall would work, even with Emory's connections. Maybe they're going to try and hide until March before sailing out? It's not that far away now."

"Which corner should we check first?" Maude asked.

"How about mine?" I suggested. "Liza found my book where I ditched it at Lily Point. We could start down there and then work our way up, and get supplies at my cottage if we need anything," I said while glancing outside. A tranquil gloominess hovered over the day with no sign of precipitation.

"Let's do it," Colette said, giving me all the permission I needed to get up so we could begin. There was no time to waste.

I stood there in the middle of the bakery as I watched the other three rise from the booth. Grant and I adjusted our jackets as Colette and Maude grabbed theirs from the stools at the counter and threw them on.

Whether or not Point Roberts was ready for us to start inspecting its every inch, we all knew one thing: it was time to go.

COLETTE

We found no sign of them at Lily Point.

After the four of us searched the park, the coast, and the surrounding forest until dark, we had to give up as heavy rain rolled in, retiring at Theodore's cottage for shelter as we planned our next move.

Time was not our friend.

Midnight seemed to hit us quickly after poring through some of the documents we'd brought over from the Moon Hotel, so we agreed to get some sleep and meet again in the morning. This time we'd scrutinize my corner of Point Roberts around Lighthouse Marine Park, the marina, and the mansions on Edwards Drive.

When morning came, I waited for Theodore, Grant, and Maude to arrive at our designated location: right in front of the Schultz house.

From where I stood on the sidewalk staring into the large bay windows, it appeared no one was home. The inside of the house was dark, still, empty.

If Emory and Amelia were stupid enough to hide Liza and Bianca in their own house, they were doing an excellent job of making it look like this was the last place they'd be.

A cold breeze pulsed through the air behind me, causing a shiver to slink across the back of my neck as I pulled my gold shawl tighter around my shoulders.

"Chilly today, isn't it?" a deep voice asked rhetorically from behind me. I startled and turned to find Grant standing there in the middle of the street a few feet from my position on the sidewalk.

"Grant! You shouldn't sneak up on people like that, especially now," I scolded him, all the while my heart melting just a little as I registered his reappearance in my life. I couldn't help it; every time I saw Grant, my insides wrung themselves out.

"I'm sorry, I didn't mean to scare you," he said sincerely, his often-harsh expression softening as he stepped onto the sidewalk beside me, placing a hand delicately on my shoulder. The warmth of his skin permeated through my shawl and caused my heart to skip a beat as my breath quickened.

I hadn't been touched like this in such a long time.

The way he looked at me in that instant, a moment of clarity washed over me.

And then it disappeared, just as quickly as it came, when Theodore and Maude arrived. The taste of intimacy with Grant dissipated, even though I realized as it left me that I didn't want it to. I wanted to be held. Comforted.

I tried to pull him back, reaching my hand up to meet his on my shoulder, but it was too late.

It was already gone.

"Hello there," Maude said as she and Theodore took their places beside us on the sidewalk.

"Good morning," I replied, trying to clear my head as I looked back to the empty house in front of us. This was not the time for romance.

We had far more urgent matters to attend to.

"I think we should try to get inside," Theodore spoke up, his first words of the day coming with no lead-up, no sugarcoating.

"Do you think that's a good idea?" Maude asked. "I don't want to put anyone in more danger than we're already in. Especially if it's not necessary. Maybe we could walk around the outside?"

"We're past the point of traipsing around delicately, Maude," Grant argued. "We'll be safe if we're together."

"As long as they don't shoot us," I said, my words haunting the inside of my mouth in their immediate absence. I couldn't believe this was the reality we'd found ourselves in.

"Let's not think that way," Theodore said, trying to calm the situation down before it grew more dramatic. "Let's just go."

With that, he walked forward, off the sidewalk, and up the driveway of the Schultz residence, heading to the front door as the three of us followed after him. There would be no more deliberating.

Continuing our search together as a team seemed to be working well. Even Theodore and Grant had fallen into step together. The previous day I'd noticed them having a conversation among themselves in the woods. The former competitors were maybe even becoming friends.

A heavy breeze rolled off the sea from behind the house, whipping around the corners of the mansion and slamming into us as we got closer to the entrance. It was a warning—that each step we took was a step closer to catastrophe.

Once we reached the front door, Theodore turned the knob without hesitation, the large glass-paned entry unlatching easily. I held my breath, waiting for a security alarm to sound, but a shrill ringing never came. The four of us quietly stepped inside the main entry hall. Theodore shut the door gently as I looked up at the glittering chandelier hung high above us.

We were inside. Why had it been so easy?

"Let's go to the kitchen," I suggested, finding my way to the large room with ease, as if I'd been in the house hundreds of times. Instead, the layout of the home was etched into my memory from the dozens of crime scene photos I'd studied, Amelia Schultz's blood smeared all over the walls. I'd reconstructed the floorplan with the pieces I'd been given; the real thing was now laid out before us.

I paused as I stood behind the large island, trying to make sense of everything I once thought I'd understood about Amelia's death. Everything that had since been proven wrong.

We gathered in the room she was once believed to have been murdered in, a cacophony of questions coming to mind, begging to be answered.

As I contemplated them, I accepted what I'd already assumed was true.

There was no way Emory and Amelia would have brought Liza and Bianca back here.

It was too closely tied to everything.

All the madness.

All the murder.

"How could Amelia have survived losing all that blood? Even without her body, the police never doubted she was dead, did they?" I asked the group, looking at no one in particular.

"I don't think there was any doubt," Theodore answered. "I mean, God, they even found her severed hand down on the beach. It seemed pretty clear someone had killed her, chopped up her body, and disposed of the pieces at sea. The hand was considered to have been accidentally left behind as the perpetrator made their way to the boat they'd anchored on the coast to dump her in the ocean. There were marks in the sand indicating someone had dragged something heavy to the water. The theory wrote itself."

"But what actually happened?" Maude asked.

"The police didn't realize what kind of psychopath they were dealing with. None of us ever thought Amelia was still alive until we came face to face with her at BGS," Grant replied.

"Hell, we never even thought of her as a suspect until a few days ago!"

"She's crazy, but she's smart," I admitted, gritting my teeth as I said it, not wanting to give the woman a compliment but knowing we needed to acknowledge this truth.

"She planned it. She must have sensed the police were circling in," Theodore went on. "She was careless killing Eddie and Alan. A reporter who'd been asking tons of questions about the town and how her husband ran it, and then the man who was challenging Emory for mayor. By faking her death in just the right way, at just the right time, she misdirected the entire search for justice by adding herself to the victim list."

"In one night, she got away with murder by murdering herself," Maude added.

"The missing pieces can only be explained by one person," I said. "We have to find her. I want nothing more than to talk to Amelia, to figure out why she did this. Why she caused this town so much pain."

"I want to know why she wrote that message on this kitchen wall," Theodore replied, his attention turning to the once-barren white wall where a painting of *The Angelus* now hung.

We knew what he was talking about, even without a full explanation. We'd seen the pictures of the crime scene. This was the wall that had once held a message you couldn't forget—where the words *It was Mallory* had been written in Amelia's blood.

I watched Theodore walk up to the wall, inspecting the small, dark painting that now hung alone in the middle of it. The size of the artwork was far too small for such an expansive space. It looked awkward and strange, the two peasants depicted bowing in a field over a basket of potatoes as they said a silent prayer. The tiny church on the horizon looked menacing in the distance.

The sight of Theodore standing there before that wall, a place where his sister's name had once been scribbled in blood, caused my chest to tighten. Acid sloshed up from my stomach, fighting against the call of gravity.

I seethed there in anger for what he'd gone through, what we'd all been put through at the hands of Amelia. We'd each lost loved ones because of this woman's diabolical actions.

"I hate this fucking painting," Theodore said in anguish as he parted from the wall, walking out of the kitchen. We followed after him. "Let's search the house high and low, and then let's get the hell out of here."

We did as he suggested, finding no trace of the four people we were seeking or any clues to their whereabouts. So we spent the rest of the day searching the nearby parts of town, with no hint of them having been present by the lighthouse, the marina, or Edwards Drive.

Another day was spent with no new leads. Yet still—together—we trudged on.

GRANT

On Sunday, February 26, we met at my cabin as the rain stopped and the clouds thinned. Peeks of much-missed sunshine slipped through, the first glimpse of blue sky returning since before the BGS meeting when everything went wrong.

I felt responsible for what had transpired that night. The kidnapping of Liza and Bianca digging into me deeper every day we didn't find them. Point Roberts was only so big, but even working together, the four us were challenged trying to figure out where Amelia and Emory were hiding.

The guilt in the pit of my stomach mixed with anger, aggression bubbling up as I tried to release it in beneficial ways, going for runs across every corner of town whenever I had excess energy when the four of us weren't together. I kept my eyes peeled as I ran, searching for clues as I jogged, never taking the same path twice, trying to cover a lot of ground as I exercised.

After my runs, I returned to the cabin and tired myself out further on the punching bag, picturing Emory Schultz's face at the point of impact where my gloves slammed into the same spot, again and again.

Even after all this, I still felt eager when I got together with the others, the desperate itch for justice overpowering everything else as I worked with Theodore, Colette, and Maude to find Liza and the Schultzes.

Our next expedition ensued as we walked through the woods near my cabin, searching outside under glimmers of sun. This time we focused on the northwest corner of town, which was mostly forest tucked between the coast and the wall. After a few minutes of looking around, I decided to offer an apology.

"I think it's important I admit you were right, Theodore," I started, looking at the man whose approval I'd once longed for so earnestly. I needed him to hear this. "The Briar's Grove Society wasn't a good idea. The secrecy, the initiations, the meetings, even the goddamn robes. It wasn't the right way to go about things. I could have done so much better without the pomp and circumstance, without the drama and mystery."

"Grant, you don't have to apologize. BGS may be a bit strange in its methods but—" Theodore began before I interrupted, talking over him.

"I just wanted to say I'm sorry. To you. To all of you," I went on, looking at Colette and Maude as they listened with cautious interest. "I guess I was looking for a sense of purpose. And maybe even a bit of power. I've felt lost ever since I was young; the murder of my grandfather, a man I never even met, haunted my life like an echo. His death destroyed my parents, and in turn, it destroyed a part of me. The Point Roberts Slayer took what could have been a far happier life away from me, and I've always blamed them. I internalized that sense of rage, and I needed to expel it in some useful way. I'm the kind of guy who has to do stuff. I can't sit still. I can't wait. I have to move. And so this all came to a head and led me to form BGS. I thought I was doing good. I really even thought throwing rocks at people in the woods was a way to deal with our collective grief. I thought I was helping people. But I wasn't. And it's sad that it took two people getting kidnapped for me to realize that."

The sound of my breath became audible as I stopped in my tracks, the understanding of what I'd said pushing down on me. Unable to look at the others, I looked down at the bright green ferns crowded in clusters around my boots where we were trekking through the woods, searching aimlessly. A sense of shame washed over me.

A moment or two passed in silence before the gulls called out overhead, and then I felt two delicate fingers under my chin, reaching out to push my head back up, urging me to stand tall.

I reached out and grasped Colette's arm, my fingers moving to her wrist as I pulled it down gently, our fingers organically interlacing at our sides as she stood by me, her hand squeezing mine in reassuring pulses of one, two, three—she was letting me know she was with me. That somehow, it was going to be okay.

Another beat or two passed, and then we released our hold of one another as Maude spoke in response to my apology.

"You're being too hard on yourself, Grant," Maude began. "Think about all the answers we found because of the Briar's Grove Society. If anyone should be apologizing, it should be me. Each of you have been working out here in your own ways, and I locked myself up in a house and helped no one—not even myself."

"Everyone deserves the right to grieve in their own way," I told her. "If that's what you needed to heal and let a part of yourself move on after your husband was killed, you deserved that, Maude."

"And maybe BGS was yours," Theodore explained, turning my advice on its head. "Your society found answers. It found Bianca. It took leads and unspooled the case. If it weren't for the racket you made, for the dramatics, Amelia might have just taken Bianca and Liza away quietly. Instead, you caused a scene. BGS danced in front of her face, it served as the best kind of low-hanging fruit, and the opportunity it presented was far too delicious for her to avoid. She had to show herself. You made her come out in the open. When we find her, the Fifteen will have you to thank. Or rather, the Fourteen."

"What's this about the Fifteen?" an unknown voice grumbled from a spot behind us. Our attention turned toward the sound, and we realized we'd wandered closer to the wall than intended.

Within a few seconds, four parlancers swarmed the spot in the forest where we stood.

We huddled together as the parlancers encircled us, forcefully pointing their batons at our chests with tasers at the ready. Wearing white helmets and opaque plastic shields to cover their faces, it was impossible to know their identities.

They could be anyone.

And of course, this was by design. No one knew who the parlancers in Point Roberts were. It was a monthly job held for only a twelfth of the year. They were sworn to secrecy in order to serve.

Even though their identities were shrouded, their mission was clear. Monitor the citizens of Point Roberts, and listen to what they spoke about, interrupting whenever the topic turned to the forbidden: the murders.

And punish them accordingly whenever caught.

"The four of you are in violation of Point Roberts Code 12.07," the same man who had first spoken up said. "As I'm sure you're well aware, speaking of the Fifteen in public is against the law. Please hold out your wrists to be handcuffed by the parlancer standing in front of you so that we may escort you back to town."

None of us moved.

I tried to rack my brain for what to do. No ideas came at first.

"There is no purpose resisting," the head parlancer said. "We have full authority."

"Like hell you do," I said, taking charge of the situation. "Where the fuck is the mayor? Your authority comes from him, doesn't it?"

"I beg your pardon?" the parlancer asked, his voice unsteady.

"The mayor? You know, that piece of shit who moves around Point Roberts like a slug? Haven't you noticed he's been missing the past three days? That the township building is on lockdown? Don't you think that's for a reason? Why aren't you looking for *him*?"

"I don't know what you're talking about," he replied.

"Don't play dumb!" I raised my voice, my fists clenched at my sides. "I may not be able to see your face, but if you have any decency, you and your team of Power Rangers will back the fuck up and leave us alone. The mayor is corrupt. We all know this. The entire goddamn town knows this. Don't be his underlings. The four of us are closer to finding justice for the victims than anyone else has been before. If you arrest us now, we're never going to catch the Slayer. We're never going to bring this town the peace it so desperately needs."

I waited for him to reply, raising my fists in front of my chest, showing him I was not playing games. Colette, Theodore, and Maude stood in stunned silence beside me.

When the head parlancer remained silent for another few seconds, I shifted my weight slightly, stretching my neck out, trying to make sure my large frame appeared as intimidating as possible. I wasn't going to leave without a fight.

Finally, he spoke again.

"Christopher Smith—victim number six—he was my cousin," the hidden voice said. "He may have been a bully, but he didn't deserve to die. I hope you find who did this. Parlancers, retreat. There's nothing to see here. Delete all recordings from the past ten minutes, starting when we began tracking these folks. Let's head back up to the wall."

"Sir, are you sure? We might want to—" a woman's voice said from behind the mask of the parlancer who had her baton trained on Theodore.

"Now!" the head parlancer screamed as he began to walk away, beckoning the other three to follow. And so they did, and we watched in grateful surprise.

We didn't move until they were out of sight, disappearing alongside the towering wall that ran through the evergreen forest.

"What the hell just happened?" Maude asked, going against her usually censored and cordial speech.

"Grant, you totally scared them away," Colette said excitedly.

This felt like quite the victory.

"See, Grant, we all have our strengths, even if they aren't always identifiable," Theodore said.

"And what strength would this be?" I asked him.

"Anger," Theodore replied. "Sometimes, anger is key."

MAUDE

We sat on the floor of my dining room among the large pillows that were usually arranged so carefully. Except now, they were in disarray. The four of us sipped tea in hushed tones, whispers coming only on occasion between gulps, the quenching of our thirsts never arriving.

It had been four days since Liza and Bianca had been kidnapped, and we'd searched every corner of town, having just come in from traipsing around the driftwood-covered shores of Maple Beach. We'd even gone as far as knocking on my neighbors' doors, but every house we stopped at in the hamlet by the water led us nowhere. Blank stares looked back at us when we showed the photos of Liza and Bianca that Colette had on her phone.

No one recognized them. No one had seen Emory recently either.

I suggested we ask about someone matching Amelia's description, but the others claimed it was too bold a move. Even without saying her name, they felt it was dangerous to plant a seed that she was alive. So we made no mention of her.

And it got us nowhere.

Instead, neighbors I hadn't talked to in decades stared at me like I was a fascinating specimen under a microscope, their eyes bulging out of their heads when they realized who I was.

"Maude Oshiro, is that you?"

"Oh my God, Maude, I didn't recognize you!"

"I'm so glad to see you've finally left that window, Maude. Good for you!"

And my favorite: "Wait a minute, Mrs. Oshiro . . . I thought you were dead?"

It was after this question that I suggested we rest back at my A-frame. I wanted to retreat from the attention, to bury it away and pretend it had never occurred.

The others could tell I was getting anxious at our lack of progress, and the pointed questions from my neighbors weren't helping. I was shrinking into an unknown oblivion, creating a future I couldn't find a path to.

We needed to make bold moves. Now was the time.

"It's been days with no sign of them," I began as I set my ceramic teacup down on the floor in front of me. "Let's be honest, we don't know where they are, and neither does anyone else in this town. We have to try something different."

"Maybe it's time we go to the police," Colette suggested, sounding resigned.

"We can't do that," Theodore said. "We've already talked about this."

"Then what do you think we should do?" Grant asked. "I have to admit, I'm running out of ideas. Where else could they be that we haven't already looked?"

An idea popped into my mind as Grant stopped speaking.

"We've focused mostly on the corners, and sure, our search has spread out from there, but the corners only reach so far inland. There's one place we stupidly haven't gone."

"Where's that?" Colette asked, her interest piqued.

"The trailer on Benson Road. The center of town."

Their eyes lit up at my idea. We'd only called Liza's foster parents that first day she went missing to alert them. The reality that we hadn't yet gone to their home was a befuddling one now that we were focusing on it. Covering the four corners of Point Roberts had seemed like a good plan initially, but it was now clear we'd forgotten one of the most important spots on the peninsula.

Within seconds, we jumped from our positions on the floor, grabbed our jackets from the hooks in the hallway, and threw them on as we left my house behind.

I couldn't move as fast as the others, but I moved as quickly as my legs would take me. I was making great strides until I noticed the state of my garden.

Every flower was dead.

Every white bloom that had burst forth over the past two weeks to interrupt the dark green canvas had wilted—seemingly overnight—shedding their petals and littering them across the ground.

They'd given up hope that continuing to live in this environment was worth it.

This discovery lit a fire under me, pushing me forward, serving as a warning sign that we could take nothing for granted.

We had to find Liza and Bianca before it was too late.

Bringing up the rear, I briskly followed the hillside stairway to the street below and took a seat in the back of Theodore's Subaru alongside Colette. He turned the ignition on and pulled out of the parking spot as we made our way to the center of town.

My nerves rattled as we drove. I was mortified I hadn't been thinking like a proper grandmother. I was still new to this, but that was no excuse. Why hadn't we gone to see Liza's foster parents in person? A phone call was not enough. They must have been worried sick.

Except they weren't.

When we stood before the trailer's creaking screen door and I told Liza's foster mother, Mary, that Liza was still missing, she stared at me like a bug she wanted to squash.

"That girl's always missing," she sneered in an annoyed tone. "I've given up on her following the rules. No matter how many times I tell her to let us know where she's off to, she never does. Liza does what she wants, when she wants. She's been gone for a few days before. But she always comes back."

"Well, she hasn't come back this time, and it's been four days," Theodore argued.

"What do you want me to do about it?" Mary asked. "Like I said, I've tried again and again with that girl but it doesn't—"

"We want you to act like you give a damn!" Colette shouted, getting heated. "She's not just missing, she's been kidnapped!"

Grant placed a hand on Colette's shoulder, trying to calm her down before things escalated. "Have you heard from her at all since the twenty-third? Has she called or anything?"

"I haven't seen her since Thursday."

"So no sign of her at all since we called you? Did anyone else come asking about her?" I said, confused as to why this woman seemed nonchalant when her foster daughter had been kidnapped. "Aren't you worried?"

"Listen, lady," she replied before taking a deep, exasperated breath and placing both arms across her chest. "Liza does this a lot. She's a wanderer. The foster system told us as much when they placed her here. She doesn't like staying in one place. She's run away before. It's what she does. I don't know squat about this alleged kidnapping, and frankly, I don't buy it. You don't need to get your panties in a twist. She'll turn up. And if she comes back here, Herb or I will call ya, like I told the French lady. Sound good?"

I could feel my forehead furrowing in frustration, my expression becoming pained. I had no way to temper my reaction. I did not like this woman.

"*This* lady happens to be Liza's grandmother, and *to be frank*, you've been a terrible foster mother," I said as the others swayed behind me, adjusting their weight on the soggy ground as they listened to my forceful rebuttal. They let me take the lead. "Liza is an extraordinary girl who you don't deserve to be in charge of. Before we leave, I'd like to take a look in her room."

Mary rolled her eyes, and I waited for her to respond, thinking she would slam the door in my face for being so honest about how I felt, but she did the opposite, stepping back from the doorway to let me come inside.

"Her room's back there," she said as I stepped into the trailer, pointing down a long hallway covered in cat paintings.

"I'll be right back," I said to the others from my new position, looking at them with a slight shrug as I registered the spot where they remained congregated together, wordlessly telling them that I wanted to do this alone.

When I entered Liza's bedroom, my eyes started to well up as if on cue.

The room had clearly been decorated before she'd moved in, the bright pink colors and lacy curtains so contrary to any design aesthetic Liza would have picked for herself.

But still, it was her room, with evidence that she'd spent a lot of time here. There were piles of books on the floor and handwritten notes littered across her desk alongside multicolored rocks arranged in neat rows. I found muddy sneakers discarded in front of the closet, one of them leaning on the other as if they'd been kicked off in a hurry.

On her bedside table there was a framed photo of Liza and an older man atop a mountain, standing before a gorgeous Pacific Northwest backdrop.

This had to be Pa.

Unsure of what I thought I'd find in Liza's room, I continued looking around, trying to take it all in, allowing my eyes to wander, hoping they'd land on something that might lead us anew.

And then I saw it, a book wrapped in a see-through plastic jacket with the words *A History of Point Roberts* across the front. It was shoved into the crevice between Liza's bed and the wall. More notes were scribbled in Liza's handwriting on pieces of paper jutting out from the book's pages.

Perhaps this book could point us to something else we'd overlooked—something forgotten in Point Roberts' history that could lead us to its future.

I kneeled on the edge of the bed, scooting my body carefully across to reach the library book and free it from the bedroom canyon it'd been held in. Once it was in my possession, I kept it close to my heart as I left the room to regroup with the others, making a final decision on what I'd been pondering.

Whenever we found Liza, I was going to adopt her.

I never wanted her to have to come back to this trailer again.

CHAPTER FOURTEEN

LIZA, BIANCA, EMORY & AMELIA

In one day's time, the wall would reopen and let people pass in either direction. The marina would allow boats to head out to sea, and the one runway in town would permit small planes to fly again.

Point Roberts' twenty-eight days on lockdown were coming to an end, and Maude worried if they didn't find Liza and Bianca before midnight on March 1, it was likely she would never see her granddaughter again.

Maude had been poring over the copy of *A History of Point Roberts* she'd found in Liza's bedroom the day before. For such a small town, it had a rather complicated history, the book coming in at over three hundred pages.

It took Maude well into the morning until she found something worth telling the others about. They had agreed to do some brainstorming and researching on their own before regrouping around lunchtime at Theodore's to search the peninsula again.

This would be their last chance.

Guidance came to Maude in the form of a handwritten note Liza had etched into the book on page 287, which showcased pictures of the old Salish Cemetery and discussed its unusual history.

Go to the cemetery.
Visit Mrs. Maguire's mausoleum.

Maude was familiar with the Salish Cemetery, but as she read, she learned more about the burial ground that had been closed for decades. Founded in the late 1800s when the town was first beginning to grow, the cemetery was used as Point Roberts' main internment for the dead until 1989, when Emory decided to no longer allow people to be buried there. He claimed the land was full and couldn't hold any more bodies. Its location high on a bluff overlooking the water near Lily Point made the ground unstable—the edge of the cemetery plummeted forty feet below its stunning vantage point, which looked out west to the mountains across the sea.

In 2003, the cemetery was closed for good after a small landslide caused a few headstones to slide down the bluff and crash along the coast. Luckily, no bodies were displaced in the incident, but from that point on, no visitors were permitted, not even to pay their respects at the graves of loved ones long since gone.

As Maude finished reading the entry on the cemetery—which only briefly mentioned Mrs. Maguire's mausoleum, naming her as Point Roberts' wealthiest resident—she plopped the heavy book on the floor, and it landed with a loud thud.

The Salish Cemetery was the perfect hiding place. Somewhere old and long forgotten, somewhere no one else was allowed to go. Another place Emory had closed off.

It was one of the only spots on the peninsula they hadn't looked.

Maude got up from where she was sitting cross-legged on the floor, her knees stiffly arguing with her as she rose; she tried to ignore the pain in her joints as she made her way to the telephone. She'd taken more steps searching for Liza and Bianca in the past few days than she'd taken over the thirty years she'd spent exiled in her house.

How her time alone had aged her.

An hour later, the four adults were gathered inside Theodore's cottage. Maude shared what she'd learned about the Salish Cemetery and explained why it was the perfect hiding place, while they passed around Liza's history book.

"And what are we going to do if we find them there?" Colette asked the group.

"I brought this," Grant replied, pulling a revolver from his coat pocket.

"Jesus," Theodore exclaimed, before tempering his surprise. "I guess . . . actually, that's probably not a bad idea. We know Amelia and Emory are armed."

"I hoped you'd say that. I brought one for you too," Grant said, pulling another pistol out of his bag and handing it to Theodore. "Have you ever shot a gun before?"

"My husband was sheriff of Point Roberts. What do you think?"

"I'll take that as a yes," Grant said with a slight smirk. "Ladies, are you okay being unarmed? I'm afraid I only have the two . . ."

"I don't think I'd trust myself with a gun anyway," Maude replied.

"Yes, that's fine," Colette added. "Let's just be sure you two lead."

Shortly after one o'clock, when the sun was beginning to sink farther behind the day's dark gray clouds, they left Theodore's cottage and began the climb to the Salish Cemetery. Instead of heading south toward the beach at Lily Point, they headed north through the woods. Theodore led the way, claiming to remember where the path through the trees would join the old dirt road that had once led visitors to the cemetery.

Within fifteen minutes, they burst forth from the thick grove of evergreens and found themselves at a clearing. What had once been a dirt road was now more of a half-covered long rectangular meadow. There were pockets of tall grass where the road had once been, with saplings dotting the route that led to their destination. About a hundred yards ahead of them, the gates of the Salish Cemetery could be spotted. Heavy black bars that had swung shut long ago blocked anyone from entering.

There was an absolute silence shrouding the cemetery as Theodore, Colette, Grant, and Maude arrived at the gates. They peered past the thick iron bars to inspect the forgotten graves crumbling before them. Although it was the middle of the afternoon, the cemetery was covered in darkness, the towering pines above having decided to block out what little sun was trying to peek through.

It felt like midnight.

It felt as if they were on the brink of an important discovery.

From the gate, they could see most of the cemetery, including the aboveground crypts and the few ornate mausoleums in the center of the burial ground that belonged to Point Roberts' deceased rich.

If they were going to break in, they would have to forge straight ahead. The rest of the fence encircling the cemetery was too high for anyone to climb over it. Written warnings ordered those who found themselves here to retreat immediately, but they said nothing about the gates being booby-trapped.

Theodore tried his luck by pulling on the metal chain that was wrapped through the gate's rungs, holding the doors together. A heavy lock was centered in the middle, tilted slightly upward as it rested on the ball of chains, creating an intimidating vise grip to dissuade anyone who wanted to get in.

Except when Theodore pulled on the chains, something unexpected happened: the large metal lock slipped off easily and fell to the ground.

"Someone's already been here," Theodore whispered. "Maude, my God, you're a genius," he said to her. "I think this might be it. Let's be careful."

Grant helped Theodore remove the chains, and together they pulled the iron gates open far enough that they could slip onto the grounds, the massive doors creaking in anguish as they moaned over their unwanted displacement.

Once inside, Colette began to study the graves closest to her, seeing dates as far back as 1895 etched into stones that were covered in green moss. Some of the headstones were in decent enough shape, but others looked like they'd been reclaimed by the forest. Pops of brightly colored mushrooms pushed themselves up from the earth where decayed bodies lay below. Maude joined Colette as they slowly tread over the final resting places of fellow Point Roberts citizens who had left many years ago.

A gull screamed and flapped its wings overhead, and Colette gasped in alarm as she looked up and watched it fly quickly through the trees. She followed its flight path as it moved toward the sea, a thin sliver of light through the nearby pines offering a preview of the ocean that lay to the west, down the steep bluff they were precariously perched on top of.

"We need to be careful," Grant whispered as he approached the two women. He motioned for them to rejoin Theodore near the gates, where he was putting the metal chains back around the previously tangled entryway, the heavy lock in his hand.

"What are you doing?" Colette asked, confused.

"We need to make this look just like we found it. Maybe Amelia and Emory are in here somewhere hiding Liza and Bianca, but it seems like they've been coming and going. I think its safest if we hide and wait. With it being February 28, they'll likely be making moves, and my guess is they'll be using this gate. If we're able to surprise them, it'll give us the upper hand."

"Where would we hide?" Maude asked.

"How about back here?" Grant suggested, pointing to a collection of large shrubs that looked dense enough to hide them in the dark filtered daylight.

"Perfect," Theodore answered as he finished securing the gate. Satisfied with his handiwork, he followed Grant and took a seat behind the bushes, Colette and Maude joining him as they settled into spots on the damp ground.

"Why do I have the feeling we're going to be here a while?" Colette asked as she tried to get comfortable next to the others.

"Hopefully it's worth the wait," Grant said.

"In the meantime, we should be quiet so we can listen for anything. We don't want to give ourselves away," Theodore suggested.

They waited in their spot on the ground behind the bushes near the gate. Remaining alert while looking past the tiny leaves in front of their faces, they gazed out to the stillness of the cemetery, trying to read the names on the gravestones closest to them, biding their time.

Hours passed.

They shifted their bodies as their backs began to ache, adjusting their posture while also trying to move as little as possible.

After the sun set and darkness blanketed the area, the four waited in blackness until the clouds burned away from the light of the moon. The full orb in the sky illuminated the hallowed ground, serving as a guide for those who were crumpled behind the bushes.

Still waiting.

Colette heard the wheezing first, and it wasn't long before Theodore, Grant, and Maude noticed it too. They shifted their positions toward the sound of a man out of breath, approaching the cemetery like it had been a terrible ordeal for him to get here.

Emory Schultz fumbled at the gates, his short arms holding a bag of food, water, and other miscellaneous supplies against his belly as he wrestled with the chains. Realizing there was no way he was going to be able to slip past the gates with his hands full, he dropped his bag of supplies and then removed the lock with ease, as if he'd done it hundreds of times before. Once the gates were open, he re-collected his supplies and walked into the graveyard, a clear destination in mind.

Theodore made eye contact with the others as he kept a finger to his lips, urging no one to move yet. Grant wanted to jump out and pounce on Emory as they watched him get farther from their hiding spot, but he understood they needed to wait just a little bit longer.

They had to see where he was going.

Emory headed straight toward the three large mausoleums congregated in the middle of the cemetery while trying to maintain the heavy bag in his arms. He grunted as he aimed to keep himself from dropping what he'd been sent to collect. When he arrived at the mausoleums, he began to climb the stairs of the one in the center.

Maude squinted from where she sat behind the bushes, focusing on the name etched in stone at the top of the mausoleum Emory was about to enter, trying to read what it said.

She wasn't sure if the letters actually ever came into focus, or if her memory just replayed them back to her. But she read the name just the same.

Maguire.

The name Liza had written about in her history book.

"It's time," Maude whispered to the others. "They're in there. They have to be in there."

Grant and Theodore looked at Maude and nodded, getting up and stepping out of the bushes, no longer trying to be quiet as they trained their guns on Emory's back. The large man, oblivious to his approaching guests, was juggling a set of keys as he attempted to unlock the doors to the underworld below.

Maude and Colette helped each other up as they followed after the men, being sure to stay close while maintaining a safe distance since they were unarmed and unsure of what Emory was capable of.

"Raise your fucking hands and turn around slowly, Emory," Grant called out as he and Theodore rushed the mausoleum. They stopped twenty or so feet away from where Emory stood on the elevated platform before the stained-glass door of Mrs. Maguire's tomb.

"Well, well, well," Emory's high-pitched voice called out, sounding not the least bit alarmed he'd been found. In one swift movement, he dropped his keys and the supplies to the floor, the echo of water bottles hitting stone vibrating across the cemetery and pushing out over the bluff. He raised his hands above his head as he'd been instructed, turning around slowly, putting his huge belly on full display.

"Are you armed?" Theodore asked.

"Of course I am, Mr. Price."

"Put your weapon on the ground," Grant ordered as he and Theodore moved closer, both of their guns aimed at his chest. "And don't try anything stupid."

Emory did as he was told, pulling a small gun from his holster and setting it down on the mausoleum's steps. Without saying anything, Grant seized the weapon, retrieving it with ease and heading back to the spot where Theodore had kept Emory in the crossfire. Grant gave Emory's gun to Colette, suggesting she move up in the ranks.

Now three of the four were armed.

And every gun in their possession was trained on the mayor.

"Tell Amelia to get up here," Theodore snarled at Emory.

"To do that, I'm going to have to unlock the door and call down to her."

At her spot behind the frontlines, Maude's stomach flipped. Amelia was down there, and she hoped to God that Liza and Bianca were too.

We've found them.

"Do it slowly," Theodore ordered as Grant nodded.

Emory cleared his throat and bent over to grab the keys off the mausoleum's stone floor. He unlocked the door.

When the stained-glass door swung open, a surprising warmth of light poured out across the cemetery, highlighting the faces of those gathered.

Mrs. Maguire's crypt had its own electricity.

A rich woman, indeed.

"Amelia!" Emory screamed, his voice bouncing down the spiral staircase that was just a few steps past the threshold. "They're here!"

Amelia would know what he meant.

"Give her a few minutes," Emory said as he turned away from the door. "She'll be here soon."

Theodore, Grant, and Colette kept their guns on Emory, their hearts beating quickly as a few moments passed before they heard someone shuffling up the spiral staircase.

Multiple sets of footsteps.

Liza came through the doorway first. Her hair was matted, and her dirty face carried an expression of torment and exhaustion, but it lit up when she saw the four people she'd missed the most standing in the cemetery, cast in an odd amber glow.

We've found her.

Behind Liza was Amelia, whose one remaining hand was handcuffed to Liza's so the teenager couldn't run away from her and into the safety of her friends' arms.

With Amelia and Liza on the portico of the mausoleum next to Emory, a final set of soft footsteps landed next to them.

Bianca's face came into focus, her dark scraggly hair backlit by the glow of the tomb's interior lighting, and the moon begged her to look at the sky.

She hadn't seen it in five days.

She wasn't handcuffed to her mother, as Amelia had no other hand to use as a means to keep her daughter at her side, but it didn't matter.

Bianca knew better than to run.

She'd run away from her mother and father and Point Roberts before, and in doing so, she'd only delayed the inevitable.

"What took you so long?" Amelia asked, agitated. "I thought we'd made it easy enough."

Theodore's mouth opened to respond, but unsure of what to say, he just stood there, gaping.

No one knew what to say.

"Shall we begin?" Amelia asked. "I have quite the story to share."

⁓

At this precipice, the future of Point Roberts would be shaped by the actions of eight people. Eight people gathered in the Salish Cemetery under the distinct moonlight.

Whatever they did—whatever they said from this moment forward—would change life on the peninsula forever.

"Liza, are you alright, dear?" Maude asked, trying to make sure the teenage girl hadn't been roughed up too much. It was clear she wasn't alright, but Maude knew asking Liza about her well-being would reinforce the idea that she cared.

"I'm okay," Liza replied before Amelia tugged her handcuffed arm back, pulling Liza closer to her and away from those who'd come to save her. She stroked Liza's gnarled hair with her other arm, the stump of where her hand had once been awkwardly knobbing across Liza's forehead.

Liza froze. This was not the first time Amelia had touched her like this, but it still gave her goosebumps.

"I've grown fond of Liza," Amelia admitted. "She's a smart girl. Lots of spunk. Reminds me of myself at her age. I am her grandmother, after all."

"You'll never be a grandmother to her!" Maude yelled back, her words coming out as growls. "*I* am her grandmother."

"Oh, Maude, don't be silly," Amelia responded with a playful tilt in her voice. "There's no reason to quarrel. Besides, you're not *actually* her grandmother. Adoptive grandmother, sure, but that's not the same as the bond Liza and I have. *Blood*. Parts of me are running through her. We all know Jon was an adopted little white boy who looked nothing like you or Toshi. Liza doesn't have a drop of your Asian blood."

"Well, I, I . . . ," Maude began, unable to finish as the daggers of Amelia's words burrowed into the space right below her ribcage, pushing her heart out of place.

"Why don't you quit with the insults, Amelia?" Grant spoke up, trying to divert the conversation back to what Amelia had hinted at before. The story behind what led her to become the Point Roberts Slayer.

"Why hide here, of all places?" Theodore asked, wondering what had brought them all to this cemetery.

"Mrs. Maguire's mausoleum is the perfect spot," Amelia replied. "That's why. Her tomb is like an underground palace. It even has electricity. Comfortable—albeit somewhat creepy—and in the middle of a closed cemetery where people can't bother us. The woman spared no expense when she was buried here. We thought we'd keep her company for a bit."

"Liza, I found her name written in your history book. Why did you want to come here?" Maude asked.

"The librarian told me about Mrs. Maguire when I asked her about the Salish Cemetery. I thought it'd be cool to see her mausoleum if I was able to get onto the grounds. So many of the Fifteen are buried here too. If I came to their final resting places, I thought it might help and—"

"When Liza told me she'd written that note in her book, I figured you'd go to her trailer and find the clue she'd inadvertently left behind . . . But I guess it took you a few days to figure it out," Amelia explained.

"Whatever the reason, we're all here now," Bianca added, her voice low and defeated.

"It's time to let them go," Grant barked, cocking his pistol as he took a step forward and lifted his arm, pointing the gun at Amelia's head.

"Oh, *my girls*? I'm not letting go of my girls. Not until I've had the chance to tell my story. And I don't think you'll kill me, especially not before hearing what I have to say," Amelia said. A smirk washed over her tight features, loosening up the wrinkles that had long ago etched themselves into her skin. She pulled Liza along with her as she moved forward, taking a seat on the steps of the mausoleum and encouraging Liza and Bianca to do the same, ruffling her long red cloak underneath her bottom and smoothing out its many folds as she tried to get comfortable. "We're going to be here for a while I think. Why doesn't everyone take a seat?"

"We can stand," Theodore replied for the group.

"Suit yourselves," Amelia said as Liza and Bianca sat down beside her on the steps. Emory took a seat on the mausoleum's flat portico, his short feet splaying out as his back rested against the gray stone near the warm light pouring from the door left ajar.

The three Schultzes and Liza sat in relaxed positions while Theodore, Grant, Colette, and Maude stood tensely on the cemetery grass, three of them with guns trained on the woman who'd taken center stage.

"You can put those things down," Amelia told the others. "I'm not going to hurt them. You took Emory's gun, and mine's down in the tomb."

"Why should we believe anything you say?" Colette asked.

"Because you've caught me," Amelia said. "And to tell you the truth, I was ready to be caught. Why do you think I came back?"

Theodore and Grant turned back to Colette, who slowly began lowering her gun. She wanted to be able to listen to what Amelia had to say. She needed to know the whole story, the *real* story, and listening while holding a gun wasn't the ideal way to focus. She nodded in the direction of the men, with Theodore also lowering his gun after another few beats. They watched as Grant overcame his hesitation and also stood down.

"Let's listen to what she has to tell us," Maude suggested from behind them. "We deserve these answers."

"Now you're speaking some sense, Maude," Amelia said as she chortled. "Where do I begin?"

Maude stepped up beside Theodore, Colette, and Grant. Now that no one was aiming their weapon at Amelia, she felt she should be in line with her friends.

"I guess I could start by admitting I was the one who called you. The voice disguiser may have been a bit intense, but hey, I wanted you to be invested. And what better way to make someone invested in a case than to tell them they're going to be added to the body count?"

"As if we weren't already invested," Theodore said, offended by Amelia's suggestion.

"Regardless, I wanted to find five people who were worthy of knowing the truth. Ever since I decided I was coming back, that was part of my plan. When I returned at the end of January, I was on the lookout. So much had changed since I left. Some candidates I'd thought of weren't here anymore, but some new folks were just perfect to add to my exclusive little list."

"Wow, should we feel honored you chose us?" Grant asked sarcastically.

"You should know I chose you for specific reasons. Theodore, of course, was the only person who ever saw me in action, even though he didn't know it was me. He has more knowledge on the Fifteen than anyone else in town and was married to the sheriff. He was my obvious first choice.

"Then came Colette, a curious outsider with a fresh perspective, someone who interacts with the people of Point Roberts daily in her bakery. When I found out she'd come to town because she was old friends with young Elsie, it made sense to add her to the mix.

"Grant, I'll admit, you were a surprise. You weren't even born when I left Point Roberts. But as I made my way around town, I heard whispers about a group called the Briar's Grove Society. A society you founded that used some peculiar methods to solve the murders. You seemed a bit off kilter, a bit wild—a strong, intimidating man with a purpose. I had to have you.

"Maude, I picked you rather easily too. With your connections to both Jon and Toshi, it was a no-brainer. I figured Jon had told you about Bianca too, before they left town together. When I came back and realized you'd locked yourself in your house, your input became even more important. You'd been around for the murders, but you hadn't partaken in the thirty years of gossip and theories. Your opinions would be unique. Invaluable. And then, of course, there was Liza."

At this point Amelia paused and turned away from the four standing before her, moving her attention to the redheaded teenager attached to her, wanting to gaze into her granddaughter's eyes as she revealed her reasoning for involving her in this insanity.

"You were the main reason I came back, Liza. The catalyst for getting me to leave the Yukon and deal with the mess I'd left. I learned I had a granddaughter and that she was in Point Roberts. Bianca's daughter would complete the quintet. I ran into her at Lily Point on the first, just as fate would have it. And as soon as I saw her, I saw myself. I saw Bianca. I even saw Jon, looking right back at me. I wanted to take her under my wing, but I accidently startled her and she ran. I watched her from afar over the coming days; I tried to find the right time to introduce myself, but I waited too long. She joined forces with Theodore, and my chance to intervene slipped away. So I monitored her actions from a distance and saw how the five of you slowly came together.

"Liza served as the cornerstone of your group. The reckless ingenue, the curious fact seeker—she quickly became obsessed with solving the case, and she was smart enough to do it. I don't know if the four of you would have figured it out without her. Liza's always been the key. And she had no idea how connected she was to everything."

Liza said nothing as Amelia's explanation ceased. She looked out at the cemetery grounds as if searching for the tiniest grave that could ever be found.

She'd been pulled away from those she cared about, and now, stuck in this terrible situation, she was nearly impenetrable. Scared, yet profound.

"That's quite the methodology," Theodore replied as Amelia's pause lingered. "If you wanted five citizens to talk to, you could have been more straightforward."

"But where's the fun in that, Theodore?" Amelia asked. "I'm all about the drama. It makes things more interesting. I could have just asked you to meet me here, but instead I kidnapped Liza and Bianca so I could lure the four of you to a spot like this—somewhere private, somewhere we wouldn't be bothered. I wanted it to be just us. *Just family.* I've thought about this night for a long time. Not necessarily because of guilt, but because I've wanted to get this shit off my chest for thirty years now. It weighs you down, you know—murdering people."

"Oh my God," Colette exclaimed, unable to deal with the candor with which Amelia was discussing having killed those they loved. "Have some decency!"

"My apologies, Colette. I'm just trying to be honest," Amelia replied.

"She's just like this," Liza responded, looking up from where she'd been staring at an old gravestone. "If I've learned anything during the past few days, she's unable to sugarcoat the way she talks."

"That's an accurate way to put it," Bianca agreed as she looked at Liza beside her, reaching out to take her daughter's free hand and holding it in her lap. Liza allowed her to do so without protest. The two had bonded during the days they'd spent together as prisoners. They'd gotten to know one another in intimate ways that likely wouldn't have come about otherwise. Liza trusted Bianca now, whereas before she had been frightened by her multitude of lies.

"I've been living in solitude in the Yukon for the past three decades. I couldn't talk to anyone about this."

"Well, now you can. We're listening," Grant said. "Can we *please* get on with it? You killed fourteen people in Point Roberts, and we all want to know one thing. *Why?*"

"It's quite simple, actually," Amelia replied, readjusting her wide bottom on the stairs, straightening out her shoulders before tossing her long auburn hair from one side to the other. Deciding she no longer needed to have Liza handcuffed to her, she pulled a small key out of her cloak's front pocket.

"Promise you won't run?"

"I promise," Liza replied. And when Amelia unlocked them, Liza kept her word, remaining seated, still holding hands with Bianca. There was nowhere for her to go. She wanted to hear this story too, maybe more than anyone. Amelia hadn't revealed anything about the murders over the past five days that she didn't already know. She was just as anxious to learn the truth.

"It all comes back to Bianca," Amelia began, getting to the bone underneath the hacked-up muscle. "From day one, I strived to be a good mother. I tried to protect her. It just got complicated rather quickly once I had to make that one difficult decision."

"And what decision was that?" Theodore asked.

"Killing your sister, of course."

After Amelia offered such a bold claim, Theodore wanted to storm the mausoleum and strangle the woman who'd killed his sister and felt no remorse for doing so. But instead, he held his ground and spoke no rebuttal, knowing he had to be patient. They had to listen and interject as little as possible. At the end of Amelia's story, once all had been revealed, they'd bring her to justice.

His body decided to offer something else in refutation: a giant fit of hacking coughs that echoed around the cemetery as if every trace of his pneumonia was leaving his body for good. The cacophony of coughs caused seagulls to stir and abandon the high branches around them. They left this weird midnight showcase and flew out to enjoy the gentle, tranquil stretches of the sea.

"You see," Amelia went on, "Bianca was a sick child. She suffered terrible seizures from birth. The first four years of her life, we barely introduced her to anyone, we were so afraid she wouldn't live for long. She was constantly in and out of the hospital. The doctors did tons of tests and offered solutions to fix her, but nothing worked. After years of never-ending frustrations, I convinced Emory to let me take care of her myself—full time, at home. I quit my nursing job and we refurbished our basement, making it as safe and sterile as possible but still a pleasant place for a young girl to grow up. We hid her away for her safety. And we told anyone who had met Bianca or learned about her that she'd died—"

"You what?" Colette interrupted, incredulous.

"It was the only way to avoid the questions of 'Where's Bianca?' 'How's Bianca?' 'Is Bianca doing better?' It was in the best interest of my child, the only way our new plan would work," Amelia offered up.

"*Vous êtes fou,*" Colette muttered, unable to help herself.

"I don't speak French, so I'll ignore that," Amelia said before moving on. "A decade of mother-daughter time went pretty smoothly from that point. Bianca still had her seizures, but I took care of her. She got a full education. She got anything she wanted—besides going outside. She assured me she was happy. But then everything changed in '87."

The year of the first five murders had finally reached her lips.

"At the end of that January, I had appendicitis, and for the first time since 1977, I had to leave Bianca alone at the house with Emory. I was in the hospital for three days. And in those three days, Emory fucked everything up."

"I don't think you can blame this on—" Emory said, speaking for the first time since Amelia had begun her story. But she swiftly raised her hand in a tightly closed fist, ordering him to silence. He knew better than to argue with her, so he said nothing more.

"Emory made some awful decisions while Bianca was in his care. The worst being hiring a babysitter to help with Bianca, even though I'd explicitly told him to take every day off and stay home. I guess he couldn't handle it. The babysitter he hired was Mallory Price."

Hearing Amelia say his sister's name aloud made Theodore want to scream, but he held the urge back. He hated it whenever anyone said Mallory's name, but he knew there would be no getting through this without people saying it.

"I told Mallory how my mother never let me leave our basement," Bianca said, adding further context, not wanting Amelia to have full control of the story.

"You shouldn't have done that," Amelia said. "It ruined everything!"

"You have no one to blame but yourself," Bianca grumbled.

Amelia ignored her daughter, continuing where she'd left off. "When I returned from the hospital and realized what'd happened, I knew nothing would ever be the same. Because of Emory's carelessness, we'd been infiltrated. And Bianca had told Mallory everything. I was *furious*. And to make matters worse, it was clear from the start that Mallory was an earnest young woman, the kind who would persist even when battered down. When I first got back to the house, she was with Bianca in the basement. I heard them laughing together, watching some stupid television show. When I confronted them and asked Mallory to leave, she looked at me with disgust. But she followed my request. As I walked her out, she paused at the door and told me she was going to report my treatment of Bianca to the police as soon as she left. I didn't know what to say. I began fumbling over my words, and the next thing I knew, I was threatening her."

"You scared her enough to convince her not to go to the police," Theodore said. "But she still knew she needed to tell someone, even after you threatened her."

"And did she tell you, Theodore?"

"She was about to, but then you killed her. To protect yourself."

"I killed Mallory to protect my family. If she told anyone about Bianca, people wouldn't understand. They'd have taken her away from me. I couldn't risk losing my daughter. She was too ill to be in anyone else's care but mine. For someone who loved his sister so much, wouldn't you do anything to protect her if she was in danger?"

"Of course I would, but I wouldn't—"

"Wouldn't kill?" Amelia asked. "Then perhaps you weren't as close as you thought you were. Mallory gave me no choice. She called me after she left, telling me she was going to tell you the truth. And oh, I'd heard about you, Theodore. I knew what kind of guy you were, the kind that couldn't keep his mouth shut. I knew my secrets would be spilling out all over town unless I stopped you. Unless I stopped her. So that's what I did."

"You killed my sister in cold blood. You murdered her right in front of me," Theodore said quietly, his words sinking into the soft earth, pulled down and absorbed by the rotted bones beneath where he stood.

"At least I was able to spare your life. As I hid in the trees, I heard your conversation and it was apparent Mallory hadn't told you yet. Her hesitation saved your life."

"Should I be grateful you didn't murder me too?" Theodore asked, his voice accentuating each syllable he spoke so Amelia would recognize the ridiculousness of what she'd just said.

"I suppose you should be. It was Mallory—her actions led us here. It was just supposed to be her. One victim. That's all it ever should have been."

"It was Mallory," Theodore repeated. "Those were the words you wrote in blood the day you faked your murder. Why bring her back into it? Why reopen those wounds two years later?"

"I wanted to bring it full circle. Because I was tired. Because I was beginning to lose my mind," Amelia spit one sentence out after the other, her stream of consciousness laid bare against the mausoleum stone.

"You told me Mallory quit. That she didn't want to babysit anymore or deal with my seizures," Bianca chimed in, once again making sure everyone was aware of her mother's cruel actions. "She was the first friend I'd ever made. And you made me feel like she was relieved to be rid of me."

"It was for your own good, Bianca," Amelia argued, turning her attention back to her daughter. "If I hadn't intervened—"

"You're a liar!" Bianca shouted, her even demeanor shifting as she forged ahead. "You've always been a liar. And you said you were going to tell the truth. I'm not going to sit here in silence. I'm going to hold you accountable. After Mallory, the murders kept happening, and I had no idea down there in the prison you'd put me in. I was kept in the dark, while people were being killed all across town—because of you. Because of me."

"What do you mean?" Liza asked Bianca, unsure of what this implication meant. "You didn't kill anyone . . . did you?"

"Of course not," Bianca replied, reassuring her daughter, wanting to safeguard the bond they'd begun to forge. "But people were killed because of me. Why don't you tell them what happened next?" Bianca asked her mother.

"That's where I was headed," Amelia said, standing up, shaking her shoulders so her cloak shimmied in the mausoleum's golden light. She pulled her arms back, placing one hand and one nub against the small of her back, trying to push the tension out of her muscles. She shifted her weight and then began again, her elevated position making it appear as if she were a political figure giving an address to those gathered in a cemetery in the middle of the night.

She was about to wake the dead.

∽

"After killing Mallory, I strangely had no regrets. I thought I'd be mortified. I'd killed a young woman who had her entire life ahead of her. I'd killed her brutally in front of her brother. I'd inflicted more pain in one minute than I had in my entire life. But instead of regretting what I'd done, I felt at ease. I felt *satisfied*. I'd taken control of the situation. I'd saved Bianca from being torn away from us. Emory hadn't done a thing to protect his daughter and had put this whole mess in motion, but I'd fixed it. After Mallory, I thought everything was going to be okay."

"How could you think that?" Colette asked, speaking on behalf of Theodore, who looked wrecked where he stood in silence beside her. Learning the truth behind his sister's murder had rendered him mute. He was stunned into a half oblivion.

"I just did. And in the days that followed, it was clear the police had no clue I had killed Mallory. I may have acted quickly, but I hadn't acted stupidly. I'd been careful. I wore a disguise. I covered up my hair, my hands, my face. I presented myself in a way that made me appear much larger than I was. I distracted Theodore, the witness I left alive. And I made sure he saw me drive away in Mallory's boyfriend's car, which I'd stolen. Even Emory had no idea what had happened. He was my husband, but it was obvious he could no longer be trusted. I thought things would go back to normal. I thought my daughter and I would resume where we'd left off before my appendectomy. But then . . . something extraordinary happened.

"For the first time since she was a toddler, Bianca went a day without having a seizure. And this was an epileptic girl who usually had three to four seizures a day. Our prayers had been answered. Or rather, something had shifted the balance of the universe. The trend continued over the next six days. No seizures. It was a miracle. Emory and I were astounded. Bianca was in shock. She had never experienced life without these painful, horrific interruptions. The week after Mallory's death, my daughter was the happiest she'd ever been. She looked healthy and talked about the future as if she would reach it. *She was excited.*"

"If only she knew her mother had just murdered her babysitter, I don't think she would have been feeling so good," Grant griped through gritted teeth, just loud enough so everyone could hear.

"Maybe that's true, Mr. Fisher," Amelia went on. "But that's not the point. Something drastic had shifted, and I couldn't help but conclude it had been my radical actions that had led us to this reality."

"You're trying to argue that killing my sister cured Bianca's illness?" Theodore snapped out of his stupor at this point, the investigator in him crawling out from underneath his sadness. "That's fucking insane."

"It probably is," Amelia acknowledged. "But that's what led me down the path I chose to take."

"A path of destruction," Maude added in, making sure that Amelia was being held accountable.

"On the seventh day—one week after Mallory was killed—Bianca had a seizure. Our brief reprieve came to an end quicker than I'd expected. I tried to convince myself she'd been healed, that taking Mallory's life had been considered an exchange by whatever forces invisibly decide our fates . . . But it wasn't so. And in my desperation, my hunger to bring happiness back to my daughter's life and keep it there, I performed what I suppose were despicable things. I convinced myself the universe wanted me to make sacrifices. I lost all sense of stability and urged myself on, believing that killing was the answer. The only solution to keep Bianca healthy. To heal her, I had to inflict damage on others."

"Do you realize how crazy you sound, Amelia?" Emory's wheezy voice inquired from where he sat, unmoving.

"I'm delivering the unfiltered truth. Maybe I sound cuckoo, but does any sane person become a serial killer? In all the years that've passed me by, I've never claimed to be stable."

"Well then, by all means, go on," he replied, with a slight roll of his eyes.

"I decided to kill again. I planned my actions carefully. I didn't want to get caught. I had to kill randomly, in different manners, at different times, finding victims who deserved it. I became obsessed. I let the madness overtake me. I drank the Kool-Aid I'd concocted, and then I dove into the empty pitcher," Amelia explained, pacing back and forth along the ten- or fifteen-foot-long portico of Mrs. Maguire's mausoleum. She passed by the three members of her family who still sat on its edges, while Theodore, Colette, Grant, and Maude remained huddled on the cemetery grass, under the moonlight.

"What made you target your next victims?" Maude asked. "There were four more murders that February after Mallory. What on Earth led you to them?"

"Excellent question, Maude," Amelia replied, still pacing. "Seems like the next logical thing to talk about, doesn't it?" she asked before pausing both her body and her mouth.

"Um, yes," Grant said, pressing her on. It already felt as if they'd been listening to this wicked woman talk for hours. At this rate, it'd be morning before she was done.

"If memory serves me right, Susan Kaiser was next," Amelia said, as if she wasn't entirely sure of the identity of the second person she'd murdered. As if you could forget such a thing. "Susan was our neighbor. A woman I'd call a *frenemy*. At times, I enjoyed Susan's company; at other times, I wanted to slap her. She was a gossip and a snitch. She enjoyed seeing others fail. So on February 10, 1987, after Bianca's seizures returned, I went over to her house, parking Robert Turner's blue car I'd been hiding in a storage unit across town in her driveway in case anyone heard anything. We chatted for a bit. I decided to tell her that Bianca—my daughter who everyone thought had died years ago—was still alive and living in our basement. Just to see how she'd react. I knew I wasn't going to let her live after I told her. And oh, *how she did react*. So I shot her in the face.

"A pattern then replayed itself across the rest of the month. I'd return home, clean up, and pretend nothing had happened. I monitored Bianca closely, and my theory proved itself true. After Susan, Bianca was granted a few more days of silent, still peace. When her seizures returned, I used them as guidance on when to act. I was directed by powers far more significant than myself.

"Brent Locke came next. He was a *homosexual*. Back in the eighties, everyone in Point Roberts just called him a silly faggot. Nowadays, most people in Washington would never utter that word."

"Were you the anonymous source who called the police and told them you saw Brent's boyfriend, Sean Jensen, dragging his body across South Beach?" Theodore asked, ignoring the awful things Amelia had said about gay men and getting to the heart of the mystery.

"That was me. I had to keep misdirecting the cops. And old Sheriff Ambrose bought what I was selling."

"I don't think I want to be here anymore," Emory interjected, his squat little body heaving in excess as he pushed his palms against the cold stone and pulled himself upright.

"You're not going anywhere, and you know that," Amelia ordered.

"Fine! But I'm not sitting here silently anymore like I have been."

"Speak as you must," Amelia answered.

Liza turned around then, looking at the spot beside the ajar mausoleum door where Emory now stood. They made eye contact as he cleared his throat. With one brisk movement, he shut the door, siphoning out the golden light and pitching the cemetery into a darker shade of night.

How could this man be her grandfather?

Just looking at him made Liza feel sick.

Amelia might have been evil, but Emory was almost as bad. A corrupt accomplice.

"I surprised Brent when he was on a late-night run to buy some cigarettes. Strangling him from where I hid in the back of his car was easier than I'd suspected it would be. I graduated from killing women to a gay man, and as he struggled to escape, it became clear I was stronger than him. After Brent, I felt like I could kill anyone.

"Jennifer Barnes came after Brent. A simple woman. A slut. The whole town knew she'd been cheating on her husband for years, so I decided to put an end to it. After one of her trysts at the Moon Hotel, I snuck into her room—after the drifter she'd been with had left—and suffocated her with a pillow while she slept."

"You're unbelievable," Colette replied, crossing her arms in disgust. Would this woman's admissions continue to pile up like this?

"Anyway," Amelia said, brushing off Colette's interruption. "The fifth and final addition for that February was William

Fisher. Grant's grandfather. And I think maybe Emory, you could add your input here as you claimed you'd like to."

"Why should he?" Grant asked, frustrated that when it came to the truth about his grandfather's death, he would have to listen to a man he despised.

"Because just as Emory's actions brought about Mallory's death at the beginning of the month, his foolishness led to William's death at the end of the month. You could say his stupidity served as bookends."

"William Fisher was a good friend of mine, whether you believe it or not, Grant," Emory began, ignoring Amelia's comments as he moved from the shadows and into the moonlight. He stepped forward on the portico and trotted down the stairs, past Amelia, Bianca, and Liza. He wanted to be closer to the four gathered on the ground. Once on their level, Emory looked up at Grant, the young man's stature towering over him as he told his part of the story from a foot below.

"I didn't know Amelia was responsible for the murders yet. Honestly, I didn't. And as mayor, I was feeling immense pressure to catch the killer. People were panicking. Hell, *I* was panicking. Every time we thought we had a suspect, something would turn up and make it clear it couldn't have been them. There were so many false leads.

"Your grandfather worked in the township building. He and I were pals. He was a smart guy, a great listener, a good friend. One day, at the end of February, I spilled my guts to him. I had to get things off my chest. I felt like I was drowning. I told him about Bianca and how strange Amelia had been acting. He offered me advice and assured me he wouldn't tell anyone about Bianca until I was ready, as long as I promised she wasn't in any danger in Amelia's care—which I really didn't think she was. The only problem was, I'd lost track of time, and Amelia had shown up at the office. She'd heard our conversation from where she stood hidden around the corner, eavesdropping."

Emory paused here, lifting his hands and placing them atop his belly, as if they had gotten too heavy to hold at his sides, needing the help of his stomach to support them. "My confession led Amelia to target your grandfather, and for that I am sorry. I think of him often. I miss him."

"You're not allowed to miss him," Grant barked at the mayor standing a few feet in front of him. "Because of you and your psychotic wife, my grandfather was drowned in a bathtub . . . his throat slit. His death ruined my parents' marriage. It made them cruel, unapologetic people. I never had a chance to be properly loved, and it's because of the pain the Schultzes caused my family, just to practice senseless voodoo to stop your daughter from shaking."

"Grant, I—" Bianca began, but Grant put a hand up, interrupting her.

"Don't talk. Not here, Bianca. Not now. I know this isn't your fault, but I don't want to hear any more excuses."

"That's fair," Amelia said, adding in her own two cents even though no one asked for it. "I think Emory covered that pretty well. I guess that brings us a third of the way through. We're at the end of February 1987. My, my, how far we've come."

⌒

Liza was tired. She'd been perched on the steps of Mrs. Maguire's mausoleum for over two hours while Amelia told her story, and to think, they were only a third of the way through. Her lower back was getting sore. For the first time since she'd moved to Point Roberts, she wanted to go back to the trailer on Benson Road. She longed for her lumpy, misshapen bed. She wished for another dream to take over, something other than this nightmare: her grandmother, the maniacal Point Roberts Slayer.

To wake herself up, she slapped herself across the face. The loud smack of her palm hitting her cheek drew the attention of the others. She saw stars as her vision refocused, with one single evergreen at the edge of the cemetery appearing to her as a golden larch, just for a second. As the tree turned dark green again, a melody played in her ears.

"Liza, what's the matter?" Bianca asked beside her.

"Sorry, I, uh, was getting a bit sleepy. I thought that would help."

"Is my story boring you?" Amelia asked, turning her attention back to where Liza sat.

"I just haven't slept well these past few nights, for obvious reasons, and it's late . . ."

"Well, the fewer the interruptions, the quicker I can get through this," Amelia replied.

"By all means, continue," Liza said, stifling a yawn as the words left her lips.

"Thank you for your permission, dear," Amelia said as she started up again, wasting no time. "When February 1987 came to an end, I reflected on all I'd done. I'd *killed* five people. Five people who may or may not have deserved it. But they were selected for a reason. Each of them. I thought those reasons would protect me and keep me from wallowing over the acts I'd committed. But after those five, I became overwhelmed. I was scared. I became paranoid that Emory would find out. And if he did, he'd report me.

"So I stopped. Or rather, the forces in control allowed me to stop. Bianca didn't have another seizure after I dealt with Mr. Fisher. A year went by, and not a single episode. My daughter's health and happiness, the look on her face . . . I'll never forget that year. It put my worries at ease. It made me think killing those five people was worth it."

"It was just a coincidence!" Bianca yelled at her mother. "You can't let your conscious rest easy just because my seizures stopped for a while after those murders. You killed people! Innocent people!"

"I did it for you," Amelia said, looking at Bianca longingly, while still keeping herself removed from where she sat, pacing along the stone. "Unfortunately, the peace didn't last. February 1, 1988, came along, and you had a seizure that morning, after going nearly a year without one. I got the urge to kill again. But I didn't think I could go through with it. I'd lost my nerve. So once you were stable, I left the house to think things over."

Amelia turned away from her daughter, her story once again directed to the others. "While sitting in my car in the school parking lot trying to collect my thoughts, feeling emotional now that February was here again, I watched in disgust as a muscle-bound jock bullied a bunch of band members while they were boarding the bus. I rolled my window down and listened to him deliver cruel insults, watching as he abused two skinny boys, pushing them down and kicking them in the ribs.

"No one did anything, so I took matters into my own hands. I had a cyanide pill with me. I'd been thinking about swallowing it. I don't think I actually would have, but I did think about it. To stop myself from acting now that Bianca's seizures were back. To stop myself from *killing*. Instead, I stuffed it into a piece of banana bread I'd brought along, scribbled a note on a scratch piece of paper, and called the bully over.

"In a split second, everything changed. I *knew* I had to kill again—to keep the demons at bay. By that point, a year removed from the first set of murders, I realized what was really troubling me: *I missed the rush that came with it.*

"Victim number six was Christopher Smith. Killing him was easiest of all. The only thing I did was compliment him, offer him the banana bread, and stick the note I'd written into his backpack pocket after distracting him. I didn't know when he'd eat the banana bread, but I knew he would eat it soon enough. He was a big boy—a hungry boy—one who'd be unlikely to share.

"He was dead that evening. Everyone in town freaked out when they found my note, and then Emory put those curfews in place, even though they accomplished nothing. Maybe it helped the people feel safe though, even if just for a few days."

"Resuming my spree softened me—which caused me to carelessly let Bianca out of the basement a week after Christopher died. She'd been begging me for months, and I finally caved. I let her out into the light of day. I walked with her down to the beach and let her put her feet in the water. Do you remember that, B?"

"Of course I remember it," Bianca replied in disgust. "It was the first time I remember being outside our house. I was sixteen years old, our house sat on the beach, and I never saw the sea until that day. You'd kept me from it. You imprisoned me."

"Don't be so dramatic," Amelia said.

"You ruined my life. You ruined so many lives. You're a monster!" Bianca screamed, the anger in her voice quaking and reverberating across the cemetery as the others watched the exchange play out.

"Well, I'm just going to ignore all of that," Amelia said as she moved away from Bianca, turning her back to her daughter and trotting down the mausoleum stairs, walking closer to where Theodore, Colette, Grant, and Maude stood. They all backed up slightly as she approached, not wanting to be any closer to her. She was the carrier of a plague they didn't want to catch.

"Letting Bianca outside was a mistake," Amelia told the four. "First of all, she didn't deserve it. And second, and more importantly, it brought up the body count. After walking back from the beach, we were interrupted by Elsie Dawkins."

Colette had known this moment was coming, but there was no way to prepare for it. She gritted her teeth and became still, her eyes locked on where Amelia stood just six or seven feet in front of her, her pale skin glowing in the dim moonlight.

How could you prepare to hear about the murder of your childhood best friend? There was nothing for Colette to do but brace herself as best she could.

"Yes, little Elsie Dawkins had stumbled into our yard, and when she saw us, she immediately ran up to us and started asking a whole bunch of questions. She introduced herself to Bianca and asked her who she was. Bianca just stared at her, not sure what to say at first, her mind probably thinking back to Mallory—the only person she'd seen besides her parents a year earlier. I thought she would think twice before spilling her guts again, but the sight of the sea made her drunk. She told Elsie *everything* before I could stop her. She unloaded it all onto that poor thirteen-year-old girl, thinking of no one but herself."

"What'd you expect her to do?" Colette asked, fighting back against Amelia's claims on Bianca's behalf. "She was a prisoner desperate for freedom. You can't blame her. You're the only guilty party in this story, Amelia, and the sooner you swallow that, the sooner you can stop blaming everyone else."

"Elsie's murder is what brought you to Point Roberts, isn't it? Coming from Montréal to dive back into the cold case of who killed your childhood chum? Well, congrats, Colette, you've cracked the case. It was me. I killed Elsie Dawkins.

"She was a bright little girl, and after she listened to Bianca divulge our secrets, Elsie said something about telling her parents, running off before I could convince her that Bianca was just a sick, confused teenager. The wheels were put in motion, and I was along for the ride. It's just a shame that victim number seven was so young."

"So you strung her up from a tree in her backyard and ripped her insides out?" Colette asked in unbottled rage, the veins in her neck bulging as spittle flew from her lips. She took a few steps forward, any fear she had of Amelia dissipating as she approached the villain who'd killed Elsie. Colette stood in front of her, her warm breath flowing like fog over Amelia's face as the two women looked eye to eye.

This was the closest any of the other four adults had come to Amelia, and she could feel the resentment bubbling off Colette's skin in such close proximity. She could sense the urge she had to bring her down.

"I had to act in random ways. Resuming my spree with Christopher had not been planned, and neither was this. I knew I didn't have much time before Elsie blabbed. So I ran into the house and locked Bianca back in the basement. I found some rope in the garage and grabbed a kitchen knife. I threw on a ski mask and some winter gloves. It wasn't a murder I'd thought about . . . And then it was suddenly upon me."

Colette was appalled and didn't want to be on the same level as this woman, or close to her at all anymore. So she turned away and retreated to the others.

"Well, you know," Amelia said, taking center stage again, no longer having to share the spotlight. "After I killed Elsie, I started to think deeply about the idea of free will. Do we get to make our own choices? I felt like I had no choice when it came to Elsie or the other murders. I was a robot in a simulation, a block of code being ordered around by a higher power. Have any of you heard of this idea? That we're just data points in some gigantic computer program we'll never see? That none of this is real?"

"For fuck's sake, Amelia, spare the people any more of your grand delusions," Emory cut in. "It's bad enough they have to listen to you talk about these things. Let's not make it any more painful by forcing them to hear your philosophic ideas too."

"Fine, fine," Amelia agreed, waving her amputated arm at Emory to concede. "It was just an idea I wanted to share—no need to get worked up. Anyway, after Elsie, the police targeted her father. He'd had the misfortune of finding Elsie. It didn't help that Elsie had mentioned him on the phone when she'd called her mother after meeting Bianca and told her to come home. Really though, the only reason she said her father was going to be mad was because he'd always told Elsie he thought I was up to something and that she should stay clear of me. Turns out he was right.

"Jason Dawkins sat in handcuffs at the police station, the third man accused of being the Point Roberts Slayer. The cops thought they had good evidence against him, but it didn't take long for the case to collapse. They weren't thinking outside the box. They never imagined the Slayer was a woman. I mean, how common are female serial killers? Can any of you name one besides Aileen Wuornos?"

Amelia stopped here, waiting to see if anyone would reply.

Silence settled across the cemetery in the forest.

"People always underestimate what women are capable of, and in this instance, it helped me. Not long after Elsie, Bianca had another seizure, the worst one since before I'd killed Mallory. She'd almost gone a year in peace, but the lion was roaring back in full force, and I knew I had to continue. I had to select more victims, more sacrifices . . . whether I liked it or not."

"She probably had another seizure because of the stress you caused her!" Theodore argued. "You let her outside for the first time in over a decade, and then you went and killed a thirteen-year-old girl the same day."

"Yes, but she didn't know that," Amelia replied.

"I might not have known you killed Elsie then, but I was beginning to understand something was very wrong. I'd be lying if I said it didn't affect my well-being," Bianca told her mother, agreeing with Theodore.

"You'll agree with whatever they say just to hurt me!" Amelia cried out, refusing to turn around to face Bianca and Liza, not wanting to look at them.

Next, Amelia explained the murders of Willow Mendez and James Turner. Each killing occurred shortly after Bianca had an episode, each seizure acting as a catalyst to drive her mother to madness. She killed Willow Mendez because she'd learned the girl was severely depressed. She justified the killing by claiming she was doing the girl a favor: putting her out of her misery. She drugged the girl and made it look like a suicide to match the motive. But when the police fell for her diversion, she grew antsy.

"When they didn't consider Willow victim number eight, I hated that. She deserved to be grouped with the others. I worried if she wasn't considered part of the Fifteen, perhaps her death wouldn't help Bianca. So I sent the police a letter, making sure they couldn't track it back to me. I included a few strands of Willow's bright blonde hair in the envelope to prove my point. It worked. She was added to the list."

And so was Jamie Turner. Amelia told the group that he was a cross-dresser, going against God's will and presenting himself as a woman when he was very much a man. She said she totally disagreed with his lifestyle, and that when she heard whisperings about the operation Jamie was going to get, it put her over the edge and gave her a reason to pick him as her next victim. She went through his mail and learned as many details as she could. And then she prepared.

Much like she had waited for Mallory along the side of the road, she waited in the dark of night for Jamie, knowing he'd be driving back from his gig in Vancouver. She'd heard he was a kind soul, and would likely stop if she flagged him down for help.

He never saw it coming.

She overpowered him and broke his kneecap with a baseball bat.

And then she ran him over with his own car—ten times—before disappearing back into the dark from which she'd emerged.

More than halfway through her murderous rampage, the Point Roberts Slayer had come entirely unhinged.

No one on the peninsula was safe.

⌒

"And what about Toshi?" Maude interjected, sticking the silence that had briefly overtaken the night with a hushed pinprick, longing for answers about what had happened to her beloved husband.

"Toshi's killing was a bit more personal."

"In what way?" Maude asked.

"During those last two weeks of February in '88, Toshi became Bianca's doctor. He made house visits. He learned about Bianca and her seizures and how she'd been confined to our house for most of her life."

"My *entire* life," Bianca stressed.

"Why did you allow Toshi into your house? I thought you were convinced doctors couldn't help Bianca?" Maude questioned.

"I insisted on it," Emory said, once again speaking from the shadows, having returned to the portico during Amelia's monologue. "Bianca had relapsed after going almost a year without having a seizure. Just like Amelia, I'd allowed myself to believe she was getting better. But when her affliction returned, I knew we couldn't keep on like we were—regardless of what Amelia wanted. I was Bianca's father, and I finally decided to put my foot down."

"Emory made me let Toshi into our house, to monitor Bianca's health and study her seizures. My husband threatened me," Amelia continued, talking to the others like Emory hadn't just spoken from behind her at his spot near the mausoleum's door. As if he weren't there. "I tried to fight against the idea, but he insisted that if I didn't agree to it, he'd report me. He threatened to take Bianca away. And from the look on his face when he confronted me, I knew he was serious. So I did the only thing I could: I agreed. Having an intruder in our house was better than having Bianca ripped away from me. But I'd be lying if I said I wasn't worried about allowing someone into our web. The next day, Toshi Oshiro came to our house. He gave Bianca a physical. He asked questions. *Lots* of questions. He took notes. And then he asked to speak with my daughter alone. I didn't want to leave her with this stranger, but Emory was eating out of the palm of Toshi's hand. Part of the agreement was that we'd do whatever the doctor requested, as long as it meant Bianca could stay home.

"I didn't have a choice. I left Bianca alone with Toshi in the basement. Later, after he left, I was frantic. But when I spoke to Bianca, she was calm. She said he'd offered her solace and suggested a few simple things she could try that might help."

"He was such a kind man," Bianca added, looking at Maude.

"He was the best," Maude replied, getting choked up as she said it.

"When my frustrations with Toshi bubbled over, I took it out on Willow and James," Amelia admitted. "Then, before long, things took a turn for the worst, as they always seem to on these dark February days. I had to act. I had to kill to protect my family."

"Why?" Maude cried out.

"Because your husband was going to expose us. *That's why.*" Amelia snapped. "It happened exactly the way I worried it would. I'd warned Emory, but he didn't listen. Just like Mallory, Toshi decided Bianca couldn't be kept a secret. He boldly said as much right to my face before storming out of the house, walking into the pouring rain.

"It was the last mistake he ever made. Just like with Mallory, I knew I had to stop him. I threw on a disguise: my hat, my gloves, my cloak. I grabbed my gun and followed him, catching up to him right before he made it to your stairs."

"You killed so many people who were just trying to do the right thing!" Maude shouted at Amelia. "Don't you see that? He was trying to help your daughter. But you wouldn't let him!"

"I *couldn't* let him. I'm Bianca's mother and I knew what was best for her. Not some doctor who'd only known her for two weeks. And so . . . he died in your arms."

"You heartless bitch!" Maude shrieked before turning her back on Amelia and moving behind the others. She crumbled onto the dew-covered grass, her lungs heaving as she began to weep next to an old gravestone. She reached out and grasped the cold gray marker to steady herself as she cried.

Seeing her grandmother in such pain made Liza spring up, jumping from the mausoleum's steps. She moved away from Bianca and jogged past the others, her fiery red hair bouncing as she went. She couldn't sit still anymore and listen to this without doing something. She wanted to comfort her grandmother. She plopped down in the grass next to Maude, delicately placing her arms around Maude's shoulders as she pulled her in, their embrace softening the blows of Amelia's disastrous story.

And then something strange happened.

A loud hooting emerged from the treetops above the cemetery. It drew the attention of those assembled, causing them to look upward, away from the land of the dead and into the unknown. The noise broke apart Liza and Maude's embrace, causing them to pull their hearts away from one another as the power of the sound took over.

With their acknowledgment—which the bird had been waiting on—the hoots transformed into a powerful flap of feathers as the owl glided down from its hidden perch high in an evergreen's branches. It flew directly to the grave Maude and Liza sat beside, its sharp talons clutching the stone as it landed.

Its bright yellow eyes stared into their souls.

A snowy owl had made its presence known, its regal face appearing unbothered as it jostled its wings, tucking them into place. The owl turned its head in both directions, demonstrating how much it could see. It took the others into account, but in the end, it focused entirely on Liza, and Liza alone.

"Pa?"

The name had come from her lips without a thought, as if the bird before her were her late father reincarnated.

A dark bird had killed him.

And now, here was a bird so light, exuding his specific energy in a way she could not explain.

A white bird to save her.

The owl hooted two syllables, the sound unlike what had come before. No one in the cemetery heard them the same way, but to Liza, the noise the owl made was as clear as day.

It had said her name.

Its message delivered, the owl pushed off the gravestone, its broad white wings allowing it to take flight as it left the cemetery behind. It followed the route the seagulls had flown earlier, heading between the two bands of trees to make its way down to the shore.

Liza stood up as she watched the magnificent bird fly away, taking its passage as a sign.

"We have to go down to the beach."

"The beach?" Amelia asked, sounding disturbed. "What for?"

"Because I said so," Liza said, knowing if she went, the others would follow. She didn't wait for the adults to respond, instead heading toward the cemetery gates, prying them open, and following the path through the gnarled trees down to Lily Point. She had trampled over nearly every inch of Point Roberts, and even though this was a trail she hadn't found her boots on previously, somehow, she knew the way.

When the tall trees parted, and the sounds of the lapping sea reached her ears, Liza was sure she'd made it to where she was supposed to be. Looking behind her for the first time since she'd left the Salish Cemetery, she saw Maude was not far behind her, with Grant, Colette, and Theodore following in close succession. In the distance, Bianca, Emory, and finally, Amelia, brought up the rear.

It had been time for a change of scenery.

Listening to the details of ten murders in a dark cemetery had been ten murders too many.

The sea, which had become Liza's enemy these past few weeks, now once again felt like home. She took a deep breath, drinking in the aroma of the unruly water she knew could never be tamed.

I should live in salt, Liza thought. The idea made no sense, but she pondered it over just the same. She took a seat on a bleached piece of driftwood, the stones covering the shore calling out to her one by one, as if each represented a star somewhere in the universe.

The owl was gone.

She accepted the fact that she was never meant to see it again.

But it had brought her here, back to the shore at Lily Point—where the month had begun—and where it would end.

As they resettled on the beach, the driftwood and the shore served as their theater. Amelia took her place with her back to the sea, standing on the tiny rocks that covered the beach; the others sat on the fallen logs.

"What made you stop again after that second February? After you killed Toshi?" Liza asked.

"Jon Templeton," Amelia replied. The answer had been ready to jump from her lips for the past three decades.

"My father?" Liza inquired, wanting to know more.

"Yes. *Him*. Bianca, why don't you tell your daughter about your late husband? I'm sure she'd like to know more about your relationship."

Liza turned to Bianca, who was sitting beside her again, a look of apprehension scribbled across her face.

"I think it'd make more sense for you to do it," Bianca said to Emory. "Everyone needs to know what you did at the end of February in '88."

Emory—from where he sat on a wide stump at the end of the row, away from the others—grunted at this suggestion. His role in the story, *this part*, could be considered the catalyst for how it all ended.

As he used his arms to push himself up, his belly almost caused him to topple over and crash against the rocks before he was able to steady himself. Being so top heavy had its downfalls.

He stood before the others, not too close to Amelia, but not far from her either. He wanted both of them in view so they could be compared.

He may have acted badly, but he wasn't *that bad*.

"Once again, Amelia had killed without much of a plan," Emory began, his squeaky voice sounding much more authoritative than it usually did. "And when she came home after murdering Toshi, I was standing in the hallway. I saw her enter in her soaked cloak, her gloves still on, a pistol in her hand, a look of weird glee on her face. When we locked eyes, *I knew*. All sorts of emotions overcame me. I felt stupid and embarrassed. I was disgusted. *I was scared.*

"My wife was the Point Roberts Slayer. And when I looked at her in that white hallway, the dark colors she wore made her appear like a stain on everything good. She was a black smudge on my existence."

"So all this time, you *knew*?" Grant called out, asking the question everyone wanted to know. "I always suspected . . . but still. You knew since '88? *And you did nothing?* You let four more people get killed?" Grant dug his hands into the driftwood, his fingers threatened by splinters as he tried to prevent himself from leaping up and strangling the mayor.

"I didn't do *nothing*," Emory replied sheepishly.

"Then what *did* you do?" Theodore demanded.

"I did what I thought was best for my family."

"You should have turned her in!" Colette shouted, upset they had to sit in front of these two evil buffoons to get the truth. She'd liked being in the cemetery much better. Here, along the sea, it felt like there was no escape.

"I was afraid she'd kill me, or worse, kill Bianca. I tried to reason with her."

"How did that work out?" Maude asked, her voice laced with snark.

"Not well, but I made some inroads," Emory replied as he turned from the others and made eye contact with Amelia for the first time in a while. "I like to think my actions brought Bianca some happiness her last year in Point Roberts. True happiness."

"They did," Bianca admitted, throwing her father a bone that caused the others to back off a bit, piquing their interest enough to no longer interrupt him.

"Once I got hold of myself after realizing what Amelia had done, I made some quick decisions. I didn't want to turn her in. I know I should have, but she was my wife. I still loved her, and it was my duty to protect her. In sickness and health.

"And oh, was she sick. *Really sick.* I didn't want her to be the only person in charge of our daughter anymore. I didn't want her interacting with Bianca at all, to be honest. Their relationship had gotten too complex. An idea came to mind, and I went with it.

"During one of his visits, Toshi told me about Jon, his adopted son. He mentioned the boy wanted to be a doctor too. He'd taught his son a lot, having him serve as an apprentice of sorts at his clinic over the years. And then I met Jon at Smith's where he also worked. Jon seemed like a smart boy—someone I could trust.

"I decided we'd bring Jon into our house, to give our daughter a friend around her age. A friend that could help take care of her, someone who knew a lot about medicine and could help Bianca in ways Amelia couldn't.

"This idea formed quickly. I told Amelia right there and then in that hallway that she would go along with it or I'd report her to the police. I wasn't sure if Jon would agree to it, but he did. He didn't even sound surprised when I first told him I had a daughter hidden in our basement."

"That's because Dr. Oshiro told Jon about me before my mother murdered him," Bianca spoke, her perspective forging the stream of her father's story. She stood up from the driftwood, moving to center stage and taking her father's place as he returned to his log, all 353 pounds of him once again resting against the grain.

"Dr. Oshiro told Jon he'd been making house visits to monitor my health. He didn't tell him everything, but he told Jon enough so that at the very least, someone else in Point Roberts knew I existed. It's why his last words to Maude were

'Tell Jon.' He was trying to alert Jon, the only other person in Point Roberts who knew about me. But because of my mother, his message never made it."

"My God . . . ," Maude whispered, her words wavering out.

"March 1988 arrived, and Jon began visiting me," Bianca explained, her starring role in the story bursting into life as her monologue began. Whereas up until this point she had appeared haggard from the shock of her kidnapping, now she looked invigorated. "At first, I was unsure of him, wondering why a teenage boy slightly older than me had replaced his father and been entrusted with my care. But it only took a few visits for me to warm up to Jon and trust him, to notice that with his presence coming to the forefront of my life, my mother's lessened. I barely saw her anymore, and when I did, it was for minutes at a time.

"Things felt new—exciting, even. It didn't hurt that Jon was a charming, intelligent, kind young man. I developed a crush on him, latching onto his compassion like a sea anemone to a shell. At first, our conversations were simple and fun. We were getting to know each other. A month or two went by without any more seizures. I'm sure my mother thought it was because she'd killed five more people that February, but I think it was because I had Jon. He brought me a kind of happiness I'd never felt before. It didn't take me long to realize I was falling in love with him. And just as I was about to profess my feelings to him that summer, everything grew more complicated.

"Jon started telling me about the murders. He'd shielded me from them those first few months, wanting to make sure I was strong enough before he shared the unbearable news. With the caring way he revealed things, I was able to take it. I didn't cry. I didn't shake.

"He told me about the most recent victim first, his father. I was shocked when I learned what'd happened to Dr. Oshiro. I'd been told Jon was replacing him because he was too busy with other patients to make house calls anymore. I'd believed it at the time. My mother's controlling effect over my life had made me so naive.

"And then slowly, over time, Jon told me about each of the other nine people who'd been murdered in Point Roberts those two years. He'd only tell me about one every three or four weeks, not wanting to overload me with too much. I dreaded the arrival of those days when I'd learn about another innocent person savagely slain, but at the same time, I looked forward to becoming educated on what was going on in my town, the land above me I wasn't able to see.

"January 1989 rolled around, and with it, I learned that Mallory had been the first victim. She'd been killed right after the last time I saw her. And as soon as Jon told me what happened to her, I put all those floating clues together. *I knew.*

"I immediately told Jon of my suspicion—that my mother was the Point Roberts Slayer. This confession frightened him, but as we talked through what we knew, sifting through the evidence that had been made public, Jon realized my claim might be valid. We knew we had to confront her. Jon said I couldn't be a part of it though, he said it had to be him. And we knew he had to do it soon . . . another February was right around the corner.

"On January 31, right before he said goodbye to me for the day, Jon told me he was going upstairs to talk to her. To tell Amelia what we suspected. I told him to be careful. I told him I loved him. What had been simmering inside me finally came to the surface. Learning about the murders in Point Roberts had stifled my feelings for Jon for too long. I didn't want to be scared anymore. I wanted to be safe, and with Jon, I knew I was. He was my home.

"We kissed for the first time then, and when our lips touched, it was like every atom in my body screamed 'This is it! *This is really it!*' I had never been so happy. But when our mouths moved apart, that pleasure quickly dissipated as I remembered what he was about to do."

Bianca paused here, looking down at her boots, kicking a few of the stones beneath her feet in frustration.

"Cat got your tongue, dear?" Amelia asked cruelly.

"You know better than I do what happened next," Bianca snapped back. "After Jon left me that day, two weeks went by before I saw him again. And this was after seeing him almost every day for a year. For fourteen miserable days, I thought he was dead. I thought you'd murdered him for confronting you."

"Well, I didn't."

"What you did was almost worse!" Bianca cried, not returning to the driftwood with the others, instead standing her ground along the sea across from her mother.

Their spirits collided.

"Your boyfriend confronted me, you're right. He told me you two had concluded I was the killer, and that he was going to bring your theory to the police. I don't know why he didn't just go to the police first. Why tip me off? This town could have saved itself all sorts of trouble if any of these people had been smart enough not to tell me what they were planning."

"That's not the point!" Bianca screamed, her voice moving out across the water, flying toward the craggy peak of Mount Baker hiding somewhere in the unseen distance.

Just because it was night, that didn't mean the mountain wasn't there.

It was always there.

Waiting.

"The point is Jon tipped me off. It was like he thought it'd be better if I knew of his plan, for whatever nonsensical reason. He was a fool, just like his father. He wanted me to promise I wouldn't kill any more people now that it was almost February again. But I surprised him. While you two were canoodling in the basement and Emory was forcing me to keep my distance, I was compiling evidence against Jon.

"I'd planned ahead, laying the groundwork for someone else to take the fall if things ever took a turn. How convenient that the first person outside my family to figure it out was Jon Templeton, who worked at the only grocery store in town where everyone shopped. Where nearly every victim had shopped right around the time they were killed. And Jon, being the head cashier in the evenings, was the one who rang them up.

"It's why I went along with Emory's plan. I'd decided to get something on Jon and frame him for the murders, allowing me to control him if it came down to it. It wasn't hard to break into the store and get the receipts. Sure, I had to fabricate a few of them, but he fell for it, and I bet the police would have too. They were so desperate to find the killer. When I pulled the receipts out of my pocket that day when he confronted me, it bought me his silence.

"I guess I frightened him a bit too much. I never told him he had to stop coming to see Bianca. I was afraid that if that happened, Emory would blame me and break our agreement and turn me into the police himself. So yes, Jon stopped coming for two weeks. His disappearance upset Bianca so much, she started saying crazy things. I tried to console her, and she accused me of murder! My own daughter!"

"You *are* a murderer!" Bianca cried, exasperated at her mother's never-ending antics.

"The next day was February 1, 1989," Amelia said, ignoring the response. "And Bianca's seizures returned, like clockwork."

⌒

Before allowing Amelia to continue discussing the final February of her murderous rampage, Maude stood up from her seat on the driftwood, pulling the small diary out of her cardigan pocket. She'd almost forgotten it was there, the piece of evidence that had revealed Amelia's guilt overshadowed by her surprising return to the peninsula. In the chaos that had ensued since the kidnapping, the group had referenced the diary for clues but had found it unhelpful. It didn't focus on places. It focused on people. With their discussion shifting back to the victims, Maude wanted to return to this primary source.

"In your diary you say you killed Diane Wertburger because she was an unfit mother," Maude began, drawing the attention of everyone on the beach. "But weren't *you* an unfit mother?"

"How dare you!" Amelia screeched, enraged by Maude's accusation. The two women both had the unique ability to get under each other's skin. "Like I've been telling you *all night*, I did everything in my power to protect my child! Diane was a monster. She *beat* her daughter. I killed her because she was an abomination to good mothers everywhere."

"You killed her with your weightlifting trophy not far from here. You smashed her in the head with it and then kicked the shit out of her. She suffered . . . ," Colette added, trailing off, disgusted by Amelia's merciless actions.

"She deserved it! And that's all I want to say about—"

"Were you starting to lose control?" Theodore asked. "You had to know your thread of carnage was about to meet its end, didn't you? Pretty soon, the police were going to connect the dots."

"I had everything under control!" Amelia argued, the whites of her eyes flaring, becoming brighter. "Where did you find that diary? I thought I destroyed it the night I left—"

"I found it on the beach the day after you *died*," Emory said, holding up air quotes as he spoke the last word. "I locked it in a vault in my office that only I know the combination to. I gave it to Bianca after we had our first talk. After all, her name's in the front of it."

"It should be at the bottom of the sea!" Amelia cried.

"I hate to break it to you, but throwing a book in the sea as a means of discarding it definitely doesn't work in Point Roberts," Theodore said. "I know from experience."

"Well, you should also know diaries are personal! I'd planned to give it to Bianca, but instead decided to use it for my own purposes. It was supposed to be for my eyes only, to process what I was doing, to justify and organize the victims so I—"

"Could try to feel better about your actions?" Grant asked. "To make it seem like the people you killed deserved it? That your *reasons for selection* were enough to give you a pass? I don't fucking think so." Grant stood up, his tall, dark frame juxtaposing dramatically next to Maude's small stature beside him. "And what about Judy Dennison? Was her eating your doughnuts like you wrote about in the diary really enough of a reason to stab her in the throat?" Grant didn't wait for Amelia to respond. Instead, he and Maude both sat down again on the driftwood. Their points had been made.

"The universe urged me to act each time Bianca's health took a turn for the worse. Fate—or whatever it was—led me to those people. Besides, with Jon's threats in the mix, I knew Judy shopped at Smith's Grocery Store almost every day, so she'd be an easy person to get a receipt for."

"So you made these victims fit into your schemes in whatever way they could? Is that it?" Liza asked. "Whichever deaths would be the most convenient for your plans, those were the ones you pursued?"

"I guess you can say that, but I don't—"

"You don't what?" Liza interrupted, not wanting her to have full control of the discussion any longer. They'd been listening to Amelia speak for hours. It was time to challenge her further. To hold her accountable.

It was time for this to end.

"I don't think you're categorizing it accurately. Things were changing that year, and I started to get nervous. It made me careless in selecting Eddie Wayne and Alan Henry. They were too close to home. I never should have gone after them, but I did have my reasons. They were threatening us. I was just trying to protect my family—I swear this was always about protecting my family."

"That's bullshit and you know it," Liza said, standing up and taking a place along the rocks next to Bianca. Three generations of Schultz women now stood along the edge of the sea. "You were protecting yourself."

"Eddie was sticking his nose where it didn't belong! He was an outsider, asking too many questions, getting people to think about the murders in ways they shouldn't have," Amelia replied, her words scrambled and anxious. "He made connections—ones people didn't think of before—he was spreading gossip, poking around town and turning over every stone. I got wind of him before he got wind of me. And when he came to my house to ask me questions, I was prepared. I took Eddie for a little ride over to the McMann house, and I dealt with him.

"And Alan was saying terrible things about Emory. He was trying to take away Emory's mayorship. I couldn't stand for that. Emory and I may have had our differences, but he was a great mayor and deserved to keep his job. If Alan took it away from him, I was worried that—"

"That Emory couldn't protect you anymore?" Liza suggested, pushing back.

Amelia stared at her granddaughter, at a loss for words. A breeze rolled off the sea then, causing the teenager's tangled red hair to wave like the snakes of Medusa, but her piercing eyes remained unhidden. They never wavered. Like a bull ready to charge, Liza was prepared to fight Amelia for dominance.

This was the first spot they had made eye contact, four weeks ago, and Liza hoped to hell it would be the last.

"Maybe my reasons were—at times—flawed, but in the thick of it, I thought what I was doing was right," Amelia countered.

"How could you possibly think that?" Bianca asked.

"She's not right in the head, Bianca," Emory added. "She wasn't then, and she's not now."

"That doesn't justify it," she replied.

"Well, if it makes you happy, killing Eddie and Alan led to my downfall. After their deaths, the police brought me in for questioning. Your husband, Bill, interrogated me for hours at the station. He made me afraid. They didn't have any physical evidence, but he had his theories," Amelia explained, directing her words to Theodore.

"I don't understand. Bill questioned you. In 1989? *As a suspect?*" Theodore asked, unable to wrap his head around this revelation.

"Yes, he did."

"He never told me, he never said *anything*. Even years after the fact, once you were gone. Why would he keep that from me?"

"Because I told him to," Emory spoke up. "You may know a lot about the Fifteen, Theodore, and I know some of your intel came from Bill, but you don't know everything. Some things are still classified. They're on the record, but they're not for everyone in town to know about, not even you. Your husband was the sheriff, and a damn good one, I must admit. He respected that this was an ongoing investigation till the day he died. He didn't tell you about Amelia being a suspect because he wasn't allowed to."

A look of anguish pained Theodore's face. The fact that Bill had been forced to keep this from him—something that might have unraveled the cases if they could have openly talked about it—felt like a regression of the loving relationship they'd shared.

"I can't believe this," Theodore whispered, in shock.

Colette scooted over on the piece of driftwood she was sharing with him, placing an arm around his shoulder. "It's okay, Theodore. Bill was doing what he thought was best. He was probably protecting you."

"After Bill and the other officers let me go, after he asked all his questions and I didn't crack—didn't confess—I knew I had to do something drastic or I was going to be locked up for the rest of my life," Amelia continued. "I didn't want to be identified as the Point Roberts Slayer. I thought the shock of it alone would cause Bianca to have a seizure so bad it would kill her. I thought about releasing the receipts I'd compiled linking Jon to the murders, but I worried it would look desperate. I thought it might incriminate me even more. So I did the only thing I could think of that might set me free: I decided to fake my own murder."

"Because of course, that was the only logical option," Grant said sarcastically.

"At the same time, Bianca was making plans of her own, weren't you dear?" Amelia asked, ignoring Grant's comment.

"Yes, I was," Bianca responded, not adding anything more.

"Care to share with the group?" her mother asked.

⌒

"In mid-February, Jon came back to me. He told me everything," Bianca began from her pulpit along the sea, standing next to Liza while facing the others sitting on the driftwood. "He told me what happened after he'd threatened to expose my mother, how she'd blackmailed him, and about the two women who'd been killed since we last spoke. We put a plan in place to escape Point Roberts. He was going to break me out of the basement so we could leave the peninsula. We thought it was the only way to end the madness. We couldn't go to the police. We were too afraid of those damn receipts—that the police would fall for the blackmail. Looking back, we should have done things differently. If we had gone to the cops instead of planning our escape, maybe Eddie and Alan would still be alive."

"You can't think like that," Liza said to her mother.

"It's hard not to," Bianca replied.

"You were okay with Jon being back in your house?" Maude asked Amelia, thinking about the last conversation she'd had with her son, when he'd told her about Bianca Schultz.

"Jon made my daughter happy. And I had gotten used to not spending much time with Bianca by that point. Jon was her caretaker, so when he returned, I welcomed him. With Jon and Bianca in the basement together each day, it gave me time to execute my plan. Faking your own murder in a convincing manner is not an easy task. The stress of it caused me to unravel a bit further, I'm afraid. I started talking to myself when no one else was around."

"And Jon and I heard you, a few days before we were planning to leave. You were basically screaming in the kitchen," Bianca claimed.

"I'm sorry you heard that," Amelia said.

"I'm not," Bianca replied. "It's how I found out *why* you killed. It convinced me that leaving Point Roberts and cutting myself off from you and the rest of the world was the only way. You babbled about my seizures and the murders and how they correlated. That killing Mallory had set a course of action in place, how you'd been trying to bring me happiness, to bring me good health.

"You made me a pawn in your game. You laid the blame on me and my affliction. You made me feel like I was just a means to your despicable end. I realized then that you never truly loved me, not like a real mother should."

"That's a lie!" Amelia screamed. The others watched all this unfold in the dark, their eyes having long ago adjusted to the moonlight. Liza took a few steps back, no longer wanting to be directly between the two women.

"Is it? We'll never know for sure," Bianca countered. "But I knew one thing right away after listening to your words get filtered down those basement stairs: I had to leave Point Roberts. If I was gone, the murders would end."

"And how funny was it that the night you two decided to escape was the same night I faked my murder?" Amelia asked her daughter with a wild grin stretched across her face.

"It wasn't funny at all. Your blood was *everywhere*. It was awful, and it always will be, regardless of it being a mirage you put in place to save yourself. In my eyes, you died that day, and that hasn't changed," Bianca said sternly. She was not amused by the carefree nature with which Amelia was discussing this. "Jon and I had to be brave to walk up those basement stairs together, afraid we might have to face you, to fight for my freedom. Instead, you weren't there, but your blood was all over the kitchen. All over the walls. The words *It was Mallory* glaring back down at us. I had a seizure once I realized what we were seeing, one so bad I nearly bit my tongue off. It was so strong it affected my memories of that evening for years to come. In the days that followed, I couldn't remember what was real and what I'd dreamed up. But two things I knew for sure: you were dead and Jon and I were leaving Point Roberts . . . forever."

"Except those two things didn't stay true, did they?" Liza asked Bianca from the spot where she stood beside her, the others looking on and listening intently, the moonlight highlighting each of their faces in soft outlines.

"No, but they lasted quite a while—almost three full decades. Jon and I got out of Point Roberts that night, and we lived a mostly happy life together on the Washington Coast. Since my mother was presumed dead, we decided not to tell anyone what we'd discovered. We wanted to start a new life. After all we'd been through, we thought we deserved that. At times over the years, I felt guilty for not allowing the victim's families to learn the identity of the Slayer. We could have brought the people in Point Roberts some peace, but we didn't. We were selfish, and for that I am sorry. But Jon convinced me to stay quiet. He thought it was safer for everyone. It wasn't until this past year that I realized exactly why he wanted us to stay silent.

"When Jon died last year, it spurred everything to fruition. I started sleuthing and asking questions—not of others but of myself. What did I remember? What actually happened? When I was going through Jon's things after he passed, I discovered the infamous receipts. It was the first chance I'd had to review the blackmail myself. Jon found them that night we left Point Roberts. My mother had left them on the kitchen counter for anyone to find. Even after choosing to fake her death, she'd decided to try to tie Jon to the crimes."

"I'd spent so much time getting those receipts. I would have been a fool not to use them," Amelia interrupted.

"You are so heartless. Even in death!" Bianca shouted back at her. Liza could tell Bianca especially hated it when her mother spoke about Jon. It was as if she were rubbing salt into an unhealed wound, one that would never fully scab. "When I saw the receipts, I was taken by surprise," Bianca continued, turning her attention back to the others sitting on the driftwood. "They looked convincing—even the fake ones. I mean, every person who had been murdered was accounted for on those pieces of paper, and Jon's name was on the top of every one. It was no wonder he'd hidden them away, never allowing me to see them. A part of me started to doubt Jon's story, making me wonder if he *was* involved in the killings. Maybe he wasn't the Point Roberts Slayer, but what if he'd been working with my mother, as an accomplice? I didn't know what to believe. I loved Jon, I always had, but I knew I had to get to the bottom of this, to uncover the truth. I had to stop hiding."

"So you came back?" Liza asked.

"I had to come back. Especially after wrestling around with what Jon had told me a few weeks before he died."

"What was that?" Theodore asked.

"That he thought my mother had faked her own murder. That there was a chance she wasn't dead."

"Why would he say that?" Colette asked.

"I don't know."

"You don't know? You mean he didn't explain himself after such a dramatic statement?" Grant inquired.

"I wouldn't let him," Bianca admitted. "I didn't want to hear it. His idea was so absurd I couldn't listen to the theory behind it. He sprang it on me one day out of the blue. You have to remember how painful this is for me. *I* am the reason all those people were killed. We left Point Roberts to escape, but more than anything, I left Point Roberts to forget.

"But Jon was right, and his words, those receipts, and a call from the universe urging me to return to Point Roberts led me here. And once I was back, it didn't take me long to realize my mother had returned too."

"How did you find me?" Amelia asked.

"I caught a glimpse of you."

"Where?"

"By the Moon Hotel, at the beginning of the month. You were watching Liza, and I was watching you. Or someone who I thought was you. I only got a look at you from behind. But the way you moved, the strands of your auburn hair in the wind—everything I saw fit.

"You didn't see me, but I convinced myself that I saw you. And from that moment on, I knew I had to try and coax you out, to be sure you were really back. Finding you alive would prove Jon had been right and clear his name for good.

"It would have been dangerous to approach you that day to confirm my suspicion, and I knew it would be risky to alert the cops. I wanted you to come out on your terms and announce yourself. I had a feeling that's what you were planning if you'd decided to come back after all these years."

"You went for the dramatic approach?" Amelia asked rhetorically.

"I put a plan in place. I aligned myself with five fellow sleuths," Bianca said, gesturing toward Liza, Theodore, Colette, Grant, and Maude. "I caused a lot of confusion, but it was necessary. And with my lies, I spilled out truths too. I shared revelations no one in town was aware of. I dropped clues and led you to evidence. I knew my actions might even lead you to suspect me, but I trusted you: individually and as a group. You're all so smart. I tried my best to leave breadcrumbs, and you followed the trail. In time, I knew the madness I was stirring up would get my mother to reveal herself."

"And it worked," Liza replied, knowing Bianca's disruptive actions had been worth it.

***

"Why did you fake your own murder, Amelia? *How* did you do it?" Theodore asked.

"Ah, yes. We did kind of skip over that part, didn't we? I promise you, I didn't forget about it," Amelia replied with a manic look on her face. "It's one of the best parts of the story.

"I made it look like I was the fifteenth victim because I was at a dead end. The cops were closing in, and there were no other options. I'd been drawing my blood and saving it for weeks, keeping it as a backup plan, one I hoped I wouldn't have to use. But as things unfolded, the backup plan slowly rose to the top. Before Bianca was born, I'd been a nurse, so I knew how to draw blood, and how much I could take out each day. I started storing bags of it in our shed, where Emory wouldn't find them. By the end of the month, I had more than enough to spill across the kitchen to make them think I was dead, even if they never found my body. Because of course, I wasn't going to actually kill myself."

"I kind of wish you would have," Liza whispered.

"Liza!" Amelia shrieked, upset at her granddaughter's words. "I thought we'd been getting along. I thought maybe we could have a—"

"A relationship?" Liza asked, unable to stop herself. "We'll never have a relationship, Amelia. *You're a serial killer!* You kidnapped me and made me sleep in an old lady's grave for five days!"

Amelia went quiet, staring at her feet, kicking the small rocks along the shore in frustration. Liza's declaration had hit her hard. She took a few moments to regain her composure in frustrated silence and then continued. "If I became a victim, people wouldn't suspect me—they'd mourn me. My murder would turn everything on its head. It would set me free."

"So you spilled your blood all over your kitchen and amputated your hand?" Colette asked, still not sure how Amelia had accomplished the feat.

"It wasn't pretty, but it had to be done. I thought the blood would be enough to convince the coroner I was dead, but if the police never found my body, there would always be that yearning for further confirmation. So I gave them my hand. I do miss it, but at least I was able to choose which one to get rid of."

"And how on earth did you do that without *actually* killing yourself?" Maude asked.

"I knew what I was doing . . . for the most part. I'd been a surgical nurse for many years and had assisted with amputations a time or two. And besides, I had Emory help me. It would have been a little hard to cut off my own hand."

"You helped her?" Grant asked. At this point, nothing the mayor had done could shock him.

"She convinced me it was for the best," Emory replied from his stump. "She kept telling me that with my help, she'd be dead. She'd leave Point Roberts and Bianca would be safe. She wouldn't kill again, and with her gone and our names cleared, I'd win the mayorship for years to come. It was a compelling argument. Sure, I was helping her, but I was also hurting her. I got to cut off her hand and listen to her shriek in pain. It made me feel like I was bringing a bit of justice to the situation, to hurt her like she'd hurt so many others."

"You people are insane," Colette cried out. "You decided to cut your wife's hand off to help her fake her own murder so she could disappear from Point Roberts . . . because you wanted justice? You know what would have been a lot easier, Emory? Going to the fucking police!"

"It may have been crazy, but it worked," Amelia said. "I was immediately considered victim number fifteen. From that day forward, I wasn't a suspect. I misdirected everyone. And sure, it meant I had to go into exile and live a secret, solitary existence, but it's what was necessary. I planned to always keep it that way, to stay up there in the Great White North, but then I found out about Liza."

"How?" Liza asked.

"I hired a private investigator to find out what happened to Bianca and Jon. I'd planned to leave them alone, but after so many years, I gave in to my curiosity. The PI was very discreet, and we had an understanding that he wouldn't ask any questions about me. I paid him handsomely, and he did his job well. He gave me a report that detailed what Bianca and Jon had been up to for the past three decades, living in Moclips, taking it easy. I even saw photos of their cute little beach house and their dog. When I got the report last month, it included a copy of Jon's death certificate, and also a copy of Liza's birth certificate. I had a granddaughter! But my joy quickly turned to anger as I learned Liza was given up for adoption. I couldn't believe it. How could you give your daughter up, B?"

"Liza, like I explained in the hotel, giving you up was the hardest thing I ever had to do," Bianca said, not responding to her mother as much as trying to build on the reasons she'd already shared with Liza. She put out her hands and Liza grasped them, giving her mother a chance to hold on to her. The others watched closely, noticing how Bianca and Liza trusted one another now.

Tiny waves churned against the shore as the wind picked up, water sifting through the stones they stood on as Bianca tried to justify her impossible decision to the person to whom it mattered the most. "I realize now that Jon, your father, pushed for us to give you away because he was worried Amelia was still alive, and if you grew up with us, there was always the chance she'd come back. You wouldn't be safe. So I did the hardest thing I ever had to do and said goodbye to you."

Liza started crying then, withdrawing her hands from Bianca's and dropping them to her sides before pulling her mother in for a hug. The others watched as the two figures embraced on the beach while Amelia looked on, discarded at their side.

"It's okay," Liza whispered into her mother's ear, her head nestled on Bianca's shoulder against her dark hair, the scent of evergreens and moist earth emanating off her skin. Bianca smelled like the forest.

"You had a good childhood, right? Walter Jennings—I got to meet him—he was the kindest, gentlest man I ever came across. I knew he would give you a good life."

"Pa was the best," Liza said, pulling back from the hug to look at Bianca directly. "I wish he were still here. Those first thirteen years with him were wonderful. It's just been the past four that have been rough."

"I'm so sorry, Liza. I never dreamed you'd lose him."

"It's not your fault."

"Walter's name was on the adoption papers the PI gave me," Amelia said, bringing the moment of reflection to an abrupt end. "And then there was the article in the *Bellingham Herald* about his death. So sad," she continued without any emotion. "Followed by a list of foster parents, the most recent being Mary and Herb Retton who lived on Benson Road. *In Point Roberts.* When I read that, well, it was a sign. A message from the universe again. I had to come back. I wanted to meet my granddaughter. So I put things in order. I sent a postcard to Emory and told him I was coming. I slipped in right before the border closed for the month."

The convergence of Amelia and Bianca in Point Roberts for the first time in nearly three decades had brought about the unraveling of the Fifteen. As one woman came down from the north, another moved up from the south, their energies coalescing on the peninsula just as February 2017 began. With both of the Schultz women within Point Roberts' borders—and a third generation present as well—the demons that had been hidden away for so long started to slink from out of the shadows. The seagulls cracked splinters in the sky, as the pebbles along the beach quivered in a forgotten fear. There had always been so much evidence to split these cold cases wide open, just on the precipice. And with Theodore Price, Colette Bernard, Grant Fisher, and Maude Oshiro coming together with Liza Jennings to investigate every single thread, the identity of the Point Roberts Slayer staying unknown a single February longer never stood a chance.

"So what's the real reason behind shutting down the town every February?" Grant asked Emory. "You've known Amelia was the Slayer since she murdered Toshi in '88. Why lock us up and keep everyone else out if you knew the identity of the Point Roberts Slayer? We only needed to be worried about one person, not every single soul who came and went."

"I'd had the idea for a while, and after Amelia left, I knew the next February would be the right time to implement it," Emory clarified. "I agreed to help her execute her plan with the understanding she would leave Point Roberts and go into hiding. She didn't tell me where she was going, and I thought it was best that it stayed that way. I never wanted her to come back to Point Roberts. Hence, the plan."

"Do you care to elaborate further?" Colette asked, trying to egg Emory on.

"I'm not as careless as you think," Emory persisted. "I closed Point Roberts down every February to keep us safe. To ensure that Amelia couldn't return during her favorite month, when she became especially crazy. I didn't want any more victims."

"So you're saying this huge charade that's been going on for nearly thirty years was designed to keep *one* woman out?" Liza asked, unable to believe the lengths the mayor had gone to to avoid telling the people of Point Roberts the truth.

"It's what had to be done," Emory replied quietly, navigating past his stomach and rubbing his palms against his thighs.

"Why didn't you just tell the border patrol to look out for Amelia and not let her in?" Theodore asked. "Wouldn't that have been simpler?"

"I was keeping people safe, Theodore. Whether you believe it or not, the February closures of Point Roberts, the parlancers, and all the other rules make people feel at ease. They've grown accustomed to it. There was no point in changing them once the murders stopped."

"Except for the fact that your rules didn't stop Amelia from slipping in this year," Maude pointed out, breaking the facade of security Emory had tried to construct.

"That's beside the point," Emory claimed, standing up from his stump. "I've kept the people of Point Roberts safe!"

"Don't try and make yourself sound like the good guy, Emory," Colette said. "You're anything but."

"You enabled Amelia. You might not have killed anyone yourself, but you protected her. You hid the truth from everyone," Theodore said, standing up and walking over to Emory. He wanted to look at his horrid face when he spoke to him. "This town deserved the truth the moment you found out about Amelia. Instead, you acted out of pure selfishness. To save yourself, to preserve your power. You're just as guilty as she is."

Emory Schultz—the man who many would have claimed was the real villain of Point Roberts—grew smaller at Theodore's words. The reality of what he'd done sank in, his guilt just now dawning on him as if he'd been asleep the entire time. Emory had been an accomplice, and no matter how unwilling he may have pretended to be, he'd been Amelia's docile servant. Without his assistance in covering up her actions, she never would have gotten away with it.

"Enough about Emory," Amelia interrupted, sounding annoyed that she had lost everyone's attention. "I've convinced him to follow my lead. We're both turning ourselves in."

"You're what?" Liza asked, surprised. Over the past five days Liza had been with Amelia and Emory, they'd never once said anything about turning themselves in. They hadn't said much at all, staying mostly quiet until this night arrived.

"I'm tired," Amelia admitted. "I don't want to hide anymore. I just wanted the chance to explain myself, to tell my story to a select few in Point Roberts so they could share the truth with everyone. That's why you're here. That's why we did this. And now we're done. There's nothing left unknown. We just have one final problem to take care of . . ."

"What on earth could that be?" Maude asked.

"Well, it's always been the Fifteen, hasn't it?" Amelia asked the group rhetorically. "It *needs* to be the Fifteen, or I fear we'll upset the universe."

Theodore turned away from Emory, sensing something sinister in Amelia's words. Colette noticed the look on Theodore's face and stood up from her spot on the driftwood, Grant and Maude following suit so that everyone gathered was now standing atop the tiny rocks adjacent to the nighttime sea.

"And since I'm not a part of it anymore, someone has to take my place," Amelia said, her statement ringing out like a decree. She pushed her remaining hand deep into the inner pocket of the cloak she wore and pulled out a small pistol. Without warning, before anyone could stop her, she pointed the gun at the person she'd decided long ago would need to take her place.

And pulled the trigger.

~

The bullet hit Bianca to the right of her heart, inflicting more damage than could ever be repaired, but not causing enough to kill her immediately.

Liza screamed as Bianca crumpled in a heap on the slick stones beneath them. Getting down on her knees, Liza positioned her mother's head on her lap and put pressure on her chest to try to stop the bleeding. Her hands turned a bright shade of crimson, visible even in the dark of night.

Bianca said nothing at first, even though Liza could tell she was still alive. Her silence served as a proclamation, one that said she wasn't surprised this had come.

The others sprang into action. Grant pulled out his gun and pounced on Amelia, wrangling the pistol out of her hand. He regretted not searching her at the cemetery—he should never have believed she was unarmed. Using his strength to corral her, Grant pulled Amelia away from Bianca and Liza, putting her arms behind her back and holding his gun under her chin so she couldn't inflict any more damage.

Theodore raised his weapon and grabbed Emory, patting him down to make sure he didn't have another gun, while Colette pulled out her cell phone and dialed 911.

It was finally time to call the police.

As Colette shouted into her telephone, Maude moved closer to where Liza sat with Bianca. Bianca's chest was blossoming red—a flower showing up on her shirt that hadn't been there previously. Maude didn't know what to do.

"It starts and ends with you, dear," Amelia shouted to Bianca from the spot where Grant had pulled her aside. She didn't resist or struggle, but she still wanted to have the last word, even if she had to speak with a gun at her throat. "I always knew this day had to come, to put everything right. To atone for my sins, I had to give up what I love most in the world, what I've always fought so hard to protect. I had to make this final sacrifice, my daughter, my dear, dear Bianca. Now . . . you're free."

"Shut the fuck up, Amelia!" Emory shrieked from the spot twenty or so feet away where Theodore was holding him. He wanted Amelia to realize that no one gathered here ever wanted to hear another word from her.

"Oh, Liza," Bianca said, the first words she'd spoken since being shot coming to her daughter's ears as a gentle whisper only she could hear. The others faded away at that moment, and it became just the two of them. A mother and daughter together on the beach, huddled against colorful pebbles that glistened if you looked at them just right.

"Hold on! Please, hold on," Liza urged, using one hand to keep pressure on the gunshot wound and the other hand to caress her mother's ghostly white face. She was dying. "You can't leave me too. Not now, not so soon. We just met, we just started to—"

"It's going to be okay. If I've learned anything about you, it's that you're strong. You can handle anything."

"You've got to hold on," Liza pleaded. "Colette's calling the police, an ambulance will be here soon and then—"

"I don't think I'm going to leave this beach. But that's okay, because I met you, and how lovely you are . . . so lovely . . . ," Bianca said slowly, straining more with each word as she lost blood. Her heart struggled to beat.

"But you're my mother. I don't want to lose my family again!" Liza cried, the tears coming hot. They stung her eyes as they left.

"You'll always have a family Liza," Bianca whispered. "You have a family right here. Theodore, Colette, Grant, and Maude. My dying won't change that. The five of you will always . . . you'll always have one another to—"

Bianca's body shuddered then, her head twitching sharply in Liza's lap as her words were interrupted by a final breath pushing itself from her lungs.

She died there on the beach, cradled in Liza's arms as midnight crashed onto the shore like a wave, the month of February ending encrusted in salt.

PART V

THE FIVE

CHAPTER FIFTEEN

LIZA, THEODORE, COLETTE, GRANT & MAUDE

Bianca had been dead for half an hour by the time the police arrived. A large swarm of officers emerged from the forest behind Lily Point, coming down from the bluff on foot, as no roads led to the secluded stone-covered beach.

They took Amelia and Emory into custody, shackling Emory with handcuffs as they read them both their rights, initially struggling with a way to secure Amelia since she only had one hand.

As Theodore watched the police take the Schultzes away, he wished Bill were present to witness it. He'd been the sheriff of Point Roberts for such a long time, and not solving the cases of the Fifteen had been one of his biggest regrets. The police force hadn't been the same since Bill retired, but Theodore hoped with Emory locked up, they'd find their way again.

Amelia and Emory went silently, having already said all they wanted to during their storytelling charade. There was nothing left to confess.

Paramedics knelt at Liza's side as her grandparents were led away, trying to convince her to release her mother's body, which she desperately clung to.

She didn't want to let her go.

If she let her go, it would be over.

It would be real, and Bianca would be gone.

Forever.

Theodore, Colette, Grant, and Maude moved to Liza's side, creating a semicircle around where she sat on the coast, cradling her dead mother. They comforted her as she loosened her grip on Bianca; the two paramedics lifted her body and placed it in a bag as black as the night.

Liza closed her eyes as they zipped it, unable to watch Bianca being sealed up like a piece of trash to be hauled away. How could this be happening?

The five of them had found answers—they'd solved the cases of the Fifteen—but at what cost?

How much had they lost?

The four adults surrounding Liza embraced her in a group hug where she sat. Their words of sympathy and solace fleeted into quiet as the soothing repetition of tiny waves crashing ashore overtook the scene.

Liza's jeans were soaked with seawater. She began to shiver.

"We'd like to question you all back at the station," a police officer with a mustache said as he approached the five.

"I'm not leaving this beach," Liza said from behind the others as they got up, ending their huddle. Liza reached her hand out to Grant, who pulled her to her feet. She wiped the tears from her face. "If you have questions for us, we can answer them here. I'm not ready to go anywhere else yet. We don't owe you guys anything."

"Alright, then," the officer said, realizing that arguing with the gutsy teenager would get him nowhere. "Why don't you come take a seat over on the driftwood, and I'll have my detectives talk to each of you separately about what happened here. The paramedics have some blankets, so we'll get those to make you more comfortable."

"We'll take the blankets," Liza said as she continued to shiver, "but we're not talking to anyone separately. The five of us solved this together. We'll talk to the detectives together."

The officer looked annoyed, but he nodded in agreement.

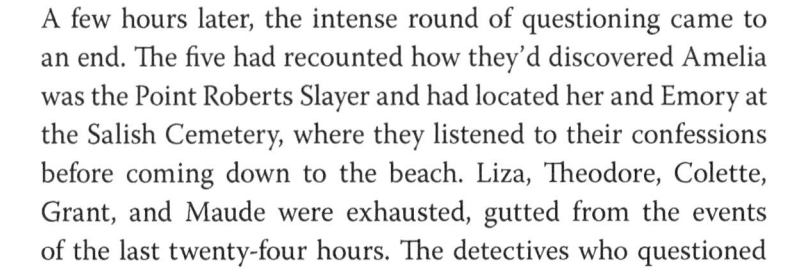

A few hours later, the intense round of questioning came to an end. The five had recounted how they'd discovered Amelia was the Point Roberts Slayer and had located her and Emory at the Salish Cemetery, where they listened to their confessions before coming down to the beach. Liza, Theodore, Colette, Grant, and Maude were exhausted, gutted from the events of the last twenty-four hours. The detectives who questioned them could tell they needed a break, so they agreed to continue the conversation later at the station, after they'd had some time to rest.

The remaining officers left with the detectives, traipsing over the driftwood and disappearing along the trail through the trees that led back up the bluff.

Only five people remained on the beach, on the edge of the sea, on the edge of everything.

"The nightmare is over," Maude said, breaking the silence.

"We solved it. We fucking solved it, and those two are going to be locked up for the rest of their lives," Grant responded, the satisfaction in his words unmistakable.

"So . . . what now?" Colette asked, pulling her golden shawl tighter as a breeze pulsed across the dawn, the darkness of the sky lessening as a new day prepared its reveal.

"It's March 1," Theodore replied, breathing a heavy sigh of relief. February was over. And if he had anything left to accomplish in this life, it would be to make sure Point Roberts was never on lockdown again. He would finish his book on the Fifteen so everyone would know what had happened here. He would run for mayor.

"We can leave," Liza whispered, the audacity of her proclamation both simple and profound.

The sun started to rise, interrupting any reply as the sky began to quiver with warm shades of pastel. It lightened further in exponential patterns, a beautiful orange glow emerging from behind the North Cascades where the five looked to the east. Overwhelmed by the pure natural splendor of the sight before them, they stood up from their driftwood seats, moving closer to the edge of the sea. They walked together to the water, their boots crunching against the rocks as the small pebbles rearranged themselves to make room for their feet.

The snow-covered peak of Mount Baker became visible in the soft morning light. Its dome arrived like a prospect to aim for, a formation that couldn't understand pain when there was such stillness and peace. The crystal-clear day was given to them as a gift. Liza, Theodore, Colette, Grant, and Maude took in the magnificent shades of the dark-blue water rippling in the bay, where each molecule at the surface fought to evolve from navy to a shimmering orange speck.

Every morning, just like water, we awake with the sun, ready to fight for our darkness to be illuminated.

"This is the first time the five of us have been together. I guess we've been together since last night, but even then, it was the first time we were all in one place. And now, it's just us," Liza admitted, revealing what she'd been thinking about as the morning continued to transform, the sky opening up to simpler shades of blue.

"Maybe that's all it took," Theodore suggested.

"Five different perspectives to solve it," Colette added.

"Our combined power," Grant said.

"Maybe it was fate that brought us together," Maude wondered. "But maybe it doesn't matter how we aligned. All that matters is we're here."

Liza laced her fingers with Maude's then, holding her grandmother's hand tightly as two pebbles at her feet caught her gaze. Still holding on to Maude, she bent down to pick them up, using her free hand to inspect them.

One was alabaster. One was gold.

One for Pa. One for Bianca.

She put them in the interior left pocket of her raincoat so she could feel them sitting against her heart.

Even though they were gone, they would always be with her.

"Liza, I know you've been through a lot, but I've been thinking, if you're interested in the idea . . . ," Maude began as Liza turned to look at her. "I'd like you to come and live with me. You're my granddaughter, and I'd be honored to welcome you into my home."

"I would like that very much," Liza replied, squeezing Maude's hand with affection as she smiled. She felt giddy knowing she wouldn't have to go back to the trailer on Benson Road or sleep on that lumpy mattress ever again.

Liza's attention was pulled out to sea then, where something glided across the water, the rising sun highlighting its shape.

A small sailboat had floated toward the shore of Lily Point for reasons unknown, as if it had realized February was over and liberated itself from the Point Roberts Marina all on its own. As the boat got closer to the coast, it became clear there was no one on board.

"How the hell did that get out there?" Colette asked the group.

"I'm not sure, but it looks like it doesn't have a captain. Luckily for us, I know how to sail," Grant told the others.

"Let's get on it," Liza suggested.

"And go where?" Theodore asked.

"We could go anywhere," Maude replied.

"We'll come back. Point Roberts is home," Liza said, reassuring Theodore as she rubbed his shoulder playfully, trying to convince him it was okay to leave.

The boat rode the next wave, coming close enough to shore that they could reach it just by wading out a bit into the sea. Grant moved into the water first, throwing caution to the wind, reaching the sailboat when he was submerged to his waist. He used his strength to pull himself aboard, motioning for the others to do the same.

"Isn't the water freezing?" Colette asked, looking nervous.

"It's not that bad!" Grant called back. "Come on! Let's go! Let's leave, just because we can!"

Colette retrieved the blankets from the driftwood and folded them up, giving half of them to Theodore as they headed into the water next, cursing aloud as the freezing water hit them. They held the blankets above their heads to keep them dry, knowing they'd all need something to warm them up once they reached the boat. When they arrived beside the hull, Grant pulled them up.

Maude went next, the water almost up to her clavicles by the time she made it to the boat. And Liza went last, purposefully, wanting to be on Point Roberts' shore for just a few moments longer than the others.

"See you soon," she said to every pebble at her feet—*not* goodbye—before pushing out into the tide, moving in opposition to the water's wishes.

When she reached the sailboat, Grant and Theodore extended their arms and pulled her onto the deck; all five of them were now aboard. Grant got the sails ready and Theodore assisted by following his orders. The white canvas caught the wind as they turned the boat around, moving away from the shore and out to the unknown depths of the sea.

Colette watched Grant move skillfully as he took control of the ship. He was at home on the water. A fisherman back where he belonged, cruising across the dark-blue salt. He felt her eyes on him, and once the boat was steadily sailing on, he turned back from the stern to where she sat at the bow watching him. He smiled at her, and her insides fluttered. He saw her. He *really* saw her.

Together, the five people who saved Point Roberts left it behind, gliding across the Salish Sea without a destination in mind. They didn't know where they were going, and they didn't care.

Liza wondered, what was a destination, anyway?

Or better yet, what was an ending?

Was it a point on the map where she wished to end up?

She knew she could never really know her own end, where the story of her life would come to a close. All she could do was live every day with gusto and barrel toward the strange and mysterious conclusions she'd write for herself.

She might not know where she would end. But one day, she would know how she got there.

And maybe that was all that mattered—that she'd use every second she was given to forge ahead into the unknown.

On the sailboat, Liza did just that, thinking of what Pa had taught her, welcoming the unidentified horizon where water and land comingled like long-lost brethren. She watched the coast of Point Roberts fade away into the distance, with two stones in her pocket and four people she loved at her side.

She had no enemies.

ACKNOWLEDGMENTS

When I learned about the existence of Point Roberts, my immediate thought was that I should write a book that takes place there. Five years ago, in a classroom in New York City, I first wrote the idea for this story down, describing five main characters and the unusual place they lived. Now, writing this in Seattle, Washington, I'd like to thank the special people who assisted me in completing the process of bringing this story into your hands:

My mother, Christine Rigby, for your unending support, love, and the honest suggestions you gave me after reading this novel.

Brian McFawn, for listening to me talk about writing this narrative over the course of three years and all the helpful edits you provided to make this book better.

Michelle Weiss, for your friendship and the attention to detail you brought to the many plotlines when you shared with me your expert reader's opinions on an early draft.

Valerie Paquin, for the wonderful job you did copyediting this manuscript, catching all the kinds of errors my eye never would have noticed. You polished this story so well.

Edward Bettison, for your incredible artistic talent and the gorgeous cover design you created for this book. It was such a pleasure to collaborate with you on this original artwork.

Rachel Marek, for your kindness in creating this crisp interior layout so that the inside of the book is as stunning as the cover.

And to Jesse Angelo, for finding me out at sea and bringing me ashore.

ABOUT THE AUTHOR

Alexander Rigby was born and raised in a small rural town in Northwest Pennsylvania. He currently lives in Seattle, Washington, with his dog, Copper Atticus, and works in book publishing. An avid outdoorsman who enjoys hiking in the wilderness, Alexander is on a mission to visit every national park in the United States.

He is the founder and editor-in-chief of *Allegory Ridge*, which publishes creative works of the millennial generation. Alexander has written four novels: *Point Roberts*, *Bender*, *What Happened to Marilyn*, and *The Second Chances of Priam Wood*.

ARIGBY.COM
ALEXANDER_RIGBY
ALEXANDERRIGBY_

Lightning Source UK Ltd.
Milton Keynes UK
UKHW010626020221
378106UK00001B/175